MARCH, A SONG AND A DANCE

A NOVEL

L. B. JOYCE

March, a Song and a Dance
Print ISBN: 978-0-9600311-3-9

ALSO BY L. B. JOYCE

Twelve Months, Twelve Love Stories

A Million Decembers

For the Love of July

February's Angel

Promise Me November

An Unexpected June

A January to Remember

September's Moonlight Serenade

Goodbye Heartbreak, Hello May

March, a Song and a Dance

~

Holidays in White Oaks Valley

A Grand Slam Kind of Christmas

PROLOGUE

Savanah Jackson and Jack Buchanan met while in line at Café Latte, their brief encounter just long enough to ignite a spark between them. That fleeting moment—recalled here from *Goodbye Heartbreak, Hello May*, Book 8—planted the seed for *March, a Song and a Dance*.

So, whether you're new to the *Twelve Months, Twelve Love Stories* series, or a long time reader—and I thank you for that—I hope this glimpse of their beginning will sweep you right into their story.

Lost in his thoughts, his fingers drumming on the steering wheel, it was a few seconds before Jack Buchanan realized the light had turned green.

A horn sounding behind him, he glanced in his rearview mirror.

For God's sake, what's your hurry buddy? Give me a break.

Though he knew the guy couldn't see him, he sent a threatening scowl in the mirror.

Then he stepped on the gas, sending his car shooting right through the intersection.

A very immature gesture…

Yes, he was aware of this. But it had been a long day, and he wasn't in the mood. He was beat, and after being cooped up in the studio for almost nine hours, a mishmash of tunes were still stuck in his head.

Since Jason had returned from his honeymoon, he had the band working on so many projects, Jack would swear he didn't even know what day it was anymore.

He knew this pace wouldn't last forever. And like his dad had always been quick to remind him, any chance to up his financial security was something he should never lose sight of, no matter how young he thought he was.

But making lots of money wasn't cutting it for him anymore.

You want more… someone to share your life. You're tired of being on your own.

He'd had the crazy thought this might be with Stephanie. But after watching her dance with this Evan—a guy who appeared out of nowhere and no one seemed to know anything about—he knew she would never be his.

He'd played at enough weddings and written enough songs to know the signs of someone in love.

Stephanie's heart was with Evan.

So, it looked like he was back to square one.

Yep, just you and your music.

Thank God he at least had that…

The car in front of him made a slow turn into the Café Latte parking lot.

Without even thinking, Jack followed him and pulled into the first parking space he saw. Coffee might be just what he needed. And even though he wasn't a dessert kind of guy, he could never pass on one of their sour cherry scones. If they had any left at this late hour.

He'd swear they were addicting.

The café was quiet on this late Wednesday afternoon. Taking advantage of this, Ellie Cook was taking a quick inventory of the available baked goods.

She was talking to herself. *"Hmm…* it looks like we'll be okay. Not the best selection, but enough to carry us through until closing."

The sound of someone clearing their throat, she glanced up from the display case to see it was Jack.

Smiling, he bided his time. He hadn't seen Ellie since she'd left Cleveland over a year ago for an internship at Ohio State. He missed her ever-present smile and cheerful banter.

She grinned. "Jack… how've you been?"

"Ellie… it's great to see you. I'm good, doing my thing, keeping busy. What about you? And why are you even here? Shouldn't you still be in Columbus? Or has your internship ended?"

She shook her head. "I'm home on a break. They needed extra help here since Laurel, the café owner, had a baby. So, I volunteered to come in for a few days."

When she saw him glance over at her left hand, she grew flustered, averting her gaze. "So, still the usual? Regular, no cream or sugar, and a sour cherry scone?"

A slight frown marked his features, noting her unease. He thought she'd be engaged to her boyfriend, Michael, by now. The one time he'd met him, he'd come across as a nice guy. Together, he and Ellie seemed like a perfect fit.

Goes to show you, when love singles you out, who knows what will happen next.

"Or maybe you want something else today?" This coming from Ellie, he shook his head. "No, what you said is fine."

Then, unsure of what to say, he fell silent, watching as she put the scone in a bag.

She was the first to speak. "Looks like today is your lucky day since this is the last cherry scone. They are by far our most popular pastry. They're usually gone by noon."

"Oh, no. Is that really the last cherry scone? Tell me it isn't so."

This disappointed comment coming from behind him, followed by a long and dramatic sigh, was enough to have Jack turn around, a smile tweaking the corner of his mouth.

This is when he'd swear everything around him came to a grinding halt. His heart pounding in his chest, he could only stare at the woman standing in front of him.

The vague thought entered his mind this must be what it felt like to be hit by Cupid's arrow.

It had zinged his heart, all right. But in a wonderful and amazing way.

He wanted to say something, if only to ask her name. But the most he could manage was a smile. So, this is what he did... he smiled like he had never smiled before in his life. While drinking in every single detail.

She was by far the most beautiful woman he'd ever seen. She was exquisite. Definitely out of his league, she was a woman he would never even think of approaching. Let alone try to start up a conversation.

Her hair was the shade of a rich, dark espresso. Pulled back in a loose bun, wispy tendrils framed her face. He wanted to reach over to tuck these behind her ears, maybe even trail his fingers over the satiny softness of her cheeks. The possibility he might lose his mind and do this, he clenched his fists to his sides.

Her face was a classic oval, a face an artist dreams of painting. A molten chocolate brown, her eyes were wide and expressive. Soft and tempting, her mouth begged to be kissed.

He'd give anything, starting with the sour cherry scone, to experience such a kiss.

But you already know it would be amazing.

When he saw his inspection had brought a faint flush to her cheeks, he cleared his throat, relieved to find his voice was ready to join him. "Hello."

Yeah, it wasn't a lot, but at least it was a start.

"Hello." She took a step closer, her move graceful as a gentle breeze.

He briefly closed his eyes.

What the hell is wrong with you? A gentle breeze? Thank goodness you didn't say that out loud. What's next? You're going to recite poetry to her?

Actually, this was something most people didn't know about him. Fascinated by the whole concept of poetry, he had fooled around a bit, writing a few lines himself.

And he could write volumes about this woman.

If he had to guess, he would say she was a dancer. But not just any dancer.

A ballerina.

The kind of ballerina everyone imagines in their mind... all beauty and grace.

Not that he knew much about dance. Or ballerinas. His sister had taken dancing lessons. Forced to sit through far too many of her recitals, what he remembered most was a lot of tulle and glitter. Along with a fair share of falls and missed cues. This invariably ended with a lot of dramatics and tears. Not at all the dancer this woman would be.

No, she would be perfection.

He just blurted it out. "You're a dancer."

She tilted her head, a look of surprise flashing across her face. Then an almost teasing smile curved her lips. "Yes, I am. And you? Are you also a dancer?"

She had moved even closer, the scent of her perfume pulling him in. A combination of lemon, jasmine and musk, it awakened his senses. Filling his mind with the possibility of long walks in the moonlight and sizzling summer nights of passion.

Again, what's going on with you? Just look at her. You don't have a chance.

He slowly shook his head. "No, I'm a musician." Then he completely surprised himself with what he said next. "I would say this means you and I are a perfect match, no? You need music to dance. And I need inspiration to write the music. I believe this is how all great love stories start."

Surprised, and even more relieved this hadn't sent her running out of the café to get away from him, he grew bolder, sending her a grin. "After all, we've already found out we have the same tastes in scones. So, imagine the possibilities."

She laughed. "But you know nothing about me. I might be a terrible dancer."

His gaze leisurely traveling over her, he slowly shook his head. "No, something tells me, as beautiful as you are, you're an amazing dancer."

He watched the color deepen in her cheeks. Amazed this was because of something he said, he was filled with a sudden determination.

You are not going to let this woman get away.

And how did he plan to go about this?

He hadn't a clue.

Ellie, who had been watching this take place, was getting more frustrated by the minute. What was Jack's problem? Why wasn't he making his move? The chemistry between them was undeniable, so what more did he need?

Enough was enough.

She cleared her throat. When Jack glanced over at her, she sent a pointed look at the bag with the scone.

He gave her a blank stare. Then, comprehension flashing across his face, he grabbed the bag from the counter.

He held it out to the woman. "Here, I believe this scone belongs to you."

She shook her head. "Oh, no… I can't possibly take it from you. I can easily find something else."

Still holding out the bag, he smiled. "Please… I insist."

She began searching through her purse. "Then let me at least pay you."

He shook his head. "No, absolutely not. My treat."

She finally took the bag from him. "Okay. And, thank you."

The smile she gave him sent a warmth through him he couldn't describe. It was a smile that had him wanting more.

You'd do anything to spend the rest of your life making her smile.

But again… this wouldn't even have a chance of happening if he let her leave without at least finding out her name.

He moved closer. "You're more than welcome. Maybe one day you can return the favor. Or we can share a scone and some conversation."

He smiled. "By the way, I'm Jack."

Her smile abruptly disappeared, panic filling her face.

Puzzled, he watched as she began backing away. Avoiding his gaze, she mumbled her response. "I have somewhere I need to go, and I can't be late. Again, thank you for the scone."

She turned, and after almost running into an incoming customer, she slipped outside.

Jack was in shock. He was also a little in denial. This wasn't what he'd expected. Was it something he said? Had he been too forward? Too familiar?

Dragging his hand back through his hair, he turned to Ellie. "Do you know her? Or, at least, know her name?"

She shook her head. "No, I don't. But I've only been filling in since yesterday." She waved her hand towards the door. "What are you waiting for? Go after her."

So, this is what he did.

As he went sprinting out of the café, he tried not to think about his behavior. Because, seriously—had he lost his mind? Chasing after a woman he knew nothing about? This wasn't something he'd do. Or even think about doing.

But, for whatever reason, crazy or not, he felt like he had no choice… it felt right.

She was his destiny.

He came to a halt in the middle of the parking lot, scanning the cars and anywhere else she could have gone.

He came up with nothing.

This is when, believe it or not, he began searching the ground, thinking she may have left some kind of clue behind.

And what are you expecting to find? A glass slipper? You're losing it, buddy, you need to get a grip.

After one last glance around the parking lot, he made his way back into the café

Crouched down in driver's seat of her car, Savannah Jackson stared at her shaking hands. Her heart was also beating so hard, and so loud, she was afraid it was going to leap right out of her chest.

Closing her eyes, she tried to slow her breathing.

The door to the café suddenly flew open. Slipping even further down in the seat, she watched as a man came running out, slowly scanning the parking lot.

It was him.

For a brief moment, she thought of making herself known. If only to thank him again for the scone. Then she'd apologize for running out on him.

But the consequences of what could happen if she did? This was too overwhelming for her.

Instead, she watched as he walked back into the café. Then, cautiously inching her way back into a sitting position, she started her car and drove out of the parking lot.

Jack shook his head at Ellie's hopeful expression.

She sighed, reaching over to pat his hand. "Oh, Jack… I'm so sorry."

He shrugged, and after leaning back against the counter, a silence fell between them. Ellie didn't know what to say, while Jack was trying to figure out where he went wrong.

He heaved a frustrated sigh. "Please don't tell me I imagined what happened. There was definitely something between us, right? A connection of some kind?"

She nodded. "Yes, I'd say there was definitely something there." Then she gave a short laugh. "But maybe I'm not the one to ask."

Aware of his concerned glance, she grabbed a cup and filled it with coffee. After slapping on a lid, she slid it across the counter to him, her smile overly bright. "Now, how about your scone? I know we still have blueberry and cinnamon."

He shrugged. "Sure, you pick."

He watched her put a scone in a bag before she rang up the sale. All while she chattered away about nothing.

But she had no reason to worry. He had received her unsaid message loud and clear. Any talk about her and Michael was off limits.

There was now a line of customers behind him, so he picked up his scone and coffee. "Well, I better be on my way. If I don't see you before you go back to Columbus, I wish you the best."

She gave him one of those big smiles he remembered. "Thanks. And I'll keep my eyes open while I'm here. You know… just in case a certain person comes in again. And don't worry, I have a good feeling about this."

As he walked out of the café, he decided Ellie's comment was proof he had every reason to feel optimistic. But this also meant he had his work cut out for him.

He needed to figure out a way to find this woman again.

Then he was going to marry her.

He stopped right in the middle of the parking lot and, raising his face to the sky, he yelled out. "It's official. You've gone absolutely insane."

He was laughing as he headed for his car. When two elderly women turned to stare at him on their way into the café, he responded with a big smile and a wave. "Have a wonderful day, ladies."

He got in his car, turned on his favorite audio track, and started the drive home.

Believe it or not, he was in a great mood.

And he had every reason to be.

He'd found the love of his life.

As Savanah drove home, she replayed every single detail of the last ten minutes in her mind. Twice, maybe three times, she did this.

What happened back there in Café Latte? This kind of behavior wasn't something she'd normally encourage. She didn't have the time, nor did she have any interest in finding a man.

Not now. This would be absolute craziness.

Her mother would be the first to remind her of this. She needed to concentrate solely on her dancing right now. Any distractions were to be avoided. She had worked so hard and for too long to let her heart fool her into thinking she could have both.

That her mother had even suggested she take a yoga class was still a mystery. But this was probably only because she thought it might help relieve the stress from all the new changes in her life.

She only hoped with her twenty-sixth birthday coming up in a few months, her mother would finally realize it was time to step back and let her run her own life.

Mistakes and all.

A faint smile touched her lips.

But, this man...

He was so handsome. And the way he looked at you. Like he thought you were the most beautiful woman in the world.

She wasn't used to this kind of attention. From her early childhood, compliments had been discouraged. Unless they were in regard to her dancing. And those had to be earned.

As she pulled into her driveway, reality kicked in. It would be best if she forgot what happened. Planned out to the smallest detail, her life was no longer her own.

There was no room in her life for a man like him.

But, try as she might, she couldn't stop thinking about his smile.

A man like him in your life?

She couldn't even imagine...

MARCH, A SONG AND A DANCE

~

Love is like playing the piano. First you must learn to play by the rules.
Then you must forget the rules, and play from the heart.
~ Anonymous

CHAPTER 1

After a sweeping glance around the small café, Jack Buchanan sighed as he turned back to the counter.

Nope, looks like it's not happening today, either.

There was no sign of the woman he'd hoped to find. The woman he'd dubbed "the dancer," sometimes even "his ballerina," a habit he knew he should break.

Nearly ten months had passed since their chance encounter here at Café Latte, yet he kept coming back, chasing that unshakable memory.

He stuffed his wallet back in his pocket. Grabbing the coffee cup and bag with the sour cherry scone, he smiled at the girl behind the counter as she held out the change from his order.

"Add it to your tip jar," he said, nodding towards it. "If only for the great smile you always have for everyone."

Her blush, making him worry he'd said too much, or lord help him, something too familiar, he turned to leave.

As a member of Cleveland's most popular and hottest band, Banded Together, he had experienced his share of crazy fans. He'd learned how just about anything, even a simple hello, could be taken the wrong way.

Stuffing the bills in the jar, she called out as he began walking away. "Thanks, Mr. Buchanan. Enjoy your scone and coffee." After a dramatic sigh, she turned to the girl working with her. "He is so dreamy, don't you think?"

Whoa… dreamy? Hmm…

A smile tweaked the corner of Jack's mouth as he pushed the button for Dark Roast and waited for his coffee cup to fill.

Was he flattered?

Of course he was—what man wouldn't be?

Curious to hear more, he slowly reached for a lid. Proof that 99.9% of the time eavesdropping leads to no good, her coworker let out a loud laugh. "*Ha…* are you crazy? I bet he's at least fifteen years older than you. Possibly even twenty.

As she set a tray of mega-sized peanut butter cookies on the counter, a customer favorite, she rolled her eyes. "With such a huge age gap, what are the chances you'd have anything in common?"

The first girl shrugged. "Well, stranger things have happened. There are tons of articles about celebrities in May-December relationships. It works for them, so why not for us?"

After she pulled an empty tray from the display case and replaced it with the tray of peanut butter cookies, her coworker frowned. "Yeah, I wonder what the real story is with those."

She grabbed a bottle of glass cleaner from behind the counter, waving the bottle to emphasize her point. "There's also a good chance he already has a girlfriend. Perhaps even a wife and a couple of kids. Think about it… he might even be on his second or third marriage. You know how those celebrities are. One of anything is never enough for them."

She was scowling as she began wiping down the counter. After her recent breakup, men had become a sensitive topic for her.

This would include *all* men.

The first girl nodded. "Yeah, you're probably right. Despite that, I'm willing to bet a cinnamon roll Mr. Buchanan is a man you can depend on. It shows in his eyes. And he has a great smile."

"*Hah…* in the beginning, they're all like that. They give you those puppy dog eyes to get what they want, and you fall for it every time. Then everything changes, and they move on."

She shrugged. "Whatever…"

After scanning the remaining pastries in the display case, she picked up the empty tray. "I'm going to the kitchen to get more sour cherry scones. I don't get it. They have been flying out of here like crazy. Have you had one yet?"

The first girl shook her head. "Nope. But they must be good, since they are the only pastry Mr. Buchanan orders. With a coffee. Dark Roast. Every single time." Her eyes grew wide. "Maybe they added in some kind of magic ingredient. Who knows? Stranger things have happened."

"Yeah, some kind of love potion."

They were both laughing as she turned to help the next customer.

A magic ingredient? Love potion?

Jack could only wish. His smile now a thing of the past, after tossing some napkins in the bag with the sour cherry scone, he pulled his keys out of his pocket.

He wasn't too happy with most of what he just heard.

Come on… fifteen or twenty years older? Not as old as you look?

He groaned.

And… dependable?

This made it sound as if he'd already settled into the middle-aged state of his life. To be clear, the last time he'd checked, he hadn't found a single gray hair. But, evidently, a man of his age, with no serious relationship in the works, or plans of marriage in the near future?

They were doomed…

Well, as far as he was concerned, he was doing just fine. Better than most, he'd say. He'd challenge anyone around town to put together a list of guys his age who still played in a band. A popular and in demand band, where age was all forgotten in lieu of talent.

All things considered, he figured he was a pretty hip and young thirty—nowhere near the fifty years the girls behind the counter guessed.

Don't forget, the one girl did say you were dreamy.

Yeah, he'd settle for this.

But they'd gotten one thing wrong. This would be his relationship status. No girlfriend, and no wife. If there was, he wouldn't be haunting Café Latte like a lovestruck fool.

Their opinion of you would change in a second if they knew the reason for your frequent visits. Dreamy would fly right out the window.

Still, he was banking on a miracle—all because of a mutual fondness for sour cherry scones.

He needed to leave. Dragging his hand through his hair, he headed for the door, pausing to send one more searching glance around the small coffee shop. There was nothing—no sign of the woman he couldn't shake, the one whose name he never got.

It's been almost a year now—what are the odds?

Frustrated, and half-convinced he was losing it, he shoved open the door and sprinted to his truck.

After he dropped the coffee cup in his cupholder and tossed the bag with the scone on the passenger seat, he glanced over at the Café Latte sign above the door. He didn't even want to think about how many stop he'd made here lately—enough to consider buying stock in the place.

He glanced over at the bag. Was he nuts, or what? The last thing he needed was another sour cherry scone. He already had over a half-dozen stashed in his freezer.

So why did he keep coming back?

It was simple. By reliving the events of that day, he would eventually get lucky—he'd turn around to find her right behind him in line.

And this time, you won't let her get away.

Yep, he was hoping for a miracle.

CHAPTER 2

Jack was about to start up his truck when his phone buzzed. He picked it up to see he had a voicemail from Stephanie.

"Hey, Jack, it's me calling to see if you got your invitation for the wedding, and if you plan on bringing a date. The wedding is less than three weeks away, so if you have asked no one yet, you're running out of time. Hold on a minute..."

Jack could hear her talking to someone before she came back on the phone. "

"Sorry about that, I'm at work. Now what was I talking about? Oh, yeah, if you don't have a date yet, I have someone who would be perfect for you, my friend from yoga class. And guess what? She doesn't have a date either. So, would you be open to meeting?"

He hit pause, and dragging his hand down over his jaw, he groaned. *Seriously?*

What the hell is going on?

First the girls at Café Latte, and now Stephanie?

Did he come across as that desperate? And this yoga friend … was there a reason she didn't have a date? He knew little about yoga people, only that they seemed to enjoy distorting their bodies in poses he wouldn't even think of attempting.

Since you also don't have a date, you have no room to talk, do you?

After staring down at the phone, wishing he'd never picked it up in the first place, he listened to the rest of Stephanie's voice mail.

*"We'll make it simple, meet at Café Latte for coffee.
So you won't feel obligated if you don't hit it off.
Even though I don't see this happening. So, think
about it. And when you decide what you'd like to do,
call me and I'll set it up. You won't have to do a
thing. Don't wait too long, though. The next three
weeks are going to fly by. Talk to you later."*

He tossed the phone on the passenger seat, and starting up his truck, he pulled out of the Café Latte parking lot. After he lowered the visor against the late afternoon sun, he thought about what Stephanie said in her voice mail.

A blind date, huh?

He thought he'd made his opinion of blind dates pretty clear… he wasn't interested.

He didn't like the pressure. the notion he needed to prove himself. Or worse yet, give the impression he wasn't desperate. That this all took place when it wasn't something he wanted to do in the first place?

This made for a very long and uncomfortable evening. And when the date ended? He was left with another sense of failure.

You're not good at blind dates. Hell, make that any kind of date.

He remembered Stephanie mentioning this woman from her yoga class. It was the night she'd agreed to be his date for the Cleveland's Elite Awards Banquet. The same night he'd realized she had fallen in love with someone else.

However, he'd been fine with this. If anything, it had been a relief. One shouldn't have to try so hard to make a relationship work. And now he and Stephanie had become close friends.

His phone rang, Jason's name popping up on the audio display.

He hit answer. "Hey, what's up?"

After a long pause, Jason's voice filled the interior of his truck. *"Umm... just checking to see if you picked up the demo. And where the hell are you, if you did?"*

At first, Jason's inquiry didn't register.

The demo?

Then he remembered.

Damn... he's talking about the new demo the band put together. You told him you'd stop by the studio and pick it up.

Jason also told him he needed it by four at the latest.

He glanced over at the clock on the dashboard.

4:28 p.m.

He groaned, and hitting the brakes, he made a sharp right into a parking lot. Tires squealing, he did a u-turn back out onto the main highway and headed for the studio.

"So, is this silence a way of letting me know you forgot?"

Jason's dry tone of voice had Jack responding with an embarrassed laugh. *"Umm... sorry. Unfortunately, I did. But don't worry, I'm already on my way to the studio. Give me about twenty minutes and you'll have your demo."*

After a brief silence, Jason gave a resigned sigh. "You're sure about this?"

"Yes, I'm sure. But then, who's sure about anything these days?"

Another brief silence passed before Jason responded. "Okay, then... I'm not going to touch that. See you in twenty."

Five minutes later, Jack walked out of the studio, demo in hand. Muttering to himself, he wondered if he was entering the early stages of dementia.

Nah... you just need to stop pushing yourself. Scale back on the workload.

But he was desperate. He hadn't had a break since he won the Cleveland Elite award for one of his original scores almost a year ago. Working long hours and pressured by deadlines, his mind was demanding a rest, his creativity begging to be put on hold.

He was almost to the point he wished he'd never heard of the damn award. Not that he was ungrateful, there was only so much one person could do.

He was reaching for his coffee when the car in front of him came to an abrupt stop. As he slammed on his brakes, he could only watch as the coffee appeared to shoot right out of the cup and into his lap.

The only positive note? The coffee was lukewarm, not hot.

A wake up call, he kept his mind on the driving and his eyes on the road.

Jack turned into The Regency parking lot. After he pulled into his usual parking space, he cleaned up as much of the coffee spill as he could.

This latest mishap had him thinking. Maybe he needed to quit being so stubborn.

Yeah, shake things up a little. Put yourself out there…

Or, as they say in his line of work… it's time to face the music.

And his first step would be?

Tonight, he would call Stephanie to tell her he would meet her yoga friend.

At this point?

What did he have to lose?

CHAPTER 3

Jack grabbed the demo from the passenger seat and jumped out of his truck. As he approached the party center, he could hear a woman talking to a small child. This came from an SUV parked in front of the main entrance.

He recognized the woman's voice as Abby Kardell's. The child's voice was her two-year-old daughter, Madeline Rose.

When she saw Jack, Madeline Rose gave an excited shriek, almost dropping the cookie she was holding. And before Abby realized what she had in mind, she ran over to him, wrapping her arms around his legs in a big hug.

"Up, up, up…" This coming in a chant, she reached up to him.

So, Jack did what anyone would when confronted by an adorable toddler with curly red hair and an angelic face. He picked her up, laughing at the big grin this brought to her face. "Well, hello little one. My goodness… life would be perfect if everyone was as glad to see me as you are."

After rewarding him with another hug and insisting he take a bite of her cookie, she patted him on the cheek.

Then, as children often do, she began a close inspection of his face. This made him nervous.

Jack had very little experience with children. Because of his father's demanding schedule and his mother's frequent travels, he and his sister spent most of their time with a constantly changing succession of nannies. And even though he had friends from school, his most cherished moments were those spent in his mother's music room, writing songs and playing the piano.

He was one of those rare kids who genuinely looked forward to practicing every day.

His mother, a well-known and popular soprano in the Denver theater scene, had encouraged his wish to be a professional pianist. While his father, a prominent criminal defense lawyer, believed his focus should be on a more financially rewarding profession.

Ideally, this would be as a lawyer.

This had been an ongoing argument between his parents for as long as he could remember.

The month before he was supposed to graduate from high school was the beginning of the end of the only family he'd ever known. On their way to San Francisco for a cousin's wedding, his mother and sister perished when the small plane they were on crashed into the mountains during a snowstorm.

Jack and his father would've also been on that plane had his father not canceled out at the last minute because of a big case he was working on. Jack's choice to stay with him would have a lifelong effect on both of them.

Overcome with grief, and filled with guilt for choosing to forgo the wedding, his father had turned into someone Jack no longer knew. He rarely left his office, ignoring Jack almost completely. If, by chance, they spent time together; they fought about everything, some of their arguments leading to full-blown shouting matches. This eventually turned into long periods of silence until they didn't talk at all.

The blame for these disagreements almost always ended with what his father referred to as Jack's "damned obsession" with music.

Jack didn't think of music as an obsession. Music made him comfortable with who he was. A life filled with music was the only career he could envision.

Music was also what had helped get him through the dark days following his mother and sister's death.

Determined to make amends, Jack set aside his dream of a career in music. He took his father's advice and enrolled in college. His plan was to earn a law degree and eventually take over his father's practice.

He lasted halfway through his first year of graduate school before he left to do what he should've done from the beginning… make music.

The day Jack called his father to tell him about his change of plans was the last time they spoke. And despite his efforts to keep his father updated on what he was doing, he'd never received a response.

No one in Cleveland knew the story of his former life. And he wanted it to stay that way. This had been his goal when he'd joined Banded Together, to make a fresh start.

His vow to put a career as a pianist behind him, his first move had been a bold one. He switched from piano to drums. Not only was the transition easier than he'd expected, he also found drumming was a great way to let out his frustrations.

And, no… he hadn't given up hope, still sending updates to his father.

"Jack? Are you okay?"

He blinked, sending his thoughts scattering. When Madeline Rose held her cookie up to his mouth for another bite, the look he sent Abby bordered on panic.

"Here, let me take her." Concerned, Abby reached for Madeline Rose, settling her comfortably on her hip. Then she sent Jack a tentative smile. "Are you sure you're okay?"

He shrugged, jamming his hands in his pockets. "Yeah, I'm fine. Let's just say it's been a long day."

He nodded toward the large bakery box on the back seat of the SUV. "I take it you're dropping off a cookie order?"

"Yes, they're for a bridal shower luncheon tomorrow. Since I'm leaving for New York in the morning, I needed to deliver them today. The guys have a three-game series with the Yankees, so Sophie, Hannah and I decided to tag along."

She grinned. "Do some shopping. Maybe even get a little wild."

Jack laughed. "Oh, boy… the three of you unchaperoned in the big city? This could be dangerous, no?"

She grinned. "To be honest, what I'm most looking forward to is some adult conversation. Along with a good night's sleep." She pressed a kiss to the top of Madeline Rose's head. "This little monkey is excited about spending time with grandpa."

"Gampa?" Twisting in Abby's arms, Madeline Rose's face lit up with a big smile. After searching the area, she turned back to Abby, her face scrunched in confusion. "Where's Gampa?"

Abby laughed, giving her a hug. "He's not here, sweetie. You'll see him when we get home." She nodded over at Jack. "Now that my father has moved closer to us, the two of them have become the best of friends."

After stuffing the demo in his pocket, Jack had removed the box from the SUV. "I'm sure you have a lot to do before you leave, so let me deliver this for you. I'm headed in that direction to meet up with Jason."

"Jack, that would be fantastic." Taking advantage of his offer, she plopped Madeline Rose in her car seat, buckling her up as she spoke. "The luncheon is in the Garden Room. There should already be a buffet table set up. This is where I told them I'd leave the cookies."

He shifted the box in his arms to get a better grip before he glanced over at her, eyebrows raised. "*Geeesh…* this is heavy. How many cookies did they order?"

"Believe me when I say too many. I don't know who's worse, the bride or groom. They've turned their wedding into a three-ring circus. It's insane."

He shrugged. "Yeah, we've seen it all, haven't we?" He shifted the box in his arms to get a better grip. "Promise you'll ask for help if you need it. There's always one of us around, so you only need to ask."

She studied him for a moment before she smiled. "People always assume guys in a band are crazy and full of themselves. But you are all so kind and always ready to help."

She pressed a kiss to his cheek. "Thank you for that."

He grinned. "Yeah? Well, I'll let you in on a little secret… we do it for the cookies."

She laughed. "*Ah…* gotcha. I'll see what I can do."

CHAPTER 4

fter Jack delivered the cookies to the Garden Room, leaving them on the buffet table as Abby had instructed, he headed for the band's equipment room where Jason would be waiting.

As he passed by Darcey's office, he glanced inside. When she looked up from her computer. he grinned, coming to a stop. "Well, if it isn't our fearless leader. How's it going? Working hard?"

"Hi, Jack." Her smile was more like a grimace as she leaned back in her chair, tossing her pen on the desk.

Concerned, he moved closer. "Hey, are you okay?"

After staring at him for what felt like an eternity, she shook her head. "I'm afraid you've caught me in one of my—what was I thinking when I agreed to take on this job—moments. Because working hard doesn't even come close to describing the past three hours I've spent with Elenore Cromley and the new chef."

She ran her hand through her hair, exhaling a long, drawn-out sigh. "It seems they are in a standoff over the new menu choices. She's all about elegance and tradition, while he's into keeping up with the latest trends. I don't understand why this didn't come up when he interviewed with her. But I guess this is to be expected. Elenore's expectations are so high, it's hard to satisfy her. It's a well-known fact she's also not one to compromise."

Then she shrugged, sending him a bright smile. "Oh, well… I told them, from now on, I'm out of it. They'll have to work it out on their own."

He chuckled. "It will be interesting to see who wins. From what little I've heard, the chef is very demanding. And Elenore? Well, she's Elenore."

She laughed. "That's as good a description as any. I guess we shall have to wait and see, huh?" Coming from around her desk, she smiled. "I'm sorry, I didn't mean to bore you with my problems. If anything, I'm glad you're here. There's something I want to show you. I believe Elenore had you in mind with this surprise.

Elenore had you in mind? You don't like the sound of this… no, not at all.

A sudden uneasiness filling him, he frowned.

Quick to notice this, Darcey put her hand on his arm. "I think you'll find it's a delightful surprise."

He dragged his hand through his hair, avoiding her gaze.

Delightful? The way this day has been going, you doubt this. Especially if Elenore is involved.

When he seemed to hesitate, she grinned. "I know Jason is waiting for you, but this will only take a few minutes. Come on…"

She left the room, giving him no choice but to follow.

She kept up a continuous chatter about the catering changes they were planning to make until they reached the Grand Ballroom. After she hit the master switch to turn on the crystal chandeliers, flooding the room with light, she again motioned for him to follow her.

She led him over to the area reserved for the band, grinning as she glanced over at him. "As you can see, we have a recent addition to The Regency."

She nodded. "Compliments of Elenore."

Where there once was an arrangement of ornamental trees, a popular setting for photo shots, the space was now occupied by a majestic grand piano.

Darcey watched as Jack walked over to run his fingers in a light caress over the keys. As he stared down at the keys, his silence confused her.

She sent him a tentative smile. "I found out only last week this would be delivered today. Elenore was very insistent it was to be a surprise. She also told me I'm to let you know you have use of the piano whenever you'd like."

When Jack still had nothing to say, she added. "From what little she shared, I got the impression you've played on a piano like this one before. So you must be very good at it."

After a slight pause, she glanced over at him. "Does Jason know this?"

He traced the familiar gilded Steinway & Sons emblem with his fingertips. After dropping his hand to his side, he slowly shook his head. "I haven't played for a long time, close to fifteen years. I guess you could say I lost interest."

He shrugged. "And no, I didn't feel the need to tell Jason. A pianist wasn't what he was looking for."

Lost interest?

Curious what he meant by that, but discouraged by the closed expression on his face, Darcey gave him a big smile. "Well, according to Elenore, when you get the urge to play again, it's only right you have this amazing piano here waiting for you."

When his only response was another nod, she was at a loss.

She didn't understand. What was happening here? She thought he'd be thrilled when he saw the piano.

She glanced up at him, her look searching. "So, what do you think? It's beautiful, isn't it? And knowing Elenore, it's the best money can buy."

He finally spoke, his words almost robotic-like. "Yes, it is." And though he wanted to say more, if only to put Darcey at ease, the memories swirling around in his mind wouldn't allow this. Blinking back the unfamiliar threat of tears, he had to clear his throat before he sent Darcey a brief smile.

"I'll have to thank her."

And that was it… he had nothing more to say.

Now even more concerned, Darcey's smile was overly bright. "Well, I should get back to work. When you see Jason, can you tell him there's no hurry? I have more than enough work to keep me busy." She turned to walk away, only to pause. "I can't wait to hear you play."

A faint smile touched his lips. "I guess we'll have to see what happens…"

Relieved to see something resembling a smile, she gave him a comforting pat on the arm and left.

Halfway to her office, Darcey remembered she'd wanted to ask Jack what he thought about Margie, the new sous chef. Only yesterday she'd confessed to having a huge crush on him since Banded Together played at her cousin's wedding. And even though Darcey knew Jack probably wouldn't be interested, she had promised Margie she'd check it out.

So she headed back to the Grand Ballroom, coming to an abrupt stop right inside the entrance. Seated at the piano, his hands resting on his knees, Jack appeared to be deep in thought.

Not wanting to intrude, she backed out of the room, almost taking off in a run back to her office.

She wandered over to the window. As she gazed out at the courtyard, she wondered… what happened in Jack's past to bring on such an emotional response to the piano?

This worried her. She liked Jack. So she'd hate to see something as simple as a piano mess up his life.

Once she was back at her desk, she refreshed her computer. She hadn't been kidding when she told Jack she had a lot of work to do. The towering pile of folders on her desk, each one containing information about an upcoming event, were a testament of this. She still couldn't believe the party center was almost completely booked into the next year.

Her phone rang. Praying it wasn't another problem to add to her list, she checked her caller I. D.

She groaned. Gloria Miller, one of their most difficult clients.

Pasting a big smile on her face, she reluctantly hit answer. "Mrs. Miller, it's so nice to hear from you. Now, how may I help you?"

CHAPTER 5

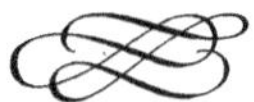

You can choose to move on,
take a chance in the unknown.
Or you can stay locked in the past,
thinking of what could've been.
~ Unknown

After Darcey had left the Grand Ballroom, Jack had planned to do the same. Yet, as though he had no control over his actions, he pulled out the piano bench.

Seated, he again reached over to run his fingers over the raised logo in front of him.

Flooded with memories, he closed his eyes. His mother's words came at him so clearly. If he didn't know better, he'd swear she was standing right next to him.

"You must never forget how lucky you are to have one of the finest hand-crafted pianos in the world at your fingertips. But the piano alone means nothing, Jacky. Your hard work and dedication will be what makes the music sing."

Jacky... this had been her nickname for him.

Against his will, his thoughts flipped right over to what could have been had his mother and sister not died in the plane crash.

A slight rustling sound told him he was no longer alone. He turned, and his gaze sweeping the room, he saw no one. Whoever it was, they had left.

This, of course, was if someone had actually been in the room.

Damn… now you're imagining things?

He groaned, dragging his hand down over his jaw.

Taking this as a sign he needed to leave, he brushed his fingers over the keys one last time. Pushing the piano bench back where it belonged, he left the room.

He was walking down the hall when he came to a dead stop.

Was this some kind of challenge? Because, for some unexplained reason, he felt this was exactly what Elenore intended it to be.

However, in his opinion, an impossible one.

He let out a sigh of frustration. He didn't like this. Until now, he had been diligent in keeping the past where it belonged, behind him, and to be forgotten. He had even convinced himself it no longer mattered.

But now? This move of Elenore's was proof he'd been fooling himself all along.

Damn…

Jack was almost to the equipment room when he realized he'd left the demo on the piano bench. He hurried back to the ballroom, and making sure not to even glance over at the piano, he grabbed the demo. Muttering to himself, once again he headed towards the equipment room.

His plan was to deliver the demo to Jason and call it a day.

Once he got home, since he'd spilled most of the coffee from Café Latte, he'd make a fresh pot.

Yeah, and he'd eat the sour cherry scone.

Heck, you might even eat two.

When Jack pushed open the door to the equipment room, he found Jason sitting at the desk, a stack of papers in front of him. He groaned, and after raking his hands through his hair, dropped his head down in his hands. The wild hair he had going on showed how frustrated he was.

Jack cleared his throat. "Hey…"

Jason lifted his head, and after throwing his pen down on the desk, he leaned back in his chair. "Well, well, well… look who finally showed up. Glad you could make it."

Choosing to ignore his sarcasm, Jack nodded over at the pile of papers. "What are you so worked up about?"

A disgusted look on his face, Jason massaged the back of his neck. "Another contract. With way too much information required." He shook his head. "I don't understand why these lawyers can't write in a language the average person can understand. Hell, I bet they don't even know what half this stuff means."

Jack wanted to tell him, from what little he remembered from his short stint in law school, knowing what half the stuff meant was a major requirement of the job.

But this might only lead to a lot of questions. Or, with Jason's current mood, a long and sarcastic commentary about lawyers in general.

Instead, he tossed the demo on the desk in front of him. "Here, this should cheer you up. Nick was pleased. He said it turned out better than expected."

When Jason didn't respond, his attention back on the contract, Jack sank down on the sofa. After a brief silence, he spoke. "I made a stop on the way. Darcey wanted to show me The Regency's newest acquisition, a grand piano, compliments of Elenore. It's one surprise after another with her, isn't it?"

Jason had picked up his pen and, with a dramatic flourish, signed the contract. After stuffing everything in a folder, he grinned over at Jack. "There, that's done. I trusted my gut and signed it. And, yeah… Elenore is something else. Darcey never knows what to expect."

The glance he gave Jack was curious. "When Darcey mentioned the piano, it occurred to me that I never asked if you play. Or if you had professional training. I play a little, yet only by ear. Now I wish I had taken lessons to at least learn the basics."

He sent Jack a thoughtful glance. "*Hmm…* how good are you? Is this something we could build on?"

Jack shrugged. "I started taking lessons when I was about four, continuing until my late teens. At one time, I had plans to take it even further." Jack shrugged. "Then I decided to go a different route."

Jason raised an eyebrow. "From piano to drums? That's quite a drastic leap in another direction, wouldn't you say?"

A sudden need to be alone with his thoughts, Jack came to his feet, pulling out his keys.

Yep, this is your cue to leave.

He sent Jason a wry smile. "Yeah, I guess you could say that. However, sometimes life gets in the way and things change." He nodded over at the demo. "So, now that you have your demo, I'm going to take off. It's been a long day."

As he began walking out of the room, Jason called out. "Hey, did Darcey say anything to you about Margie, the new sous chef they hired a while back?" He grinned. "Believe it or not, for some strange reason, she's interested in you. "

Holding back a groan, Jack came to a halt.

Here we go again. The perfect way to top off your day.

He turned to Jason. "I'm sure Margie is a fantastic person, and I'm flattered, but she's not the woman for me."

Then a sharp laugh escaped him. "What is it with you and Stephanie? She left me a message for the same reason. She wants to fix me up with a woman from her yoga class, so I'll have a date for her wedding. I assure you, I will be fine. I don't need a date. And who knows, I might even surprise both of you and find a date on my own. Stranger things have happened."

He walked out of the room, with Jason staring after him, a confused expression on his face.

He didn't understand.

What was Jack so fired up about?

Almost an hour later, Jason walked into Darcey's office.

Engrossed in her work, her face scrunched up in concentration, she was unaware of his presence.

And, just like that, he fell even more in love with her. A smile spreading across his lips, he shook his head. He was living the life in all the love songs he'd always wanted to write.

You are one lucky guy...

Sauntering over to her, he cleared his throat.

Darcey glanced up, his bemused expression making her laugh. "My goodness, what are you thinking about? You look like you're not sure about something. Or you're hiding some kind of secret."

Not sure about something? With her, you've never been more sure.

He cleared his throat. "A secret? Me?" Slowly shaking his head, he came around the desk and pulled her up from her chair. After he wrapped his arms around her, he dropped a kiss in her hair. "Ah, gorgeous, it's no secret how much I love you."

"*Hmm...* I love you, too." Her head tilted, she gazed up at him. "So, did you ask Jack about Margie? Did he say anything to you about Elenore? Or, the piano?"

He chuckled. "*Wow...* that's a lot of questions to throw out all at once. About Margie? Despite being flattered by her interest, Jack claims she's not the woman for him. He also said he doesn't need a date for the wedding. And if he did, he'd be more than capable of finding one on his own."

He smiled at her disappointed expression. "Sorry, gorgeous... these are his words, not mine."

Darcey sighed. "Oh well, we tried. But, wait a minute, what did he mean, she's not the woman for him? Is there someone else we don't know about?"

He shrugged. "Hell if I know. Jack isn't one to share details about his personal life. And Margie? She'll get over it." Then he frowned. "Jack seemed all rattled up about something. What happened when you showed him the piano?"

"I'm not sure. At first, it was if he'd found an old friend, one he never expected to see again. Yet, when I told him Elenore said it was his to use whenever he pleased, he acted like he didn't care. While at the same time, he seemed so sad. And when I returned to the ballroom because I'd forgotten to ask him about Margie, I found him seated at the piano, staring down at the keys. So, I left."

She sighed. "I got the impression he was re-living a lot of memories, good and bad. It made me sad."

After pressing a kiss to the top of her head, Jason smiled. "An old friend, huh? I guess we'll have to wait to see what happens next. It will be interesting to see if he takes Elenore up on her offer."

He pressed another kiss in her hair. "I've always felt there's a lot we don't know about Jack since he always changes the subject when you ask about his past. But I can't imagine what he told Elenore to have her bring in a grand piano." He shook his head. "I mean, who does something like that? I only know she has a way of getting information out of people. Even their deep, dark secrets."

He shrugged. "Maybe Jack is a famous pianist. This wouldn't surprise me in the least. Like they say, it's always the quiet ones that surprise you."

She studied him, a smile curving her lips. "*Hmm…* deep, dark secrets, huh? And did you share any of these secrets with Elenore that I should know about?"

She could see the teasing glint in his eyes before he laughed. "*Ah…* I'll have to think about that and get back to you."

Then, after giving her another kiss, he nodded over at her computer. "Now, are you about done here? I want to go home and spend some time with my gorgeous wife." He grinned. "I'll even make dinner."

He winked. "Or at least call in the order."

CHAPTER 6

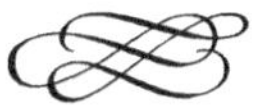

After spending too much time on his computer, yet accomplishing nothing, Jack decided to call it a night. Before he signed out, he sent a text to Stephanie.

This accomplished, he shut off the computer, plugged it into the charger and turned off the light.

After the day he'd had, he figured he'd have no problem falling asleep.

No such luck. An hour later, he was still awake.

Wide awake...

All because of the damn piano.

Every time he closed his eyes, an image of the piano popped up in his head. The vision was so real, he could almost feel the smooth ivory veneer of the keys under his fingertips.

Or catch the fleeting scent of beeswax and turpentine in the furniture polish his mother had used to maintain the piano's beautiful shine.

Stop it—don't go there.

Giving his pillow a few punches to knock it into shape, and adjusting it more comfortably under his head, he closed his eyes.

Fifteen minutes later, he was still staring wide-eyed up at the ceiling.

He didn't get it. What was Elenore Cromley up to?

Because, *come on...*a grand piano isn't something you send to someone on a whim. This would be the act of a person who is a bona fide and dedicated pianist.

Or, like Elenore, a lifelong patron of the arts with more money than they knew what to do with.

Grand pianos don't come cheap.

There was only one explanation he could think of. About five months ago, he'd stopped by The Regency to get Jason's input on a jingle they were putting together for a local company. After they wrapped it up, Jason left for the studio, but he stayed behind to make a few phone calls.

The signature loud squeak of Elenore's rubber-sole shoes was his only warning before she marched into the room. When he'd asked if she was there for Jason, she told him no, he was the person she wanted to see.

She then settled on the sofa and pulled out a bottle of water from her sweater pocket. After she took a drink, she started right in with the questions.

Had he always lived in the Cleveland area?

And if not, where was he from?

What was his favorite kind of music?

Did he always want to be in a band?

What made him decide to play the drums?

Was anyone else in his family musically gifted?

Despite keeping his answers short, he'd somehow ended up sharing almost his entire life story.

It wasn't until Elenore asked what made him choose a career in music, he opened up; the words flowing easy as he reminisced about the hours he'd spent at his mother's grand piano. Gifted by a long-time friend and mentor, the piano was her pride and joy.

When it appeared Elenore had run out of questions, for a few minutes, a companionable silence fell between them.

Elenore had been the first to speak. In her usual style, direct and to the point, she'd asked if he was still open to a career as a concert pianist.

The intense anger he first felt at her inquiry had shocked him. Resisting the urge to tell her it was none of her business, he'd barked out a resounding no.

He had then changed the subject, inquiring how the party center renovations were coming along.

Not long after that, Elenore announced it was time for her to leave. After coming to her feet, with a little help from Jack, she'd thanked him for taking the time to answer, as she put it—an old lady's meddling questions.

She'd paused at the door, sending him a stern look over the top of her glasses. "You realize it's never too late to go after what you want. Think how happy your mother would be to know you never gave up on your dream."

After she left, he had thought long and hard about she'd said.

And he decided she was wrong.

For him, it was too late.

Now beyond exhausted, he closed his eyes.

The dream started as soon as he fell asleep. Seated at the piano and about to play the beginning notes of his first song, his mind went blank. His fingers poised over the keys, for the life of him, he couldn't remember the notes.

He sent a glance out at the packed auditorium and the first person he saw was Elenore.

She nodded.

As his hands were about to come down on the keys, he woke in a sweat, his heart galloping in his chest.

It took him a long time to fall asleep after that.

CHAPTER 7

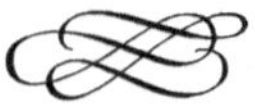

*A*cross town, on her way to the nurses' station to sign out for the night, Stephanie Bennett was checking her phone for messages.

She had a text from Jack. Her steps slowing, she checked it out.

> Okay, I give in. I'll meet this woman from your yoga class. But don't get your hopes up—my track record isn't good. Pick a time and let me know. And the invite looks great. It's getting real, kid. Sweet dreams.

Grinning from ear to ear, she dropped the phone in her pocket. She had a hunch, call it women's intuition, that this time was going to be different. Jack would discover she was right, he and Savanah were a perfect match.

At the sound of someone clearing their throat, she saw Evan leaning against the counter at the nurses' station. His arms crossed, he was smiling.

He tucked a wispy strand of her hair behind her ear. "Hey, beautiful… what's on your phone that brought on such a big smile?

She pressed a kiss to his cheek. "A text from Jack."

He nodded. "*Ah…* Jack."

Five months ago, this information would have had him up in arms.

Admit it, you were jealous as all get out.

Not anymore. Over the past few months, after working on a couple of projects together, they became good friends.

He wrapped his arms around Stephanie, smiling down at her. "Let me guess… he finally caved and said he'll meet Savanah." He shook his head at her grin. "I can't believe I'm about to say this, but you could be right about those two. They just might hit it off."

"They might?" She laughed. "How can they not? They're perfect for each other. I can't wait to text Savanah. But since it's late, I'll do that tomorrow. Don't let me forget, okay?"

He grinned. "Sure, but I doubt that's going to happen."

She slipped out of his arms and, taking a seat at the counter, signed into the computer. "Once I finish up here, we can leave."

About to hit the keys, her fingers stilled. A thoughtful expression on her face, she turned to him. "I wonder… can you do something for me?"

He'd be willing to wager everything he owned she was about to tell him someone needed her help. A smile tugging the corner of his mouth, he leaned against the counter. "*Uh, oh…* what's up?"

"Remember, I told you Nathan was back for another operation?"

He nodded.

Her forehead creased with worry, she continued. "Well, he's having a hard time with this latest surgery, slipping back to where he was right after the accident. I'm pretty sure this is because Elenore and Dr. Davis decided it would be best if Oreo wasn't around for a few days."

She frowned. "Though, I don't agree. He's so attached to that little dog."

She tilted her head, gazing up at him. "So, I think it might help if he had some interaction with someone besides a staff member. With the pain he's experiencing, we aren't at the top of his list of favorites right now. So, would you mind spending a little time with him? Talk to him, try to cheer him up?"

She had that look on her face… the one that had him ready to do anything she asked.

Anything…

So how could he refuse? Brushing his knuckles along the curve of her jaw, he smiled. "Okay, I'm on it. What room is he in?"

"Room 312. Take your time. I don't mind waiting." As he began walking down the hall, she called out to him. "Evan…"

"Hmm…" He turned, greeted by her smile.

"Thank you." She mouthed the words, *"I love you,"*

"You're welcome." The warmth of his smile traveling the distance between them as he mouthed the same to her.

She watched until he turned the corner. She still found it so hard to believe in less than a month they would be married.

Still smiling, she refreshed the computer screen.

The TV was on, the sound turned on low, when Evan walked into Nathan's hospital room. His one leg in a full cast up to his hip, he appeared to be sleeping.

But when Evan settled in the chair next to the bed, his eyelashes fluttering open, he glanced over at him.

The faintest of smiles flitted across his face. Then he frowned, his eyes closing again.

Evan leaned closer, his voice a whisper. "Hey, buddy… I heard you're having a hard time, so I thought I'd stop in to keep you company for a while."

When Nathan's only answer was a shrug, he reached over to brush his hair off his forehead. "I know you miss Oreo, and I'm sure he's missing you even more. Yet I assure you, everyone here is going to try their darnedest to get you feeling better so the two of you can be together again. You need to hang in there, okay? We're all pulling for you."

Nathan opened his eyes, searching his face before he spoke. "Will you come visit me again?"

Evan reached over to hold his hand. "Of course I will. In fact, next time I come, I'm going to bring you something I believe you'll like."

An actual smile flitted across Nathan's face. "You are? What is it?"

"Nope, you'll have to wait." Evan shook his head, chuckling at the disappointed expression on his face.

When he'd first entered the room, he noticed the dinner tray on the bedside table. He lifted the cover to reveal a dried up toasted cheese sandwich and a cup of cold tomato soup. It was obvious they had been there for a quite a while.

He glanced over at Nathan. "I take it this means you've had nothing to eat?"

Nathan shook his head.

Evan seemed to think about this before he nodded. "Okay, if I ask them to bring you something, will you try to eat? This will start the healing process and get you out of this bed even faster."

Fingering the blanket, Nathan shrugged. "I can try, I guess."

Evan grinned. "Good. Because you gotta eat if you want to get better." He raised an eyebrow. "Pancakes? Ice cream? Or maybe even French fries?"

When this only brought on another shrug, Evan pulled out his phone and sent Stephanie a text. Then he smiled over at Nathan. "Okay, now we'll find out if I've got any influence around here."

Within seconds, Stephanie responded with a thumbs up emoji. When he showed it to Nathan, this brought yet another smile to his face.

It was a step in the right direction.

Twenty minutes later, Stephanie walked into the room carrying a tray. In the middle of telling Nathan about his recent photo shoot at the Cleveland Aquarium, Evan was standing in the middle of the room. His arms held out wide, he was explaining how big the sharks were in the shark exhibit.

After watching this for a moment, she laughed. "Is this your typical fish story? The more you tell it, the bigger the catch?" She sent a wink over at Nathan. "It looks like I got here just in time."

The glance Evan sent her was one of mock disbelief. "Are you suggesting I might be exaggerating?" He frowned, shaking his head over at Nathan. "And here I thought she liked me."

Puzzled, Nathan glanced over at Evan. "She doesn't? Aren't you getting married?" Then he grinned. "Oh, I get it... you're joking, aren't you? My dad used to tease my mom all the time. He would..."

A stricken expression on his face, his words died. His bottom lip beginning to quiver, he closed his eyes.

As Evan reached for his hand, Stephanie set the tray down on the bedside table. She kept her voice low. "Do you want me to stay?"

He shook his head. "We'll be okay. Give us a little more time."

She pressed a kiss to his cheek and left.

A half hour later, Stephanie glanced up from the computer. Walking towards her, Evan was smiling. It wasn't a big smile, but it was enough to let her know whatever happened, for now, Nathan was in a better frame of mind.

She walked right into his arms. After she reached up to give him a kiss, her whisper brushed across his cheek. "Thank you."

He pulled her against him, his response also a whisper. "I feel like I can relate to what he's going through. I remember when I felt so alone, as if I had been abandoned. But where I had nothing to compare, for Nathan it's so much worse. He knows what he lost."

He sighed. "We're two of a kind, two kindred souls trying to deal with what life gave us. We understand each other."

He pressed a kiss in her hair. "But now, I'm the lucky one. You came along and life is good."

He leaned back to smile down at her. "Are you ready to go home? I know I am. After Nathan ate most of what you brought for him, he struggled to keep his eyes open. So, I think he'll sleep tonight. I told him I'd stop by sometime tomorrow to check on him."

He chuckled, shaking his head. "But I don't think he heard me."

He sent a quick glance around them before he lowered his voice. "There's something I want to give him. And I want to see if I can convince Elenore to let Oreo come back."

"You're the best." She linked her fingers behind his neck and gave him a kiss that had him wishing they were already in the privacy of their condo.

And Stephanie?

Never had she loved anyone as much as she loved him right now.

CHAPTER 8

$\mathcal{A}$s far as days went, Savanah Jackson would rate this one as a four out of ten.

Maybe even a three…

Sinking down onto the bench lining the one wall of the dance studio, she leaned her head back and closed her eyes.

She was furious, her heart pounding in her chest. And despite her attempt to conceal this, the anxious glances from the other dancers were a sign she wasn't doing a very good job.

Honestly? She didn't care. She was tired of pretending everything was okay.

And what was the cause of all this anger?

Two words… Léon Pantonelli.

The principal male dancer, he had recently joined the company. His movie star good looks, and the toned body of a dancer, may have won over the other dancers, but she saw right through him. She'd dealt with his kind in the past.

His presence alone brought on a toxic energy that had the dancers on edge. The most fitting words she could think to describe him would be downright nasty. Along with arrogant, uptight, and sarcastic, to name a few.

At least, this was her opinion.

She was also willing to bet that accent of his? It was fake. And his name, Léon Pantonelli? This wasn't his real name.

He isn't any more Italian than you are.

Suspicious of him from the start, when she realized she wasn't the only one affected by his unpredictable personality swings and irrational behavior, she decided it was time to check him out on the internet.

Her search had turned up tons of information about his long history of broken relationships. Along with dozens of photos of him with different women to validate this. Yet there was little about his success as a dancer. Most likely because he never stayed with a dance company for more than a year before moving on.

She found this information disturbing.

The bottom line?

Léon Pantonelli was trouble.

Sensing someone had come to stand in front of her, Savanah opened her eyes. Iris, a long time dancer and member of the company, plopped down on the bench beside her, handing her a bottle of water.

Savanah smiled over at her as she uncapped the bottle. "Thanks. I need something to cool me down." Her sigh was frustrated. "He makes me *so, so* angry."

She had just raised the bottle to her lips when Iris spoke. "What's going on with the two of you? With all the negative energy you're throwing around, my guess is that you were in a serious relationship that didn't end well."

A mouthful of water, Savanah almost spit it all over Iris. Wiping her mouth with the back of her hand, she choked out a groan. "*Oh, please...* don't even suggest such a thing." Her face scrunched up, she shuddered. "I don't know what his problem is, and I'm to the point, I don't care."

Iris nodded over to where Gayle, the director of the studio, stood watching them from the door to her office. "Well, she cares. Yet even when there are so many red flags, she still thinks he walks on water." She frowned. "I don't get it."

"I know. And it's so frustrating." After taking another drink, Savanah turned to Iris. "We've waited a long time for this chance, and I have no intention of letting some egotistical man take it away from us."

Iris was confused. "We?" Then she nodded. "*Ah… yes, your mother is very involved in your career, isn't she?*"

Savanah's response was curt. "My mother has dedicated her life to me. As she was also once a dancer, her advice and support have been the driving force that got me to where I am today."

Iris sighed, and after giving Savanah's knee a pat, she came to her feet. "I don't know what to tell you, except there comes a time in every mother's life she needs to let go. And you need to think about what you want, not what someone else thinks you should want."

She walked away, only to turn back, a hesitant smile on her face. "I'm sorry, I didn't intend to lecture you. But sometimes, we fail to notice what's right in front of us." She shrugged. "I hope you're not mad."

After blowing her. kiss, Savanah watched as he walked over to join the other dancers. Then she shook he head. Perhaps there was some truth in what she said. But right now? She had a bigger problem on her hands.

Léon Pantonelli was here to stay.

She glanced over to where Léon was talking with Gayle, whatever he said, making them both laugh. As though they hadn't a care in the world.

She'd had enough. It was time to pack up her stuff and go home.

After retrieving her bag from beneath the bench, she kicked off her ballet shoes and massaged her tired feet. With the longer than usual rehearsals the past week, her whole body ached from head to toe. All she wanted was to go home and indulge in a long, relaxing bubble bath.

She exchanged her ballet shoes for flats and was searching through her bag for her keys when she realized there was a loud argument across the room. It appeared Gayle and Léon's laughter from a few minutes ago had now escalated into a heated dispute.

Just be happy this time he isn't angry with you.

Unfortunately, it turned out he was…

As if on cue, Léon sent an angry string of Italian in her direction, waving his arms for emphasis. While Savanah couldn't make out what he said, it was clear she was the reason for his rant.

Well, too bad… whatever he's worked up about, you don't care.

She sighed. If only this were true. Because, no matter how much she tried to deny it, she did care. To the point she dreaded coming to the studio every day.

If she could only figure out what his problem was. Then they could talk it out, maybe even settle on a truce.

She sighed again.

You're dreaming. You know this isn't going to happen.

Now even more determined to leave, shrugging into her coat and grabbing her bag from the bench, she headed for the exit. Her hand on the doorknob, she was about to open the door when Gayle called to her.

In the uneasy silence that followed, feeling as though all eyes were on her, she shook her head and slipped outside. Whatever Gayle had to say, it would have to wait until tomorrow.

The rain of earlier had ended, although the temperature had dropped. Wrapping her coat even tighter around her, and dodging the puddles as she ran, Savanah headed for her car.

Her evening was all planned out. After a quick dinner, she would indulge in a soothing bubble bath to ease her aching muscles. Then she'd go to bed. Not the most exciting way to spend her time off, but to her, right now it sounded wonderful. And after the past few nights of the same reoccurring dream, Léon's presence sending it spiraling into a nightmare, she could use a good night's sleep.

With him as her partner, the dream always began as a normal dance routine. Moving as one, they surrendered to the music.

Suddenly seized by a fit of uncontrollable rage, his movements became frantic, a whirlwind of uncontrolled energy, his steps almost too erratic to follow

Fear racing through her, she tried to persuade him to slow down. However, as dreams go, her warnings went unheard. Instead, he lifted her up, his muscles straining as he tried to hoist her even higher.

And then?

He let her go.

Making no move to catch her, he threw back, roaring with laughter.

Just as she was about to hit the floor, she jolted awake, her mouth open in a silent scream. Her heart pounding, it took her a long time to fall back asleep. Only to fall back into the same dream.

So, of course, she was worried.

Only yesterday she'd pulled Léon aside to ask if he had concerns with their routine. Or if they needed to make any changes.

He'd stared at her for so long, she didn't think he was going to respond. Then he gave a harsh laugh. "There's nothing wrong with the routine. So, instead of blaming others, maybe you should wonder if the problem is with you?"

A look of contempt on his face, he'd turned and walked away.

The problem is with you? Was the man crazy?

So she had no alternative except to talk to Gayle, something she'd wanted to avoid. And she needed to do this soon.

You are professionals, not children.

So, this shouldn't be happening.

Now waiting for the traffic light to turn green, Savanah glanced over to see Café Latte coming up on her right. Since her encounter several months ago with the man who gave her his sour cherry scone, she'd avoided the coffee shop.

To her, it was a moment best left behind.

Out of sight, out of mind, right?

But she was kidding herself. This would never happen. She would forever remember what happened that day.

Beginning with his name…

Jack… he told you his name is Jack…

A wistful smile curved her lips. She remembered every word he'd said, the way his gaze held hers, he'd had her so she couldn't even think straight.

He embodied everything she had always imagined the man she'd fallen in love with would be. The fact he was a musician had her dreaming even more.

How perfect was this? Hadn't he said so himself?

*"I'm a musician. I'd say this means you and I
are a perfect match, no? You need music to*

dance. And I need inspiration to write music.
I believe this is how all great love stories start."

And if that wasn't enough, he'd gone on to say…

"After all, we've already found out we have the
same taste in scones. So, imagine the possibilities."

She closed her eyes, her thoughts running wild.
Imagine the possibilities...
She groaned. What was she thinking? This encounter had taken place months ago. No doubt he had already forgotten all about her.
A relationship with him was out of the question.
Remember? Your career is still your top priority.
Her fingers tapping on the steering wheel, she sent another glance over at the coffee shop. The half-empty parking lot meant the after-work crowd hadn't arrived yet. So, what were the odds she'd run into him again? Highly unlikely, right?
Coffee and a sour cherry scone sounded really good right now. And after the day she had? If anyone deserved a treat, it would be her.
One more glance over at the coffee shop, and before she could change her mind, she pulled into the parking lot. One quick check in the rearview mirror, and satisfied with what she saw, she marched across the parking lot and threw open the door. A determined smile on her face, she headed over to the counter to place her order.

Fifteen minutes later, Savanah was back in her car. A cup of coffee and a bag holding the sour cherry scone sat on the console beside her.
She rested her head back against the seat and closed her eyes.
Well, that turned out to be a complete waste of time, didn't it?
She had hoped the woman from last time would be behind the counter. By the cheerful banter she and Jack shared, it was obvious they knew each other fairly well.
Instead, a teenager had taken her place.
Did this even matter? What would you have said to her if given the chance?
No doubt she would've come across as desperate—even humiliating

herself to the extent she could never show her face in the coffee shop again.

Although she knew what she planned to order, she'd stalled for time, signaling for the other customers in line to go ahead of her as she checked out the display of baked goods.

When she was the only person at the counter, she knew she couldn't wait any longer without coming across as crazy. So, she placed her order for a sour cherry scone and a medium coffee to go.

In an attempt to stall even longer, she had then engaged the girl behind the counter in a conversation covering everything from the benefits of coffee to the unpredictability of the weather. This was while she kept a close eye on the entrance, checking out everyone who entered the shop.

And, once again, disappointed, it wasn't Jack.

With nothing more to say, and one more sweeping glance around the café—you know, in case she had somehow missed him—she'd left.

She groaned, dropping her forehead to the steering wheel.

This is insane. Why are you torturing yourself like this? You need to forget about him, because it's not going to happen…

Because as unforgettable as those few minutes had been for her, she found it hard to believe it meant the same for him. Nor did he come across as a man who lacked female companionship.

There was also the possibility sour cherry scones weren't even his thing. Instead, he had stopped in to pick up one for a co-worker, or his girlfriend. Perhaps even his wife.

No wife, remember? You checked his left hand, and there was no wedding band.

She watched as a man got out of his car and headed for the café entrance. Once again disappointed it wasn't Jack, she started her car.

She needed that bubble bath now more than ever.

Her decision to drop in Café Latte for coffee and a sour cherry scone?

It certainly hadn't been one of her better ideas.

CHAPTER 9

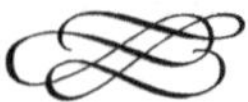

After dinner and a relaxing bath, Savanah glanced over at the clock on the microwave.

It was still early, not even nine o'clock yet.

Filled with a restless energy, she tossed a load of clothes in the washer. Grabbing a broom, she swept the kitchen floor.

The broom put away, she wandered over to the fireplace. Wrapping her arms around herself, she gazed around the room. Six months had passed since she'd moved into the condo, yet she still found it hard to believe it was really hers.

She loved everything about it. The cathedral ceiling, along with the large Palladium window overlooking a wooded backyard, made the great room and kitchen area seem larger than it was. While the marble fireplace, built-in bookcases, Brazilian wood flooring, and white woodwork, gave the room the clean and traditional look she wanted.

A quartz topped island, with seating for six, divided this space from the kitchen. The appliances were stainless steel, the cabinets a soft white.

A master bedroom with an en suite bathroom, a second bedroom, bathroom, and a laundry room made up the rest of the condo.

It was perfect.

There was one drawback. And it was a big one. This would be the non-ending argument with her mother about the move.

She failed to understand why Savanah needed a place of her own. She believed marriage was the only reason for a woman to leave home. As old-fashioned as this sounded, to her it made perfect sense.

And with Savanah's dream of becoming a professional ballerina now a reality, this was her time to shine. She certainly didn't need the additional stress of being a homeowner. Nor did she need any added distractions.

By distractions, her mother meant a relationship. A man would only complicate her life now. Since this was what led to the end of her own career in dance, she wanted to make sure Savanah didn't follow in her footsteps. Time for that would come later.

Since it was obvious they would never agree, whenever her mother began with another one of her lectures, she quickly changed the subject.

She picked up the remote. After she watched the latest saved episode of Dancing With the Stars, she'd go to bed. She needed to be at her best tomorrow to handle Léon.

Just as she was plugging her phone into the charger, she saw she had a text from Stephanie.

> Hey, I feel like we haven't talked in so long. I know you can't make yoga this week, but can you do coffee at Café Latte on Thursday around five? It's my day off. Let me know if this will work for you. Miss you—

Her first reaction? With rehearsals for Swan Lake now in full swing, this was impossible.But after reading Stephanie's message again, she thought, why not? She hadn't missed a day since joining the company. So, if only to escape the drama with Léon, perhaps it was time to take a break.

She missed talking to Stephanie. They had become friends when signing up for the same yoga. The weekly class had now become her one chance at a social life.

Well, maybe it's time for a change.

She typed out her answer.

The text sent, she turned out the light.

She was drifting off to sleep when her lashes flew open.

What about Jack?

What if he showed up at the coffee shop?

But isn't this why you stopped there today? Hoping he might be there?

This was different. She'd told Stephanie almost nothing about that day in Café Latte, how she secretly cast her encounter with Jack as the start of a modern-day fairy tale. Jack, of course, was the charming and handsome prince, while she slipped into the role of Cinderella, fleeing the coffee shop with him in pursuit. But, unlike Cinderella, she had left no clues behind.

Fairy tales don't usually end in awkward reunions. Yet, the thought of Jack showing up at the coffee shop sent her bolting upright in bed, her heart racing. Surely, she would embarrass herself again.

Stephanie would think you were crazy—there's no way you can do this.

She grabbed her phone from the nightstand, her fingers hovering over the screen to text Stephanie she had to cancel. But then she groaned, tossing it aside as she fell back on the bed.

This was ridiculous. She was freaking out about something that probably wouldn't even happen. What were the odds he'd remember her—or that instant chemistry that sparked between them before she went and ruined it?

Worse yet, if he did, he'd recall her running off—reason enough to avoid her like the plague.

And whose fault was that?

Remember, you were the one who ran…

She placed the phone back on the nightstand and snuggled back under the covers. She closed her eyes, letting her mind transport her to a familiar haven that always brought a sense of peace in troubled times.

Her own private dance floor.

She didn't know where it was, or how she found it, only that the dreams she had always lulled her to sleep.

She took on the part of Odette, the role she was hoping to earn in the ballet company's upcoming production of *Swan Lake*. And although Jack was a musician, and not a dancer, she gave him the role of Siegfried.

Remember, it was her dream. This meant she could pick or choose whatever she wanted.

Imagine the possibilities, right?

Minutes later, she drifted off to sleep.

Across town, Stephanie's shift had ended. As she was waiting for the elevator, she checked her phone for messages.

Savanah had answered her text.

> I miss talking to you, too. With all the drama going on in the studio, I could use a break. So, count me in. See you Thursday at five.

She immediately sent a text off to Jack. The first part of her plan in place, she was smiling as she ran out to her car.

Stephanie Bennett—make that soon to be Stephanie Marshall—you are a genius.

Jack and Savanah?

Again, she had a good feeling about this.

CHAPTER 10

*S*tephanie was the first to arrive at Café Latte Thursday afternoon. In fact, she was fifteen minutes early.

The enticing aroma of freshly brewed coffee and homemade baked goods greeting her when she walked into the little café, she headed right for the counter, eager to place her order.

A chocolate chip muffin and a cup of hazelnut flavored coffee—her favorite and a Café Latte exclusive blend—on her tray, she grabbed the last table by the window. With a clear view of the parking lot, she'd be able to see Jack and Savanah when they arrived.

She was early only because she was nervous. Even though she had no reason to be. After all, she hadn't done anything illegal or sneaky.

Well, in a way, you have. At least with Savanah. She doesn't know you've asked Jack to join you.

What's the worst that could happen? In the event they didn't hit it off, something she couldn't see happening, there was no pressure.

Right?

No, it would be a well-deserved break for all of them. They'd share a lighthearted conversation, drink their coffee, and when the time seemed right, they'd leave. If they didn't want to see each other again, so be it.

She'd given it her best shot.

But why was she even questioning this again? A dancer and a musician? This was almost too good to be true. Evan had even agreed you couldn't ask for a more perfect match.

She eyed her muffin. It wouldn't hurt to have a few bites while she waited, right? After a small salad for lunch, it's understandable she was hungry. More like famished.

She picked up her knife, her plan to only eat half.

Ten minutes later, and still no sign of either Jack or Savanah, she decided she might as well finish the rest of the muffin.

After another five minutes passed by, and still alone at the table, she pulled out her phone to check her messages.

There was only one. The florist who needed to confirm the final flower order for the wedding.

After sending a response, she glanced out at the parking lot just in time to see Savanah had arrived and was about to enter the café. So, after dropping her phone into her pocket, she waved to get her attention.

When Savanah reached the table, Stephanie gave her a big hug. "I'm so glad you made it. I was wondering if I goofed up the time."

After setting her purse on the table, Savanah pulled out a chair. Once seated, she sent Stephanie a smile. "No, you're fine. I'm late, and I apologize for that. You can blame this on Léon. I swear, as soon as he found out I had plans to leave early, he decided we needed to go over the end of the second act one more time. He claimed I was off on the count."

She frowned. "He's the one out of sync, not me. For some unexplained reason, he thinks he can do a better job than the choreographers. Instead, he's turning the production into a complete disaster. No one knows what they're supposed to be doing anymore."

Then, after shrugging off her coat, she sent Stephanie another smile. "But enough about him. I'm so glad you suggested this. As you can tell, I need this break." She glanced over at the long line at the counter. "Since they're so busy, I'll wait a few minutes before I go place my order. I'd rather talk to you than eat. Even though I've been thinking about their sour cherry scones all day."

Her brow creased in thought, Stephanie studied her. "*Hmm...* speaking of scones, what happened with the guy you met here a while ago? Have you seen him since then?"

Still reluctant to share any details of that day, Savanah shook her head. "No, I haven't. And it's been months since that happened. For all I know, he was from out of town, here on business. Which means it's unlikely I'll ever run into him again."

You might be a little superstitious, but why jinx it? This way, you can keep the memory to yourself a little longer.

She changed the subject. "Before I forget, your invitation came yesterday, and it's beautiful. I already mailed my response. How are the rest of the wedding plans coming along?"

A topic Stephanie never tired of, she began filling Savanah in on all the details.

Jack started up his truck. The sound of screeching tires and flying gravel filled the air as he made a sharp turn out of The Regency parking lot.

He frowned at the cloud of dust visible in his rearview mirror.

Take it easy, buddy. A ticket for reckless driving isn't something you want right now. You'd never live it down.

His excuse?

He was late.

And what was the reason for this?

He had no one to blame but himself. Had he gone straight to his truck after he left Jason, he wouldn't be driving like a maniac, trying to make up for lost time.

Their plan to dedicate the entire afternoon to a new project the band was working on, things had progressed at a much faster speed than expected.

This was fine with Jack.

Even though it's possible he imagined this, he'd swear Jason was acting a little strange. More than once, he caught him studying him, an almost gleeful smile flashing across his face before he averted his gaze.

As though he was in on some kind of secret. Or he was waiting for the right time to bring up something he knew he had no business talking about.

Jack had a hunch this "something" had to do with Stephanie. Given the close brother-sister relationship she and Jason shared, there was a strong possibility she had told him about his meeting at Café Latte with her friend.

Well, he was out of luck. Because no way in hell would he bring it up. The last thing he wanted was advice from Jason.

As you've already told Stephanie, it's a long shot. So, your expectations are low.

Again? It wasn't a big deal.

Period.

Following their decision to call it quits for the day, and with Jason's cheerful good luck following him out the door, his plan to hop in his truck and head for the café got sidetracked.

Before he could convince himself otherwise, after a quick glance to make sure no one else was around, he made the impulsive decision to take a detour, slipping into the Grand Ballroom.

And there it was… the grand piano, in all its glory.

It drew him like a magnet.

However, as he stared down at the keys—reminding himself it was no big deal, he only needed to hit the damn keys and play something, anything—he couldn't do it.

It appeared he'd forgotten everything he'd ever learned.

So, after flexing his fingers, he tried again.

Yet again, there was nothing.

Five minutes later, still staring down at the keys—in what he now thought of as an unspoken apology—he brushed his fingers over the keys and left the ballroom.

Perhaps his father was right. He was obsessed. How else could you describe his behavior?

Again, it was only a piano.

Yet you're letting it take over your life…

This explained why, almost fifteen minutes past the time he was to meet Stephanie, he was only now pulling into the Café Latte parking lot.

For a few minutes, he remained in his truck, wondering what in *God's* name had convinced him this would be a good idea. After a quick check in the rearview mirror and making a few passes through his hair, he took a deep breath and got out of his truck.

You've got this, you're going to be fine.

Remember… he wasn't expecting much.

Savanah didn't mind listening to Stephanie chatter on about her wedding plans. She understood how excited she was. But after watching her add another reminder to this pocket size wedding planner she had? A notebook she said she'd die if she lost it?

She wondered if all the fuss was worth the anxiety.

When she caught Stephanie glancing out at the parking lot again, following with a frustrated sigh, she placed her hand on her arm. "Hey, is there somewhere else you need to be? If so, I understand. I know you have a lot going on. We can always do this another time."

Mortified, Stephanie shook her head. "Oh, no… Savanah, I'm so sorry. And no, I don't have any other plans, only dinner later with Evan. I thought I saw… well, what I thought… there's someone…"

She shook her head, pressing her lips together to keep from blurting out the truth. Regardless of how trivial, telling a lie was way out of her comfort zone, her guilty expression always giving her away.

She sent another desperate glance out the window, almost diving out of her chair when she caught sight of Jack's truck pulling into a parking spot.

Now more angry than worried—thinking he'd better have a really good reason for being late—she picked up her empty cup, sending Savanah a cheerful smile. "The line is going to get any shorter, so I'm going to get a re-fill. Tell me what you want and I'll get it for you."

Savanah stood, reaching for her purse. "That's okay, I can get—"

Stephanie cut her off, almost shoving her back in the chair. "No, you stay here." She said this so loud, the people at the next table glanced over to see what was going on.

Savanah sank back in her chair, a nervous laugh escaping her. "Are you sure?"

After Stephane sent another glance out the window, where she could see Jack was now making his way across the parking lot, she sent Savanah an even brighter smile. "We don't want to lose our table, so you should stay here. This will be my treat. It's the least I can do after boring you with wedding plans for the last ten minutes."

Savanah nodded, thinking it might be best to humor her. "Okay, I'll guard the table with my life. I'll have a regular coffee and a sour cherry scone. If they're sold out, you choose. I trust your judgement. And thanks you for treating."

"Gotcha." Stephanie turned and took off in a sprint to join the line at the counter.

While she was waiting, Savanah checked her phone. The only message of importance was from Gayle regarding the costume fittings for Swan Lake. The plan was for everyone to meet at the dance studio tonight at seven. Because of a mixup with scheduling, this was now the only time available.

The time was now 5:30 p.m.

So, as she tucked her phone back in her pocket, she wasn't worried.

She had plenty of time.

CHAPTER 11

Jack had barely stepped foot into Café Latte when Stephanie appeared at his side, latching onto his arm. He raised an eyebrow. "Well, hello there."

"Jack…" She glared up at him. "Where have you been? Whatever the reason, it better be good. I was wondering if you weren't coming."

"Whoa… I'm sorry. Unfortunately, the reason I'm late is a lame one." He shrugged. "But I'm here now."He sent a brief glance around them. "Is your friend here?"

She nodded. "She's saving our table."

"Okay, tell me what you both want so you can go join her."

She sighed, shaking her head. "No, this is supposed to be a random meeting, remember? The story is I ran into you while waiting in line and you looked so lonely, I suggested you join us."

He sent her a long look, unable to hide the smile tweaking the corner of his mouth. "Are you sure about this? Because I don't see how making me sound desperate will help my case."

She laughed. "Don't worry, I'll let her know, even though you may seem hopeless, you're still a great catch."

She sent a glance around the room before she smiled up at him. "And seriously? You can't tell me you haven't noticed almost every woman here has had their eye on you the moment you walked in. I'm willing to bet most of them would jump at the chance to have coffee with you."

He acknowledged Stephanie's comment with a shrug. "You're exaggerating."

She laughed. "You're something else. Then again, perhaps this is what makes you so charming."

"And now I'm charming?" Running his hand through his hair, unaware this gave him an even more disheveled and sexy kind of look, he rolled his eyes. "Okay, if this is some kind of pep talk, there's no need. Just be glad I'm here, ready to please, and as usual, expecting little."

"I know, I know… you've made that very clear." Then she frowned. "Please promise you won't hurt her."

He glanced at her in surprise. "What makes you think I'd do that?"

She studied him for a moment. Then she nodded. "I'm sorry, you're right. Forget I even said that. It's only that she's gone through a lot of changes over that past few months… moving across country and starting a new job. Then, there's her mother. Don't even get me started on that woman."

"Her mother? What does her mother have to do with this?" He groaned, massaging the back of his neck. "*Geeez…* this is not what a guy likes to hear. What's up with her mother?"

He frowned, peering more closely at her. "And what else haven't you told me I should know?"

He groaned. "Please don't give me the dreaded—she has a great personality—line no one wants to hear."

She shook her head. "Nope, it's all good. In fact, I'm confident you'll be thanking me before the day is over."

He laughed. "You're pretty confident about this, aren't you?"

"Yes, I am." Smiling, she handed him her empty cup. "Here, I need a refill of hazelnut. Savanah wants a regular coffee and a sour cherry scone if they still have any left. If they don't, any scone will be fine."

A faint smile coming over his face, he appeared lost in thought. She nudged him with her elbow, "Hey, what's with the smile?"

He blinked. "Sorry, I guess I got distracted for a moment. So, your friend's name is Savanah? That's a pretty name. And she wants a sour cherry scone, huh? How ironic. One would almost wonder…"

Then he shook his head. "Nah, that's crazy."

Puzzled, Stephanie wondered what he was mumbling about. But before she could ask, he'd turned to place their order.

Savanah slipped her phone back in her pocket. Wondering why Stephanie had been gone for so long, she glanced over to see she had left the counter, now on her way back to the table.

Stephanie began chattering the moment she reached Savanah. "Sorry for the delay. I ran into a good friend of mine. With the wedding taking up so much of my time, I haven't talked to him in a while. So, I invited him to join us. I hope you don't mind?" Without waiting for a response, she moved aside so Jack could set the tray with their orders on the table.

Her heart leaping to her throat, Savanah stared in disbelief at the man standing in front of her.

"Jack?"

His concentration on the loaded tray, every nerve in Jack's body jumped to attention at the sound of Savanah's voice.

It was a voice he'd hadn't been able to forget. And the fact she had remembered his name made this moment so much sweeter.

Somehow, and he wouldn't be able to tell you how he managed this without dropping the tray, he lifted his head to look right into her eyes. As if no time had passed, he found himself right back to when they first met, the world and everything around them coming to a grinding halt.

Except for his heart. Thundering in his chest, so fast and so hard, he found it a struggle to even breathe.

He was in disbelief.

My God… the dancer…

He opened his mouth to say hello. Yet, as had happened before, even this one simple word failed him. Instead, with what he was sure had to be a goofy smile on his face, he could only stare.

His gaze roaming over her, he took it all in. If possible, she was even more beautiful than the image he'd kept tucked in his mind over the past months.

And now he had a name to put to this vision of loveliness in front of him.

Savanah...

He smiled. Already the lyrics of a song were rolling around in his mind, making it hard for him to think straight. He looked down at the tray he was holding, if only to take a few moments to regain his composure. Then he glanced over at her. The dazed expression on her face told him the connection he'd been so sure of when they first met?

It was still there.

And even better, it was obvious she felt the same.

This had to be some kind of sign, right? A second chance of sorts? Because, what were the odds this woman would be the same person Stephanie wanted him to meet?

A memory clicked in his mind. The Cleveland Elite Awards Dinner last May. Nominated for an award, he'd asked Stephanie to be his date. This is when she told him there was a woman in her yoga class she wanted him to meet. Since she was a dancer, and he was a musician, she had predicted they were a perfect match.

Damn... you should've taken her up on that. Look at how much time you've wasted.

He shook his head. Could it be that women really did have this intuition thing going for them? If so, he was now a believer. From now on, he'd take Stephanie more seriously.

Of course, he'd never tell her this. He'd never hear the end of it if he did. Instead, a huge smile on his face, he turned to her. "So, this amazing woman is your friend?"

Unable to hide her jubilation, Stephanie nodded. This was turning out even better than she had hoped. Jack's elated expression, along with Savanah's flushed cheeks, was all the proof she needed. Though Jack and Savanah might not know it yet, they couldn't be any more perfect for each other.

Yep, your intuition has come through big time.

So, her smile was big enough for both of them. "*Hmm...* even though it appears you've already met, and introductions might not be necessary, Jack, I'd like you to meet Savanah Jackson. And Savanah, this is Jack Buchanan."

Worry creased her forehead. "Please don't tell me you've met before and it didn't work out."

The corner of Jack's mouth quirked up in a smile. "*Ah...* on the contrary, something definitely 'worked out' for us. At least for me, it did. Something wonderful. Right here in Café Latte, while in line to place our orders."

He glanced over at Savanah, a slow smile curving his mouth. "But, for some unknown reason—and I hope it wasn't because of something I did—this beautiful woman ran off before I even had the chance to get her name. And I've been hoping to run into her ever since."

He chuckled, shaking his head. "I've lost count of how many times I've stopped by here on the chance this might happen."

He sent a nod towards the tray. "And to think this all came about because of our mutual fondness for something as simple as a scone."

He sent Savanah a wink. "A sour cherry scone. Something I will be forever grateful."

He gestured to the chair next to her. "May I?"

That he would be so close, her heartbeat jumped right into high gear, her reply a breathless whisper. "Yes, yes... of course. Please sit..."

He waited. Then he cleared his throat. "Savanah?"

She glanced up at him.

"Your purse?" He gave a nod toward the table.

When she realized he was waiting for her to move her purse to make room for the tray, she became even more flustered. She made a grab for the purse, almost knocking the tray out of his hands and sending coffee sloshing over the rims of the cups.

Then, to heighten her anxiety even further, as he placed the tray on the table, his hand accidentally brushed against hers, sending a tremor rippling through the both of them.

Her breath catching in her throat, she sneaked a glance up at him.

Had he felt it, too?

His response?

He winked, his nod confirming he did.

Now blushing like crazy, she lunged across the table and grabbed a napkin, mumbling as she tried to wipe up the spill. "Oh my gosh, I made a mess, didn't I? Let me go get more napkins."

As she made a move to stand, he put his hand on her arm, and darn if this didn't send another one of those tremors racing through them.

"Hey, it's okay. Please, sit down." Then he aimed a smile right at her. The same smile she'd filed away with all the other memories of that day, in case she never saw him again.

Sitting back in her chair, unaware she was twisting the napkin in her hands, she gave him a weak smile. "I'm sorry. I have no idea what my problem is."

He placed his hand over hers. "It's okay, Vanababe. No harm done."

Vanababe?

He realized what he'd said the moment the word flew out of his mouth. And now he was the one to panic.

What in God's name are you doing? Trying to scare her away again? You better hope she didn't catch what you said.

The likelihood of this happening vanished when she turned towards him, wide-eyed with surprise.

He cleared his throat. "I'm sorry, that sort of slipped out. I have a tendency to play around with words, and how they might work in a song." He shrugged. "I guess you could say it's all part of my job."

Aware he was rambling, and eager to change the subject, he zeroed in on the tray, and reaching for a cup, he handed it to Stephanie. "Here you go, Steff. Hazelnut as requested."

Then he set a cup in front of Savanah. "And I believe you're the regular coffee and a sour cherry scone. A perfect pairing, if I may say so." And even though he'd claim this was purely accidental, again his hand brushed against hers.

This sent another tremor, or maybe even what he'd like to think of as a spark, traveling through them. However, it was the blush rising in her cheeks that had his smile grow even bigger.

Now, he could be wrong, but this led him believe fate was on their side.

Savanah was struggling. That the attraction she felt for this man was even stronger than she remembered? This had her so rattled she couldn't even look at him. Heaven knows what might come out of her mouth if she did. And if the opportunity arose? She'd try to make a run for it, like she had the first time she saw him.

Yes, the connection was present.

So, what's the problem?

Nothing had changed.

Remember? The timing was off. At this stage of her career, there was no room for a man like Jack. It didn't matter how well-suited they were. Or how wonderful it would be to have him in her life. It couldn't happen.

End of story.

Unfortunately, it appeared her heart had no intentions of going along with this.

And Jack?

Surprisingly, given his track record in this kind of situation, his confidence was high as he waited for Savanah's response. As long as he didn't goof it up, everything should fall into place.

So, yes… his hopes were high.

CHAPTER 12

$\mathcal{A}$fter mulling it over, Savanah decided it might be wiser to let Jack's use of endearment slide.

Why even mention it? Especially when she'd already convinced herself that nothing could come from this fleeting encounter??

Vanababe…

It wasn't that she disliked it—because in all honesty, she liked it a lot. And try as she might, she couldn't ignore that something had shifted in her. With just that one word, she was hit with this rush of emotions, butterflies fluttering in her chest.

Was this what they called falling in love?

But even if it was, it didn't matter. Tomorrow, this moment would be only a memory, and she'd return to her life as a dancer.

So, no—she told herself, love had nothing to do with how she felt.

Taking Savanah's silence as a sign she was okay with his blunder—as he rather liked that it had come to him so naturally—Jack was smiling as he turned to her. "So, you and Stephanie met in yoga class?"

Wrapping her hands around her coffee cup, the glance Savanah sent Stephanie bordered on a glare. That Jack knew they did yoga together proved Stephanie had planned this meeting.

Nope, Jack's presence was no accident.

Her smile stretching from ear to ear, Stephanie sent Savanah a nod of encouragement. *"Hmm... I think I'll let you answer this."*

Savanah made a face at her before she smiled shyly at Jack. "When I moved to Cleveland, outside of the dance studio, Stephanie was the first person I met." She grinned. "We tend to be the troublemakers of the class. When we goof up, we laugh. Sometimes, a lot. And this doesn't go over well with the rest of the class."

She shrugged. "They take it so seriously.

Stephanie laughed. "I goof up, you mean. You put everyone to shame at how graceful you are. You've impressed even Melody."

"Ah, yes... Melody, the infamous yoga instructor." Jack nodded before he glanced over at Savanah. "Stephanie has tried to convince me many times to come to a class. And just as many times, I've refused." His head tilted, he studied her before his lips slowly curved into a smile. "If only I had known..."

He watched as the color again filled her cheeks before she grabbed her cup, bringing it to her mouth for a drink.

This only made his smile grow bigger.

Not that he wanted her to feel uncomfortable. It was more that he couldn't keep his eyes off her, fascinated by every move she made.

No doubt you're scaring her to death. Don't forget how she ran away from you once.

This was why he was determined to find out as much about her as possible. That she'd only just moved to the Cleveland area, was a dancer, shared his fondness for cherry scones, and did yoga, but didn't take it seriously?

This wasn't enough.

To prove his presence had no effect on her, Savanah reached for her scone and cut it in half. As she began buttering it, she peeked a glance over at him.

He was watching her, the intensity of his gaze enough to have her set the knife back on her plate. After she dropped her hands to her lap, hoping he hadn't noticed they were shaking, she sent him a shy smile. "You should come. You'd be a welcome addition to the class."

He nodded. "You think so, huh? Well, I might just do that."

Stephanie, who was following their conversation, laughed. "Hey, all the times I've asked you to come to a class, only to be shot down, and now you're suddenly on board? *Hmm...*"

After a drink of coffee, she glanced over at Savanah. "Like Jason, Jack is a superb dancer, so I think some of the moves would come easy to him." Her brow furrowed in thought. "Now, he may not be as flamboyant as Jason, but he is definitely better than most. Why, I remember the one time he..."

Before Stephanie shared another personal or embarrassing fact about him, Jack cut her off, directing his comment to Savanah. "About dancing, when we first met, in what now feels like ages ago, I believe you told me you're a dancer. Is this with the Cleveland Ballet?"

She shook her head. "I wish, but, no. The company I'm with is a spin-off of the Cleveland Ballet." She shrugged. "I guess you could call us the second string? Or a backup option? Not quite good enough for the real thing, but still hoping to get that big break."

He leaned back in his chair, shaking his head. "As beautiful and graceful as you are, I find it hard to believe you'd be second to anyone. I bet you're an amazing dancer." As he said this, he reached for her knife and, after buttering the scone, he cut off a piece and handed it to her.

He did this as if it was the most natural thing in the world.

She watched, almost mesmerized, as he cut another piece of scone for himself. After he popped it in his mouth, realizing what he did, he sent her a guilty glance. "*Oh, geeez...* I'm sorry. Again, I don't know what came over me. I should've asked."

She laughed. "It's okay. If you think about it, I do owe you." And following his example, she popped the piece of scone into her mouth.

Watching this, he chuckled. "Can I let you in on a little secret? I have more than enough scones for both of us stashed away in my freezer. These would be from the many trips I made in the past few months, hoping to run into you again."

He refused to share his theory about why he did this. At least not yet.

God, no... she'd run off for sure if you did.

Instead, he cut off another piece of the scone and, after popping it in his mouth, he gave her a very mischievous smile.

And it was at this moment, despite her effort to convince herself otherwise—as falling in love wasn't an option—Savanah's emotions took over. And she felt herself slowly slipping under his spell.

Yes, she was falling in love with Jack Buchanan.

Overwhelmed by this newfound knowledge, the smile she sent him was a shaky one.

She didn't have a chance, and she knew it.

She was in trouble... *big trouble.*

CHAPTER 13

I like her because she smiles at me and means it.
~ Anonymous

A sip of his lukewarm coffee had Jack coming to his feet. "I need a refill.

Can I get anything for either of you?"

When Savanah and Stephanie shook their heads, he turned to leave. Only to pause, sending a grin to both of them. "If you're planning to talk about me while I'm gone, please be kind."

Stephanie waited until he was far enough away before she turned to Savanah, a gleeful expression on her face. "I knew it, I just knew it. You and Jack are perfect for each other, the chemistry between you is off the charts. And don't deny it, because you know I'm right."

Her eyebrows shot up. "And then it turns out you've already met? I can't understand why neither of you ever mentioned this to me. Imagine how this could've changed things if you had."

Then she grinned. "And then to find out all this time Jack has been coming here hoping to run into you again? Seriously, Savanah… this is the closest thing to a modern day fairy tale you could ask for."

Think of the possibilities…

Murmuring this, Savanah smiled. Then she sighed, shaking her head. "Stephanie, I can't do this. I need to focus on my dancing. It wouldn't be fair to either of us."

Stephanie sighed. "I want you to look me in the eye and tell me you there's nothing between you. No spark, no connection, and most of all, no regrets if you never saw him again." She tilted her head, a thoughtful expression on her face. "Or, better yet, you wouldn't mind if I fixed him up with someone else. I can think of a few…"

Savanah's head shot up, her eyes narrowed. She didn't like the sound of this. Fix him up with someone else? Who did Stephanie have in mind? "You don't mean Melody, do you? Because she would be all wrong for him. She's nice, but…

Her words faded at the big smile on Stephanie's face.

Stephanie laughed. "She's not you, right? And I agree. Because it's obvious he's fallen for you big time. He looks at you as though he wants to devour you." At Savanah's worried expression, she added, "but in a good way, of course."

After glancing over to where Jack was at the coffee station, she turned back to Stephanie and sighed. "He is perfect, isn't he?"

Her finger to her lips, Stephanie nodded over to where Jack was now about to approach their table. She whispered. "Shh… here comes your perfect man now."

Once Jack had set his cup on the table and took his seat next to Savanah, he grinned at both of them. "So, what did you girls talk about while I was gone? Should I be worried?"

Stephanie laughed. "I assure you, it was all good. Right, Savanah?"

The color rising in Savanah's cheeks, evidence he had indeed been the subject of their conversation, Jack chuckled. "Since I'm outnumbered here, I won't press for more details." His glance slid over to Savanah. "That can wait."

A thoughtful expression on his face, he began tapping his fingers on the table. Maybe he was over-reacting, but he had this sudden need to make sure his time with Savanah didn't end here.

You will not let her disappear from your life, not again…

He glanced over at Stephanie, her slight nod the boost he needed.

He went with a casual approach. Leaning back in his chair, and crossing his arms, he nodded over at Stephanie. "So, have you shown Savanah around this wonderful city of ours?"

A guilty expression on her face, she shook her head. "No, I haven't. My life has been so crazy with all the wedding plans. It's also been busy at work."

She sent Savanah an apologetic smile. "After the wedding, we'll do that for sure."

"*Oh, no…* I never expected that. And I've been busy, too. With opening night a little only two weeks away, it seems like I've been at the dance studio twenty-four-seven. Besides our yoga class, this is the first break I've had in weeks."

Stephanie nodded over at Jack. "I have an idea. Jack, since you're familiar with all the hot spots in Cleveland, why don't you show Savanah around? After all, you're quite the man about town."

Jack sent her a warning glance. "That's a bit of an exaggeration, don't you think? 'Man about town' is definitely not how I'd describe myself."

She laughed. "Oh, come on… the stories I could tell. Hmm… starting with that charity bachelor auction you were in right before Christmas."

Jack groaned.

Oh boy, here we go…

She grinned over at Savanah. "Jason actually had to step in to rescue him. It was wild." She shook her head. "I still can't believe those women almost got into a fight over you. And then—"

He quickly interrupted her. "I'm sure Savanah isn't interested in hearing about that. And if you remember, alcohol played a huge part in what happened that night."

He shook his head over at Savanah. "Picture a large group of women, out on the town, minus their kids or significant others, and ready to party. Let's just say the evening got a little wild, not how I expected it to go. So, now I'm a lot more cautious when agreeing to any fundraisers or special events."

He shuddered at the memory. He still considered himself fortunate to be alive and in one piece after the way those women came at him that night. Thank goodness the highest bidder—who'd paid a ridiculously large amount he still couldn't comprehend—had placed the bid only to make her boyfriend jealous. Even going as far to make him propose.

A few weeks after their dinner date, she sent him a text she was engaged. So, at least there was a happy ending.

"Jack? Is there something else you'd like to add?"

He blinked. "Nope. Trust me, that was an experience best forgotten." Then he promptly changed the subject. "A tour? Sure, I can do that."

This had Savanah all flustered. "*Oh, no, no…* that's not necessary. I'm sure you have better things to do than wander around the city with me."

He appeared to think about this. Then he shrugged. "Nope, I disagree. Wandering anywhere with you is something I'd be more than happy to do. In fact, I insist. And I know the best place to start… dinner at Jake's Place. Have you been there yet?"

"No, I haven't. Though I've heard all the rave reviews.

"It's settled then, we have a plan. If I can get a reservation, Jake's will be our first stop of the tour. You can't start off with a better introduction to our city than that. Of course, this all depends on your schedule. I assume you have performances scheduled for the upcoming nights?"

She shook her head. "There are no performances until April. This month we're rehearsing for Swan Lake, which opens on the first. After that ends, we'll jump right into rehearsal for Cinderella, opening in mid-June."

Jack was checking his phone. "*Hmm…* tomorrow night is the only booking the band has this weekend. So, if I'm able to get reservations for Sunday night, would this work for you? Say, around seven?"

Savanah hesitated. Was his offer only because Stephanie put him on the spot? The nice guy he was, he wouldn't dream of refusing?

She glanced over to see he was watching her, waiting.

He smiled. "So? This would be the perfect start of our tour. You can't experience the true ambiance of Cleveland without a visit to Jake's for dinner."

Ah… so it's only part of the tour.

So, as long as she didn't let herself believe it could be the start of something more, she should be okay.

Right?

So, she took a leap of faith and nodded a firm yes.

Relieved, Jack leaned back in his seat, exhaling the breath he wasn't even aware he was holding. Had she turned him down? He didn't know what he would've done.

He glanced over at Stephanie.

She mouthed the words, you owe me, big time, before she glanced down at her watch. After she grabbed her cup and took one last gulp of coffee, she scrambled to her feet. "Oh, geeez... I'm meeting Evan for dinner, so I need to leave. There's no reason the two of you shouldn't stay, since I'm sure you'll find a lot to talk about."

She grinned. "Maybe even share another scone."

She nodded toward the window, frowning at the stalled traffic. "And better yet, you'll avoid the rush hour."

She turned to leave, blowing a kiss over her shoulder. "Bye, I'll talk to both of you soon."

CHAPTER 14

*A*fter watching Stephanie drive out of the parking lot, knowing she was safely on her way to meet Evan, Jack glanced over at Savanah.

A smile tweaked the corner of his mouth. "Savanah Jackson, it appears we've been set up."

"I believe you're right." She laughed. "Tell me, were you as clueless as I was?"

Even though he wanted to deny it, his guilty expression gave him away. "I must confess, I wasn't. However, I never expected you would be the woman Stephanie wanted me to meet."

He smiled. "She can be quite persuasive."

Savanah grinned. "Yes, she can. And she's determined I have a date for the wedding." A look of horror came over her face. "Not that I'm suggesting this would be you. Or I want it to be you."

She groaned. *"Oh, no…* that's not what I meant."

He laughed. "That's okay, I understand what you're trying to say." His eyes met hers, a teasing glint in his. *"Hmm…* would this be so bad? I'm not one to brag, but I bet you'd find I'm the perfect date."

She laughed. "Oh, really? And why would this be?"

Pondering over this, he nodded. "Well, to start, I like to dance. I would even go as far to say I'm quite good at it. And given your love of dancing, what more could you ask for?"

She nodded. "Interesting. So you consider yourself as, shall we say, this amazing dancer—"

He laughed, holding his hand up to cut her off. "Now wait a minute… I said I was good at dancing, not a superstar. Though I have been told I'm better than most."

She tried to hide a smile and failed. "How do I know you're telling the truth?"

"So you need proof? *Hmm…*"

He rose to his feet, and with a small bow, extended his hand. "Savanah Jackson, would you do me the honor of sharing this dance?"

Then he waited, his gaze holding hers in a dare.

Open-mouthed, she stared at him. It was only when she glanced around the room to see his behavior had attracted quite a bit of attention, she finally stuttered out her response.

"Jack… are you serious? Here? Everyone will think we've lost our minds."

He didn't agree.

"*Ah*… I believe you're wrong about that. Instead, I'm sure they would congratulate me on my choice of such a beautiful dance partner."

He tilted his head, as if listening for something, before he sent her another smile. "I can't quite hear the music, nor do I recognize the song. But it doesn't matter, we can make our own music."

He moved closer, still holding out his hand. "So, what do you say?"

And now, all eyes were on Savanah.

As a professional dancer, Savanah was more than familiar with performing for an audience. So, that she was hesitant to accept his offer to dance for the small crowd gathered in the coffee shop?

This didn't make sense.

Eager to move things along, the woman at the adjacent table leaned in closer to Savanah, speaking in a loud whisper. "Honey, what are you waiting for? If he asked me to dance, I'd jump out of my seat, go right into his arms, and let him take the lead for as long as he wanted."

Jack grinned over at her. "Thank you for the support, ma'am. I appreciate it." Then he glanced back at Savanah. "Well?"

For the briefest of moments, she considered accepting his invitation. Instead, overcome by a sudden shyness, she shook her head. "I'll make you a deal, the next time we're together, and we have the right music, then we can dance."

His raised eyebrows prompted her to hold out her hand. "I promise."

He gave her hand a firm shake. "It's a deal."

After acknowledging the collective sigh of disappointment from the woman and her friends at the adjacent table with a shrug, he sat back in his chair, a smile on his face.

Uh, oh…

His smug expression had Savanah a little nervous. "Why do I feel like we're not on the same page? It's only a dance, right? Your typical everyday kind of dance. "

He lifted his shoulders in a shrug. "With you, I would never consider it as only a dance.

She studied him, a faint smile on her face.

He cleared his throat. "So what's the verdict? Maybe I can help? Ask me anything."

The blush in her cheeks giving her away, she voiced her true feelings. "I've never met anyone like you before. Are you always this spontaneous? Dancing in coffee shops?"

She sent him a mock frown. "Helping yourself to someone's scone?"

He laughed. "*Ah…* if you only knew. Most of my friends would tell you I'm more the quiet type. Yet with you? I'm that man who wouldn't even hesitate to share a dance in a coffee shop. Music or no music. And the scone? Remember, you did say you owed me for that."

"Yes, I did. And I do. Owe you a scone, that is. Don't worry, I won't forget." She grinned, crossing her hands over her chest. "Cross my heart."

He had moved closer. His elbow on the table, and his chin resting in his hand, his gaze roamed over her face before he smiled. "That's good enough for me. However, may I ask you something?"

The musky scent of his cologne—a subtle combination of sandalwood, leather and patchouli—had her moving even closer. The thought flitting through her mind how easy it would be to kiss him now that he was close, her reply came out a little breathless. "I guess it would only be fair?"

He reached for her hand, smiling when her fingers curled around his. Such a simple move that, for an instant, had him staring down at their hands, his mind suddenly blank.

He finally lifted his head, tightening his hold on her hand as he spoke. "I've had a lot of time to think since that day we first met, and I keep going back to how you left. What made you run off like that? Was it something I said? Or something I did? Because, if I insulted you, I apologize."

His mouth twisted in a wry smile. "I even ran out to check the parking lot, hoping to catch you before you drove off. But, no such luck."

"I know, I saw you." Horrified that she blurted this out, she pulled her hand away. Reluctant to even look at him, she grabbed her napkin and began wiping up the few crumbs on the table.

After what felt like forever, she stole a glance at him.

Jack didn't understand.

She saw you?

He cleared his throat. "You saw me?"

And, again the words flew out of her mouth. "I was in my car. I waited until you went back inside before I left."

Comprehension dawning on his face, he groaned, dragging his hand back through his hair. "Oh sweetheart, I'm sorry. I frightened you by coming on so strong, didn't I? I assure you, that's not what I meant to happen."

She dropped the napkin, shaking her head. *"Oh, no, no, no...* it was nothing you did. You're fine."

He waited. When it became obvious she had nothing more to say, he nodded. "So, I take it that's all you're going to tell me?"

She took a deep breath. "I'm sorry. I panicked. Everything happened so fast. And, it seemed too perfect, so unreal."

Avoiding his gaze, she shrugged. "I guess I was afraid."

For Jack, this was when everything fell into place. Believe it or not, that she left was a good thing. It was proof she had been just as overwhelmed as he was by that day's events.

Well, she's never going to run from you again. Not if you can help it.

He stared down at their hands. If he could, he'd freeze this moment in place forever. Instead, he lifted his head, his gaze locked with hers. "I'm pretty sure it's real, Vanababe."

Bringing her hand to his mouth, he brushed his lips over her fingers in a kiss. "Very real…"

In a daze, she watched as he reached for what remained of the scone. After cutting it in half, he handed one piece to her and raised the other in a toast. "Cheers to the mighty scone. But most importantly, here's to the start of something wonderful."

And he popped it in his mouth.

Her heart skipping a beat at what he was suggesting, she did the same.

Jack was grinning as he settled back in his chair. "So, tell me more about Savanah Jackson. Was it always your dream to become a dancer?

It was in this moment, as he watched the play of emotions on her face as she spoke, that he realized his life was about to change forever.

This breathtakingly beautiful woman, once lost to him, had now come back into his world.

Destiny?

Fate?

It didn't matter what they called it.

All that mattered was that the story ended with her.

CHAPTER 15

Other than the low buzz of conversation from the few occupied tables, an occasional customer takeout order, or the distant sound of activity from the kitchen, Café Latte had settled into a cozy early evening silence.

This was the time of day the staff welcomed, as it provided a much needed break before the late night run of customers began filing in.

After Stephanie left, Savanah and Jack's conversation had covered just about everything—their work, favorite foods, movies, songs—along with all the little things that defined them. They even shared a second sour cherry scone.

There was only one topic they'd both avoided.

This would be anything about their immediate families.

Jack worried his past would come across as too depressing. He'd found whenever the topic of his mother and sister came up, this made people upset. It then fell on him to reassure them, resulting in a flood of memories he'd tried so hard to put behind him.

While Savanah was unsure how to explain the complicated relationship she had with her mother, fearing it would make her seem over-bearing and out of touch.

Even though she'd be the first to admit her mother could be both.

Now, in the easy silence that had fallen between them, Jack glanced over at Savanah. Running her finger along the edge of her coffee cup, she saw him check his watch.

She glanced over at the clock behind the bakery display case. It was already past seven.

"Oh my gosh, I didn't realize it was that late. I hope I haven't bored you with my life story." She began piling their cups and napkins on the tray, in her haste sending a pile of napkins fluttering to the floor.

He retrieved the napkins, chuckling as he tossed them on the tray. "*Ah…* I guarantee this will never happen. You could never bore me, Savanah Jackson. This time I've spent with you has been amazing. Unfortunately, I have a recording session scheduled at the studio, and I need to leave now if I want to get there in time."

A smile lit up his face. "This has turned out to be the perfect intro-duction to your tour of Cleveland, hasn't it? And, now that you know what a great guy I am, there's no reason for you to run off again."

Yes, he was teasing her, but never had he been more serious.

Though she tried, she couldn't hide her smile. "You're not going to let me forget that, are you?"

He grinned. "Let me put it this way, I don't think I can fit any more scones in my freezer."

With a dramatic sigh, she dropped the last napkin on the tray. "Okay, I promise. I'm done running. And I understand if you need to leave now, since I should be at the dance studio as we speak. The wardrobe designers are doing the final alterations tonight for our Swan Lake costumes."

She glanced over at the clock again before she reached for her coat. "In fact, I'm already late."

"*Hmm…*" His head tilted, he appeared to be listening to something.

She waved her hand in front of his face. "A penny for your thoughts?

His answer was to take her hand, and before she realized what he had in mind, his other hand had slipped to her waist to pull her against him. After gazing down at her long enough to send her heart beating in a frenzy, he smiled. "If I remember correctly, you made a promise to me. You said the next time we were together, and the music was right, you'd dance with me."

His hand drifting down her back to hold her even closer, the huskiness of his voice had her closing her eyes. "*Sooo…* I believe this meets the requirements, no? We're together, the song is a classic, and you have to agree you're a perfect fit in my arms."

In the time it took him to twirl her around before pulling her back into his arms, she recognized the song.

"Can't Help Falling In Love…"

Her heart now up to a million beats a minute, maybe even more, she closed her eyes, resting her head against his shoulder. So many times over the past few months, she had let her imagination carry her away, fantasizing about how it would feel to be in his arms.

Yet, she had never imagined it could happen.

Nor did you imagine it would feel like this.

She lifted her head to fall right into his gaze. He smiled. "This is nice, isn't it?"

Her nod had him twirling her around again, this time dipping her almost to the floor.

"Jack…" She was laughing when he pulled her back against him. His cheek resting against hers, he sang softly along with the words of the song

"Take my hand,
Take my whole world, too.
For I can't help falling in love with you…

She was completely smitten.

She'd had many dance partners over the years, but dancing with Jack felt effortless. She surrendered to his lead, her feet skimming the floor as his steps guided them through the maze of tables and around the room. And even though his eyes never left hers, he didn't miss a beat, his steps never faltered.

One with the music, they moved as though they had danced this same dance countless times before. And, in a way, they had. Yet this time was for real, not only a fantasy in their dreams.

"Just as I thought, you are a beautiful dancer." His whisper brushed her cheek before he guided her into another spin.

A laugh bubbling up in her throat, she gazed up at him. "And, you were right… you're also quite good at it."

He pulled her a little closer, a warmth spreading through her at the tenderness in his voice. "*Ah, Vanababe…* you make it easy."

There it was again… *Vanababe.*

It was almost frightening how much she liked it.

And then they were dancing again, the rhythm now a part of them, each step, and every turn, more confident than the last.

It was at this moment Savanah let go, ready to embrace this unexpected chance at love.

Nothing mattered except the man holding her in his arms. No matter what the future held, she wanted to follow his lead, let him take her anywhere.

This wasn't just a dance, it was a new beginning.

For both of them.

The song had faded into silence, his steps slowing to a stop. Reluctant to break the spell, it was only after she realized how tightly she was clinging to him, she lifted her face to his.

The seriousness of his gaze was so unexpected, she had to turn away to regain her composure.

While Jack slowly began to smile.

That he was holding her in his arms seemed surreal. And by her reaction, he was pretty sure she felt the same.

Savanah slowly untangled herself from Jack's hold. Resisting the urge to reach up and stroke his cheek to smooth away his bemused expression, she searched his face.

"Jack?"

He blinked.

Still processing his emotional reaction to their dance, wishing she was still in his arms, he reached for her hand. After he brought it to his mouth for a kiss, the warmth of his smile echoed in his voice. "Thank you for the dance, Savanah Jackson. When I'm ever in need of a dance partner, you will be my one and only choice. But, as much as I'd love to dance the night away with you, if we intend to keep our jobs, we should leave."

Once they were outside, he held out his hand. "If you give me your phone, I'll add my number. Once I make the reservation, I'll call you for directions to your place."

"I'm excited about dinner at Jake's Place." She was quick to add, "and that it will be with you, of course."

He laughed. "Well, that's good to hear." He handed back her phone, and coming to a stop, he searched the parking lot. "Where did you park? I'll walk you to your car."

"You don't have to do that. I'll be fine."

"I'm sure you would be. But after the long wait to see you again, I have no intention of letting anything happen while you're under my watch. So, lead the way."

After she unlocked her car, she turned to him. "I want to thank you."

She looked so serious, he tried to hide his smile as he casually reached over to tuck a loose curl behind her ear. "*Hmm...* and this would be for?"

He had moved closer, bringing her to do the same. For a fleeting moment, she let her mind wander again, thinking how she'd like him to kiss her. It didn't have to be a big kiss. Any kind of kiss would work. It only had to be long enough for her to find out how his lips felt against hers.

That this even crossed her mind, she grew flustered, color staining her cheeks. She took a deep breath. "For listening to my silly stories, making me laugh, and most of all, going along with Stephanie's plan." She nodded. "It was nice... really nice."

And even though she knew she was on the verge of making a fool of herself, she nodded again.

To her relief, he seemed to understand.

"Yes, it was nice, wasn't it?" The need to touch her again, he reached over to tuck a curl behind her other ear.

This is when common sense kicked in. He'd be a fool not to know he should leave before he did something stupid. Like give into what he'd wanted to do the moment he first saw her. This would be to pull her into his arms and give her a kiss. Right here in the Café Latte parking lot.

This would be to make up for all the time they'd lost. And a move he couldn't afford to make.

Lord, no… this could send her running off even faster than the last time.

He waited until she'd started up her car before he tapped on the window. "About dinner," and again he was careful not to refer to it as a date—even though, as far as he was concerned—it definitely qualified as one. "Once I make the reservations, I'll let you know the details."

She grinned. "Yes, you've already told me that."

"*Ah…* and so I have. But this is only because I'm determined to make this happen." He bent down, his lips brushing against her cheek. "Until Sunday then. Drive safe."

In the event she was watching him in her rearview mirror, he waved before heading over to his truck. He started it up, and leaning his head back against the seat, he closed his eyes. He needed time to think about what just happened.

All because of a sour cherry scone? Who would have thought?

Maybe a scone shouldn't get credit for today. But it definitely had a big part in starting it all.

All those sour cherry scones stashed in his freezer?

His patience had paid off.

CHAPTER 16

*A*fter Savanah pulled into a parking space outside the dance studio, like Jack, she lingered in her car, reluctant to make the move back to her everyday life.

The studio door flew open.

The scowl on his face visible even from across the parking lot, Léon stormed out of the building and headed for his motorcycle. After he raced out of the parking lot, the loud roar of the engine fading into the distance, she left her car to go inside.

As soon as she walked into the studio, a hush fell over the room. Immediately sensing something was wrong, Gayle confirmed this when she beckoned to Savanah from her office. She closed the door, gesturing for Savanah to take a seat.

Nervously capping and uncapping her pen, she smiled.

It was a strained smile.

Thinking this was because she was late, Savanah nervously tucked her hair behind her ears as she apologized. "I'm sorry I'm late. I met up with someone and lost track of time. It won't happen again."

Yes, you lost track of time. But because you were with Jack, you're not sorry.

Gayle waved her hand in dismissal. "That's not the reason I called you into my office. Though in the future, please remember I expect you to be on time. I ask this of all my dancers."

Her hands clasped together in front of her, she studied Savanah for a few moments before she continued. "This is about you and Léon. He insists you're impossible to dance with. You refuse to follow his lead, your moves are off sync, and this hinders his performance. He claims your dancing is not up to what is expected of a principal dancer."

She paused, waiting for Savanah to respond.

Savanah was at a loss for words. In all honesty, what she really wanted to do was to get up out of her chair, walk out of Gayle's office, and never return.

Instead, she shook her head, no.

Gayle persisted. "Savanah? Have you nothing to say? If not, I find it hard to doubt the validity of Léon's accusations.

Again, Savanah shook her head.

Accusations? They were more like lies...

And now she was mad. No, she was beyond mad. She was furious. Her hands clenched in her lap, she took in a deep breath. "Léon may be a premier dancer, but this doesn't give him the right to keep making changes, to then not follow his own directions. He has everyone in the studio so confused, they don't know what they're doing anymore."

She shrugged. "I don't know, it's possible he might think I'm beneath him because I'm only a soloist. Or maybe this is his normal behavior. However, if he finds me unacceptable as a dance partner, so be it.

After a long silence, Gayle sighed. "But this negative energy between the two of you is a problem we can't afford. We both know making changes at this late date is out of the question."

She leaned back in her chair. Tapping her fingers on the desk, she got right to the point. "I'm giving you a week to work out your differences. And if you don't? We may have to make those changes after all. Because we can't lose Léon. We need him as our premier male dancer if we hope to keep the company afloat."

The look she leveled at Savanah said it all.

She was expendable.

Léon was not.

A first year dancer poked her head in the door. "Gayle, they need your opinion on a costume."

Not even hiding her eagerness to end to their meeting, Gayle practically leaped out of her chair and headed for the door. There she turned to Savanah. "Please think very seriously about what I said."

Savanah couldn't seem to move. Her anger had disappeared, leaving her in a state of disbelief. Was this what she'd worked for her whole life? To be pushed aside because of a temperamental and egotistical principal dancer? One who, for some unknown reason, had decided he didn't like her?

Doubt pushed its way in. Maybe Léon was right, and she had been fooling herself? She had always known she had a lot to prove in order to win the coveted title of premier ballerina. And until now, she was confident she'd finally made this a reality.

The possibility she could lose her soloist status and find herself back in the corps de ballet?

She didn't want to even think about this.

Well, as her mother was always quick to remind her, the life of a dancer has its ups and downs.

But you're already in your late twenties. And the majority of female dancers retire before the age of forty.

Suddenly, her future no longer felt secure.

She stood, wanting to be anywhere else. However, the chatter coming from the other room was a reminder she couldn't leave until she was fitted for her costumes.

Forcing a smile on her face, she left Gayle's office.

Other than responding to the seamstress when necessary, Savanah had little to say. Instead, in her mind, she was back in Café Latte. Closing her eyes, she could almost feel Jack's arms around her as they danced, the song he sang, a soft brush of words against her cheek.

It would be three days before she saw him again.

This seemed like a lifetime.

CHAPTER 17

When Savanah arrived at the Chic Boutique on Saturday morning, a steady rain was falling. Her head down, she made a mad dash across the parking lot to the entrance.

She was still trying to justify her dinner date with Jack required a new dress. She had two perfectly good dresses, maybe even three, hanging in her closet she could wear.

Remember? It's not a date. It's just dinner. Or according to Jack, an introduction to a tour of the city.''

That she was even here at the boutique was because of Stephanie.

When she found out Savanah hadn't even thought about what to wear, she'd insisted a trip to the boutique was necessary. Co-owned by her friend Sophie and Sophie's Aunt Louise, they would find Savanah the perfect dress.

She wanted to look her best, didn't she?

One glance around the small shop and she understood why Stephanie insisted she check it out.

The merchandize, displayed by color, resulted in a feast for the senses. She hadn't been in the little shop for five minutes, and already she'd spotted a cute little jean jacket and a red embroidered peasant skirt she wanted.

She was checking out a rack of dresses labeled with a sign—*Dresses for that Special Night Out*—when a middle-aged woman appeared at her side.

She smiled, holding out her hand. "You must be Savanah. I'm Louise, Sophie's aunt. Stephanie called to let us know you might pay us a visit today. Unfortunately, Sophie just left. She had to take the twins for their checkups."

At Savanah's questioning look, she explained. "Trevor and Hudson, her three-year-old twin sons. A real handful, those two. And growing up so fast."

She laughed. "I told her it's time she had another baby. I guess we'll have to wait and see what happens."

She reached for the glasses perched on top of her head. After adjusting them comfortably on her nose, she smiled. "Stephanie also mentioned you're a dancer, but I would've known this by the way you carry yourself."

A thoughtful look came over her face. "*Hmm…* have you ever done any modeling? I could've used you last month for our annual fashion show. A fundraiser, the proceeds go towards scholarships for the fashion design school. This is where both Sophie and I got our degrees. With the show becoming more popular every year, we're always on the lookout for new models."

Savanah shook her head. "I've never done any modeling, but it sounds like it would be fun."

"*Hmm…* yes, it's an amazing event. However, I bet by adding someone like you and incorporating some dance moves into the walk— you know, just to spice things up a bit—we'd have a big hit on our hands."

Savanah was skeptical. "I'm not sure if that's…"

Her words trailed off when she realized Louise had already moved on, mumbling to herself as she searched through the rack.

Fascinated, Savanah trailed behind her, watching as she pulled out two dresses, holding them up for Savanah's inspection. "I was told you're looking for a dress to wear for a dinner date with Jack Buchanan. Am I right?"

She laughed at Savanah's surprised expression. "Honey, nothing gets by this group of friends. Jack is one of their favorites. That someone hasn't grabbed him up yet is a mystery."

She smiled, shaking her head. "He is such a handsome young man, with the almost tragic hero vibe he has going on. And talented in so many ways. The woman that catches his eye will be a lucky one, indeed."

She took a moment to think about this before she shrugged. "But back to why you're here. This bronze dress would be perfect. But then again, so would the coral, though it's just a tad more formal."

She held up the dresses, studying each one.

Then she nodded. "I think I have a solution. Do you have a dress to wear for Stephanie's wedding? If not, I think the coral would be perfect. That leaves the bronze for your date with Jack. Either way, you couldn't go wrong."

A pleased expression on her face, she nodded. "Well, that was easy, wasn't it? Let's get you into the dressing room so you can try them on."

She took off, giving Savanah no choice but to follow.

After Louise hung the dresses in the dressing room, she turned to Savanah. "Start with the bronze. Once you have it on, come out so we can get the full effect in the big mirror. And if you don't think it's what you want? We'll find something else. In the meantime, I'll be in the back unpacking new merchandize. So call out when you're ready."

After adjusting her glasses, and flashing a huge smile, she left.

As she removed her coat, Savanah glanced over at the dresses. She had a hunch when she left the boutique, she would be taking them with her.

One look in the mirror and Savanah fell in love.

The dress Louise had suggested for her dinner with Jack fit as though it had been made for her. The bronze silk fabric shimmered in the light, but not to the extent it was too flashy. But what she liked best were the simple lines. Fitted, and hitting a little above the knees, the ruching down one side hugged her body just enough to show her curves. This, along with the scalloped v-neckline and three-quarter length sleeves, added up to a look of total sophistication.

"I've never had a dress this color before, but I like it. What do you think?" She smiled over at Louise as she said this.

Her arms crossed over her chest, and a serious expression on her face, Louise nodded. "It suits you. And if I didn't know better, I'd think it was tailored to fit. This is a big plus, since your date is tomorrow."

After adjusting the ruching, she stepped back to take one more look before she smiled at Savanah. "So, is this a go?"

Savanah turned away from the mirror, a hint of uncertainty in her voice. "There's only one problem…"

Busy adjusting the neckline of the dress, Louise's response was distracted. "*Hmm…* and what would that be?"

Savanah hesitated, to then blurt it out. "I'm not sure if Jack considers this a date. It was only after Stephanie suggested he show me around town he offered to take me to Jake's for dinner. He said I could consider it as part of my tour of the city. So, maybe this is a bit over the top? Too dressy?"

She ran her hands down over the skirt of the dress. "I love the dress, but I don't want to come across as expecting too much."

Louise peered at her over the rim of her glasses, eyebrows raised. "Sweetheart, you're overthinking this. Trust me, when a man asks a woman to have dinner with him—especially at a restaurant like Jake's Place—it's considered a date. And the dress? It's definitely not too much. Jack will take one look at you, and he'll be hooked."

Her smile was teasing. "Though from what I've heard, that's already happened."

Smiling at the blush rising in Savanah's cheeks, she kept up a constant chatter as she herded her back into the dressing room. "Let's get you out of this dress and into the coral one. I know your plan was to buy only one dress today. But as long as you're here, you might as well pick up one for the wedding, too. Think about it. Then we'll talk about accessories."

A bell rang, announcing someone had entered the shop. After stretching her neck to see who it was, she groaned, her voice low. "It's one of Sophie's clients, here to pick up a dress she left to be altered. She's quite demanding, thinks everything is about her."

After shoving her glasses back on top of her head and fluffing out her hair, she turned to Savanah. "Let me take care of her. I shouldn't be long."

And again, just like that, she was gone.

An hour later, Savanah left the boutique carrying a garment bag with the two dresses, the jean jacket and red peasant skirt. Along with a pair of strappy high heels in a beautiful shade of bronze.

Once she was in her car, she decided to check her messages before starting her drive home.

There were three texts from Jack.

> As promised, I made a reservation at Jake's Place for seven tomorrow night. So, I'll pick you up at six-thirty.

> I'm really looking forward to seeing you again.

> Also, if I remember correctly, you still owe me a dance. Because, the dance we shared in Café Latte? Since you didn't ask me, I asked you, I've decided it doesn't count. So, I hope to remedy this tomorrow night.

She looked up from her phone, a laugh bubbling up in her throat.

After reading the texts one more time, she started up her car and drove out of the Chic Boutique parking lot.

She sang as she drove. Something she hadn't done for a long time.

Take my hand,
Take my whole world, too
For I can't help falling in love with you.

CHAPTER 18

$\mathcal{J}$ack was ready

Truth be known, he had been ready for his date with Savanah for almost an hour. This was after he'd shaved, showered and spent a longer time than usual putting together a look he was finally happy with.

This would be his favorite dark gray sports coat, his lucky white oxford shirt, and his best dress jeans.

And, yes… the shirt was lucky. Every time he wore it, something good happened. So, you can bet for tonight, the shirt was his first and only choice.

He gave one last swipe through his hair before he tossed the comb on the vanity. His reflection in the mirror meeting his approval, he turned out the bathroom light and sauntered down the hall to the kitchen.

His mouth felt dry.

So, after grabbing a bottle of water out of the refrigerator, he took a long drink as he walked over to pick up the TV remote from the sofa. After scrolling through the channels and finding nothing of interest, he shut off the TV and tossed the remote back on the sofa.

He checked his watch.

Only five minutes had passed. After another swallow of water, he wandered over to the floor to ceiling windows that made up the one wall of the main living area.

He watched as a van pulled into a guest parking spot below, a family with four kids piling out all at once. Because he lived on the top floor, and the windows were double paned and sound proof, he couldn't hear their conversation. But judging by the gift bags the father unloaded from the trunk, handing one to each of the family members, they had come for a celebration of some kind. Sure enough, the father pulled out what looked like a large cake box, closed the trunk, and they all headed for the entrance of the building.

This was when Jack realized the scene he just witnessed? This was what he wanted... a family, kids, and all the gatherings, celebrations, and even challenges that came along the way.

You want it all.

Because of his parents' demanding careers, his mother's performance schedule monopolizing most weekends and holidays, there had been little time for family celebrations

Guilt pushing Its way in, he turned away from the window, He had no right faulting his parents. They'd provided him with everything he needed, and then some. However, he couldn't help but imagine how things could have been different had his mother and sister not died in the plane crash.

After throwing the empty water bottle in the trash, he gave the lid an extra hard push. Then he groaned, running his hand through his hair. He needed to let it go. The past would never change.

He shoved his hands in his pockets and wandered back over to the window. Watching as the sun dipped slowly beneath the horizon, he felt a sudden surge of hope.

It's time to focus on the future... starting now.

A reminder of the time, he checked his watch again. If he left now, he'd have twenty minutes to spare. This would be enough time to stop at the florist to pick up flowers for Savanah.

Keys in hand, he headed for the door.

You're not going to mess this up.

Nope, he was going to do it right.

If you were to ask, Savanah would tell you the last three days had been the longest three days of her life. Jack had taken over her mind, her thoughts no longer hers to control. When she wasn't reliving every minute they'd spent at Café Latte, she was thinking about their upcoming dinner date.

How had he slipped into her life as though this was where he belonged? She felt like she was living on the edge of a dream. Many times she'd caught herself staring into space, a smile touching her lips when he popped into her mind, flashing that sexy smile of his.

And her dancing? Her steps had become lighter, even the more complicated dance routines coming easy to her. That Léon couldn't find fault with any of her moves was driving him crazy.

If this is what it felt like to fall in love, she never wanted it to end.

But now, standing in front of the bathroom mirror, with Jack due to arrive in about twenty minutes, something didn't feel quite right.

This wasn't because of the dress from Chic Boutique. No, the dress was perfect. After a long and critical inspection in the mirror, she decided it was her hair. She'd styled it in a French twist, and this suddenly seemed all wrong. She pulled out the bobby pins and, combing her fingers through her hair, watched it tumble in a riot of waves to her shoulders.

Yes, this was much better. No longer was she the ballerina who believed romance blossomed only in the stories she danced to on stage.

Instead, she was a woman about to go out on a date with the man of her dreams.

No, she didn't need to be reminded it wasn't a date.

Yet, there was no harm in pretending it could be.

She gathered up her evening shaw, slipped her phone into her purse and turned out the light.

CHAPTER 19

Each time I look into your eyes I want to kiss you.
~ Anonymously Yours

Jack had been sitting in his truck for at least five minutes. He planned to wait for another two before ringing Savanah's doorbell.

He glanced over at the bouquet on the passenger seat, shaking his head.

It might be a long time before you get up the nerve to visit that florist again. You almost made a complete fool of yourself.

The first thing the florist asked was if the flowers were for a special occasion. Or was there was a special message he wanted to convey?

He should've said yes and left it at that. Instead, thrown by the question, he said he wasn't sure. Feeling the need to explain, he told her this was why he steered clear of giving flowers.

Now this wasn't because he didn't like flowers. He only found it confusing they each had their own special meaning. The possibility of coming on too strong, or sending the wrong message by gifting the inappropriate flowers?

The conscientious guy he was, this worried him.

After he had rambled on about this, the confusion on the florist's face a sign he wasn't making sense, he'd cleared his throat. "I'm sorry. As you can see, I'm not good at this dating thing. Only this time, it's important I do it right. This means I can't make any mistakes."

This finally brought a laugh from the florist. "As charming as you are, I don't think you need to worry. The woman who receives these flowers from you will be thrilled."

"I hope you're right." He grinned. "So, what do you suggest?"

She turned, heading for the back of the shop. "Come with me."

He followed her over to the glass coolers lining the back wall of the shop, filled with flowers in every color of the rainbow. After pointing out at least a dozen different blooms, the majority with names he'd never remember, she turned to him and shrugged. "I think we're making this more complicated than it is. Instead, why don't I make up a bouquet filled with a little of everything? This way, you'll have all the bases covered."

A smile lit up his face. "Exactly. That would be perfect since she's everything I could ever want."

Her smile telling him he'd shared more information than necessary, he zeroed in on a huge container filled with dozens of roses in all different colors. "Now here's a flower I recognize. Can you add in some of these?"

She'd nodded. "Yes, of course I can. Give me a few minutes and I'll make up the perfect bouquet."

Ten minutes later, he was back on the road. The flowers, wrapped in florist paper and tied with a white satin bow, were on the passenger seat.

And now, glancing over at the dashboard, he saw his two minutes were up.

He grabbed the bouquet and sprinted up the walk to Savanah's front door. With the flowers held behind his back, he took a deep breath and hit the doorbell.

So far, so good.

A car door slammed, sending Savanah in a panic, her heart beat careening out of control. To pace herself, she started counting to ten as she left her bedroom. When, if she could, she'd rather run over and fling open the door.

"Eight, nine, and ten…" After following this with a deep, calming breath, she opened the door.

In the midst of brushing a speck of lint off the sleeve of his jacket, Jack lifted his head.

Oh, my…

The Savanah standing in front of him was a woman he didn't know. As this was the first time he saw her with her hair down, for a good ten seconds, he could only stare.

She looked amazing. Gone was the prim ballerina, her hair pulled back in the usual low chignon. Instead, her hair falling to her shoulders in soft waves, the woman standing in front of him was stunning. She was also the sexiest woman he'd ever seen. A description he knew would have her blushing in denial were he to tell her this.

A slow smile working its way across his face, he moved closer.

"Hi…"

Color already staining her cheeks, her smile was shy.

"Hi…"

They continued to smile at each other until he cleared his throat, though not enough to clear the huskiness from his voice. "You look absolutely amazing, Vanababe." After edging a stray strand of hair from her face, he smiled. "I like your hair down like this."

"Thank you." She tilted her head, studying him. "That's the second time you've called me that."

He shrugged, unable to hide his smile. "Yes, I know."

She laughed. "You know?"

He shrugged again. "What can I say? It just happens." He grinned. "And I like that it does. However, like I said before, if you'd rather I stopped, tell me and the word will never cross my lips again."

Before she could respond, his intention to wow her with his suave demeanor as he handed her the bouquet, instead he dropped it. Swiftly snatching it up from the steps, he presented it to her with a flourish. "Here, this is for you. A beautiful bouquet for an even more beautiful woman."

He closed his eyes, holding back a groan.

A little over the top, don't you think? You better get your act together.

She surprised him. After a smile that had him almost forgetting his name, let alone remember who or where he was, she pressed a kiss to his cheek. Then, taking the bouquet from him, she beckoned for him to follow. "Come on in so I can put these in water before we leave."

After the kiss she gave him? Even if only to his cheek?

He'd follow her anywhere.

In the kitchen, she took a vase out of the cupboard. As she began filling it with water, she glanced over at him, a shy smile curving her lips. "Thank you for the flowers, they're beautiful. No one has ever brought me flowers on a date before."

He smiled, moving a little closer. "*Hmm...* is that so? Well, knowing I'm the first makes me very happy."

Determined to help, he untied the bow from the bouquet, his arm brushing against hers as he unwrapped the flowers from the florist paper. Encouraged by the shiver that coursed through her with this simple touch, he was smiling as he sent her a sidelong glance. "So, you consider this a date, huh?"

She turned to answer him. Startled to find him so close, she pulled her arm back, knocking over the vase, and sending a spray of water right at him.

"*Oh, no...*"

"*Whoa...*"

Once he got over his initial shock, he righted the vase and shut off the water. He was laughing.

While Savanah couldn't be more embarrassed. Mumbling over and over how sorry she was, she grabbed a dishtowel from the counter. Before she could even wipe the water from Jack's jacket, he gently pried the dishtowel from her grasp and threw it back onto the counter.

He was still laughing. "Hey, it's okay. It's only water." He smoothed his hands down over his jacket. "See? I'm perfectly fine."

"Even your hair is wet," she said, reaching up to brush the few drops of water still lingering in his hair. "Again, I'm so sorry. I'm usually not this clumsy. I just... well..."

Her voice fading off, she turned to add more water to the vase.

Watching this, he picked up a rose, twirling the stem between his fingers before he cleared his throat. "So, what would you say makes this time so different?"

She hesitated, staring down at the vase.

Tell him the truth, that he's turned your life upside down. And now you want more of everything, as long as it's with him.

Beginning with a kiss.

Yes, this was exactly what she wanted.

"Savanah?" Leaning against the counter, he had that quirky smile of his going on. The one that told her he knew how flustered he had her.

Their eyes meeting, he offered her the rose. Another shiver running through her when his fingers brushed against hers, she closed her eyes.

This is ridiculous. If you're going to make your move, you better do it now.

She tossed the rose on the counter. And before she could change her mind, rising on her tiptoes and framing his face in her hands, she claimed his mouth in a kiss.

In a state of shock, at first he didn't move. Not only was her move so unexpected, he was also having a hard time accepting it had indeed happened.

But in less time than it took to inhale his next breath, he pulled her against him. And, after what Savanah liked to believe was a groan of surrender, he kissed her back.

Was this how she had imagined their first kiss would be like?

She hadn't even come close.

Jack lifted his head. When he saw Savanah's eyes were closed, he rested his forehead to hers, his whisper brushing over her cheek. "*My goodness...* I never expected that. But I believe you've given me your answer. We can now officially call this a date."

In her dazed state, the only thing registering in Savanah's mind was the smile in his voice.

Again, she panicked.

My God, you keep doing one crazy thing after another. What is he going to think?

She backed away from him and, grabbing the rest of the flowers off the counter, shoved them in the vase. She turned to leave the kitchen, her attempt at a smile pretty much a failure. "We should leave. Let me get my coat."

Oh, no you don't…

Jack was having none of this. In a flash, he was behind her, his arms wrapping around her. "Hey, hold on here. You can't give me a kiss like that and then run off, expecting me to act like it never happened."

He paused, a hint of doubt in his voice. "You meant for it to happen, right?"

She shrugged, avoiding eye contact. "I'm not sure what came over me. I've never done anything like that before. Not with anyone." Then, in a voice so soft he had to lean in even closer, she added. "Until you."

This a tremendous boost to his confidence, his lips settled a breath away from the curve of her ear. "*Hmm…* so what you're telling me, the flowers and now this kiss, they're a first? And both with me?"

Without realizing it, she leaned against him as she nodded. The warmth of his embrace, the beating of his heart, so steady and sure… she wanted this moment to last forever.

On the contrary, he was more than aware of every inch of her pressed against him. That she was a perfect fit in his arms was all the proof he needed to know she belonged there. After he dropped a kiss to her cheek, a soft laugh escaped him. "This leads me to believe we're off to a great start, wouldn't you agree?"

She sighed. "Considering I can't even remember the last time I went on a date, I wouldn't be able to say." Once she found the courage to look up at him, her smile was wistful. "Unfortunately, my life revolves around dancing."

"Well, we're going to change that. There's no reason you can't do both." He smiled down at her. "First, you need to promise me something."

"I do?"

Her wary expression had him dropping a quick kiss to her cheek before he answered. "Yes, and this would be all the dates will be with me, and me only."

She tried to hide her smile, yet failed. "Jack Buchanan, why do I get the impression you're going to drive me crazy?"

He laughed. "I assure you, the feeling is mutual. However, you haven't given me your answer yet. Are you in?"

Yes, he was pushing it. But after the kiss they shared, the possibility of her going out with someone else wasn't even an option. So he needed her promise.

She nodded. "We have a deal."

Tempted to validate this with another kiss, instead, he checked his watch. "So, now that we've got all that settled, if we intend to make our reservations on time, we need to leave."

He grinned. "I can't wait to show you Jake's. I hope you're hungry."

CHAPTER 20

On this chilly Sunday evening in March, Jake's Place was a hub of activity, both the waiting area and bar packed with diners waiting for their tables.

His goal to get within speaking distance to the reservation desk, Jack reached for Savanah's hand. "Hold on to me, Vanababe. I don't want to lose you."

Vanababe... The tenderness in his voice wrapping around her like a caress, she was smiling as he navigated them through the crowd.

While he confirmed their reservation, she gazed around the bustling restaurant, taking it all in.

In the main dining room, the colorful Tiffany chandeliers, crafted by local artists, and the clear glass candle centerpieces on each table created a warm and inviting atmosphere. Crisp linen tablecloths added a touch of elegance, while the custom designed chairs upholstered in a soft burgundy leather promised a comfortable dining experience.

And though the restaurant didn't have a dress code, this was not a shorts and tee shirt kind of place.

The dress Louise had convinced Savanah to purchase was perfect.

A familiar laugh caught her attention, sending an unpleasant chill running through her. Coming from across the room, it was a laugh that, to her, spelled danger.

Leon's laugh…

Hoping she was wrong, she turned her head just a fraction to scan the room.

She froze.

Seated at the bar, Léon was with a woman she recognized as one of the costume designers at the ballet fittings for Swan Lake.

And like every other time he showed up in her life, her hands trembled, while her heartbeat sped up, anticipating the worst.

She closed her eyes and, taking in a deep breath, she told herself she had nothing to worry about. It was highly unlikely he'd notice her in the crowded restaurant.

Right?

She glanced over again in his direction.

Wrong…

He was staring at her. And before she could turn away, his mouth twisting in a mocking grin, he raised his glass in a toast.

This told her he had every intention of using this opportunity to cause trouble.

Forcing a smile on her face, she edged closer to Jack.

Unaware of the events unfolding around him, after confirming their reservation, Jack turned to Savanah and smiled. "The hostess said they're setting up our table right now, so we shouldn't—"

His smile disappeared, his words coming to an abrupt stop. Moving them off to the side, he searched her face. "Sweetheart, what's wrong?"

She shook her head. She certainly couldn't tell him she was afraid of some guy sitting over at the bar. He'd think she was crazy.

Isn't it a bit late for that? You've already given him enough reasons to question your sanity.

Her attempt at a smile failing miserably, her answer came out more frantic than she intended. "Nothing is wrong. I thought I saw someone I know, but I was mistaken."

Before he could respond, the hostess tapped his shoulder. "Mr. Buchanan, if you'd like, I can show you and your guest to your table now."

Jack glanced back at Savanah. "Are you sure you're okay? If not, we can leave."

Her smile overly bright, she nodded. "Yes, yes… I'm fine. Please, don't worry, everything is fine."

Jack hesitated. He was far from convinced. She sounded more desperate than confident. Yet not wanting to upset her any further, he decided to wait until they were seated to find out what was going on.

After the hostess seated them, Savanah began talking non-stop. Unable to get a word in, Jack did the only thing he could—he settled back in his chair and listened.

He watched as she re-arranged her silverware, folded her napkin, and then folded it again. This all happened between the backward glances she kept sending over her shoulder.

Curious, he scanned the area. Apart from a heated argument between a man and a woman seated at the bar, everything seemed normal.

At that moment, the man turned, and they locked eyes. A slow and almost menacing smile creeping across his face, he raised his glass in a toast. After finishing his drink in one gulp, he turned back to the bar and called out for another round.

Jack was confused.

Does he think he knows you? Because you have no idea who he is. Maybe he's a friend of Savanah?

He glanced over at the bar again. This turned out to be a mistake. Now a fresh drink in his hand, the man again raised his glass in another toast before making a comment to his companion.

Jack turned back to Savanah. An anxious look on her face, she was watching him. She had such a tight grip on the stem of her glass, he feared it might snap in her hands.

It was at this point he realized, if he wanted to salvage the rest of the evening, he needed to say something.

Otherwise, this could end up just like all the other disastrous dates you've had.

He moved his chair closer, his plan to take the water glass from her "Here, let's take your glass and set it out of the way."

Her reaction surprised both of them. Jerking her hand away, almost toppling over the glass, her voice shook with anger. "Stop, I can handle it. I'm not going to spill water on you again."

After another glance over her shoulder, she gave a frustrated sigh. "This is a mistake. We never should've come here."

He was silent, weighing his words. Then he reached for her hand again. "Hey, come on… talk to me. Tell me what's going on."

She opened her mouth, only to close it again, shaking her head.

"Savanah? Come on, sweetheart… look at me."

She lifted her head, her eyes pleading with him. "I'm sorry, I didn't mean to snap at you like that. I—"

"Stop." Encouraged she hadn't pulled her hand away again, he reached for her other hand, holding them both in his. "Before you say more, there's no need to be sorry. Whatever the reason, I'm on your side. But it would help if you told me what's wrong, so we can join forces and fix it together.

She took a deep breath, exhaling it slowly. "Léon Pantonelli is here."

He was confused.

Léon Pantonelli?

Who the hell is Léon Pantonelli?

He cleared his throat. "I'm sorry. Léon Pantonelli? Is he an old friend? Boyfriend?"

She shuddered. *"Oh, no… please, no.* He's the premier danseur in the dance company. When his original partner injured her knee and required surgery, they offered me her role. Yet, for whatever reason, Léon has developed this immediate dislike for me and tries to humiliate me whenever he can.

She sent another nervous glance over her shoulder, the words flying out of her mouth. "I've tried to talk to him, get him to tell me what's wrong, but he refuses to even listen to me. It's to the point I dread going into the studio every day."

She glanced over her shoulder again. "And now he's here."

Maybe it was her way of convincing herself she had no reason to worry, but for whatever reason, she couldn't stop talking. "I'm sorry, you probably think I'm over-reacting, but his behavior is so unpredictable. And it's getting worse."

She began fingering the stem of her glass again. Then she frowned, pushing it away. "Maybe he thinks dancing with me, a mere soloist, is beneath him. Well, I have news for him. Even though he's very talented, he's not as good as he thinks. If he was, a higher ranked dance company would've signed him."

Gently releasing her hands, Jack sat up straighter in his chair. His eyes narrowed, his gaze was fixed on something behind her.

He nodded. "*Ah…* it appears he's on his way over here as we speak."

"*Oh, no, no, no…*" A look of pure panic on her face, she sent a frantic gaze around them. "We should leave. Now, before—"

Pressing his fingers to her mouth, he shook his head. "Savanah, sweetheart, look at me." His gaze holding hers, he smiled. "It's going to be all right."

"No, you don't know what he's like." She was gripping the edge of the table, her gaze darting around the room, checking for the fastest escape route.

He knew if she could, she'd be gone in a second.

With one finger, he lifted her chin to look into her eyes. "I promise I won't let anything happen to you. So, trust me, okay?"

Once she nodded, he tried to get a read on Léon, who was now making his way over to their table. Judging by his unsteady gait, he'd already had a few drinks and was feeling pretty good about himself.

This was confirmed when he tripped and had to grab onto the edge of their table to keep from falling. After mumbling a long string of cuss words, he zeroed right in on Savanah.

He laughed. "Well, well, well… look who's here? My elusive little dance partner. Funny, I don't recall ever seeing you here before. Because I'm sure I'd remember if I had."

His hand coming down on her shoulder, he gave it a squeeze. Hard enough to make her flinch.

His anger just barely in check, Jack came to his feet and extended his hand. "Jack Buchanan here. And you? Are you a friend of Savanah's?"

His eyebrows raised, Léon ignored his offer of a handshake. After Jack merely shrugged, shoving his hands in his pockets, the two men sized each other up, their instant dislike vibrating between them.

His jaw clenched in anger, Léon was the first to look away. That Jack didn't seem the least bit intimidated was a reaction that was completely foreign to him.

His gaze shifting to Savanah, his expression was one of mock disbelief. "What's this? You haven't told your date about your dance boyfriend yet? This needs to be remedied." After a quick glance around the room, he turned back to them. "I don't think the pianist is scheduled to set up for another twenty minutes. When he does, I'll see if I can convince him to play a special song for us."

Nodding over at Savanah, his smile bordered on a smirk "Then we can show your friend some of our moves."

Her smile was strained. "Léon, please… there's no need to do this."

He shrugged. "Do what? Help out a fellow dancer? If nothing else, think of it as good publicity for the company. Until you finally get it together on the dance floor, we need all the press we can get."

Jack was livid, the muscles in his jaw pulsing in response. Because, *come on…* who the hell did this Léon think he was? That he thought he could talk to Savanah in such a demeaning manner was unacceptable.

However, he'd be a fool not to know that getting into a fight with him wouldn't help matters. Though in his present inebriated state, it wouldn't take much to bring him down.

He groaned.

What are you doing? You need to put an end to this before it gets out of hand—or you do something stupid.

He issued what he felt was a clear warning. "Since Savanah has made it clear this isn't something she wants, there's no need for you to talk to the pianist."

He sent a nod over to the bar, where Léon's companion was glaring in their direction. "It also appears your friend misses your company. So, please don't let us keep you."

To his relief, after a long, hard stare, Léon turned to walk away.

He came to a sudden stop, his words holding a definite threat. "Since I call the shots when it comes to dance, we'll see about that, won't we?"

He directed his next comment to Savanah. "So, be ready for that dance, my little ballerina friend. Think of it as a gesture of goodwill to dancers everywhere."

Laughing loudly at his attempt at humor, he spun around and strutted back to the bar, already calling for another drink.

CHAPTER 21

Love is not about how many days, months,
or years you have been together.
Love is about how much you love each other every single day.
~ Unknown

Slowly sinking back in his chair, Jack glanced over at Savanah. Her head bowed, her eyes were closed.

"Are you okay?"

When she didn't answer, only shaking her head, he moved his chair even closer, covering her hands with his.

He frowned. "You're shaking."

"I know. I'm sorry, I don't know why I let him get to me like this, but I—" She pressed her lips together.

"And?" His head tilted, he searched her face.

The genuine concern she saw in his eyes was almost enough to send the tears flowing, but she blinked them away. "I don't want to dance with him. Not here. I just can't. He might, oh I don't know, trip me. Or make me look as if I don't know what I'm doing. This is what he does."

After tucking her hair behind her ear, he gave a casual shrug. "Then you refuse."

"But—"

"No 'buts' about it."

Problem solved—at least as far as he was concerned—he reached for a menu and handed it to her. "Right now, let's decide what we want for dinner. This way, when the server returns, we'll be ready to place our orders. And if you're still worried? I think I may have a way to fix that."

After he opened the other menu, relieved to see she did the same, he smiled over at her. "Whatever you choose, you can't go wrong. Everything here is excellent. Just make sure you save room for dessert. Chef Amber Snow is famous in this part of town for her amazing creations."

While they placed their dinner order, Jack caught Savanah stealing nervous glances over to where Léon was still at the bar. He also witnessed the mocking smile Léon gave her, raising his glass in yet another toast.

This had him furious.

My God… how many drinks has this guy had?

Given this was a clear sign Léon had no intention of letting up, Jack caught the server's attention, keeping his voice low. "I have a favor to ask. It appears we've had a change in plans and need to leave as quickly as possible. Is it possible to have our meals, along with a bottle of your featured red and one of your signature desserts, packed up for takeout?"

Once the server had left with their order and his credit card, Jack focused his attention on Savanah, his intent to take her mind off what had happened.

After a drink of water, he smiled. "So here we are… the first stop of your tour of Cleveland. Even though I think we can now both agree, it's officially a date."

Her emotions still running high, her response bordered more on a sob than a laugh. "You're just not going to let that go, are you?"

Relieved that she laughed, even though it was on the shaky side, he grinned. "It only makes sense, right? All these firsts… first date, first time at Jake's, first flowers, and my favorite… first kiss."

He tilted his head, his gaze settling on her mouth. "And you? What is your favorite?"

Of course, this had her all flustered. So she went for the safest. "The flowers?"

He laughed. "Really? The flowers?"

Before she could answer, he leaned closer. His mouth brushing over hers, the huskiness of his voice sent a shiver down her spine. "*Hmm… I guess I was hoping you'd go with the kiss. Instead, it seems I have some work to do.*"

She waited, thinking he was about to kiss her.

Instead, he sat back, a smile hugging his lips. "*Sooo…* since I chose this restaurant as the first stop of your tour, I think you deserve a brief history of how it even came into existence."

"You have my undivided attention." Her elbow on the table, and her chin resting in her hand, she gave him a flirty smile.

At least this is the way he saw it.

He smiled, his voice calm and unhurried. "Even though this building had been empty for years, long-time friends Jake Martin and Joe Kennedy believed it had potential. After investing a good chunk of their savings and spending countless hours on renovations, they opened for business about three years ago. They became an instant success."

He smiled. "If you ask Jake, he'll say they got lucky. However, I think it has more to do with his talent as a chef. This, along with Joe's law background and keen business sense, has earned them quite a few awards. Best Cleveland Restaurant, Best Ambiance, and Top Chef, to name a few."

He nodded over at the large windows, offering a view of Lake Erie. "We'll have to come here in the summer for dinner out on the deck. And on weekends they have live music." He chuckled. "It could be my chance to get in that dance you owe me."

Greeted with silence, this is when he realized she probably hadn't heard a word he said. Instead, her focus was on their hands, his thumb massaging slow circles in her palm.

He gave her hand a gentle squeeze. "Hey, are you still with me?"

She lifted her head and, caught up in the warmth of his gaze, her smile was as genuine as it gets.

This was all he needed to blurt out what he had no business saying out loud. Even though it was the one thing that hadn't left his mind since the first time he saw her.

"Marry me…"

And even with the odds only at one in a million—no, make that one in a billion she'd give him the answer he wanted—he held his breath, waiting.

Marry me?

Her head jerking up, Savanah's first thought was she'd heard wrong. Then a horrible thought entered her mind. Was this his way of offering a solution to protect her from Léon?

Asking her to marry him?

Oh, God… the last thing you want is for him to feel sorry for you.

She dropped her gaze back to their hands, searching her mind for a response.

Her reaction had Jack feeling like a fool. What in God's name had he been thinking?

You're out of your mind. That she hasn't taken off, like she did the day they met in Café Latte, is a miracle.

They both spoke at the same time.

"Jack, I…"

"Love, I'm so…

And Savanah would swear her heart skipped a beat.

Love? And again, this is the problem… this guy has more charm than you can handle

She smiled. "You go first."

He shrugged. "I apologize. I hadn't planned to say that. But when I'm with you, before I know it, the words fly right out of my mouth."

Her forehead creased in concern, she wasn't sure if she liked what he said.

What does he mean, he hadn't planned to say that?

He moved closer, clearing his throat. "Don't get me wrong. The possibility of that happening sounds wonderful to me. But…"

He paused, a look of bewilderment on his face. "What have you done to me, Savanah Jackson? I've known you for what, only a few hours? And you have me so that I can't even think straight. Yet at the same time, I can't imagine a life without you."

A laugh bubbled up in her throat. "I'm sure once you get to know me better, you'll think differently."

"I can't see that happening. Not when you've already captured my heart. And do you know what?" He brought her hand to his mouth for a kiss. "I think I've—"

"Mr. Buchanan? After placing the receipt and Jack's credit card in front of him, their server sent them both a big smile. "Your orders are ready and waiting for you at the hostess stand. Thank you, and I hope to wait on you the next time you come to Jake's."

Jack chuckled. "I promise you'll be our server of choice."

The receipt signed and his credit card back in his wallet, he stood. Holding out his hand to Savanah, he smiled. "Come on…"

And now she was confused. "We're leaving?"

He chuckled. "Yeah, like I said, I have a plan. If I have my way, nothing will ruin this night, Léon included."

Across the room, Léon watched them leave.

Damn…

A scowl twisting his face, he grabbed his glass, tossing back the contents in a single gulp.

He stared down at the empty glass, turning it in his fingers. The sudden urge to fling it across the room, he slammed it down on the bar instead.

He groaned. His date. He forgot all about her. Dragging his hand down over his jaw in a half-hearted attempt to compose his features into a smile, he turned to find she was gone.

What the hell?

His scowl now even more pronounced, he signaled to the bartender for another drink.

It looked like he would be dining alone again.

CHAPTER 22

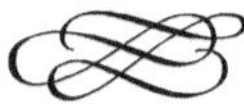

While waiting to turn out of the restaurant parking lot, Jack stole a glance at Savanah.

There was a hint of a smile in his voice. "So, are you ready for a new adventure?"

Tucking her hair behind her ear, she gazed over at him. "I feel like I've ruined everything. I shouldn't let Léon get to me, but…"

Her words trailing off, he reached for her hand, linking their fingers together. "*Remember what I said?* You have no reason to feel sorry about anything. Léon's behavior was unacceptable. When it became obvious he had no plans to let up, I thought it might be best to leave. I think you'll like what I have planned.

"It's all good." If only to convince himself, he nodded.

She glanced over to smile at him. "I'm not worried.

"Good." He grinned. "And it's worked out in my favor, since I now have you all to myself."

She laughed. "Are you sure this is what you want? So far, being in my company has only resulted in one disaster after another. Heaven knows what might happen next.

He shook his head. "I disagree. I don't see this evening as a disaster." Then he grinned. "And even if it was? If the result is spending more time with you, I'm more than up for the challenge."

After he had to let go of her hand to make a turn, he sent her another smile. "Only a few more minutes and we'll be there."

A silence falling between them, she stared out the passenger window. Those two little words were still echoing in her mind.

Marry me…

Perhaps she was making too much of what he said? After all, even he admitted he hadn't intended to say it out loud.

Yet, this meant it was on his mind, right?

She peered over at him in the dim interior of the truck. He was smiling as if he hadn't a care in the world.

Proof of this, he reached for her hand again, giving it a gentle squeeze. "We're going to rock this date, beautiful. You'll see, nothing can ruin this time I get to spend with you."

And like every other time he gave her a compliment, she was blushing.

Jack was feeling pretty good about his plan. Yeah, it would've been nice to have dinner at Jake's as planned. But, as dates go, this could turn out even better.

It was definitely unique.

And yes, he now considered this an official date.

The first of many, he hoped.

Jack turned into The Regency parking lot. With no events scheduled for the evening, the venue was shrouded in darkness, giving it an almost haunted look.

Once he pulled into a space close to the main entrance and shut off the ignition, he glanced over at Savanah. "Well, here we are."

She peered out through the windshield at the empty parking lot before she looked over at him. "Are you sure about this? It's awfully dark."

Since the band had used the venue numerous times for late night practice sessions before moving to their new studio, Jack wasn't worried.

However, now viewing it through Savanah's eyes, he wondered if maybe this wasn't such a good idea after all. As far as first impressions go, this would be a huge fail.

Well, you're here now, so you better make it work.

He got out of the truck and opened the passenger door, Noting her skeptical expression, he chuckled, brushing his knuckles along the curve of her jaw. "It may be a little unconventional, yet as far as first dates go, I think it will be perfect."

Her eyes wide, she gazed up at him. "If you're sure…"

Caught up in her eyes, and under the cover of darkness, how could he not take advantage of this opportunity? Reaching over to cup her chin in his hand, the kiss he gave her was long enough for her to sway towards him, her hands gripping his arms for support. He lifted his head, his answer ready.

"I'm sure."

He helped her out of the truck. After catching the corner of her mouth with another kiss, and grabbing the bag with their dinners from the back seat, he reached for her hand. "Come on."

He kept up a constant flow of words as they ran up the steps to the main entrance. "Again…," he stated, "we'll be fine. I have the lock combination to get in, and I'd never do anything that could get us into trouble." He grinned. "Let's say I have connections."

She eyed him cautiously. "Well then, I guess I'll have to trust you."

"*Hmm*… is this another first? A very important one, I believe."

"I guess we'll have to wait and see…"

And damn if she didn't give him another one of those flirty smiles of hers.

Jack punched in the combination to open the door to the main entrance, and reclaiming Savanah's hand, he led her down the dark hallway to the Grand Ballroom.

With a flip of a switch, the chandeliers burst into light, sending a warm glow over the room.

He grinned over at her. "Another bit of history here… this building was once home to The Cleveland Chandelier Company. Established back in the early nineteen hundreds, they were famous worldwide for their elaborate custom lighting fixtures. For whatever reason—when they closed after almost a hundred years in business—these chandeliers were left behind. Elenore had them restored and now they're as good as new."

Her hand still clasped in his, he led her through the maze of tables to the far corner of the room where a pair of ornate French doors opened into an attached sunroom. The focal point of the room was an elaborate stone fireplace, framed by floor-to-ceiling arched windows. The same style of windows lined the remaining walls, offering a view of both the ballroom and surrounding courtyard.

In one corner, a small round table was set for two. A plush cream-colored sofa and matching armchairs were grouped around the fireplace, while potted greenery and scattered throw pillows added the finishing touch.

Jack set the carryall bag on the table before he turned, arms outstretched and a boyish grin on his face. "Behold… our own private dining experience awaits us."

After slowly turning around, taking it all in, Savanah's hand went to her mouth, an awed sigh slipping out. "Oh, Jack… this is amazing."

He nodded. "It is, isn't it? This is all Darcey's work. At one time it was used as the showroom for the lighting company. She saw it as a place for guests to share quiet conversations, take photos, or just take a break from the reception." A guilty expression on his face, he shrugged. "Once Jason gets going, it can get really loud and crazy in the ballroom."

He pointed to the small chandelier hanging from the center of the domed glass ceiling. "Elenore had this smaller version made to match the chandeliers in the ballroom."

She smiled. "It's such a beautiful space. I'm sure it's very popular with guests."

"Well, since the remodeling was only recently completed, I'm not sure if anyone has even used the space yet. Which means we may be the first." He winked. "How about that? Another first."

He gestured to the bag. "If you'd like to take out the food, I'll hunt down some silverware and glasses. And when I get back, I'll turn on the fireplace."

Then he did what had now become almost as natural to him as taking his next breath. He caught her by surprise, his mouth swooping in to caress hers in a sweet, lingering kiss. "*Hmm…* nice. And on that note, I'll be right back."

Her fingers slowly going to her lips, she watched him leave.

She was smiling as she began taking the containers out of the bag.
Then she shook her head.
Savanah Jackson, you are in big trouble.

CHAPTER 23

*J*ack poured what remained of the wine into their glasses. Once he set the bottle on the table, he smiled over at Savanah. "So, love… what's the verdict?"

As always, his use of endearments had her blushing, her words nearly tripping over each other. "It's perfect. Everything… the food, this place, and you… especially you." Thinking she may have said too much, she quickly nodded over to where music was coming from where his phone was setting on the table. "And we even have music."

He laughed. "*Ah, yes…* sorry about that. After all this time, you'd think I'd know where the control panel for the audio system is in this room, but I don't." He shrugged. "Though you're right, it has worked out rather well, hasn't it?"

He set his wineglass aside and reached for her hand. "I know this wasn't the date you envisioned, but I wanted to make this a night to remember, not one to forget. I promise we'll get to Jake's soon."

"It's okay—it wasn't your fault. If anything, I should apologize to you. I think this is a perfect first date, very memorable."

For a few moments, he studied her, his expression unreadable. Then he nodded, doing so slowly. "Yes, it is, isn't it? Very memorable. The start of many, I hope?"

"That sounds nice." Unsure of what else to say, she nodded.

Then he frowned, cocking his head as he listened. "But I see we've lost our music. My phone must have died."

She stood. "That reminds me, while I waited for you to return, I noticed there is a grand piano in the corner. Was it also left behind by the previous owners?"

She had already left her seat to walk over to the piano. He followed more slowly, stopping about ten feet away, watching as she trailed her fingers over the keys.

He cleared his throat, shoving his hands in his pockets. "No, as a matter of fact, it arrived only a few days ago." He shrugged. "It's a long story."

The reluctance in his tone a hint he wasn't eager to elaborate, after a slight hesitation, she pressed on. "When I was a child, the woman who lived next door had a grand piano on display in her front window because she gave lessons. I was so jealous of the people who came for those lessons, I wanted to be one of them. But my mother said I needed to focus on my dancing."

She shrugged. "So that's what I did." After running her fingers over the keys again, this time sending a rippling of notes echoing into the silence, she flashed a grin at him. "I've always wanted to learn how to do that."

He laughed. "Although it requires a bit of practice, I believe you could master it."

Walking over to him, she tilted her head, her expression completely innocent. "Do you play?"

Jack's first impulse was to do what he always did when asked about his past. This would be to change the subject, something he'd become very good at after all these years.

However, with Savanah? He couldn't do that. He didn't want to keep any secrets from her, his hope she would'd be just as open with him.

He pulled out two chairs from one of the ballroom tables, and once they were seated, he began to speak. "I started piano lessons when I was three-years-old, continuing until my junior year in high school." Fiddling with the stem of his wineglass, he sent her an embarrassed smile. "I had such big plans back then. I was going to be the best concert pianist ever, take the world by storm with my amazing talent."

He shrugged. "I guess it wasn't meant to be." His mind traveling to another time and place, he grew silent, staring down at the wineglass.

Savanah moved closer, reaching for his hand. "What happened?"

And with this simple touch, the words he found so hard to share came pouring out.

He told her everything, beginning with the tragedy that befell his mother and sister, and ending with Elenore gifting the piano. An exact replica of his mother's grand piano, this brought back so many of the memories he'd worked so hard to forget.

He glanced over at the piano, shaking his head. "According to Darcey, Elenore said I'm free to use the piano whenever I want. Years ago, my hands would've been on the keys before those words had even left her mouth. But now? I can't bring myself to even touch the keys, let alone play."

Dragging his hand down over his jaw, he groaned. "Not even one single damn note…"

His gaze traveled over the grand piano; the polished wood gleaming under the dim lights. Then he gave her hand a gentle squeeze. "But this isn't your problem, love, I need to work this out on my own."

"Would you play for me?"

As surprised as he was when this slipped out, their eyes locked; hers, shining with hope; his, revealing a flicker of panic. He cleared his throat. "Oh, Vanababe… I don't know if…"

She pressed a kiss to his cheek, and coming to her feet, she smiled, holding out her hand. "Come on—it doesn't matter what you play. Or if it's perfect. You just need to take that first step, and everything will fall into place."

She tilted her head. "Please? For me?"

A slow smile spread across his face, while at the same time, he shook his head. "*Ah, love...* you're not playing fair. By now, you have to know you have me under your spell and I'll do anything for you."

She only continued to smile, holding out her hand.

He rose to his feet, letting her lead him to the piano. Before he could pull out the bench, she did it for him, gesturing for him to sit.

That familiar onslaught of anxiety took over, his mind warning him this wasn't a good idea. But with Savanah gazing up at him, her smile so hopeful, how could he refuse?

He slid onto the bench and patted the space next to him. "Sit here with me. You can be my inspiration."

Once she was seated, he took a deep breath and exhaled slowly. And for a few moments, the silence surrounding them stretched on, making his pause seem even longer as he stared down at the keys.

Then, raking his fingers through his hair, he let out a long groan. "I can't do this. *God, Savanah…* I don't even know where to begin or what to play. It's as though I've forgotten everything I ever learned."

She studied him for a few moments. "What was the last song you played? Do you remember?"

He nodded, a wry smile twisting his lips. *"Yes… it was 'Greensleeves.' Do you remember?*

Of course he did. How could he not? Even the mention of this song was enough to flood his mind with so many memories.

A favorite of his mother's, he'd worked long hours on his original arrangement, his plan to surprise her at an upcoming competition for amateur composers.

Unfortunately, this event had been scheduled the week after what should've been her return from that fatal trip to San Francisco.

Since his mother had always accompanied him to these events, his father had offered to go in her place. Distorted by grief, he saw this as his father's insensitivity to their loss and refused his offer. After an exchange of angry words and accusations, he had pulled out of the competition. This was also when he'd closed the door to the music room, the piano too painful a reminder of what he'd lost.

So, yes…

He had mixed feelings about "*Greensleeves.*"

Unaware she was now leaning against him, Savanah nodded. "*Hmm… 'Greensleeves,'* huh? My nemesis would be '*The Music of the Night,*' from '*The Phantom of the Opera.*' It was the song I chose for the very first audition I ever did for a dance company."

"And can I assume you wowed them right from the start?" He

smiled down at her. Now that she had moved closer, he was having a hard time concentrating on what they were talking about. He was too caught up in wondering what she would do if he pulled her into his arms for a kiss. If only long enough to make him stop thinking about the kiss she gave him earlier.

That's not going to happen, and you know it.

She laughed. "Unfortunately, no. They weren't impressed. I was devastated, ready to quit dance right there on the spot. It was only when I later found out the company was in debt and on the verge of filing for bankruptcy, I was able to put it behind me."

She didn't tell him it was the worst performance of her life. Or that she almost walked off the stage halfway through the audition when the director of the dance studio suggested she might be better off choosing a new career.

The unwanted thought that this might've been an early warning of what was to come, she shook her head.

No, that's silly. You've come a long way since then. You're different now, tougher.

Pushing this thought aside, she glanced up at him. "Since you never got to play it for your mother, perhaps 'Greensleeves' would be a good place to start. Think of this as your chance to pay tribute to her, show how much you loved her."

His lips curved into a smile. "What did I do to deserve this moment with you?"

Thinking he was teasing, her face scrunched up in concern. "I'm not trying to tell you what to do, I—"

He pressed his fingers to her lips, shaking his head. "Hush, I know you aren't."

"But wait… you need a proper introduction." She slid off the bench and, facing the room full of empty tables, held out her arms. Her voice rang out, surprisingly loud in the empty room. "Ladies and gentlemen, tonight we have an impromptu concert by none other than the renowned pianist and man of the hour—Mr. Jack Buchanan."

Reclaiming her place on the bench, she grinned. "Okay, you're all set."

His kiss brushed her mouth. "We've got this."

Exhaling a long breath, he closed his eyes. His arms relaxed and held out in front of him, he dropped his hands to the keys.

After the first notes faded into silence, he raised his hands again. And this time, when they came down, there was no hesitation. His fingers glided over the keys, flowing effortlessly, and right into his arrangement of *"Greensleeves."*

As though no time had passed, the more he played, the more the music spoke to him. Each note, every pause, and shift in momentum he remembered came to life under his fingertips.

He didn't stop when he came to the end of the song. Or maybe it was more like he couldn't. The notes flowing from his fingertips, he played from memory, skipping from song to song, if only for one or two refrains. It was as though a dam had burst, every song he'd ever learned was clamoring for attention, begging to be set free.

He'd compare it to being reunited with a long-lost friend.

And it felt so good…

As the last note died away, Jack lowered his hands onto his lap. It wasn't until he took a deep breath and let out a long, healing sigh he remembered Savanah.

Mesmerized by the movement of his hands, his fingers dancing over the keys, Savanah had been content to watch him play. His touch appeared effortless, the notes flowing into each other with a simplicity that was beautiful to behold.

That he had kept such an amazing talent hidden all these years was incomprehensible to her. And to have the privilege of sharing—what could be this life-changing moment with him?

It was a gift she would treasure forever.

If only she had something to give him in return.

It was at that moment she realized she did.

A stricken look on his face, Jack turned to Savanah. "I'm so sorry. I didn't mean to go off like that, but once I started, I couldn't stop."

He looked down at his hands before gazing up at her, a look of wonder on his face. "I swear, it was as though my fingers took on a life of their own, I—"

Her hand going to his arm, she shook her head. "Please, you don't need to apologize. You have such an amazing talent, you play beautifully. That I could share this with you has been an honor. I could listen to you play forever."

She reached up to frame his face with her hand. "But now, will you do something for me?"

He captured her hand, bringing it to his mouth for a kiss. "Anything, for you I would do anything." A smile tweaked the corner of his mouth. "I'm thinking, you and I? Together, we could take on the world."

She laughed. "*Umm…* maybe? But right now, do you know the score for '*The Music of the Night?*' If you do, could you play the first two verses, ending with the refrain?"

"I could do that. And if I do?" His eyebrow raised, he waited.

"Let's just say I want to honor a promise." Her smile was infectious. "More like part of a promise."

"*Ah…* okay then." Since he had a pretty good idea what this promise was, he was more than happy to honor her request.

After a quick kiss to his cheek, she slipped out of her shoes and ran to the center of the dance floor. Once she assumed her starting position —her back straight, her chin held high—she sent him a nodAnd as his hands came down on the keys, sending the opening notes of the song floating through the room, she danced.

She poured everything she had into the dance.

Her body in sync with the music, she moved effortlessly across the dance floor. With every step, turn, and twirl, she expressed the emotions of joy, laughter, love, and grace.

In her mind, this was her validation of how far she'd come since that first disastrous dance audition.

But in her heart? Even though she'd deny this if asked, she was dancing for the man she was falling more and more in love with each breath she took.

It was, without a doubt, the best she ever danced.

Even before the last note had faded, Jack was at Savanah's side. That he'd even waited until then was a miracle.

Never having known someone who was a genuine ballerina, he hadn't expected to be so moved by her performance. And now he wanted to take her into his arms. If only as proof this beautiful and talented woman was real, and not just a figment of his imagination.

He pulled her close. His cheek resting against hers, his whisper brushed across her face. "Dance with me. If only to fulfill the rest of that promise you made to me."

So, with his heart beating so close to hers, and humming bits and pieces of whatever song came to him—because everyone knows you can't dance without some kind of music—they danced.

The melody wrapped around them like a quiet spell , the world beyond fading away as they swayed together, her feet brushing the floor in time with his. Her hand rested lightly in his, her head settled against his shoulder, and in that moment, what they shared was so much more than a dance—it was an unspoken promise of their love.

Little by little, he slowed his steps, reluctant to end the magic, until they stood still. After dropping a soft kiss in her hair, he leaned back just enough to gaze down at her.

"What?" she asked, and as a grin spread across his face, she laughed, her joy spilling over.

He cleared his throat, his voice warm but teasing. "I must say, this is by far the best first date I've ever had. It's going to be hard to top."

When her brow furrowed, a flicker of doubt crossing her features, he was quick to add, "I'm sure we will, though. I know I'm all in."

Her arms going up to wrap around his neck, she whispered. "Then kiss me."

"*Hmm…* with pleasure." And in less than a heartbeat, his mouth captured hers in a kiss that went soul deep.

It's safe to say this turned out to be the best first date for both of them.

CHAPTER 24

*A*fter Jack refused Savanah's help clearing away the remains of their dinner, humming along with the music still playing from his phone, she wandered over to the piano.

Lightly fingering the keys, she glanced up to see he was watching her.

Her smile was shy. "Do you think you could teach me how to play? Just the basics?"

"Sure, if it means spending more time with you, I'd be more than happy to give you lessons." He grinned. "Something tells me you'll be a quick learner."

His head tilted, he studied her. "*Hmm…* maybe I'll have you sign up for a life-time plan. That way, I'll be able to keep you around." He smiled. "You will be my inspiration."

She frowned. He obviously didn't know her as well as he thought he did.

You are far from being anyone's inspiration.

And what brought on this sudden feeling of self-doubt?

As she'd watched Jack's fingers glide gracefully over the smooth ivory keys, his love for the music in every note, she realized his passion for what he did was the key to his amazing talent. He threw himself into the music, giving his all.

Above all else, his playing came from the depths of his heart.

While for her, somewhere along her journey, the joy she once found in dance had dimmed. And as much as she hated to admit this, she'd lost the drive to be the best dancer she could be.

This scared her.

For as long as she could remember, her life had revolved around dancing. This was all she wanted, all she knew. She had never envisioned a future doing something else.

Shaken by these thoughts, she feigned interest in the inner workings of the piano.

Her sudden silence had Jack wondering if he had gone a little too far with what he'd said.

Come on, didn't you tell Stephanie to stop overthinking everything? Maybe it's time to follow your own advice?

He picked up the carry-out bag filled with the used dinner containers and utensils. Grabbing the empty wine bottle, he waved it to get her attention. "Hey, I'm taking this to the trash. When I get back, if you'd like, we'll get a start on that first lesson."

She called out just as he reached the door. "Jack, wait… you need to see this. It looks like someone carved their initials and a heart next to the serial number. I wonder if it's the person Elenore Cromley—"

A loud crash echoed through the room. She whirled around just in time to see the wine bottle roll across the floor and under a table.

The bottle forgotten, she watched Jack toss the bag on the table before making his way over to her in record time. After leaning inside the piano to get a better look, he turned to her, his expression one of shock.

He dragged his hand through his hair. "What the hell?"

He took a second look, this time reaching over to trace the carvings with his fingertip. The entire time, he kept shaking his head, mumbling under his breath. "No, no, no… how can this be possible? I don't understand. This is crazy, it makes no sense."

His gaze returned to her, but she realized he was oblivious to her existence. Instead, he was ransacking his mind, scrambling to find a likely explanation.

His gaze shifted to the piano bench. "I wonder if—" His sentence left unfinished, within seconds, he was lifting the lid of the bench. He leafed through the stack of sheet music stored inside, a brief laugh escaping him as he glanced over at her. "This is insane. I thought I'd never see these again."

After shaking his head, he returned the sheet music to the bench and closed the lid.

He sank down on the bench, staring into space. Unsure of what to do, Savanah sat beside him.

They sat in silence. He was trying to make sense of what had happened. While she was searching for the right thing to say.

She made the first move. Resting her head on his shoulder, she slipped her hand in his.

With this simple gesture, Jack's trance-like state broke, his voice unsteady. "This is my mother's piano. The initials and heart?"

He glanced up at the ceiling, a shaky laugh escaped him. "I'm the one responsible for those. When I was about eight years old, she was on tour so much, I accused her of loving the piano more than me. I still remember how angry this made her. She even threatened to get rid of the piano."

A faint smile flitted across his face. "So, I decided to put my mark on it, claiming it as my own. Remember, I was only a child. And in the end, I got my wish. The piano stayed, and my mother cut down on her engagements. At least for a while."

He groaned, dragging his hand down over his jaw.. "What possessed Elenore to do this? It couldn't have been easy. That she got my father's consent is a miracle in itself."

He gave a bitter laugh. "Unless he thought this would be the perfect way to cut ties with me for good."

"*Oh, Jack...* I don't think..." When he only stared at her, his expression resigned, she squeezed his hand. "What did you and Elenore talk about?"

After he filled her in with what he could remember, he grew silent. Then he groaned. "*My God*, she's probably wondering why I haven't thanked her. But in my defense, the thought never entered my mind it could be my mother's piano."

He nodded, as if to re-assure himself. "Yes, I need to pay her a visit soon. Not only to thank her, but to find out how she did this."

Savanah sighed, resting her head back on his shoulder. "I'm sure she knows you would have thanked her had you known. But what a nice thing for her to do. Whatever you said must have made her see how much the piano meant to you."

He pressed a kiss to the top of her head. "I told her things about my life I've told no one else. I don't know how she does it, but she has a way of getting you to bare your soul and share your deepest secrets."

He glanced down at his watch, springing to his feet. "Oh, geeez... it's late. Really late. It won't be much longer before the kitchen crew shows up for the early morning shift. So, I need to get you home."

He glanced over at the piano, then at her. "Unfortunately, this means your piano lesson needs to be put on hold."

She tried, but couldn't hide her grin. "I'm sorry, I don't mean to laugh. But I think we can both agree this has been a crazy, but very interesting, first date. All beginning with Léon at Jake's Place."

He reached for her hand to pull her up and into his arms. He was grinning. "Ah, love, yes, it's been crazy. But a wonderful crazy. And I disagree. For me, our date began with the kiss you gave me before we even left your condo."

After pressing a quick kiss to her mouth, he retrieved the wine bottle from under the table and picked up the carryout bag. As he headed for the door, he grinned at her over his shoulder. "Let's try this again. I'll be back in a couple of minutes."

After she watched him leave, she again wandered over to the piano. As her fingers trailed over the keys, she glanced over at the vacant dance floor, the memory of dancing for Jack still vivid in her mind. And now, in the hushed middle-of-the-night silence, she'd swear there was a hint of magic in the room. She saw this as an invitation to re-capture the joy she'd felt earlier.

So, once again, she kicked off her shoes and ran out onto the floor. Assuming her starting position, she closed her eyes.

And, once again, she danced.

This was the scene that greeted Jack upon his return to the ball-room. Even without music, or perhaps because of its absence, she danced with a reckless abandon. Leaving him reluctant to interrupt, captivated by her every move.

Sensing his return, after a series of spins and one final graceful leap, she finished with a low, sweeping bow. It wasn't until she returned to a standing position, she opened her eyes, watching as he closed the gap between them.

Planting a gentle kiss on her forehead, the gruffness of his voice betrayed his emotion. "I could spend the rest of my life watching you dance. Your beauty floods my mind with so many possibilities, the lyrics and notes begging to be heard."

Her smile was wistful. "I haven't danced like this for such a long time. Where I can do whatever I want—with no demands, or constant criticism—becoming the dancer I always believed I would be." She shrugged. "Maybe things will get better. I'll just have to wait and see."

He brushed a kiss over her mouth. "Whatever you need, I will always be here for you."

A smile curving her lips, she linked her fingers behind his neck. "Always?"

He nodded. "Always."

"Then kiss me."

As their lips met in a long kiss, he knew this was a moment he would always remember.

It was also when he finally understood how it felt to have fallen truly and deeply in love.

After Jack pulled into the parking spot in front of Savanah's condo, he looked down at the hand Savanah had placed on his arm.

Concern furrowed her forehead. "I'm sorry, I've been talking non-stop since we left the party center, haven't I?"

A grin appeared on his face. "You can talk as much as you want. I'm the one who should apologize for being so quiet. I think it's because I'm still trying to take everything in with you right up there at the top of the list."

He pulled up in front of her condo, and after he helped her out of his truck, he walked her to her door.

With a sigh, he rested his forehead against hers. "The past few hours have been like heaven to me. If only the evening didn't have to end." He leaned back, his gaze searching. "I can't wait to see you again. My schedule is packed tomorrow, but I'm free Tuesday after-noon. Could this work for you?"

The soft kisses he pressed along the curve of her jaw sent her thoughts scattering. This made it impossible to concentrate on anything but the feel of his lips. She sighed, closing her eyes.

His kisses slowed, his whisper brushing right below her ear. "You need to help me out a little, love. Lunch? Dinner? Both? You name it, my time is yours."

The playful tone of his voice jolted her back to the present. "Tuesday would be perfect because we only have rehearsal in the morning. Gayle needs the studio for new auditions in the afternoon.

At the reminder of this, she frowned.

The addition of new talent certainly won't be a help to your career.

Unsure whether her expression was about him, or if she was about to change her mind, Jack's responded quickly. "Okay, lunch it is. You can text me with a time and I'll pick you up at the studio. Until then, sweet dreams, Vanababe."

After a quick kiss to her cheek, he ran to his truck.

Once Jack's truck had disappeared from view, Savanah was hanging up her coat when she noticed the note from her mother on the kitchen table.

> Savanah,
> I stopped by to drop off these banana muffins I
> made, but you weren't home. Remember,
> bananas are an excellent source of
> potassium. I put them in the fridge.
> Call when you get the chance. We need to talk.

Talk? About Jack, no doubt.

But she didn't want anything to spoil the mood she was in, so she decided to call her mother in the morning.

When she finally fell into bed, she was out within seconds.

And all her dreams were sweet.

CHAPTER 25

Jack couldn't sleep. Never had he felt so wide awake.

After checking the time for what had to be the umpteenth time, he tossed his phone back on the nightstand.

4:26 a.m.

Propping himself up on his elbows, he glanced over at the windows. But since it was still dark, there really wasn't much to see. He groaned, and falling back on the bed, he dragged his hands back through his hair.

He stared up at the ceiling.

Who would have thought a piano would cause so much trouble?

After dropping Savanah off at her condo, he almost drove back to The Regency. This was because of—yeah, you guessed it—the damn piano.

Turns out overcoming his fear wasn't enough.

He wanted to make up for lost time, find out if he could recapture the joy music used to bring him. Or maybe it was that he needed to prove, if only to himself, he still had it.

So, go ahead, make it happen…

Other than the caterer's early morning bakers, a crew who rarely ventured out of the kitchen, the party center would be deserted at this hour, This meant he'd have a few hours to himself before anyone else showed up for work.

Then what the hell are you waiting for?

He ran his hand down over his jaw, checking to see if he needed a shave. But then decided, if he was going to do crazy, he might as well look the part.

He threw on a pair of jeans and a sweater, did a quick comb through of his hair, and pulled on his boots. After searching for his keys for a good ten minutes, to finally find them in his jacket pocket, he headed for his truck.

Even with a spur-of-the-moment stop for coffee, in less than twenty minutes he was back in the Grand Ballroom seated at the piano, his fingers flying over the keys.

From classical to modern—Chopin, Beethoven, Bach, Ravel, Gershwin, Andrew Lloyd Webber, the Beatles, Elton John—to name a few.

He wanted to play them all.

Yeah, he knew he was insane.

But sometimes a man's gotta do what a man's gotta do…

Right?

Fast forward about three hours when, a takeout cup of coffee in her hand, Darcey unlocked the main entrance to The Regency. She was walking down the hall to her office when she came to a stop, listening.

She could hear piano music. And if she wasn't mistaken, it was coming from the Grand Ballroom.

A big grin lit up her face.

Maybe it was Jack?

Determined to find out, she headed for the ballroom to investigate. Opening the door as quietly as possible, she peeked inside. Just as she suspected, Jack was at the piano.

Not wanting to disturb him, she remained by the door as she listened.

It was clear he was a gifted pianist.

And to think he'd kept this to himself?

This was borderline criminal.

However, as much as she wanted to stay and listen, she had work to do. Her plan to leave as quietly as she had arrived, she reached for the door handle.

Her phone rang, shattering the early morning silence. In a rush to get it out of her pocket to turn it off, she lost her hold on the takeout cup of coffee. The cup hit the floor, sending a wave of hot coffee splashing across the hardwood floor.

"Oh, no…"

Caught up in the music, Jack had no clue Darcey had come into the room. Startled by her cry, he turned to see she was crouched down on the floor.

Even he would admit he'd overreacted at this point. But in his defense, he wasn't sure what happened, only that Darcey was on the floor and appeared to need his help.

He took off in a sprint across the room, and coming in contact with the wet floor, his feet flew out from under him, sending him flat on his back.

"What the hell?"

In the silence that followed, his eyes closed, he didn't move.

"Oh, no… Jack, are you okay? Talk to me." This anxious whisper had him opening his eyes. A horrified look on her face, Darcey peered down at him.

He opened his mouth to answer. Instead, he started to laugh. And he kept on laughing. A laugh almost bordering on insanity, it was a laugh he couldn't control for the life of him.

But this was understandable.

Because, come on… who gets all this thrown at them in such a short time?

He groaned, throwing his arm across his forehead. "Are you kidding me? What's next?"

This was when he realized Darcey was sitting on the floor next to him. Only she wasn't laughing. Instead, she had a very concerned expression on her face.

With another groan, this one louder, he pulled himself up into a sitting position. After he wiped his wet hands on his jeans, he sent her what he hoped was a reassuring smile. "I'm fine. Let's just say it's been a long and crazy night." He shook his head. "I honestly had no idea you were here until I heard you cry out. When I turned to find you on the floor, I thought you fell or something. I guess my gallant plan to rescue you was a little over the top."

"I think it was a very kind and gracious gesture. So, thank you." Now that Darcey knew he was okay, she was smiling. "When I realized it was you playing the piano, I intended to listen for only a few minutes and then leave. Instead, my phone rang. And when I tried to take it out of my pocket to turn it off, I dropped my cup of coffee".

She frowned. "I'm so sorry. And I'm even more sorry I interrupted your playing."

He shook his head. "No harm done. It's about time I left, anyway." He glanced around at the wet floor before he looked over at her and grinned. "And now I really want coffee."

She laughed. "I know. I was really looking forward to that coffee." She looked down at the empty cup she was holding. "French vanilla, my favorite."

She shrugged. "I guess it wasn't meant to be."

She abruptly laid her hand on his arm, a serious expression on her face. "You need to let Jason hear how beautifully you play. You have an amazing talent, one that needs to be shared. Now I understand why Elenore had the piano sent here."

A wry smile on his face, he shrugged. "Yeah, I didn't realize how much I missed it until now. And regarding the piano…" Reluctant to say more, he shrugged. He needed to talk to Elenore first.

"Well, what do we have going on here? An early morning picnic?"

They both turned, watching as Jason sauntered over to them, an amused expression on his face. His arms crossed over his chest, the glance he sent Darcey was teasing. "*Hmm…* and why do I get the feeling you're the instigator here? Didn't you learn your lesson after the fiasco in the equipment room?"

Once he helped her up off the floor, she stuck her tongue out at him. "Long story short, I heard piano music and thinking it could be Jack, I decided to check it out. After listening to him play for a few minutes, my plan was to leave. But my phone rang, I tried to shut it off, and dropped my coffee instead. Being the gentleman that he is, Jack came to help, and slipped on the wet floor."

Jason grinned over at Jack. "You gotta be careful around this woman. I swear, she causes havoc wherever she goes." At the same time, he pulled Darcey into a hug, pressing a kiss in her hair. "I never know what to expect, one of the many things I love about you, gorgeous."

Now back on his feet, Jack shook his head, a sheepish smile on his face. "Believe me, the blame is all mine with this one. I over-reacted."

He glanced down at his watch, then over at Darcey and Jason. "I need to go, there's something I need to do. But first, let me help you clean up this mess so no one else falls."

Darcey shook her head. "No, I'll get someone to take care of it." She peered more closely at him. "Are you sure you'll be okay?"

"Yeah, after a shower I'll be good to go."

Although Darcey wasn't convinced, she nodded. "Good. Because you look a little frazzled."

He laughed.

Frazzled? Yeah, I guess you could call it that.

Her phone rang. Checking the screen, she groaned. "*Oh, geeez...* I'm sorry, I need to take this call. If there's anyone who deserves the Bridezilla of the Decade award, this woman would win, hands down. Whatever she's dreamt up, I need to nip it in the bud. Don't worry about the coffee spill. I'll get someone to take care of it."

After a quick kiss to Jason's cheek and a wave to Jack, she left the ballroom, already speaking into her phone.

Jason nodded over to Jack. "I only stopped by to pick up something I forgot, so I'll walk out with you."

He glanced over at Jack as they walked down the hall. "*So,* what are you doing here? It's not like you to show up so early. And more importantly, how was your date with Savanah?"

The mention of Savanah brought a smile to Jack's face. "It was good... fantastic, in fact."

"She liked Jake's?"

Jack hesitated. He wasn't sure if he wanted to tell Jason what happened with Léon. But since there was a ninety-nine-point-nine percent chance he'd find out from someone else—remember, there are no secrets in this group—he'd rather it came from him first.

He cleared his throat, aiming for nonchalance. "Well, she did. But we ended up coming here instead."

Confused, Jason came to an abrupt stop. "Here? You brought her here? Why?" He grinned. "Certainly not to use the kitchen to impress her with your cooking skills. Because from what I remember, you're not much of a cook."

Jack gave him a long look. "No, I did not. I'm not stupid. We got dinners to go from Jake's."

Jason laughed. "That's a relief. But what made you decide to leave Jake's?"

Jack gave him a summary of their encounter with Léon, along with Savanah's obvious fear of him.

Just thinking about this, he shoved his hands in his pockets, his voice vibrating with anger. "The guy was a complete jerk. I swear his only goal was to intimidate Savanah and ruin her dinner."

A faint smile touching his lips, he shook his head. "Instead, it was an evening I don't think we'll ever forget. At least, I know I won't."

Jason's calculating look, suggesting he was about to ask for more details, Jack promptly changed the subject. "So, after I took her home, I couldn't sleep. All these songs kept running through my mind, begging to be played. You, of all people, know what that's like. So, I came back here and let the music take over. Then Darcey showed up."

He shrugged. "And there you have it, that's everything."

Granted, this wasn't entirely true. But again, until he talked to Elenore, he had no plans to share what he'd learned about the piano.

Jason was nodding. "*Hmm...* that's great news about the piano. I can't wait to see what you've got." He grinned. "And it seems you and Savanah hit it off, big time. So, when are you going to see her again?"

Jack checked his groan. Jason had no plans to give it up, did he?

Once they were outside on the front steps of The Regency, he pulled his keys out of his pocket. "If you must know, the plan is to meet for lunch on Tuesday. So, I guess we'll have to wait until then to see what happens."

He shrugged. "And for now, that's all I've got."

He sent Jason a nod as he started down the steps. "Catch-ya later."

Jason was grinning as he watched him run down the steps to the parking lot. The guy was an open book. The smile that touched his lips whenever he said Savanah's name? This was a dead giveaway he had already fallen for her like a ton of bricks.

He yelled out. "Hey, don't forget we're meeting at the studio later."

Already at his truck, Jack responded. "Yeah, yeah… don't worry, I'll be there. Two-thirty, right?"

It was only after Jack had pulled out onto the main road, Jason headed back inside the party center.

Since it looked like he'd be working late, he decided to pay Darcey one more visit before he left.

He could use another kiss or two to tide him over.

CHAPTER 26

Savanah's phone was ringing.

Then it stopped.

Relieved, because the last time she checked, she still had another hour before she had to get up, she burrowed back under the quilt and closed her eyes.

The alarm had interrupted her dream. Following the same pattern as most of her dreams, she was dancing on stage. There was one difference. This time her partner wasn't Léon. This had her working the floor with ease, her confidence at an all-time high even when performing the most complicated of steps. So, it's understandable she wanted to know who her dance partner was.

She hoped it was Jack.

The ringing started up again. Grabbing the phone from the nightstand, her mother's number jumped out at her from the screen.

Geeez… now she's even interfering in your dreams?

The possibility of discovering the identity of her dream dance partner now out of the question, she threw aside the quilt and headed for the bathroom. There, she hit the answer button on her phone and put the call on speaker.

Not a fan of greetings, her mother started right in, her voice amplified in the small room. "Savanah, let me begin by saying how inconsiderate you've been. You know how I worry when you don't answer my calls. Someday when you become a mother, you'll understand."

Resisting the urge to ask how the possibility of children even existed when her whole life revolved around dance, Savanah splashed cold water on her face.

Her mother was now on a roll. Half listening to her lecture—where, according to her mother, she was going about her life all wrong—she leaned in closer to get a better look in the mirror.

She didn't understand. How was it, the woman staring back at her looked so different? She looked younger, happier. As if she had awakened to a whole new world.

It was official… the time she'd spent with Jack had changed her forever. The events of last night flooded her mind, a smile playing on her lips as she closed her eyes, remembering

"Savanah, are you even listening to me? Honestly, this is exactly why I tried to talk you out of moving. Already, your priorities have shifted."

Savanah blinked.

Yes, your priorities have shifted. And it's the best thing that ever happened to you.

She picked up her phone and headed for the kitchen. "Mother, it wasn't a mistake. I love my new place. And I'm sorry you were so worried. That wasn't my intention. I got home late and didn't want to wake you."

"*Hmph…* where could you possibly be late on a Sunday night?"

With a flick of the switch, Savanah started the coffeemaker. Once the familiar whirring sound filled the quiet kitchen, she sent a nervous glance over at her phone. Given her mother's animosity towards just about every man on earth, she was reluctant to tell her about Jack.

But since nothing will change how you feel about him, it doesn't matter, right? So, go for it.

She took a container of yogurt out of the refrigerator and, setting it on the counter, she took in a deep breath. "I had a date."

The silence seemed to go on forever, with Savanah the first to speak. "His name is Jack Buchanan. A friend of Stephanie's, he offered to show me around the city."

A little unnerved when her mother still hadn't responded, she pushed on. "He's very nice. I think you'd like him. He's what you would call a perfect gentleman."

When this resulted in even more silence, she added. "He's a musician. You should hear him play the piano. He plays beautifully."

Her mother let out a dramatic sigh, the sound amplified on speaker-mode. "Savanah, we talked about this. Your career is at a critical point right now and needs your complete attention. This is not the time to be gallivanting around the city with someone who chose such an unpredictable career. That phase of your life can wait."

Confused, Savanah stared down at her phone.

Unpredictable choice of career? Isn't becoming a dancer just as risky?

As she reached into the cupboard for a cup, she sighed. It was obvious her mother would find fault with Jack no matter what he did.

The sudden need to make her mother understand how serious she was, she gave it one more try. "Mother, I like Jack. I like him a lot. And I know he'd never do anything to jeopardize my career." She paused to add under her breath. "It seems I'm already doing a good job of that on my own."

Unfortunately, her mother heard this. "What do you mean? Did something happen at the studio?"

Still holding the cup, Savanah leaned against the kitchen counter. her eyes closed. She couldn't even imagine what her mother would do if she found out about the warning Gayle gave her and Léon.

A vision of her mother barging into Gayle's office, demanding who-knows-what, she shuddered.

As a result, her answer was vague. "Everything is fine." However, her frustration couldn't be silenced. "Except for the new dance moves Léon thinks we need, adding more work for everyone."

"Well, I'm sure the two of you will figure it out. Never forget how lucky you are to be working with such a well-known dance partner."

Looking up at the ceiling, Savanah rolled her eyes.

Was she serious? She thinks you're lucky?

The tone of her voice was curt. "I don't consider myself lucky. While he may be talented, his personality has much to be desired. He's the rudest person I've ever known."

This brought another dramatic sigh from her mother. "Savanah, you need to remember once your name gets linked with Léon's, a whole new world will open for you. So, try to ignore his flaws the best you can and concentrate on your dancing."

At the loud beep from the coffee maker signaling the coffee was ready, Savanah filled her cup and set it next to the yogurt. Only to realize, her mother wasn't finished yet.

"Now getting back to this John, the man who has so graciously offered to show you around the city. Is he aware of your full schedule?"

"It's Jack, mother… Jack. And, yes, he is. We made plans to meet for lunch tomorrow. Gayle is using the studio in the afternoon for auditions, so our rehearsal was cancelled.

"A true gentleman would pick up a woman up for their date. Never would he ask her to meet him somewhere."

Unwrapping the muffins her mother had left, she frowned as she put one on a plate. Did her mother have to find fault with everything?

She glared over at the phone. Well, she wasn't going to win this one. She smiled. "Well, I guess Jack must be a gentleman because he's picking me up from the studio. In fact, he insisted."

Yes, this was stretching the truth a bit. However, since they hadn't even discussed the possibility of meeting at the restaurant, this was good enough for her.

She glanced over at the clock. "I need to take a shower and get dressed, or I'll be late. Thanks again for the muffins, and stop worrying so much."

"I'm your mother, so I will always worry. Starting with the reminder, you should always start your day with a nutritious breakfast. That's why I dropped off the banana muffins. You can always use the extra potassium in your diet."

"I know, I know… I have a muffin in front of me as I speak. I'll talk to you later. Love you…"

"Love you, too."

Cora Jackson set her phone on the kitchen counter. She gazed around the room, zeroing in on a photo displayed on the refrigerator door. Taken of Savanah at her first dance recital at the age of seven, she had a huge smile on her face.

And now this happens?

She groaned, and dropping her head in her hands, she closed her eyes. She needed to calm down.

It was only after she heard the school bus come to a grinding stop in front of the neighbor's house, she lifted her head.

Tea… you need a cup of tea.

She filled a cup with water and, after putting it in the microwave to heat, she pulled out her basket of tea bags.

She was a long-time believer of the power of tea. And based on her tea chart, a guide she swore by, peppermint tea would be her best choice. Known to help combat anxiety, it was also one of her favorites.

At the rate you're going, you'll need more than a cup.

After almost knocking over the cup as she removed it from the microwave, she dropped in the peppermint tea bag.

She sat at the counter, and stirring the tea, she inhaled its refreshing, minty scent. This ritual alone was usually enough to bring a sense of calm to her life.

But not this time.

She was trying not to worry, but this Jack? Appearing out of nowhere? There was no doubt in her mind, attracted to Savanah's beauty, he'd wasted no time in sweeping her off her feet with a long line of compliments.

This was exactly what she'd tried so hard to protect Savanah from over the years. And to have everything fall apart at this level of her career just because of a man?

You don't want to even think about this happening.

Then to find out this Jack was a musician? This sent a vision of wild all-night parties and clandestine meetings at sleazy hotels skittering through her mind.

Yes, she knew some people thought of her as being overbearing and controlling, but she didn't care. She did what she did only because she wanted the best for Savanah.

And she had no intentions of letting up now.

Like you've told Savanah many times, you're only doing your job.

She took out the tea bag and set the cup next to the plate with a banana muffin. She cut the muffin in half, and after spreading it with a generous layer of cream cheese—a sure sign she was feeling stressed—she set the muffin back on the plate.

Before things got out of hand, she needed to put a stop to this infatuation of Savanah's

Her plan?

She would start by gathering as much information as possible about this Jack. Then, as soon as he arrived at the dance studio to take Savanah out for lunch, she would engage him in conversation, and inquire what his intentions were toward her daughter.

You can bet she was going to be there.

Forty-five minutes later, Savanah's phone beeped as she was about to leave for the studio.

She had three messages, all from Jack.

> Hi beautiful, I wanted to let you know how much I enjoyed what we've both now agreed was our 'official' first date. I also need a time to pick you up for lunch tomorrow. Which, by the way, will be our 'official' second date.
>
> I believe we've got this, Vanababe. Until tomorrow then.
>
> One more thing, I can't believe how much I already miss your smile.

After about ten minutes or composing and then deleting what she wanted to say, she finally sent him a response

> I also enjoyed our 'official' first date. And I'm really looking forward to lunch. Will 12:30 work for you? If not, let me know. Until our 'official' second date, then. XOXO

As she was wondering whatever had possessed her to add the XOXO to the text, her phone beeped. It was another text from Jack.

> 12:30 p.m. it is. XOXO

CHAPTER 27

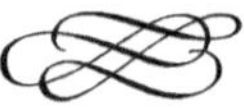

*A*cross town, after glancing at her watch, Stephanie slipped into the hospital staff lounge. Covering for a nurse who had called in sick, and unfamiliar with her routine, this was the first chance she had to take a break.

An intern, sprawled out in a chair and fast asleep, was the only other occupant in the room.

Not wanting to disturb him, she tiptoed over to the coffee station, made a cup of tea, and helped herself to one of the chocolate chip cookies she brought for the staff.

A peek over at the intern to see he was still out cold, she grabbed another one.

Not that she had any reason to feel guilty. After the morning she'd had, she deserved a whole plateful.

She kicked off her shoes, and after settling comfortably on the sofa, she pulled her phone from her pocket.

She had a text from Jack.

Hey, I hate to bother you, but if you're at the hospital, can you tell me if Elenore is there? I need to talk to her.

She typed out her response.

She just informed us she will be leaving at noon for a lunch date. Do you want me to ask if she can see you?

He answered within seconds.

That's okay, I'll take my chances. See you soon.

Wondering what he was up to, she dropped her phone back into her pocket.

She finished the first cookie and after taking a bite of the second, she smiled. She couldn't wait to hear how his date went with Savanah. She was still patting herself on the back for arranging their meeting at Café Latte.

It confirmed what she'd said all along… this was a match made in heaven.

Seriously? You could have left, and they wouldn't have noticed.

She sighed. Love was such a funny thing. Look at her and Evan… in the beginning, she'd fought him every step of the way.

And now you can't imagine life without him…

She pulled out her phone and sent him a text.

I wanted to let you know I love you. And miss you. XOXO

Before her phone was even back in her pocket, Evan answered.

I love you, too. And always will. XOXO

Not even bothering to hide her smile, she popped the last bite of cookie into her mouth and drank the tea. According to the bright yellow smiley face clock on the wall, she had about fifteen minutes before she had to be back out on the floor.

So, she rested her head against the sofa cushions and closed her eyes. She intended to take advantage of every single one of those minutes.

It took Jack about ten minutes before he found an available parking spot in the hospital lot. He grabbed two bakery boxes from the passenger seat, hit the lock button, and headed for the hospital's main entrance. After he took the elevator to the third floor, he searched the reception area for Stephanie.

Unfortunately, she was nowhere to be found. Instead, the first person he saw was Lucy.

He groaned, running his hand back through his hair.

Aw, geeez… this isn't good.

He'd met Lucy only once, at Stephanie and Evan's engagement party. For him, this had been one time too many.

Not that he disliked Lucy. No, if anything, she could be very entertaining. And since she tended to monopolize any conversation she was in, this meant he didn't have to say much. She also had the annoying habit of getting right in your face. And that drove him crazy. After a few minutes of this, he was ready to run right out of the room.

Once he saw she was busy with another staff member, he took off in a sprint to the nurses' station.

He found Stephanie on the phone. Waiting until she finished her call, he tapped her on the shoulder. "Hey, Steff…"

"Jack…" After she gave him a hug, she grinned. "So, tell me… what's so important that you need to see Elenore? When I let her know you would be stopping by, she told me to bring you to her office the moment you arrived. Then she smiled before she said, "I wondered how long it would take him to figure it out."

She tilted her head. "Figure out what? Does this have something to do with the piano?"

His glance was teasing. "Maybe, maybe not."

She nodded toward the boxes he was holding. "Well, it must be important if you need to bribe her with Abby's cookies."

He grinned, handing her a box. "This is for you and your co-workers. And no, there's no bribery involved. It's just me, being nice."

She peeked inside the box. "These are sure to be a hit with everyone. However, you better not leave without telling me whats going with you and Elenore. Otherwise, there will be no more favors. No matter how many boxes of cookies you bring."

Then she grinned. "I also want to hear all the details about your date with Savanah."

He laughed. "Again, maybe, maybe not."

She placed the box of cookies on the counter and gestured for him to follow her. "Come on, I'll show you to Elenore's office."

When they reached Elenore's office, after again reminding Jack he better not leave without stopping by to see her, Stephanie left.

Jack found Elenore at her desk, working on her computer. He cleared his throat to get her attention.

When she glanced up, he sent her a tentative smile. "Good morning. Is this a good time? If not, I can come back later—"

She cut him off, waving him in. "No, no… please have a seat. I'll be with you in a minute."

As promised, she turned off her computer with seconds to spare. She pushed it aside, and after removing her glasses, she sent him a smile. "And a good morning to you, too."

He placed the remaining bakery box in front of her. "This is a little something to make your day even sweeter… cookies from Abby's."

Elenore opened the box, and after *oohing* and *aahing* over the cookies, she placed them on the corner of her desk. "These look amazing. Thank you."

She came right to the point. "So, am I to assume this visit has something to do with the piano?"

He nodded. "Yes, it has everything to do with the piano. I want to start by thanking you for having it delivered to The Regency. The move couldn't have been easy. I also want to apologize for not coming to see you sooner.

He shrugged. "To be honest, it was only last night I finally worked up the courage to even put my fingers to the keys. And when I discovered it was my mother's piano? Well, I gotta tell you, I was beyond surprised.

He shook his head. "I don't know what else to say, except… how were you able to accomplish this?"

A smile touched her lips. "Before I go into the details, when did you realize it was your mother's piano? And how?"

He told her about the initials and heart he'd scratched on the inside of the piano, along with his reason for doing this.

Elenore nodded. "*Hmm…* perhaps this was something you needed to do at that time in you life in order to arrive at this point in time?" She shrugged. At my age, I've seen a lot. And I've come to the conclusion everything really does happen for a reason."

Allowing Jack some time to think about this, she reached for a folder on her desk. After a quick scan through the contents, she pushed it across the desk to him. "This is for you. Everything you need regarding the piano is in this folder, including the papers verifying you as the rightful owner. According to your father, this is what your mother would've wanted."

She shrugged. "As for that matter, his sentiments were the same."
Your father agreed to this?

Jack found this hard to believe. "Well, since he hasn't responded to any of the texts or emails I've sent for almost the past fifteen years, I wonder if this is his way of cutting ties with me for good."

Again, he shook his head. The more he learned, the more confused he became. "I figured he'd given the piano away long before this.

And now Elenore was the one shaking her head. "*Ah, Jack,* it makes me so sad thinking of what you and your father have lost because of your stubbornness. And yes, you're just as guilty of this as he is."

She sighed. "Unfortunately, grief has a way of doing this to a person, if only as a way to deal with their loss."

His head tilted, Jack studied her. "You still haven't told me why you did this. I'm curious, what is your connection to my father?"

She removed her glasses and sat more comfortably back in her chair. "I've never actually met your father, but I did meet your grandfather many years ago at a charity event here in Cleveland. He and my husband Peter were business colleagues. Unfortunately, like my Peter, your grandfather also died at an early age. Besides his wife, he left behind a son who married a well-known opera singer."

Jack's eyes lit up. "That would be my mother. I never met my grandparents. My grandfather died before I was born, and only a short time later, my grandmother moved back to Vienna to be with her family. This is what I was told."

Elenore nodded. "Unfortunately, there was the tragic passing of your mother and sister. As an opera fan, I'd followed your mother's career and remembered when it happened. Loved by so many, fans from all over the world mourned her passing."

She smiled. "Then you came along, and I recognized your last name, Buchanan. Since you're also a musician, I wondered if there could be a connection. This explains all those questions I fired at you that day at The Regency.

She shrugged. "And the nosy old lady that I am, after listening to you reminisce about the time you spent at your mother's piano, I wondered what happened to it. And the only person who might have the answer to that would be your father. So, I found his number and called him."

She sighed, shaking her head. "We talked for a long time. He told me how difficult it was after your mother died, the rift between you. But even before that, for your father, music had become the enemy. Unfortunately, it caused a huge argument he had with your mother right before she left for the wedding. He didn't give me any details, nor did I ask. However, I got the impression this led to a long period of whys and what ifs. And a lot of guilt."

She clasped her hands together, leaning closer. "Jack, your father knows he should've done more to help you through that awful time. However, he was grieving, too. And when you chose music over law? For him, that was the final blow."

She shrugged. "I truly believe, even though he hasn't shown it, he's very proud of the man you've become."

Jack closed his eyes. He felt as though enormous weight had lifted from his shoulders, bringing a long-overdue sense of relief. Elenore had given him the confirmation he'd been waiting for so long—his father had finally accepted his choice of career.

And this was all he'd ever wanted.

"Jack?"

He opened his eyes, sending her a rueful smile. "I'm sorry. It's only that I've waited so long to hear this. And you're right, he isn't the only one at fault. I'm sure I made it very difficult for him."

He groaned, dragging his hand down over his jaw. "*God*, we really made a mess of things, didn't we?"

"You're only human, and that was a terrible time for both of you." Elenore shook her head. "After Peter's accident, there were some days I didn't get out of bed. I blamed everyone. His doctors for not knowing he had a heart condition… the ambulance for not arriving soon enough, and so on. It was a long, painful journey before I finally rejoined the living. Only when I became involved with the Children's Hospital, the satisfaction of helping others was what got my life back on track."

She smiled. "But getting back to you… when I told your father you said the time you spent at your mother's piano was the happiest of your life, he agreed the piano should be with you. So, I made all the necessary calls."

She shrugged. "And you know the rest."

Her voice took on an almost threatening tone. "This means the ball is now in your court. You need to reach out to him, tell him how good it feels to have his blessing. I realize he hasn't responded in the past, but take it from me, as you grow older, learning to forgive becomes a little easier."

Elenore didn't feel it was necessary to tell Jack his father had to be the most stubborn person she'd ever dealt with. He didn't like to be proven wrong, and apologies weren't part of his vocabulary. She had to do a lot of fast talking to convince him the piano belonged with Jack.

And with no guarantee he'd hold up his end of the bargain, it was only after the piano had arrived and was set up in The Grand Ballroom, she could finally relax.

This, along with Jack's heartfelt appreciation, was enough to know her decision to contact his father had been a good one.

Jack nodded. "Yes, I'll talk to him. I just need a little time to figure out what I want to say."

"Good, but don't wait too long."

Then, clasping her hands together on the desk, she leaned closer, sending him a huge smile. "So, tell me… what prompted you to even look for the heart and initial carvings? And how did it feel to play again? Did the notes come easy? Or have you given any thought how you plan to use this new found opportunity?"

He laughed. "*Wow...* where do I start? Let's see, I wouldn't be here without the help of a very special woman."

This had Elenore's immediate attention. She liked nothing better than an honest-to-goodness love story. She wasn't one to brag, but she considered herself quite the matchmaker. Proof of this was Stephanie and Evan. If there were any two people in desperate need of her help, it had been them.

So, with Elenore occasionally interrupting him for more details, he told her how Savanah had not only found the carvings, but she'd also convinced him to play again. And much to his surprise, as if no time had passed, he had no difficulty playing the songs he remembered and loved.

However, as to what came next, he wasn't sure. Right now, his only goal was to make up for lost time, rediscover all that he'd lost.

They were discussing their favorite songs, surprised to find how many they had in common, when Elenore glanced down at her watch.

"*Oh, no...* where has the time gone?" She came to her feet, prompting Jack to do the same.

He watched as she gathered up the papers on her desk and stuffed them into a folder. After pulling her purse out of the desk drawer, she picked up the box of cookies.

She smiled. "I'm so sorry. I have a luncheon date at noon and if I don't leave now, I'll be late." She grinned. "Since I'm a great believer in punctuality, I better practice what I preach, right?"

After she'd waved him out of the office, locking the door behind them, he accompanied her to the elevator. She looked up at him. "I'm so glad you came to see me. Please keep me updated on the situation with your father. I also expect an update on this new woman in your life. By chance, is she a music lover?"

A smile flashed across his face. "I guess the answer to that would be a yes, since she's a dancer. A ballerina, to be exact."

Her hand going to her heart, Elenore came to an abrupt stop. "*Oh, Jack...* how romantic. Think of what you could accomplish together, blessed with such talent. Promise you'll let me know what happens. At my age, it's always exciting when a good love story comes along."

He waited until she'd stepped into the elevator and pushed the button for the main floor before he responded. "I promise to keep in touch. Have a great lunch, and again, thank you."

After the elevator doors closed, he turned and headed back to the nurses' station. And as dramatic as this may sound, this meeting with Elenore had left him feeling like a new man. Just like that, all the years of self doubt and regret were gone.

And he was ready to take on the world.

Yep, life was good.

Now he only had to find Stephanie. Hopefully she hadn't taken her lunch break yet.

He was starving.

CHAPTER 28

*U*nfortunately, this time it was Lucy who was manning the nurses' station, not Stephanie. And before Jack had the chance to make his escape, she looked up and right at him.

A huge smile crossing her face, she jumped up from her chair and scooted around the counter until she was only inches away.

"It's Jack, right? Remember me, Lucy? What can I do for you today?"

He countered by taking a step back and, jamming his hands in his jacket pockets, gave her a wary look. "Hey, Lucy… you haven't seen Stephanie, have you?"

Unfazed by his brief answer, she moved a little closer. "She's around here somewhere. My gosh, it seems like we met only yesterday. Remember? It was at Stephanie and Evan's engagement party. And in about two weeks, they'll be walking down the aisle, ready to begin their happily ever after."

She gave a long and dreamy sigh. "It's all so romantic, isn't it?"

Her good mood abruptly flip-flopping, she frowned. "Of the two of us, I thought for sure I'd be the first to get married. And now I'm not even sure I'll have a date for the wedding."

She glanced over at him, her brows furrowing. "*Hmm… I wonder…*"

Her mouth curving in a smile, she put her hand on his arm.

Uh, oh...

Whatever Lucy was about to suggest, Jack wanted no part of it.

Jamming his hands even deeper in his pockets, he took another step back, searching the surrounding area. "*Umm...* I promised Stephanie I wouldn't leave without saying goodbye. Could she be on her lunch break?"

Suddenly dropping her hand from his arm, Lucy gave an annoyed jerk of her head, implying he should look behind him. "I believe that's her coming down the hall now." She walked back behind the counter and all but threw herself in the chair. "Don't worry, I get it. You don't need to make excuses for why you can't be my date for the wedding."

Stephanie joined them. "I heard what you said, Lucy. Have you already forgotten I told you Jack has a date?" She glanced over at Jack, an eyebrow raised. "A very special date, I hope?"

Lucy's eyes lit up with excitement, her lack of date forgotten. "Really? You've met someone? Well, don't keep us in suspense, we want details. Who is this mysterious woman?"

She snapped her fingers. "I bet it's Melanie, the infamous yoga instructor." She frowned. "You better be careful. From my experience, I've found most yoga instructors aren't as sweet as they let on."

Stephanie laughed. "Lucy, you know that's not true. You're bent out of shape because someone told you they saw Melanie and your ex having dinner at Jake's Place. Since you're the one that ended the relationship, you have only yourself to blame."

"I don't want to talk about it. That ship has sailed." Leaning back in the chair, Lucy sent Jack a coy smile. "I want more information about you and this mystery woman."

Jack was shaking his head, no. The idea of discussing Savanah with the two women, especially Lucy, had him sending a longing glance over at the elevator.

Remember, he was running on very little sleep. This combined with everything he'd had to process over the last several hours, his mind was no longer working at full capacity. This meant he needed to leave before he started talking stupid.

He dragged his hand through his hair, sending Stephanie a silent plea for help. "I promised I wouldn't leave without saying goodbye, so here I am."

She tucked her arm in his, giving it a reassuring pat before she turned to Lucy. "I'm going to lunch and I'm taking this cutie with me. I have a favor to ask him. So, if anything important comes up, you know where to find me."

Lucy leaned over the counter, calling out as they turned to leave. "Wait, you're not going to tell me who it is?" Upon being ignored, she crossed her arms over her chest and let out a long, dramatic sigh. "Why does everyone else has a special someone, except for me?"

Then, remembering where she was, she scanned the area. Relieved to see no one was around to have witnessed her lament—after all, she had a reputation to keep up—she grabbed her phone and headed for the staff lounge.

She had some detective work to do. There had to be someone on her contact list she'd overlooked as a possible date. And if she wasn't mistaken, Stephanie had brought in a plate piled high with cookies. Chocolate chip, her favorite.

If anyone needed a pick-me-up right now, she'd qualify hands down.

She plopped down on the sofa, cookie in hand. After taking a big bite, she closed her eyes, a blissful sigh escaping her.

She needed to learn how to bake.

How hard could it be?

Their choices made, a chicken sandwich for Jack and a salad for Stephanie, they grabbed the first available table they found in the crowded cafeteria.

Stephanie had been talking non-stop since they left the nurses' station. So, giving a nod here and there, if only to show he was listening, Jack picked up his sandwich and took a big bite. Breakfast had been a long time ago, and he was hungry.

As she added the dressing to her salad, Stephanie chattered on about how she didn't understand why people waited so long to send in their response cards for the wedding. Didn't they realize the caterer needed this information so they wouldn't run short on food? And could you imagine the uproar if they did?

This wasn't how she wanted their wedding to be remembered.

She shook her head, sending a glance over at Jack. When he only shrugged before taking another bite of his sandwich, she sat back in her chair, her face scrunched up in dismay. "Oh, Jack… I'm so sorry. I'm talking too much, aren't I? It's only when I think about everything that can go wrong, I get so nervous. Then I can't shut up."

He chuckled. "Don't worry about it. Since I was starving, I'm perfectly content to listen while I eat. But, a little advice here? You need to step back, take a big breath, and stop worrying. The wedding is going to be perfect."

"You're right." Then she followed his advice. She took in a deep breath, and after slowly letting it out, she sent him a big smile.

He gave her a thumbs up. "There ya go. And trust me, even if you forget something, you'll be the only one to notice." About to take another bite of his sandwich, his forehead creased in thought. "Speaking of wedding plans, what's this favor you want from me? Or was that your way of changing the subject to get Lucy off my back?"

He held his hand up in denial. "Not that I needed your help."

"Oh, really? I'm pretty sure I heard her trying to con you into being her date for the wedding. You had that 'deer-in-the-headlights' look when I saw you. Don't even try to deny it."

She laughed, waving her fork to make her point. "Who knows what you might've agreed to had I not stepped in to save the day?"

He frowned, a little insulted by what she said. "I'm pretty sure I had everything under control, making it very clear I didn't need a date."

"*Hmm*… that's not what I saw." She grinned. "But I hope this means everything went well with Savanah and she agreed to be your date for the wedding?"

Oh, boy…

He hadn't even mentioned to Savanah they attend the wedding together.

And you wonder why you don't do well with dating.

He set the sandwich down, and after wiping his mouth with his napkin, he cleared his throat. "We, uh… no, we did not. I think we both took it for granted? At least I did."

Stephanie nodded, slowly she did this. "*Sooo*… you took it for granted. Seriously, Jack? This was the whole point of getting the two of you together. And trust me, no woman takes something like that for granted."

Convinced this wouldn't be a problem, he picked up his sandwich again. "We'll be fine. We're having lunch tomorrow. I'll bring it up then."

"You realize the wedding is less than three weeks away, right?"

He sighed. She wasn't going to let up on this was she? Avoiding eye contact, he tucked the lettuce back in his sandwich before he responded. "Yes, I'm well aware of that. How would I not, since you keep reminding me?"

"Jack, you're making me nervous." She looked him straight in the eye. "You do still like her, right?"

This was when Jack realized she had no intentions of letting up until he shared details about his date with Savanah. And he wasn't sure he wanted to do that. At least, not yet.

Stalling for time, he took another bite of his sandwich, chewing slowly.

He finally swallowed what was in his mouth, washed it down with a gulp of coffee, and wiped his mouth with a napkin. After throwing the napkin on his plate, he glanced over at her.

She was staring him down.

Oh, boy…

He cleared his throat. "The only reason we didn't get together today is because she has rehearsal." He glanced down at his watch. "And I need to be at the studio in about an hour. It's going to be a late night with this new project we took on."

She raised an eyebrow.

This is when his mind betrayed him and he just blurted it out. "If I had my way, I wouldn't have let her out of my sight. She's like no woman I've ever met, and I don't intend to lose her."

And if that wasn't more than enough information to share, he couldn't seem to stop. "The moment I turned to find her standing behind me in line at Café Latte, I knew she was the woman I wanted to spend the rest of my life with. One look, and I was hooked."

A faint smile curved his lips. "I've never been one to believe in all this fate and destiny stuff, yet now I'm thinking differently. Because how else would you explain this?

Then, damn if he didn't throw in the pièce de résistance. "And between you and me? If I could get her to say yes, I'd marry her in an instant."

Then, as though nothing unusual had happened—he hadn't just poured his heart out, sharing his innermost feelings about the woman he loved—he picked up what remained of his sandwich and popped it in his mouth.

Stephanie slowly sat back in her chair, her mouth open in shock. "*Oh, my...* when I suggested the two of you should meet, I never, *never,* envisioned this happening. However, I think it's absolutely wonderful, because you really are perfect for each other."

She grinned. "Again, what would you do without me?"

He chuckled. "Yeah, I'll give you this one. Only remember, I did find her first. And on my own. I just didn't act on it fast enough."

He grinned. "Now I know better."

She smiled. "Yes, and now I want you to follow the advice you gave me the night of the awards dinner. Do you remember what you said? You told me to dive in, let go of any trust issues I had, and enjoy the moment. Those were your exact words."

He laughed, reaching across the table to give her a high-five. "*Wow...* I said all that? Pretty deep, huh?"

He chuckled, shaking his head. "I surprise myself sometimes. But hey... whatever works, I'm all for it."

She laughed. "Good. And now that you're sitting on top of the world, ready to dive in and enjoy the moment, I think this is the perfect time to ask you about that favor I want."

She pushed her salad aside, suddenly serious. "Evan and I have chosen the song "*Endless Love*" for our first dance. I assume you know the song?"

He nodded. "Good choice. A tribute to true love."

She smiled. "Yes, it is. And we've been thinking how great it would be if you played your version of the song for us. This would make our dance even more special.

He fingered his cup, a teasing glint in his eyes. "*Hmm...* special, huh?"

Stephanie nodded. "Yes, *very* special. I know how much you enjoy composing your own version of a song. And you're so good at it."

He raised an eyebrow. "Oh, really? And how would you know this? Or are you trying to win me over with flattery?"

She laughed. "No, no, no... there's no flattery involved. I'm repeating what Jason told me. He said you had a gift for bringing music to its highest potential. And he should know, right?"

"Highest potential?" Jack burst out laughing. "Well, it would be nice if he told me that himself."

Encouraged by his laugh, she was grinning. "You know how he is with the band. He doesn't want to come across as a softie."

She pushed her salad aside, an earnest look on her face. "The band we hired said they would be more than happy to play the original song. But Evan and I think our first dance would be more memorable with you on the piano, playing your version." She leaned forward, a hopeful look on her face. "Please? It would mean so much to us."

He was silent. It was only when she thought he was about to refuse, he smiled. "I'd be happy to do this for you. I'll get to work on it as soon as I can."

He wasn't going to tell her this, but already, different variations of the song were popping up in his mind, making him eager to get started.

Must be the magic of the grand piano.

Stephanie was ecstatic. "*Oh, Jack...* thank you. This was the one part of our wedding that didn't feel right. Yet, now it does." She clasped her hands to her heart. "Thank you, thank you, thank you... I'm *so* excited."

She glanced at her watch. "Okay, now that we have that settled, I've still got ten minutes. Tell me what happened with Elenore."

Still reluctant to share any information of his past, Jack gave her only a brief summary of his meeting with Elenore. He said little about his father and his part in the delivery of the piano, as this might lead to questions he wouldn't want to answer. Or—and he'd be willing to bet on this—Stephanie would insist he call his father, right her and now in the hospital cafeteria to make things right between them.

As he told Elenore, he had plans to do that.

He just needed a little more time.

With Jack's promise he'd call the moment he finished the revision, Stephanie was all smiles as she returned to work.

As promised, Jack sent Savanah a text before he started up his truck. Then he turned on the audio and hit a few buttons, sending *"Endless Love"* through the interior of his truck.

As he headed for the studio, already the notes were starting to come together in his head.

On the other side of town, Savanah's day wasn't going that great.

Léon had shown up at the studio, the unmistakable signs of a nasty hangover evident in his every move.

Obviously, he had continued to drink long after she and Jack left the restaurant last night.

The good news—if you want to call it that—was that his focus wasn't only on Savanah. The nastiest he'd ever been, he found fault with everyone in the studio. This had all the dancers so nervous, they were at the point they couldn't remember what was what.

When this resulted in Gayle calling for another break, Savanah checked her phone to find she had a text from Jack.

> Hey beautiful. I thought you might be interested to know I talked to Elenore, and all is good. I'll fill you in when I pick you up tomorrow. Until then, save one of your beautiful smiles for me, okay? XOXO

She typed out her response.

> Your text couldn't have come at a better time. Léon is on a rampage today, but now you've given me a reason to smile. I can't wait to find out what happened with Elenore. Until lunch tomorrow. XOXO

It was only after she sent the text, she became aware of the uncomfortable silence now filling in the room. She glanced up from her phone to find all eyes were on Léon..

Glaring at her from the other side of the room, his crossed arms and sarcastic tone immediately had her on alert.

"So, Savanah… will you be joining us on the dance floor? Or have you decided you'd rather spend your time on the phone? I know keeping up with social media is important, but in case you've forgotten, we're here to dance. And this includes you."

He raised an eyebrow. "Or maybe it's your boyfriend you're texting?"

She held him in a long stare before she tucked her phone back in her bag. Carefully adjusting her leotard and smoothing back her hair, she strolled out onto the dance floor.

Her hands on her hips, she sent him a huge smile. "Sorry about that. I'm ready if you are."

Léon was not going to ruin her good mood.

Not now…

Not ever.

CHAPTER 29

When Savanah's alarm went off Tuesday morning. the sky was overcast. Now, pulling her car into the studio parking lot, a steady rain was falling.

She considered making a run for the entrance. However, since she was early and there was no sign of Gayle's car, this suggested the studio entrance was probably still locked.

She figured she'd have about twenty minutes before the other dancers began arriving. This would give her enough time to alert Gayle about Léon's increasing erratic behavior.

Their encounter Sunday night at Jake's Place had concerned her, but as he was on his own time, she had no grounds to criticize him.

It was what happened during rehearsal yesterday that worried her. When he'd returned to the studio after their lunch break, the over-powering smell of alcohol on his breath more than explained his erratic moves and distracted state. But when this led to several missed cues, and a near fall almost taking her down with him, she'd suggested they take a break. Mumbling profanities, he'd stormed out of the studio.

To return over an hour later, behaving as if nothing had happened.

This, along with his actions the night before, raised too many red flags. So, for her safety, and that of the other dancers, she wanted to make Gayle aware of the situation.

A car pulled into a space not too far from hers. After she watched Gayle jump out and run through the rain to unlock the studio door, she reluctantly did the same.

Ten minutes later, Savanah plopped down on one of the chairs lining the back wall of the studio. After kicking off her shoes, she pulled her ballet slippers out of her bag, jamming her feet into them.

She was trying to calm down.

Her meeting with Gayle hadn't gone well. If anything, she'd brushed aside Savanah's suggestion there even was a problem. According to her, every dancer has their own way of dealing with the long hours and constant stress involved. For Léon, maybe this was by indulging in an occasional drink or two.

An occasional drink or two?

Savanah didn't even know how to respond to that.

Now, if he continued this behavior, Gayle had said, she'd talk to him. But, as she was quick to remind Savanah, Léon was their ticket for a successful season. And with the full schedule of auditions now taking up so much of her time, she'd hoped the dancers were professional enough to work out any problems on their own.

Then, a sign their conversation was over, she picked up her phone to make a call.

So, it was a frustrated Savannah that left Gayle's office. Her message couldn't have been more clear.

It looks like you're on your own.

Ignoring the chatter of the other dancers now filing into the studio, she started right in on her barre workout.

Once finished, and calmed by the familiar routine, this all but disappeared when Léon stormed into the studio. A sign his disposition hadn't improved, he immediately began barking out orders, sending the dancers scattering.

She glanced over at the clock hanging above Gayle's office door. It was about 9 a.m. In less than four hours, she would be with Jack.

This is what she was going to hang onto.

Four hours… what could go wrong?

The clock on the dashboard of Cora Jackson's 2006 Camry read 12:30 p.m. when she pulled into the studio parking lot.

Relieved the rain had ended, and she wouldn't need her umbrella, she grabbed the tray of banana muffins from the passenger seat.

She was about to open the car door when an unfamiliar black pickup truck pulled into a nearby parking space. She watched as a man got out of the truck and began walking towards the entrance to the studio.

He was holding a single red rose.

She leaned forward to get a better look at him through the windshield.

Humph… this must be the man Savanah was talking about.

He was very attractive, she'd give him that. Yet, given her experience with good-looking men over the years, she viewed this as more of a disadvantage than a plus.

Piling on the charm to get what they want comes easy for them. Then, with no warning, they're gone.

She watched as he came to a halt and pulled his phone from his pocket. When he began typing something, she saw this as the perfect opportunity to get his attention before he entered the building.

Just to ask a few questions, discover his true identity.

Tossing the tray of muffins back on the passenger seat and scrambling out of the car, she called out. "Sir, excuse me… sir?"

Dropping his phone back in his pocket, he continued on his way to the entrance.

Maybe he couldn't hear her?

She called out even louder. "Hello, you with the rose… I need to talk to you."

Again, there was no response. And this made her angry. How could he not hear her? She had yelled as loud as she could. The possibility she was being ignored had her even more determined to catch up to him.

She ducked into the car and grabbed the muffins. Unfortunately, in her rush to get back out of the car, she smacked her head on the door frame… hard. Stunned by the impact, she moaned, and clutching her head, she collapsed into the driver's seat, all thoughts of confronting the enemy now on hold.

For a few minutes, she didn't move, waiting for the pain to subside. Finally, blinking her eyes open, she glanced at her reflection in the rearview mirror. Apart from the huge bump, on her forehead, she looked normal. Thankfully, there was no blood.

She closed her eyes again.

Where most people would take this as a warning to leave things alone, she saw it as an omen. This man Savanah liked?

He was trouble.

So, when she finally entered the studio, her mood had dipped to a dangerous low.

And who was to blame for this?

Why, Jack, of course.

Fortunately, Jack was completely unaware of this. Had he known what Savanah's mother was thinking, he would've been horrified.

His excuse? Though he was physically present, his mind still hadn't left the Grand Ballroom.

He had spent most of the morning working on a revision for the song Stephanie and Evan had chosen for their first dance. From the moment he sat at the piano, a sudden eagerness had consumed him. And once his fingers found the keys, he let the music do its thing.

Even after the drive across town to the dance studio, the notes were still bouncing around in his head, clamoring for attention.

As his mother used to say, he'd found his happy place.

And now, the knowledge he would be sharing the day with Savanah?

Could life get any better?

He didn't think so.

CHAPTER 30

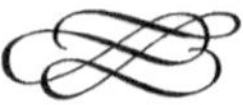

a young girl was seated behind the counter when Jack entered the dance studio's reception area. Her back to him, she was talking on her phone.

When a few seconds had passed, and she still hadn't acknowledged his presence, he cleared his throat.

She whirled around, and letting out a piercing shriek, she dropped her phone.

Almost as traumatized by this as she was, Jack held his hands up in defense. "*Whoa…* I'm sorry. I didn't mean to startle you. But no one else seems to be around?" Glancing around the room as he said this, he turned back to find he was talking to empty air.

She had disappeared.

A few seconds later, she popped up from behind the counter, holding her phone and checking it for damage.

Finally satisfied it still worked, she glared at him. "You shouldn't sneak up on people like that. You scared me half to death."

And you should pay more attention to your job instead of gabbing on your phone.

Of course, he didn't say this aloud, but you can bet it was what he was thinking.

After one more anxious inspection of her phone, the girl set it on the counter. She sent him a bright smile. "So, may I help you?"

His patience beginning to wane, his smile was less sincere. "Yes, my name is Jack Buchanan, and I'm a friend of Savanah Jackson. I'm here to take her to lunch. She's expecting me."

She shoved a pen and clipboard across the counter to him, giving a curt nod to the sign displayed on the counter.

Visitors must sign in
with receptionist before
entering the studio area.

With his usual flourish, Jack added his signature to the list and shoved the clipboard back to her.

After she checked it out, she looked up, a snort-like laugh escaping her. "Are you kidding me? You call this a signature? You need to come up with something better than this."

He sighed, and pulling out his wallet, he began leafing through it as he spoke. "Once again, my name is Jack Buchanan."

He handed her his driver's license. "And this should be the proof you need."

Again he waited.

She looked up from the license, her eyes narrowed.

Now he was getting irritated.

What is she doing? If she's looking for an exact match, the photo is from almost three years ago. So, you better hope you haven't changed much.

Unfortunately, this was exactly what she was doing. And by the huge frown on her face, she wasn't happy with what she saw.

"How is it you look like a movie star in this photo? Mine looks like I stuck my finger in a light socket, my hair one gigantic mass of frizz. And they refused to take another photo. Wait, I'll show you how awful it is."

She was pulling her purse out from under the counter when her phone rang. Dropping the purse to answer the call, she held her finger up as a sign he should wait before she turned away.

Jack had reached his limit. He grabbed his license off the counter and walked over the door to the studio. One hand on the doorknob, he sent her a wave. "Now if you don't mind, I'm going to let Savanah know I'm here. Have a great day."

When she didn't even glance up from her phone, he slipped into the studio, closing the door behind him.

He came to a dead stop, instantly on guard.

Whoa... this brings back some pretty scary memories.

The last time Jack had been in a dance studio was for one if his sister's dance recitals. As a shy and gawky soon-to-be-teenager, he'd laid low, his eyes glued to the games he was playing on his phone. It's safe to say no one had even noticed he was there.

The same didn't hold true this time. Aware of a sudden hush falling over the room, he looked up to find all eyes were on him. The news an attractive man was now on the premises had made the rounds in record time.

His gaze sweeping the room, he almost panicked when confronted with the room swarming with dancers. With their pulled back hairstyles and almost identical leotards, tights, and leg warmers, they all looked alike.

Reluctant to leave his place by the door—since one never knows when a fast exit might be needed—he scanned the room again, searching for Savanah.

As if she sensed this, Savanah turned, her gaze locking with his.

He sent her a tentative smile.

With a smile that lit up the room, banishing all other thoughts from his mind, she made her way over to him in a graceful, leaping dance.

Her fingers brushing lightly against his arm, she gazed up at him.

"Hi..."

He gently tucked an errant strand of her hair behind her ear. Then, unable to resist, he leaned in to drop a kiss to the corner of her mouth.

"Hi, beautiful..."

A shiver coursed through her at the deep huskiness of his voice. When a smile tweaked the corner of his mouth, a sign he was aware of this, she grew flustered. She reached up to smooth her hair in place, her reply breathless.

"I'm sure I look far from beautiful." She wrinkled up her nose. "And I'm sure I don't smell very good since we've been rehearsing all morning. But don't worry, I'll take a quick shower before we leave."

When he only continued to smile, thinking this was because of what she said, she closed her eyes, color filling her cheeks.

Really? was it necessary to give him all that information?

Now totally embarrassed, searching for something to say, she zeroed in on the rose in his hand. Her head tilted, she smiled up at him.

"Is that for me?"

Jack was on the verge of losing his mind. Her flushed cheeks, the damp curls framing her face, and the intoxicating blend of sweat, perfume, and soap came across as so incredibly sexy.

Never had he wanted a woman as much as he wanted her right now.

This wasn't like him.

At least until now, it wasn't.

Luckily, the background sounds of the studio were enough to remind him of where he was, common sense kicking in.

He handed her the rose, watching the color deepen in her cheeks, a shy smile touching her lips.

"Thank you, it's gorgeous."

He smiled. "You're welcome." The need to touch her now even stronger, he brushed his knuckles over the curve of her jaw. "And a mess? You couldn't look like a mess even if you tried."

And when she swayed towards him, her lips parted? He decided it would only be fair to meet her halfway.

So he leaned in to give her another kiss.

This time, she was ready.

She kissed him back.

Léon had spotted Jack the moment he walked into the studio. However, that he was there wasn't a surprise.

He'd found with the long hours spent at the studio, the dancers were a very close-knit group. This meant there were no secrets, gossip running rampant. So, if he wanted the latest news, he only needed to keep his eyes and ears open.

Based on what he'd heard, this Jack was a musician, the rumor he might even be famous. And since there would be no afternoon rehearsal, he planned to take Savanah to lunch.

Léon had laughed at the possibility Jack might be famous. No doubt the guy made this up to impress Savanah.

He could understand this. With his own relationships numbering in the dozens—an accomplishment he took great pride in—he'd found most women would do just about anything for a date with a celebrity.

He shrugged.

So, you embellish a little, no big deal.

He massaged his jaw, frowning when his fingers encountered the sandpaper-like stubble. Yet everything about the past few days had been rough, so this seemed fitting. The way he looked at it, that he even showed up, was a damn miracle.

His mood was at an all-time low. He'd even considered blowing off rehearsal when he woke this morning, feeling like he was at death's door. Then, as if nursing another hangover wasn't enough, he'd pulled something in his shoulder during rehearsal yesterday, and it still hurt like hell.

This is supposed to be the prime of your career. Instead, you're like an old man.

So, if he was miserable? He was going to make sure everyone else suffered right along with him.

His head pounding with each step, he walked out onto the dance floor. The sharp, angry tone of his voice commanded everyone's attention.

"Heads up, everyone. We still have time before we turn the studio over to Gayle. So, let's not waste it. Everyone on the floor for Act IV at the lake. You know your places."

A collective groan greeting this announcement, he clapped his hands. "Come on, no whining. Just do it."

He watched the dancers take their positions on the floor. All except for Savanah. She hadn't moved. Naturally, he saw this as a dare. His arms crossed, he nodded over at her. "I believe this also includes you, no? Unless you can't pull yourself away from this new man of yours…" He left his words hanging, a mocking smile on his lips.

All eyes had now shifted to Jack. However, he was unaware of this, the play of emotions on Savanah's face—resignation, frustration, and anger—his only concern. He leaned in to whisper in her ear. "Maybe it would be better if I left? It seems my presence brings out the worst in Léon."

There was a smile on his face as he said this when, in fact, he was furious. He had no intention of leaving Savanah alone with this man. Not after witnessing his behavior at Jake's Place, and now this?

Absolutely not.

Savanah whirled around. Her eyes pleading with him, she shook her head. "No, please stay. You make me feel safe."

He held out his hand. "Let me hold on to the rose. And promise you'll let me know if I need to step in."

"I promise."

The impulsive kiss she planted on his cheek came as a pleasant surprise.

He was smiling as he watched her join the other dancers on the floor.

CHAPTER 31

The same girl was behind the counter when Cora Jackson walked into the studio reception area, her head still throbbing from her run-in with the car door.

Once she gave the girl a lecture on the importance of making a good impression for visitors—beginning with limiting her personal phone calls—she took the muffins into Gayle's office. As she set them on her desk, she saw Gayle had left out the cast list of dancers for Swan Lake.

She glanced over her shoulder. The girl wasn't paying attention, already back on her phone as she searched for something in her purse.

So, she picked up the list, scanning the names.

She drew in a sharp breath.

Why was there a question mark behind Savanah's name?

She checked Léon's name. She found nothing. In fact, the only other dancer with a question mark was new to the company, someone she didn't know.

What isn't Savanah telling you?

Her headache intensifying with this revelation, she set the list back down on Gayle's desk. She would ask Savanah about this later. No doubt it was nothing important.

Now wishing she hadn't even seen the list, she left Gayle's office. Lost in thought, she didn't even notice the girl was back on her phone. Instead, sending her a vague smile that left the girl staring after her in confusion, she walked over to open the studio door.

Cora entered the studio, surprised the dancers were still on the floor. According to her watch, they should be done for the day. Once she spotted Savanah, she searched the room for the man from the parking lot.

No, she hadn't forgotten about him. If anything, she was even more determined to have a word with him.

She found him within seconds. Standing in the back of the room, casually leaning against the wall, his attention was on the dancers as they waited for their cue to start.

She watched a smile flash across his face, and after touching the rose to his lips, he sent Savanah a nod.

She glanced over at to Savanah. A radiant smile on her face, she responded by blowing him a kiss.

A groan escaped her.

This is worse than you thought.

Her lips pressed in a thin line, she walked across the room to stand a few feet from him.

Caught up in the energy emanating from the dance floor, Jack wasn't aware that Savanah's mother had come to stand next to him. He watched as the dancers assumed their positions, their chatter coming to a sudden halt when the lights dimmed in a warning they were about to begin.

For a moment, there was only silence. Then the opening notes of the music filled the room.

And they danced…

Even though Jack had seen Savanah dance before, the polished elegance of her moves in a professional setting left him awestruck. He watched, mesmerized, as she embraced the role of Odette. Surrounded by an entourage of dancers, they appeared to float across the floor in unison, their synchronized steps creating the illusion they were one.

Again, the little Jack knew of ballet was from what he remembered of his sister's recitals. And if he remembered correctly, he had not been impressed.

Now he thought differently.

"Beautiful... so incredibly amazing..."

Cora viewed his whispered comment as the ideal opportunity to speak her mind. Moving even closer, her gaze fixed on the dance floor, she spoke in a loud whisper. "Yes, you're right. She's exquisite, isn't she? And also extremely talented, as only the most dedicated of dancers can carry off the intricate steps of this ballet."

She paused, a warning tone creeping into her voice. "Mind you, this requires a work ethic unlike any other. So, outside distractions are discouraged. One poor decision, and her career could be over."

With a curt nod, and still avoiding eye contact, she walked away.

Jack watched as she found a place to sit, never once giving a backwards glance.

He shook his head.

Well, it seems you've just met Savanah's mother.

This was all forgotten when Léon burst onto the dance floor, his arrival bringing a toxic energy to the room. He took over the floor, going right into a sequence of jumps called cabrioles. This sent all the dancers, except for Savanah, scattering in every direction.

His arms outstretched, and again traveling across the floor in a dramatic combination of jumps and double tours, he swept Savanah into his arms. In sole possession of the floor, they danced as Siegfried and Odette in a celebration of their new love.

At least this was the plan...

Yet something wasn't right. Even to Jack's untrained eyes, it was obvious what was playing out on the dance floor was a disaster waiting to happen. A tension radiating from Léon, his moves were erratic, his steps heavy and out of sync with the music. This had Savanah stumbling as she tried to follow his lead.

Aware of the growing sense of anxiety among the dancers, Jack glanced over at Savanah's mother. Following the frantic display of leaps and lifts across the room, she rose from her seat and took a few steps closer to the dance floor.

His concern escalated.

If her mother is worried, something isn't right.

Unlike Savanah's mother, he took a step back, shoving his hands in his pockets. If only to keep from making a fool of himself and charging onto the floor like a lunatic.

Little did he know, he would later regret that decision.

Savanah was struggling. Léon's footwork was far from what they'd rehearsed, making it hard for her to maintain her balance. Anger flared inside her, her self-control on the brink of collapse.

Is this Léon's way of making you look like a fool in front of Jack?

Well, he wouldn't win this one. It was time for someone to put Léon in his place.

And it might as well be you.

This was when she realized he'd upped the tempo. He was no longer dancing with her as Odette, but as Odile, his moves now even more reckless. And when he lifted her high into the air, higher than he'd ever attempted, she knew she was in trouble.

It's the same nightmare, all over again. Only this time it's for real…

"Léon…" At her frantic plea, their eyes met. For a moment, he seemed to hesitate. Then, his expression going blank, he took her through another series of high and low lifts across the floor. Once again, he seemed to hesitate. But after a huge grunt, he raised her up even higher.

The *Dance Gods* protested, sending him stumbling as his feet hit the floor. As he tried to re-gain his balance, he lost his grip on Savanah, sending her flying through the air.

Time seemed to stand still, leaving her suspended in mid-air. Then, with a sickening thud, she hit the floor. Her eyes closed, she didn't move.

A deathly silence filled the room.

Then all pandemonium broke. Her anguished cry echoing through the room, Savanah's mother ran to her side, only to find Jack was already there.

Even though he knew he'd never catch her, Jack somehow reached Savanah almost the second she hit the floor. Crouched next to her, murmuring words of comfort, he willed her to open her eyes. It was only when she uttered a soft moan, her lashes fluttering, he let out a long ragged breath.

He reached for her hand. "Hey, sweetheart, open those beautiful eyes for me. Let me know you're going to be okay."

A searing pain shooting through her hand, she sucked in a sharp breath, jerking her hand away. "No, please don't… it hurts. And my head…" For a very brief moment, their eyes met. Then, after a shuddering breath, she closed her eyes.

"Stop. What do you think you're doing? Don't you dare touch her." This coming from behind him in a loud hiss, he turned. Trembling with rage and her fists clenched at her sides, Savanah's mother glared at him. "This is all your fault. You've come into my daughter's life, luring her with all these promises. It's no surprise something like this happened."

Luring her in with all these promises? What the hell is she talking about?

He shook his head. "Hey, now wait a minute. I've made no promises…" As soon as this left his mouth, he knew it was a poor choice of words.

Oh, geeez… you need to stay calm.

His hand held up in denial, he kept his voice even. "What I meant, I—"

She cut him off, almost spitting out the words. "You said exactly what you meant to say."

Her laugh was harsh. "Admit it, for you, this is just a fling, isn't it? Another beautiful woman to add to your list of conquests. And when it's over, you'll move on. After all, it's not your career that's on the line."

He came to his feet, his voice clipped with anger. "I would never, never, do anything to hurt Savanah. And there's nothing you can say or do that will keep me from being with her. The only person to do that would be Savanah."

Then, before he could reign in his anger, everything he was thinking came out uncensored. "You need to stop interfering in Savanah's life and let her make her own decisions. Instead, you're trying to turn her into the person you wanted to be, the dancer you never were. Proof of this is when Savanah told you how worried she was about Léon's behavior, and what did you do? You brushed it aside.

How could you do this to your own daughter, knowing her life could be in danger?"

He shook his head. "So, if there's any blame to be had, it should go to you."

"How dare you…" Her voice rose almost to a shriek. *"Go… I want you to leave now. Or I'll call the police. And if you come anywhere near Savanah again, I'll file a restraining order against you, claim you've been stalking her. I won't have you ruining the life she's worked so hard for."

Gayle had joined them.

After shaking her head over at Jack, she turned to Savanah's mother. "Cora, you need to calm down. Everything is going to be okay. We called for an ambulance, and they should be here shortly. Savanah will be in excellent hands."

Cora shook off Gayle's hand and pointed at Jack. "You need to tell this man to leave. None of this would have happened if he hadn't been here."

Gayle hesitated before she shook her head. "Cora, you know that isn't true. He isn't the problem, Léon is." She glanced around the room. "Where did he go? I need to find him."

"Mother, *please*…" This faint whisper coming from Savanah, Jack squatted beside her, his whisper brushing her cheek. "Sweetheart, it's okay. I think it would be best if I left. Though I promise I won't go far."

At the sound of loud voices, he glanced over his shoulder to see the EMS crew had arrived. He gave Savanah a reassuring smile. "The paramedics are here. So, you need to let them take care of you, okay? And I promise, the first chance I get—the absolute second—I'll be with you."

He smiled, brushing her hair back from her face again. "Then we'll get in that lunch date, okay?"

When she responded with a faint nod, he rose to his feet. Following a vague response from a paramedic about what hospital they planned to take Savanah, he turned to her mother.

"You've got your wish, I'm leaving. Only because I want Savanah to receive the urgent care she needs as soon as possible. But don't think you've seen the last of me. I love your daughter, and I plan on sticking around for a long, long time."

He turned and left the studio.

When Jack passed through the reception area, the same girl was behind the counter.

On her phone, she glanced over at him, wondering if he might be the one to ask why the paramedics were called. However, it only took one look at his angry expression for her to decide this might not be a good idea. Instead, she remained silent, holding her breath as she waited for him to slam the door.

But he didn't.

Thank goodness his departure was a lot quieter than Léon Pantonelli's only minutes ago. Muttering in some foreign language— maybe Italian, she wasn't sure—Léon had stormed past her, slamming the door so hard she had ducked behind the counter, fearing for her life. She'd swear he almost knocked the photos off the walls.

But it was the paramedics, ignoring her request to sign in as they rushed by, that had her questioning why she'd ever thought this would be a great place to work. Not when no one would tell her what was going on. Or listened to a word she said.

Therefore, when the paramedics passed by on their way out, she didn't even glance up from her phone. She figured, why bother?

After a long and dramatic sigh, she hit her friend's number.

She recently got a job at Target.

Maybe they were still hiring.

CHAPTER 32

Still reeling from what had happened in the studio, Jack just barely escaped being hit by a speeding motorcycle as he left the dance studio.

The driver had missed him by only inches, giving him a clear view of his face as he raced by.

It was Léon Pantonelli.

Jack's first impulse was to go after him. So he could ask him what the hell he'd been thinking when he tried such a stupid move on the dance floor. He had to have known it could only end in disaster.

Again, he wasn't familiar with ballet, so he wouldn't be able to tell you one move from the next. What he did know, that dance move Léon had attempted with Savanah?

It was a no-brainer.

This wasn't the Cirque du Soleil, this was ballet. A normal person wouldn't even think of trying something that stupid.

When have you ever thought Léon was normal?

And now that Léon and his motorcycle were long gone, he had more important things to do. Like finding out what hospital the paramedics planned to take Savanah.

So, right now, he did the only thing he could… he sat in his truck and waited for them to come out of the building.

Five minutes later, as he followed the ambulance to the hospital—their sirens on and lights flashing—he told himself he had no reason to worry.

Everything was going to be just fine.

Right?

Of course, it would be.

Yep, that's what he kept telling himself.

An hour later, Jack pulled into The Regency parking lot. After he parked in his usual space, he turned off the ignition.

Overcome with a sudden weariness, he remained in his truck, staring out at the lake. With the rain and heavy cloud cover of the past few days, the water had taken on a gray hue, the waves choppy and unapproachable.

The perfect match for your mood.

He leaned his head back against the headrest and closed his eyes. The image of Savanah hitting the floor kept playing over and over in his mind. And when she didn't move, lying lifeless on the floor? This alone sent his stomach churning, his heart pounding in response.

Never had he felt so helpless.

Or even more, so, *so* angry. .

He groaned, dragging his hand back through his hair.

Didn't you make things worse?

Yeah, what had he been thinking, confronting Savanah's mother? If he had remained silent, or at least civil, there was a possibility he'd be with Savanah right now.

But now, any updates on Savanah's condition would be hard to come by with all the hospital's privacy rules and regulations.

Stephanie… you can call Stephanie.

The medical profession was a tight-knit group, ready to help their own, so maybe she could help?

He pulled his phone out of his pocket and hit Stephanie's number. Unfortunately, his call went straight to her voice mail. So, he did the only thing he could.

He left a message.

He got out of his truck. His mind still on Savanah, he slowly made his way up the steps to the main entrance. There, he encountered a woman and a young girl about to enter the building. His manners kicking in, he sprinted over to hold open the door.

The girl gazed up at him, a huge smile on her face. Then she frowned. "Are you having a bad day?"

"Lexi..." Horrified, the woman groaned before turning to Jack. "I'm so sorry. My daughter has a habit of saying what's on her mind. No matter how often I remind her it might not be what people want to hear." She shrugged. "I'm afraid she's inherited this from me."

When he saw the stricken expression on the girl's face, Jack smiled. "As a matter of fact, I'm having a less than stellar day. However, that you cared to ask has already made me feel better."

This earned him another big smile.

The woman held out her hand. "Hi, I'm Raegan O'Connor. I just accepted the job as Darcey Bennett's assistant. I'm here to fill out all the necessary paperwork."

She put her hand on Lexi's shoulder. "And this is Lexi, my very inquisitive—or should I say nosey—eight-year-old daughter." Her head tilted, she peered more closely at him. "You're a member of Banded Together, aren't you? I heard you playing the piano when I was here earlier this morning. You play beautifully."

"Thank you. I'm Jack Buchanan. And yes, I'm with Banded Together." As he was one to shy away from compliments, he changed the subject. "I'm sure you'll like it here. You couldn't ask for a better person to work with than Darcey."

Lexi squinted up at him, a serious expression on her face. "Do you have a girlfriend?"

"Lexi..."

Rolling her eyes, Raegan grabbed Lexi's hand. "I believe on that note, we'll leave you to enjoy the rest of your day. It was nice meeting you."

"Same here." His hand lifted in a wave, Jack watched them disappear down the hall before he slipped into the Grand Ballroom.

He walked over to the piano. After he took a seat, he flexed his fingers. Exhaling a long breath, his hands came down on the keys, starting right in with the opening notes of his version of Clair De Lune.

A song that never failed to calm him, he gave it all that he had.

Remember, music was Jack's way of dealing with his emotions. By taking his frustration out on the keys, he was able to clear his mind, ready to deal with whatever came his way.

And right now, he needed all the help he could get.

On his way to the recording studio, Jason stopped by The Regency. Greeted by the sound of piano music as soon as he entered the building, and his curiosity piqued, he headed for the Grand Ballroom.

There he found Jack seated at the grand piano, his fingers dancing across the keys.

He listened as the notes shifted from an intricate classical piece to a more relaxed and peaceful rhythm. But then, the music abruptly changed course; the rapid string of notes injecting a burst of unleashed energy into the music.

Intrigued even more, he moved closer.

At one with the music, Jack was oblivious to his surroundings. It was only when Jason had come to stand next to him, he realized he was no longer alone. He dropped his hands to the keys, bringing about a jarring mix of notes. After the last note faded into silence, he turned to acknowledge Jason.

"Hey…"

"Hey to you, too." Casually leaning against the piano, Jason gestured to the piano. "What brought this on? You're pounding the keys like a man possessed. If this is a new piece you're working on, I'm not impressed. It sounds like a bunch of songs all rolled into one."

Jack dragged his hand through his hair. "I was just trying to figure things out, you know, let the music lead the way."

Jason gave a half snort, half laugh. "Well, it's taking you down the wrong path, man."

He studied Jack again, longer this time. "What's really going on?" Then he raised his hand. "Wait… let me guess. It involves Savanah." He grinned. "When there's trouble, it's common knowledge among men that a woman is involved. So, spill…"

Jack gave him a brief summary of what took place at the dance studio.

Massaging his temples, Jason's look was one of disbelief. "Okay, let me see if I've got this right. A woman you're madly in love with—and don't try to deny this, because you know it's true—is in the hospital because she was injured by her maniac dance partner. A man who then left the scene to do who knows what. Yet you're here? Playing the piano?"

He scratched his head. "I'm sorry, but I don't understand. Shouldn't you be with Savanah? And more importantly, why haven't you already figured this out for yourself?"

Jack groaned, pushing away from the piano and coming to his feet. "Because I acted like an idiot, tearing into her mother and basically putting all the blame on her. So, of course, she retaliated, threatening to call the police if I didn't leave. She accused me of every crime in the book... stalking, harassment, lying, you name it. The woman was a screaming lunatic."

He shook his head. "And this all took place while Savanah was in pain and on the floor. Not one of my prouder moments."

He began pacing back and forth. "But, in my defense, I had no choice but to leave." He turned to Jason, dragging his hand through his hair. "That's the last thing I wanted to do."

His pacing coming to a stop, he uttered a sharp laugh. "Then I almost got run over by Léon on his motorcycle as I came out of the studio."

He shook his head at the shock on Jason's face. "I like to think this was because he was in a hurry, not intentional. I even considered going after him, but what good would that have done?"

Jason exhaled a huge breath. "Thank God you didn't. That would've only made things worse." He took a moment to consider this before he glanced over at Jack. "What about Savanah? Where is she? Is she going to be okay?"

"I honestly don't know. Since I followed the ambulance, I know they took her to University Hospital. After that, I'm clueless. When I called for an update, I was told that's only available to the immediate family. They wouldn't even confirm if she was a patient."

He was pacing again. "So, I called Stephanie, hoping she could find out what's going on. Only the call went to her voice mail. So I left a message." He glanced over at Jason and shrugged. "So, that's where I am right now."

Jason nodded. "I think she and Evan have something going on tonight, so she traded for the afternoon shift. Since she has that rule about no calls or texts when she's covering for someone new, I guess you can only wait."

He glanced down at his watch. "It's almost four, so unless she gets roped into staying longer, and with Stephanie this is always a possibility, you should hear from her soon."

"Let's hope you're right." After staring into space, Jack abruptly turned to him, pulling out his keys. "Hey, I you don't mind, I'm going to take off. I have some files I want to deliver. There are a few other things I have to do, too."

He shrugged. "Not knowing is driving me crazy. So, I need to keep busy, hope for the best, I guess."

Jason put his hand on his shoulder, giving it a reassuring squeeze. "It will all work out. You'll see." With Jack already halfway across the room, he had to yell out his next words. "If I hear from Steff, I'll make sure she calls you."

Now alone, hands shoved in his jeans pockets, he gazed around the room where so many memories had been made over the years, Darcey and his wedding reception included. And in less than a week, Stephanie and Evan would be celebrating their wedding, too.

He grinned. He'd be willing to bet another wedding would soon follow.

He left the ballroom. A quick stop in to see Darcey and then he would be off to the studio.

Life was good.

When Jason walked into Darcey's office, a young girl looked up from where she was sitting at the small table in the corner. A wary look appearing on her face when she saw him, she set the colored pencil she was using on the table.

Almost as uncertain about this encounter as she was, Jason's reaction was just as cautious. He cleared his throat. "Hey, there… may I ask who you are?

Before she could answer, he grinned, snapping his fingers. "I bet you're Darcey's new assistant, aren't you?"

"Me?" Her eyes going wide, she giggled. "I can't work here. I still need to finish school." She shrugged, twirling a strand of hair around her finger. "I'm only in second grade, and I'm only eight. My birthday was weeks ago."

Jason massaged his chin. "*Hmm...* you seem older. I thought you might be a new employee. So, if you're not here to work, what brings you here?"

"My momma got a new job working for Darcey. She had to pick me up from school since we only had a half day. Do you know Darcey?"

"Yes, I do. In fact, I'm her husband, Jason. And your name is?"

"Lexi."

"*Ah...* Lexi, that's a pretty name. It's perfect for you."

"Thank you." And as always happened when Jason complimented a member of the opposite sex, she blushed, twirling her hair around her finger even faster.

A silence fell between them while Lexi studied him with the frank curiosity of a child.

After jamming his hands in his pockets, Jason gazed around the room, searching for something to say. Where the hell was Darcey?

You're not the best with kids. At least not one on one.

He cleared his throat again. "So, Lexi... what are you working on? It looks interesting."

She sent a furtive glance over at the door before she held her finger up to her lips. "*Shhh...* I'm making a birthday card for my momma. It's tomorrow."

She frowned. "She said she doesn't want anyone to know because she isn't in the birthday mood. No cake, no balloons, no nothing. I don't get it. How can you have a birthday without balloons or a cake?"

After a long and over-exaggerated sigh, she shrugged and picked up her pencil. "So, I guess this card will have to do."

She looked so sad, the words popped right out of Jason's mouth. "I'll tell you what, I'll talk to Darcey and we'll see if we can get some balloons. And a cupcake from the kitchen. No one should have a birthday without balloons or some kind of cake."

Her eyes lit up with excitement. "You will?" Then, just as quickly, she looked worried. "But I don't want her to be mad at me."

He drew his finger over his lips. "Mums the word, your name will never come up. This will be all on me and Darcey, okay?"

The smile back on her face even bigger, she nodded.

A voice came from behind them. "Well, I see you two have met."

Jason and Lexi both whirled around to face Darcey. They both looked so guilty, she laughed. "What are you two up to?"

The worried expression back on Lexi's face, Jason shrugged. "Oh, nothing much. We were talking about normal things. You know, school, friends, homework, blah, blah, blah."

Darcey nodded." She turned to Lexi. "Your mom and I should be finished in about twenty minutes. I only came back here to get something. Is there anything you need?"

Lexi shook her head.

"Okay. And remember, we're only two doors down the hall if you have any questions."

After another nod from Lexi, Darcey turned to Jason. "And how may I help you?

Aware that Lexi was watching them, he had to be satisfied with giving Darcey a quick kiss to her cheek. "Just keep being you, gorgeous. I had to pick up something here on the way to the studio and I ran into Jack, pounding away at the piano. He told me that Savanah was taken to the hospital after getting injured during rehearsal.

Her hand going to her mouth, Darcey shook her head. "Oh no, is she going to be okay?"

"He's pretty confident she will be, but isn't sure. That's why he was taking it out on the piano." He looked down at his watch. "But I gotta go. I'll let you know if I hear anything. And we need to talk about balloons and cupcakes. Don't let me forget."

"What? Balloons and cupcakes? I'm confused."

"I'll fill you in later." Then he moved even closer, his voice dropping to a whisper. "I also wanted to tell you how much I love you."

After another kiss to her cheek, he smiled over at Lexi. "I enjoyed meeting you, Lexi. And I won't forget what we talked about."

With a wink, he walked out of the room.

Puzzled, Darcey watched him leave.

Balloons and cupcakes?

She smiled, shaking her head. With Jason, it could be anything.

Her elbows on the table and chin resting in her hands, Lexi watched Darcey search through the folders on her desk. She grinned. "I like him. He's nice."

Darcey turned to smile at her. "I know, he is nice, isn't he?"

After she found the folder she was searching for, she paused at the door to smile once again at Lexi. "See you in a little bit."

As she walked down the hall, she thought about what Jason had told her about Savanah.

She hoped it wasn't serious.

CHAPTER 33

*A*fter Jack delivered the files, relieved to find his client was out to lunch and he wouldn't have to be sociable, he headed for home.

Once there, he tried calling Savanah again. If he had to guess, he'd say this was his fifth or sixth try.

However, it didn't matter, since there was still no answer.

He'd left two messages, both the same.

Call me. We need to talk.

Yes, this was the extent of the message. When he sent it, in his frustrated state, it seemed like enough. Now he wondered if this came across as too demanding.

Or worse yet, threatening.

Against his better judgement, he tried one more time. When the call again went to her voice mail, he hit end and tossed the phone on the counter. He groaned, massaging the back of his neck.

Almost five hours had passed since he'd stormed out of the dance studio. Yet it felt more like days, or even weeks.

And you still know nothing…

There was so much going on inside of him, he couldn't even think straight.

He was angry. He was worried. And, that he hadn't been strong enough to take a stand against Savanah's mother, instead letting his emotions take over? Never had he felt like such a loser.

To be fair, you had no choice but to leave. Who knows what else you might have said had you stayed?

Either way, it was a no-win situation.

He was about to pour out yet another cup of coffee when his phone rang. He grabbed it from the counter, relieved to see it was from Stephanie.

"Stephanie… hello." This came out almost in a shout.

There was a slight pause before she responded. "Jack, where are you? Have you talked to Savanah? I thought for sure you'd be here at the hospital."

Pacing back and forth, he raked his hand through his hair. "Believe me, I've been trying to reach Savanah. But every call had gone straight to her voicemail. So, I could only leave a message. I left a message for you, too."

Then her words registered.

Wait a minute… Savanah is still in the hospital?

He didn't understand. "You talked to Savanah? And why is she still in the hospital?"

"No, I missed her call." She gave a long sigh before she continued. "Today has been crazy. We got two new patients and there was a mix-up with rooms. Then everything else started going wrong, and I didn't have time to check my messages. It wasn't until my shift was over I saw Savanah left a voice mail. But it turned out it was her mother who left the message. Savanah had asked her to let me know she had a fractured wrist and a possible concussion. This was a due to—and these are her mother's words, not mine—an 'unfortunate incident' at the dance studio. So, I rushed over here, not knowing what to expect."

Frustration came through in her voice. "I thought you'd be here. Instead, it was her mother who gave me the news Savanah just came out of surgery. The operation on her wrist a success, but the plan is to keep her overnight because of a possible concussion. This is the normal protocol when there's trauma involving the head."

Briefly closing his eyes, Jack groaned *"Damn...* I didn't know. Honest, I had no idea. After the altercation with her mother, I thought she wasn't answering her phone because she didn't want to talk to me. Had I known her injuries were serious, I would've been there in a heartbeat. Even if it meant another possible run-in with her mother."

Stephanie sighed. "Well, her mother left about five minutes ago. The doctor convinced her to go home so Savanah can rest. So, get here as soon as you can. This way, when the anesthesia wears off, you'll be the first person she sees."

She glanced down at her watch. "I'll wait, if only to make sure there won't be any trouble. From what I was told, what Savanah's mother told the staff about you was less than complimentary."

When this was greeted with silence, she glanced down at her phone. Jack had already ended the call.

She found a seat in the waiting room and checked her phone for the time. Since it was rush hour, she'd give him about twenty-five minutes to get to the hospital.

Stephanie's calculations were almost spot on. It was twenty-three minutes later when she glanced up from her phone to see Jack striding in her direction.

"Stephanie..." He came to a stop in front of her, and dragging his hand through his hair, he managed to look relieved and worried at the same time.

Taken aback by his appearance, her initial reaction was to stare. The Jack she knew was always meticulous and put-together. Casual or formal, his finished look was always perfect.

But the Jack standing in front of her now?

He was a mess.

His shirt tail was only half tucked in, his sweater inside out. Her guess was the second he'd ended their call, after a quick finger comb through his hair and grabbing his keys, he was in his truck and on the road.

That, along with the anxious state he'd worked himself into, had her re-thinking the lecture she'd planned. This would be how he needed to be a man and stand up to Savanah's mother. Let her know that no matter what she thought of him, he was here to stay.

She patted the chair next to her. "Here, sit down and take a deep breath. Then you can tell me what happened."

He sank down in the chair and after exhaling a huge breath, he filled her in on what happened at the studio leading to Savanah's accident.

"So now my only hope is you." He shrugged. "Because right now, I have no idea what to do next. Talk about feeling helpless…" His voice fading off, he shook his head.

Stephanie was horrified. *"Oh, my gosh…* poor Savanah. But she's going to be okay. Her injury was to her wrist and not her ankle, so as long as she follows the recommended therapy and doesn't rush things, she should be back to dancing in no time. At least that's what Savanah's mother told me."

Her brow furrowed. "The woman needs to let Savanah live her own life. She's too controlling. Savanah told me she was also a dancer when she was young. Then, for some unknown reason, she quit. So, maybe she's trying to recapture what she lost through Savanah? Instead, she's lost sight of what Savanah wants."

"Unfortunately, I told her the same thing in a more threatening way, and right to her face." His mouth twisted in a wry smile. "As you can imagine, she didn't appreciate my input."

Stephanie put her hand on his arm. "Oh, Jack… you didn't…"

He nodded. "I'm afraid I did. And it wasn't pretty."

She searched his face. "What did you say?"

He leaned back in his chair, giving a frustrated sigh. "Well, for starters, I told her if there was any blame to be had for what happened, it should go to her. I then accused her of being a terrible mother, putting her daughter's life in danger when she ignored her concerns about Léon."

He sent her a guilty look. "I'm afraid I then said a lot more, most of which I'd rather not repeat. Let's just say her threat of legal action if I ever came near Savannah again was what made me leave."

"Well, you're here now." She shrugged. "And the worst thing for Savanah would be to see you looking like it's the end of the world. Believe me, after everything that happened, she needs all the positive reinforcement she can get. It doesn't help you haven't talked to each other since you left the studio."

He slowly nodded. "Yeah, I'm aware of that. Believe me, I tried." His voice trailed off as he watched her pull a phone out her pocket, holding it out to him. "That reminds me, her mother gave me this. No doubt the reason you haven't heard from Savanah."

It was Savanah's phone. He recognized the bright flowered cover. As he took the phone from her, his laugh bordered on a groan. "Why am I not surprised? And how did you persuade her to give this to you?"

She laughed. *"Ha...* it was more like I took it from her? She told me she's had it since Savanah's accident. She only volunteered this information after I noticed it sticking out of the side pocket on her purse and asked if it was Savanah's. At first she got all huffy, claiming Savanah didn't need to be talking on her phone. Especially to certain people. Then, after almost throwing the phone at me, she stomped off."

She sent Jack a sidelong glance. "I'm assuming she was referring to you with that 'certain people' remark."

He turned the phone around in his hands, examining it as though it held the answer to his problem. Then he shrugged, slipping it in his pocket. "Maybe her mother is right, I *am* responsible for what happened. Though a distraction is the last thing I'd ever want to be."

He closed his eyes. *"God, no..."*

Stephanie patted his arm. *"Oh, Jack,* I don't think..."

He looked over at her. "Have you seen Savanah dance?"

She shook her head. "No, I haven't." Then she smiled. "Evan and I have tickets for the ballet's production of Swan Lake. I can't wait."

He nodded. "Even though Savanah will deny this, she's an amazing dancer. It's almost magical how she becomes one with the music, her moves so effortless and graceful. She makes it look easy."

He smiled. "It was only after I watched her dance with Léon, I realized how difficult it must be to dance with a partner. Each move has to be perfect, down to every single little detail... the jumps, the lifts and so on. Timing means everything, every second counts."

He shrugged. "Where music is more forgiving. Sure, a mistake can stall the tempo of a song. However, this doesn't lead to a disaster. Nothing comparable to what Savanah experienced."

He frowned. "Speaking of Léon, after witnessing what happened on the dance floor with Savanah, I'm not sure it was an accident. I want to believe, as a professional, Léon would never harm Savanah on purpose. Yet I can't shake the feeling he did. And after the way he behaved at the restaurant, I wouldn't put anything past him."

Stephanie nodded. "I'm also struggling with that. I haven't met him, but from what Savanah has told me, he doesn't seem like a nice person. She brushes it off, insisting he's just another temperamental dancer, and she isn't worried."

His head tilted, his expression was puzzled. "Is this normal in the dance world? It doesn't seem to fit the whole picture."

Stephanie shrugged. "I guess when you're good—and according to Savanah, he's known to be one of the best—you can get away with almost anything. If there's one positive note, he's never with the same company for long. He jumps from job to job, with always some drama or scandal involved. So, maybe this will have him on the move again."

She glanced over at Jack. "I wonder what he's running from? Or what he's hiding?"

He frowned. "I don't know, and I don't care. I only want him to stay away from Savanah."

Caught up in their thoughts, it was a few moments before Jack spoke. "So, you said I can see her? They won't try to stop me? No restraining orders from the boss?"

He tried to make light of this reference to Savanah's mother, but his frustration came through in his voice.

She gave his hand a reassuring pat. "From what I've been told, Savanah's mother started ordering everyone around the moment she walked through the doors. This didn't leave the best impression with the staff. And lucky for you, I graduated with a nurse on duty tonight, so I was able to put in a good word for you."

She smiled. "In fact, right before you arrived, she texted me that Savanah had been moved to a room."

She glanced at her watch. "Evan and I are meeting with the caterer to finalize the menu. I should have left five minutes ago, but I'll walk you to Savanah's room."

She grinned. ""If she could choose anyone to see when she wakes, I'm certain you'd be her first choice—you'd win hands down."

"I hope you're right." Coming to his feet, and after taking her hand to pull her up out of her chair, he gave her a hug. "It looks like I owe you once again. And don't worry, I promise not to cause any trouble while I'm here."

Stephanie laughed. "Let's hope not."

He glanced over at her as they walked down the hall. "Not too much longer, huh? Is everything falling into place?"

"Yes, it's finally beginning to feel real." Her smile brilliant, she chattered on as they took the elevator up to the fourth floor. After escorting him down the hall, she pointed to a room, the door slightly ajar. "This is it."

She pressed a kiss to his cheek. "Let her know you're here for her. That you'll love and support her no matter what, okay? Because even though the outlook is good, an injury of any kind has to be a dancer's worst nightmare."

She walked away, only to turn to him. "And if her mother shows up? What is it they say? Treat her with kindness. Maybe this is all she needs?" She shrugged. "You'll never know unless you try."

Jack didn't buy this. Treat her with kindness?

Ha, it will take a lot more than kindness to get the woman to like you.

But the smile he sent Stephanie was upbeat. "Don't worry, I've got this."

She blew him a kiss and was gone.

CHAPTER 34

With the shades drawn, Savanah's room was a serene sanctuary amid the hospital's everyday bustling activity.

Respectful of the silence, Jack carefully closed the door before making his way over to the bed. Her left arm wrapped in a bulky gauze dressing and propped up on pillows, Savanah was sound asleep.

Unable to resist the urge to touch her, he trailed his fingers along the curve of her cheek in a soft caress.

She stirred, a faint smile flickering across her lips

Encouraged by this, he pulled the chair closer to the bed. After he leaned his arms on the side rail, his gaze traveled over her face, drinking it all in.

Even after the trauma of surgery, she was still beautiful. Her cheeks flushed, her hair framed her face in wispy tendrils.

But the dark circles under her eyes were new.

Dropping his forehead to his arms, his groan was muffled against the sleeve of his sweater.

Her mother is right … you're responsible for this. You've caused nothing but trouble since you've come into her life.

Then, sitting back in his chair, he drummed his fingers on the armrests.

No…

Whatever her mother believed, he didn't agree. How could wanting to be with her be wrong? He loved her. He'd do anything for her. And he was pretty sure she felt the same about him, based on the little things she did when they were together.

Beginning with the way she always leaned into his touch, as though she wanted to be closer. Or the many times he'd turn to find her watching him, a wistful smile on her face. Only to become flustered, avoiding his gaze when she realized he'd caught her in the act.

And don't forget the color that flooded her cheeks when he gave her a compliment. She had to know this only made him want to shower her with even more flattery. To the point, he knew he should stop.

Again, he could be reading too much into this. But he didn't think so.

He stood, and jamming his hands in his pockets, he strolled over to the window. A smile tugging at the corner of his mouth, he watched as Stephanie emerged from the building. As if she sensed he was there, she glanced up and waved before she took off in a run to her car.

He watched her drive away, filled with an overwhelming sense of gratitude for the friendship they shared. He honestly didn't know what he would've done without her these past few weeks.

Startled by the urgent beeps from the heart monitor next to the bed, he turned around. Her face scrunched up in discomfort, Savanah was pulling at the blankets.

True to form, when it came to Savanah, Jack over-reacted, interpreting this as a desperate plea for help. He lunged across the room and, in his haste, banged his shin against the corner of the bed frame.

Not good…

Hopping on one foot and muttering a few choice words as he massaged his shin to ease the pain, he glanced over at Savanah. At least his shenanigans hadn't disturbed her slumber.

He moved closer, and brushing her hair back from her face, his voice dropping to a whisper. "Hey, sweetheart … it's all good. You're only dreaming." After adjusting the blanket and pulling it up to cover her, he went to tuck her hand without the cast under the blanket.

He frowned. Her hand was ice cold.

frowned. "*Oh, Vanababe…* you're freezing. Let's see if I can warm you up a little." He pulled the chair even closer to the bed, massaging her hand until he felt the warmth return to her fingers.

After he carefully tucked her hand back under the blanket, he sank back into the chair.

For a few minutes, he sat there, his body motionless, his gaze fixed on nothing. The weight of everything that happened had left him totally depleted, both mentally and physically. Add in the enormous amount of coffee he had consumed since he'd left the dance studio?

Simply put, he was wired for disaster.

"Jack?"

His eyes flew open at this faint whisper to see Savanah's eyes were open, searching.

A huskiness in his voice, he smoothed her hair back from her face. "Hey, beautiful… how are you doing?"

"You came…" A faint smile playing across her lips, her lashes fluttered in her struggle to regain consciousness

He knew little about the aftermath of surgery, his only hospital experience the summer before his junior year of high school, when he broke his arm playing baseball. After a quick x-ray to confirm the break, they'd slapped on a cast and sent him home.

With youth on his side, he'd heal fast, they claimed.

His mother had been frantic, fearing this would end his dream of becoming a concert pianist. But after a dreadful summer spent wearing a cast, and forbidden anywhere near the music room, he was right back doing what he loved… playing the piano. And, for some unknown reason, he played even better than before.

Unfortunately, it turned out life had another plan for him, shattering his dreams in an instant. So, in a way, he could emphasize with what Savanah was going through, wondering how this injury might affect her career.

His heart ached for her.

She stirred, giving a faint moan. Still holding her hand, he pressed another kiss to her fingers.

Again, her eyelashes fluttered open. She gazed intently at his face, a hint of recognition in her eyes. "I thought…" She struggled for words. "I didn't know…"

Her eyes closing again, he responded as if she was still listening.

"Yeah, I finally showed up. You didn't answer any of my calls, so I wasn't sure what to do. Then I talked to Stephanie, and here I am."

Her lashes flew open at this. She didn't understand. What did he mean? What calls? Her lips parted as if she wanted to say something, but exhausted by even this slight effort, and unable to put her thoughts into words, she closed her eyes again.

For some reason, and she wasn't sure why, she felt weighed down, everything moving in slow motion. Even keeping her eyes open required too much work.

Thinking she was drifting off again, Jack pressed a kiss in her palm, his lips brushing over her wrist.

This tickled.

She giggled, her lashes flying open.

He chuckled. "You're feeling pretty good, huh? This is from the medication they have you on."

She tugged her hand from his, reaching over to stroke his cheek before she dropped her hand back on the bed. "You're so cute." She murmured this in a soft, whispery sigh.

He couldn't remember the last time someone told him he was cute. But hey, coming from her, he'd be more than happy to be cute. He reached over to once again brush her hair back from her face, not even attempting to hide his smile. "So… you think I'm cute, huh?"

She nodded. "And *sooo* perfect…" After another giggle, her lashes drifted shut again.

Perfect?

Well, this was promising, as up until now, his imagination had him thinking the worst. This would be that she might never want to see him again. And though he knew the chance she'd remember this, or any of their conversation, was pretty slim, he needed this moment.

More than anything.

And, come on… what man wouldn't be thrilled to have a beautiful woman tell him, not only was he cute, he was also perfect?

Yeah, this is good… really good.

He claimed her hand again, pressing another kiss to her fingers. "*Ah*… thank you, sweetheart. And you are the most beautiful woman I've ever known. You are amazing, Savanah Jackson. I can't believe how happy you've made me since you've come into my life."

She opened her eyes. Her gaze settling on his mouth, she reached over to trace his lips with her fingertip. "Kiss me... please?"

He didn't even hesitate. His hand cradling her face, his lips brushed against hers in a whisper of a touch.

Now he honestly intended this would be it. His plan was to go easy, give her only a hint of a kiss, nice and gentle. Yes, a mere brush of lips was what he had in mind. After all, he didn't want to take advantage of her vulnerable state.

But the moment his mouth touched hers, warm and so inviting, he was consumed. And when her lips parted, opening to him? He took this as an invitation for more.

That plan he had?

It didn't have a chance.

It didn't help when he ended the kiss, a soft moan rising from deep in her throat, she lifted her head, her mouth searching for his. "Again, please?"

So, what other option did he have, other than leaning in to kiss her again? And this time, he kept the kiss going longer. A sweet, lingering kiss that ended in a long sigh from both of them.

He lifted his head, smoothing back the hair back from her face as he spoke. "*Ah, Vanababe...* I swear you've put some kind of spell on me. If I could, I'd be happy to stay here with you forever, kissing you for as long as you'd let me. But right now, you need to get some rest."

Her gaze holding his, she trailed her fingertips down the side of his face. "I love you."

He stilled, his heart crashing in his chest. These were the same three little words that had been swirling around in his mind, waiting to be set free from the first moment he saw her. How many times he'd almost blurted them out, only to hold back, afraid this might be moving too fast?

This was only because he had never been so sure of anything in his life.

It's bad enough you ask her to marry you every chance you get.

His emotions getting the best of him, he had to clear his throat. Even then, his voice was still gruff. "I love you, too. More than all the stars in the sky."

A faint smile touching her lips, her lashes drifted shut. "That's a lot of stars." Her eyes opening again, another giggle escaped her. "I really do love you."

"I really do love you, too. But right now, even though it's the last thing I want to do, I think I should leave. You need to get some rest so we can get you home."

"Home… that sounds nice ." Anxiety spreading across her face, she tightened her grip on his hand. "Don't leave. Stay with me, please?"

He pressed a kiss to her hand. "Only if you promise to close your eyes and go to sleep."

"Okay, you're the boss." And like a child, she squeezed her eyes shut and was silent.

His arms resting on the bed rail, he watched as her facial features relaxed, surrendering to the healing sleep she needed.

He dropped his chin to his arm, his eyes closed. His mind was racing, his heart beating a mile a minute.

She loves you…

Yeah, don't worry, he got it. The medication she was on had her feeling a little drunk. This meant her declaration of love had a little help. Who hasn't experienced someone sharing their entire life story, or their most intimate secrets, after a few drinks?

But, he'd take it. Gladly, he would. He planned to hold on to every single one of these moments, no matter how many or how long it took to win her love.

Her even breathing a sign she was asleep, he eased his hand away. Only to have her become aggravated, searching for his hand. So he pulled the chair close to the bed and, linking their fingers together, settled in for what could be a longer stay than he'd intended.

Finding solace in the silence, and comforted by the warmth of her hand in his, he closed his eyes. He only knew there was no where else he'd rather be.

An hour, maybe two at the most. Then you'll leave.

Who would've thought the sound of a heart monitor could be so soothing?

He didn't have a chance.

The events of the day catching up with him, he dozed off.

CHAPTER 35

"Mr. Buchanan… hey, come on, hon. Can you wake up for me?"

Hon?

Still not awake, and not sure who he was dealing with, Jack opened one eye just a crack.

A rather large woman was standing beside him. Her gray brown streaked hair pulled up in a messy bun and her arms crossed over her generous bosom, she peered down at him through a pair of large red-framed glasses.

He groaned.

He wasn't in the mood to carry on a conversation, let alone with someone he didn't know.

Certainly not with this woman who looked like she meant business. He'd seen his share of bouncers while on tour with the band, and she'd be an excellent fit for the job.

So, a slow shake of his head was his only reply.

Not the least bit discouraged, she gave a grunt. "Good… you're waking up."

Now checking the monitor, she sent him a glance over her shoulder. "You poor thing, how long have you been here? It always amazes me when someone falls asleep in one of these chairs. I can't tell you how many times I've told the big guys in charge they need to replace them with a more comfortable model."

She shrugged, a resigned look on her face. "But, do they listen to me? Nope, of course not. What do I know?"

Jack opened his mouth to tell her it didn't matter, he was perfectly fine. However, she was on a roll, not to be interrupted.

As she checked the status of Savanah's IV, she continued in an exaggerated whisper. "This isn't my usual shift. I came in three hours early to fill in for one of the nurses who didn't want to miss her daughter's dance recital."

Satisfied everything seemed in order, she nodded over at the empty bed occupying the other half of the room. "Since no one is assigned to this room, you could've slept there. I'm surprised no one told you that, since the staff has been buzzing ever since you arrived. They think it's so romantic, you being famous and all."

You? Famous?

He cleared his throat. "*Umm*… I don't know about that."

"Yep, they're all looking for that fairy tale ending. At their young age, I guess that's to be expected." She shook her head. "A girl can dream, right?"

After he checked her I.D. tag to see her name was Diane, he sent her a smile. "Diane, as tired as I was, I'm pretty sure I could've slept anywhere."

"*Hmph*… maybe." After she placed her hand on Savanah's forehead, finding it cool to the touch, she sent him a smile. "She's coming along just fine."

Then she shook her head. "It's you I'm worried about. You're looking a little ragged. When did you last eat?"

His gaze going to Savanah, he shrugged. "A cup of coffee and I'll be good to go."

Her sharp laugh, more like a bark, was a sign she didn't agree. "Honey, something tells me you've already had way too much coffee."

He smiled. "Don't worry, I'll be fine."

She crossed her arms, studying him. Then she sighed. "I hope when Savanah wakes up, she realizes how lucky she is to have you. And since it looks like you have no plans of leaving—which is okay, you're welcome to stay as long as you want—let me see if I can get something nutritious sent up from the kitchen."

He gave her one of his most winning smiles. "Thanks, Diane. That would be great."

"*Oh, lordy…* this man has no clue how charming he is. No wonder the nurses are all riled up." Mumbling this on her way out the door, she pointed her finger at him. "Don't you dare wake her."

It was only after he nodded, she left.

Jack came to his feet, his cramped muscles protesting the move. Diane had called it right with the chairs, they were only meant for a brief visit. After a long stretch, he dropped a gentle kiss to Savanah's forehead, his whisper brushing her cheek, "I'm still here, like I promised I would be. So, sleep on beautiful."

He walked over to the window, watching the activity in the parking lot. When in reality, the conversation he'd shared with Savanah was all he could think about.

She loves you…

But what if she doesn't remember?

"Jack?"

He turned.

Her eyes open, Savanah was watching him.

Smiling, he made his way over to her. "*Hey…*"

A smile touched her lips. "You really are here. It wasn't a dream."

So, here's your proof… it was real for the both of you.

This giving him every reason to smile, he leaned in to press a kiss to her mouth. "I promised I wouldn't leave, didn't I?"

Then he couldn't help it… he kissed her again. A little longer this time.

Jack woke to the buzz of a loud conversation from the hallway outside Savanah's room. For a moment, disoriented, he didn't move, unsure of where he was.

The sound muted on the wall-mounted TV, he watched Martha Stewart and her co-host wrestling a massive turkey into a roasting pan before shoveling it into the oven. A commercial for insurance flashing across the screen, he grabbed the remote and shut off the TV. Tossing the blanket aside, he sat on the edge of the bed and checked his phone.

5:04 a.m.

Damn... who would've thought a hospital bed could be this comfortable?

Raking his hands back through his hair, he glanced over at Savanah. She was still out, her breathing deep and steady.

Earlier, he'd flagged down the night nurse, uneasy about all that sleep.

She'd shrugged it off. "For some reason, people think too much sleep is bad for a concussion, but that's a myth. Savanah needs sleep—especially after her surgery and the trauma of her injury." Patting his arm, she'd added. "So, let her rest so she can heal."

Relieved, he'd settled in. After he polished off the dinner Diane had sent up, he decided to take advantage of the empty bed, maybe watch a little late-night TV.

But, now? Massaging the back of his neck, he frowned.

What about Savanah's mother?

She struck him as a morning person, that is if she even slept. The thought of her barging into the room and finding him with Savanah, his gut clenched

He shrugged on his jacket, and rummaging through the pockets for his keys, pulled out Savanah's phone instead. After he set it on the bedside table, he leaned down to press a kiss to her forehead. "Your phone is right here," he whispered. "Call me when you can, love."

Halfway to the door, he doubled back, grabbed a pen and notepad from the table, and wrote a note to Savanah. About to leave it by her phone, he hesitated before slipping it into his pocket instead.

After one last glance, he left.

CHAPTER 36

A container of her homemade banana muffins in her hands, Cora Jackson stepped off the elevator on the hospital's fourth floor.

A man came around the corner. His head down, and his hands jammed in his pockets, he seemed to be in a hurry.

As he drew closer, she drew in a sharp breath.

It was Jack. Her immediate instinct to hide, she ducked into the nearest room.

She scooted behind the door, where she tried to calm down. She didn't understand… why was he here? Hadn't she made it clear to the staff that Savanah wasn't to have visitors? With him at the top of the list?

Since it looked like he was leaving, she decided she'd wait until she heard the elevator doors close before she continued to Savanah's room.

On his way to the elevator, Jack stopped off at the nurses' station. Seated behind the counter, the nurse on duty smiled up at him. "I didn't know you were still here. What can I do for you?"

He handed her the note he'd written to Savanah. "I wonder if it is possible for you to deliver this note to Savanah when she wakes up. It's sort of important and I'm afraid it might get lost if I left it in her room."

She slipped the note in her pocket, giving it a reassuring pat. "I will deliver it to her in person."

Secure in the knowledge at least now there would be less chance of any interference from Savanah's mother, he gave her a thumbs up. "Thank you. I appreciate it."

As he waited for the elevator, he felt as though he was being watched. His eyes narrowed, he spun around to check out his surroundings. Apart from the nurse he just spoke with, no one else seemed to be around.

He groaned, running his hand through his hair.

You're being paranoid. Savanah's mother has better things to do than follow you around. Then again…

After taking the elevator down to the main floor, he took off in a run to his truck. It wasn't until he drove out of the hospital parking lot and headed for home, he finally relaxed.

He had every reason to smile.

Remember?

She told you she loves you…

It was only after Cora heard the telltale swish of the elevator doors closing that she knew the coast was clear. Despite this, she decided to wait a little longer before leaving the room.

If only to be sure Jack had left.

A voice came from behind her. "May I help you?"

She almost dropped the muffins. Her mouth opened in a silent scream, she whirled around. Seated at a table, a cup of coffee in front of him, a young doctor was watching her.

She recognized him as the same doctor on call when Savanah arrived at the hospital.

He raised an eyebrow. "So… clue me in. Are you running from the law or something?"

As was usually the case when confronted, she went right into an attack mode, starting with a complaint. "You need better security in this hospital. Anyone could walk in here and do who knows what. For example, the man who just walked by—why is he allowed to wander around the halls at this early hour? As my daughter is a patient here, I have a right to be concerned."

He nodded. "*Ah, yes...* you're Savanah Jackson's mother. If I remember correctly, you're not a fan of how we do things around here, are you?"

She drew in a sharp breath, ready to defend what she believed were her reasonable demands. However, before she could even open her mouth, he cut her off. "Mrs. Jackson, I assure you our security is aware of every single person in this building, twenty-four-seven. And the man you saw? Jack Buchanan? I believe he's on your daughter's list of allowed visitors. So again, I assure you, it's all good."

He rose from his seat and, ignoring her furious expression, gulped down the rest of his coffee before he threw the empty cup in the trash.

He paused at the door to send her a big smile. "Have a great day."

"Wait..." Her plea ignored, she watched as he left the room. Frustrated she didn't get his name, and determined his disrespectful behavior would not go unnoticed, she marched down the hall, planning her complaint as she went.

Yes, marched. If she had been holding anything else besides the muffins, there's no doubt she would've flung it in anger. This was because she realized she now had one more thing to be mad about.

Why was Jack added to Savanah's visitor's list? And more importantly, who added him?

You can bet she was going to find out.

When Cora entered Savanah's room, she discovered she was asleep. So, she set the muffins on the bedside table.

This is when she also saw Savanah's phone. She picked it up, and for a few moments, held it in her hand, weighing her options.

Then she sighed. This situation—or whatever you wanted to call it—was getting worse by the minute. It looked like she and Savanah needed to have another serious talk about priorities.

But for now? Why even chance it?

She dropped the phone in her pocket.

Did she feel guilty about this? No, of course she didn't. As Savanah's mother, it was her job to protect her.

It's safe to say, Jack had no clue what he was up against.

CHAPTER 37

Patience is when you're supposed to get mad, but you choose to understand.
~ Anonymous

ednesday dawned unusually warm for late March, bringing a promise of spring in the air. The sun was shining, the sky a brilliant blue.

It was not the kind of day to be cooped up in the hospital. Gazing out the window of her fourth-floor room, Savanah would vouch for this.

At the sound of someone talking outside of her room, she glanced over at the door, an expectant smile on her face.

But, whoever it was passed by, their voices fading as they continued down the hall.

She turned back to the window, this time searching the hospital parking lot.

She was looking for a truck.

A black pickup truck.

Jack's truck.

Her search coming up empty and after giving another sigh—one of many in the past few hours—she wandered over to sit on the bed. Dragging her hand through her hair, she gazed up at the ceiling.

If only she could remember more of what went on in the past twenty-four hours. Instead, most of it was a complete blur. She wasn't sure if what she thought she remembered was real. Or it was only a dream.

Consider her phone, for example. Maybe she dreamt Jack had left it there so she could call him, his whisper brushing over her cheek.

However, when she woke this morning, the phone was nowhere to be found.

Instead, seated in the chair next to the bed, her mother was working on one of her many needlepoint projects.

After Raegan reassured her that, aside from a lingering headache and a dull ache in her wrist, she'd be fine, she braced herself for another one of her lectures. Sure enough, according to her mother, what happened was an unfortunate accident. Yes, Léon may have miscalculated on that last lift. However, this is what professional dancers do. They take risks, strive to be the best.

So, instead of dwelling on what happened, it would be best if they let it go. After all, with Savanah's dancing career on the line, their only priority should be her swift recovery.

Savanah stared at her. Had she heard right?

Unfortunate accident? Let it go? You don't think so. Not if Léon is still in the picture.

But before she could voice her thoughts, there was a knock on the door, followed by the sound of a male voice.

"Hello… Dr. Davis here. Is it okay to come in?"

Without waiting for an answer, and accompanied by a crew of interns, the doctor sauntered into the room. He glanced up from his phone, his gaze resting on her mother.

"Hmmph… it's you. Not who I wanted to see." Muttering this under her breath, she glared at him a good five seconds before she returned to her needlepoint. Jabbing the needle through the fabric, almost injuring herself in the process, she made her dislike more than clear.

He watched this, an amused smile on his face before he nodded. "Well, well, well… so we meet again, huh?" Then, ignoring her, he turned to Savanah.

His demeanor flip-flopped, a slow smile traveling across his face.

"*Ah...* the smile I see on your beautiful face tells me you're doing much better today."

His fingers gently probing her wrist, he gave her one of his most charming smiles. "You're very lucky, as it could've been a lot worse. We'll leave this dressing on for now, but before you go home, we'll replace it with a removable brace. This will make taking a shower, and life in general, much easier for you."

He continued to talk as he re-wrapped her wrist. "As long as you don't rush things, I see no reason you shouldn't be back to dancing by mid-summer."

He was aware of the sharp gasp from Savanah's mother, a clear indication she disagreed with his assessment. But once again, he ignored her, his attention on Savanah. "Right now, I'm more concerned about your concussion. So, I'd like to ask you a few questions. If you find it's too much, let me know, and I'll stop."

He began firing questions at her, one after the other. And though she tried to keep up, she found it hard to concentrate, her answers coming out slower and more confused.

He held up his hand, acknowledging this. "Okay, let's take a brief break. Close your eyes and take some deep, cleansing breaths."

Not used to being ignored, Savanah's mother had remained silent for as long as she could before she began rolling up her needlepoint. After making quite a production out of stuffing it in her tote, she cleared her throat. Loudly, she did this. "Don't you think you've asked more than enough questions? It's obvious they're only making Savanah feel worse. What she needs is to go home. This would be the best place for her."

"*Mother...*"

Savanah's groan earned her a sharp retort. "Savanah, you know I'm right. I can just as easily take care of you at home. How hard can it be?"

Dr. Davis again ignored her as he checked Savanah's vital signs. Only after he'd entered the results on his tablet, he responded. "I'm sorry Mrs. Jackson, but I disagree. Savanah is not ready to go home. The lingering effects from the concussion can't be ignored. So, in order to monitor her recovery, the hospital is the best place for her. We'll evaluate her progress again tomorrow."

Savanah's mother was shaking her head. When what she really wanted to do was scream. This was not what she'd planned. Sending him one of her most threatening expressions, one that always got her the respect she deserved, she nodded. "We'll see about that."

Closing his eyes, Dr. Davis massaged the back of his neck. His offer to fill in for a fellow doctor on a paternity leave now seemed like a big mistake With his already heavy workload at the Children's Hospital, he had no time to himself. And, as evidenced by his behavior with Savanah's mother, he was finding it hard to be civil.

He was exhausted. But then he was always exhausted. Fatigue had become his constant companion. And he'd wondered if it would ever end.

Then, out of the blue, yesterday had been different. As the doctor on call when they brought Savanah to the emergency room, captivated by her exquisite beauty, he'd insisted on taking over her care.

Unethical? Maybe. Yet, what man doesn't dream of having their own personal ballerina in their life? And never one to pass up on a new opportunity, he saw this as the perfect chance to make this fantasy a reality.

However, any hope of a relationship with Savanah had dwindled when he overheard a few of the nurses raving about her hunk of a boyfriend, Jack Buchanan. You'd think the man was a saint, the way they carried on about him.

And the pièce de résistance? After making the promise he wouldn't leave, he had stayed by her side all night, holding her hand while she slept.

The vote was in, the entire staff agreed… one can't get anymore romantic than that.

Well, he wasn't impressed. He could be romantic with the best of them. Make that better. Proof of this would be the long line of broken hearts he'd left behind.

There was also the problem of Savanah's mother. From what he'd experienced so far, she was a very angry woman. And if he had to make a list of what scared him the most, angry women would fall into the top five. He'd tangled with quite a few over the years, in both his work and personal life, and it never seemed to end well. So, with her dislike of him already so obvious, he wondered if, for now, it might be best to lie low.

Aware that the interns were getting restless, he slipped the tablet in his pocket before he reached over to give Savanah's hand a reassuring pat. "Don't worry, another night's stay isn't that bad. Think of it as our way of making sure you're on the right track to the best you can be. Are you on board?"

At Savanah's nod, he winked before heading for the door. "Good. Now close those beautiful eyes and get some rest."

Again, unethical. Yet, as far as he was concerned, he was only speaking the truth. He'd swear a man could drown in her eyes and die happy.

With the interns following behind, he paused at the door. "I'll be by later to check on you."

They had no sooner left the room when Savanah's mother started in with a whole new string of complaints. This Dr. Davis needed to be brought down a notch. An I.D. tag on his jacket, with Dr. in front of his name, didn't give him the right to be so rude. And if she wasn't mistaken, he had been flirting with Savanah. This was not an acceptable behavior for someone of his status.

Savanah wasn't listening. A harsh reminder her concussion was still hanging on, her lingering headache had now developed into a sharp throbbing pain.

She closed her eyes. Only seconds before she dozed off, it flashed through her mind she'd forgotten to ask her mother about her phone.

When Savanah's mother saw she was asleep, she gathered up her bag, pressed a quick kiss to Savanah's forehead, and left. She had work to do, starting with a stop at the nurses' station, where she intended to find how to contact the hospital director to voice her concerns.

As she would be quick to remind everyone, as Savanah's mother, she knew what was best for her.

And right now?

This would be for Savanah to go home.

CHAPTER 38

Savanah turned off the TV, dropping the remote next to her on the bed. The Hallmark movie with its picturesque setting, flawless actors and an impossibly happy ending was too much of a reminder of what she'd lost

She frowned, Who came up with the plots for these movies? It had to be someone who knew very little about what really happens when you fall in love. This would be where a woman meets a man, only to scare him away with all her problems. Then, to make things even more complicated, add a run-in with a co-worker, and a meddling and demanding mother.

And there you have it—a movie about real life… her life.

And you wonder why you haven't heard from Jack?

She picked up the magazine the nurse gave her to read, only to toss it next to the remote.

Settling back against the pillows, she closed her eyes.

"Hello… Savanah, are you awake?"

Her lashes fluttering open at this soft greeting, Savanah glanced over to see Stephanie enter the room. Holding an enormous bouquet and a white bakery box, her smile was tentative. "Do you want me to come back later?"

Savanah burst into tears.

Once Stephanie set the flowers next to the other floral arrangements Savanah received, she grabbed a handful of tissues from the table by the bed and handed them to her.

Still holding the bakery box, she sat in the chair next to the bed, reaching over to pat Savanah's hand. "Go ahead, let it all out. After what you've been through, you deserve a good cry."

Savanah wiped her eyes and blew her nose before she managed a weak smile. "I'm sorry, I wasn't sure if you got my message…" Her forehead creased, and for a second she seemed confused. Then, just as quickly, she smiled. "I'm just so happy to see you."

Stephanie grinned. "And I'm happy to see you, too." She handed Savanah the box. "Here, this is exactly what the doctor—or should I say nurse—ordered."

Savanah peeked in the box. After breathing in the heavenly aroma of Sweet Abby's frosted sugar cookies, she glanced over at Stephanie. "Oh my gosh, thank you. They smell amazing. I can't wait to try one.."

"Why wait? There's no reason you can't have one now."

Savanah held the box out to her. "Only if you have one, too."

Their choices made, Stephanie took a big bite of her cookie, studying Savanah as she chewed. Then she smiled. "So, you look pretty fantastic for someone who recently had surgery. But, more importantly, how do you feel?"

Savanah sighed. "Everything hurts… my head, my wrist, everything. Now I know what people mean when they say they felt like they got hit by a truck."

Stephanie shrugged. "That's understandable after what you've been through. From what you told me in your message, you had quite a fall." She leaned forward, her expression serious. "Savanah, what happened?"

Still finding it hard to comprehend what took place in the studio, let alone talk about it, Savanah gave her a brief account of what led up to her injury.

Reluctantly meeting Stephanie's gaze, she shrugged. "I guess Léon thought he could pull it off."

Stephanie's silence had Savanah feeling the need to explain. "But that's not unusual. Injuries in the dance world are more common than you'd think. As my mother would say, this is to be expected, as impossible is not a word in a successful dancer's vocabulary. The best are those who are always striving to reach that elusive high."

Again, she shrugged. "It was unfortunate I was with Léon when he made that attempt and failed."

Stephanie was skeptical. She didn't even want to think about what could've happened. Nor was she impressed with how talented Léon was.

After popping the last bite of cookie into her mouth, she shook her head. "Savanah, I know it's not for me to say, but maybe you need to take a break from this Léon. What if something like this happens again? You might not be so lucky."

Raising her hand with the cast, Savanah's smile was wry. "Well, it looks like I won't have to worry about that for a while. Instead, that will fall on the shoulders of his new partner."

She frowned. "It wouldn't surprise me if Gayle had already selected my replacement."

However, she didn't want to talk about this. Not when she couldn't shake the thought she might be partly responsible for what happened. She should've stood her ground, refused to dance with Léon until he behaved like the professional he claimed to be.

Sensing her reluctance, Stephanie changed the subject. "So, have you talked to Jack? You did get your phone, didn't you? Jack said he left it here after he stayed the night with you. It turns out your mother had it. She gave it to me, and I gave it to him."

She sighed. "Because he refused to leave—not even to get something to eat from the cafeteria—the staff has crowned him as the hero in all of this. And I have to say, I agree with them."

Savanah's smile was brilliant, Léon and the subject of dance forgotten. "Jack was here? He really was? I wondered if it was all a dream. Because I couldn't find my phone anywhere."

Stephanie shook her head. "Nope, it wasn't a dream. He followed the ambulance to find out the hospital they were taking you. But because of privacy laws, they couldn't give him any information. And I was at work, so by the time I read your voicemail, you were already out of surgery."

"I sent you a voicemail, too?"

"Well, it came through your phone. Even though the message came from your mother. So, as soon as I got out of work, I came here."

"My mother called you from my phone? I don't understand…"

Noticing Savannah's worried look, Stephanie changed the subject again. "That's when Jack came to the rescue. So, knowing that you were in expert hands, I left.

Savanah rested her head back against the pillows, a long sigh escaping her. Then she glanced over at Stephanie. "I wish…"

Stephanie cut her off, giving her hand a gentle squeeze. "Things will work out, I know they will."

Her face brightened. "Completely off topic, here's some good news. Jack has agreed to play the piano for our first dance. He's composing a revised score of the song we chose. I tried to convince him to sing, but he wouldn't."

She shrugged. "It's okay. That he agreed to play the piano is enough."

Savanah smiled. "He is so talented."

Stephanie laughed. "And so are you. Like I've said before, you're perfect together. Speaking of that, what did the doctors tell you?"

Leaning back against the pillows, Savanah sighed. "Well, they said the surgery on my wrist was a success. But they're concerned about the concussion. At least this is according to Dr. Davis. He insisted I stay another day so he can keep an eye on me."

"Dr. Davis said he wants to keep his eye on you?" Stephanie rolled her eyes. "Why am I not surprised?"

"Why? He seemed nice."

Stephanie raised an eyebrow. "I guess it depends on how you define nice. How much time do we have?"

After she glanced at her watch, she settled more comfortably in her chair before she grinned over at Savanah. "So, you thought Dr. Davis was nice, huh? *Hmm…* where shall I begin."

Dinners had been served. The trays cleared away, the hospital was settling down to its normal evening routine.

Stephanie had left over an hour ago.

And Savanah still hadn't heard from Jack.

She'd tried calling him using Stephanie's phone, but there was no answer. So, she tried to leave a message, only to find his mail box was full.

As a last resort, she'd called her own phone. If her mother answered, then she'd know where her phone was. But again the call went to voice mail. She decided not to leave a message.

How ridiculous would that be? Who responds to their own voice mail?

She propped up the pillows behind her and closed her eyes. Ever since Stephanie told her Jack was going to play his original version of the song she and Evan had chosen for their first dance, an idea had been rolling around in her mind and it wouldn't leave.

It's a crazy idea. Just let it go.

Instead, she made a mental note, as soon as she had her phone back, she would call Stephanie.

She closed her eyes again.

You really need to go home…

The sound of someone clearing their throat, she opened her eyes.

Dr. Davis stood at the foot of the bed. He smiled. "I'm sorry. I hope I didn't wake you?"

She struggled into a sitting position, shaking her head. "No, no… you're fine."

Now standing next to her, he placed his hand to her forehead. "Nice and cool. A good sign."

He withdrew his hand, and after sinking into the chair and stretching out his legs, he let out a long sigh. "It's been a long day. In fact, this is the first break I've had. I can only blame myself, since I should've gone home long ago. But I wanted to check up on my new favorite patient before I left."

Unsure of how to respond, she only nodded. This resulted in an uncomfortable silence.

He didn't understand. Had she misunderstood him? Because this certainly wasn't going as he hoped.

He usually held the advantage, his charming personality winning over a woman's heart within seconds of meeting.

He leaned forward in his chair, his voice taking on a more serious tone. "As your doctor, in order to make this visit legit, I need to ask you a few questions. Such as… have you noticed any unusual, or worsening pain in your wrist? Blurry vision? Severe headaches? Or sudden episodes of dizziness?"

Stephanie shook her head. "No, I'm feeling much better."

"*Ah…* this is what every doctor likes to hear." His head tilted, he studied her with an intensity that had the color flooding her cheeks. Then he shrugged. "I apologize. I don't mean to stare, only I've never met a real ballerina before. Are they all as beautiful as you?"

She laughed at this.."I hate to disappoint you, but we're just like everyone else."

Encouraged by her laughter, he grinned. "*Ah…* I doubt that. Though I'd be willing to have you prove me wrong."

She laughed again. But this time it was a nervous laugh

He chuckled. "I'm serious. I'd love to take you out dancing sometime. I fall short in that area and I could use some pointers."

Wow… Stephanie was right about him. You can understand why women fall for him.

She gave him a bright smile. "Oh, I'm sure you're much better than you're letting on. And if you are serious about becoming a better dancer, I think you'd learn more from dance classes than you would from me."

Again, not the reaction he expected, he was silent. This beauty was going to be a lot harder to win over than he expected. This didn't mean he wouldn't try. Remember, there was nothing he enjoyed more than a challenge.

He decided it might be time to dazzle her with stories of his many accomplishments. It also couldn't hurt to let slip he was the youngest CMO in the history of the Children's Hospital, as this never failed to impress.

He reached for her hand. "Here, let me check your lifeline."

He was in the middle of sharing the conversation he had with a patient who claimed she could predict his future through palm reading, when he realized Savanah wasn't listening. Focused on something behind him, her face lit up with a radiant smile.

He turned to check it out.

Damn…

It was the boyfriend…

Jack Buchanan.

CHAPTER 39

On the way to the elevator, a container of pink roses on display in the hospital gift shop window caught Jack's eye. Propped up against the container was a small stuffed bear wearing a pink ballerina tutu.

A smile traveling over his face, his steps slowed.

Ten minutes later, he walked out of the gift shop carrying the entire container of roses; the bear peeking out of his jacket pocket.

It seemed like an eternity since he last saw Savanah.

He had accomplished very little since he left the hospital in the early morning hours. Not that he hadn't made the effort. *God knows*, he'd tried. However, his mind had refused to cooperate, instead choosing to replay the events of the last twenty-four hours.

Over and over and over again…

And now he only wanted to be with Savanah.

Somehow, he was confident, together, they'd find a way to make everything right.

He stepped off the elevator onto the third floor

"Mr. Buchanan, excuse me… I need to talk to you."

He turned to see a nurse waving from the nurses' station. She was the nurse he'd asked to give Savanah the note he'd written.

He walked over and set the container of roses on the counter. "These are for you and the other nurses on the floor. I hope there's enough for everyone, since I took all the gift shop had. Think of them as a token of my appreciation for all you've done for Savanah."

This was when he realized the nurse seemed upset. A pained look on her face, and wringing her hands, she came from around the counter.

Not the response you expected. Is it the hospital policy not to accept gifts?

He gestured to the flowers. "I'm sorry. Are these not allowed? Perhaps I should have asked first?"

"*Oh, no, no, no…* they're beautiful, and I know everyone will love them. It's something I did."

"Okay…" A little worried, he waited.

She reached into her pocket, and pulling out the note he'd left for Savanah, she handed it to him. "I never gave this to Savanah. We got busy, and it wasn't until I saw you, I remembered. So, I certainly don't deserve a rose. I'm so sorry."

He took the note, and after stuffing it in his jacket pocket, he pulled two roses out of the container, handing her one. "Nope, if I'm not mistaken, this rose has your name on it. And don't worry about the note. I'll give it to her now."

He grinned, holding up the other rose. "I better not forget to give a rose to Savanah, right?"

She gave a sigh of relief. "Thank you. And no, you can't forget Savanah."

He turned to leave, only to have her call out to him. "Mr. Buchanan?"

His grin was teasing. "I hope this is good news?"

She laughed. "Yes, it is. I thought you'd like to know Savanah will be so happy to see you. Even though she didn't actually come out and tell us this."

She shrugged. "We're pretty good at sensing what's going on with our patients. It comes with the territory."

"Thank you for sharing that." He followed this with a wink before he continued down the hall to Savanah's room.

He was going to be happy to see her, too.

The sound of a male voice suggesting Savanah had a visitor, Jack cleared his throat before he ventured into her hospital room.

He came to an abrupt halt.

Dr. Davis was sitting in the chair next to the bed.

Jack was okay with this. What he didn't like was that the doctor was holding Savanah's hand. As far as he was concerned, this was taking a bedside manner a little too far.

Nope, not on your watch. Dr. Davis picked the wrong woman to flirt with this time.

Stephanie had filled him in about the doctor's history as a heart-breaker. From what she'd said, commitment wasn't something he believed in.

And now, turning to see Jack standing by the door, he slowly let go of Savanah's hand. After rising to his feet and checking his watch, he glanced over at her and grinned. "*Whoa...* I can't believe it's almost seven. Where has the time gone? I've definitely overstayed my welcome."

He inclined his head towards Jack. "It also looks like you have a visitor, which means it's time for me to leave. But I'll be back tomorrow morning to check on you."

As he started to walk out of the room, he glanced over at Jack, his arrogant smirk a promise of trouble. "You must be the boyfriend every-one's talking about. You're one lucky man. Take good care of her while I'm gone."

Jack saw this as a threat. Experiencing a level of jealousy he had never felt before, he wanted to confront him, challenge him, or do whatever was necessary to keep him as far away from Savanah as possible.

To keep from making a foolish mistake—such as ordering the doctor out of the room and forbidding him from ever speaking to Savanah again—a curt nod was his only answer.

Savanah remained silent, watching the two men. Only after Dr. Davis had left, she glanced over at Jack, her forehead creased in concern.

"Jack?"

Their eyes met. An unspoken rush of emotions passing between them, in a matter of seconds, he was at her side. Tossing the rose on the chair, and framing her face in his hands, he touched his mouth to hers in a soft kiss.

"Vanababe..." he whispered. Relief poured through him when she seemed to melt against him, her soft sigh followed by a breathy explosion of words. "*Hi*... I didn't know... I wasn't sure... especially after what happened with my mother... And then I lost my phone... "

He pressed his finger to her lips. "*Shush*... there's no place I'd rather be than here with you." His smile matched the teasing gleam in his eyes. "When a man proposes to a woman as many times as I have to you? That's all the proof you need."

She reached for his arm, her plan to pull him closer for a kiss. Instead, thrown off balance because of the bulkiness of her cast, she fell back onto the bed. And somehow, she managed to take him with her.

He was the first to move. His gaze fixed on her face, his voice slipped to a husky whisper, brushing over her cheek. "*Ah, love*... I'm not sure if this was what you intended. I only know I'd be foolish not to seize the moment."

He swooped in, claiming her mouth in a kiss. A kiss they both so desperately needed, if only to erase the uncertainty of the past twenty-four hours.

He lifted his head, watching her lashes flutter open. Brushing a strand of her hair from her face, the corner of his mouth curved in a lopsided grin. "Well, I must say... that was the best answer you've given me so far. Enough to give me reason to hope."

His playful smile made her laugh. "Oh, Jack... I'm so glad you're here."

He chuckled. "Like I've been trying to tell you, I'm here to stay." He leaned in to give her another kiss. Only to stop short at her sharp intake of breath, her face twisting in pain.

He began inching his way off the bed, all the while keeping up a running apology. "*Oh, my God*... what am I doing? The last thing you need is for me to injure you even more."

Once he had her settled back in the bed, he frowned. "It's a good thing your Dr. Davis didn't witness that. He'd have me escorted out the building in no time, banning me from you for life."

With that, he sank down into the chair, having forgotten this was where he tossed the rose.

He dove out of the chair, feeling like a fool.

"Are you okay?" Wide eyed, she was trying not to smile.

Totally embarrassed, he raked his hand through his hair. "*Geeesh…* I don't know what the hell my problem is. It seems like I cause trouble with everything I touch, including you. Let me go get you another rose. It will only take a—"

"Jack, stop…" She reached for his hand, and pulled him close. "I don't need another rose. You are the only thing I need… the only person I've been able to think about since I've been here. Every time I heard someone talking out in the hallway, I waited, hoping it was you. Only you."

Leaning back against the pillows, her face scrunched in disbelief. "And Jack, seriously? Dr. Davis? Give me some credit. Why would I even be the least bit interested in him when I already have you?" She paused, studying him before she added. "That is if you want me, too."

Jack was grinning.

That she even had to ask?

Lost in her eyes, daring to believe the love shining there was for him, he finally gave her that kiss.

CHAPTER 40

"Well, if I didn't already know better, I'd think this was a scene out of one of those romance movies you can find on TV."

A hearty laugh following this, both Savanah and Jack turned to see Diane, the nurse on duty the previous night, standing at the entrance to the room.

She was holding a pink rose.

Her grin was huge. "Sorry for the interruption, but I wanted to check on you before I left, if only to make sure you're all right. I see I had no reason to worry."

She held up the rose. "I also wanted to thank you for this. It was a rough day here on the floor, so your kind gesture helped put a smile back on everyone's face."

"Of course, there are those that won't crack a smile no matter what you do." After mumbling this under her breath, she shrugged. "However, that's neither here nor there. We all know you can't please everyone."

She directed her next comment to Savanah. "I hope you realize how special this guy is. He spent the entire night by your side. Refused to leave. If I hadn't convinced the kitchen to prepare a plate of food for him, he might have starved to death."

Jack laughed. "I'm sure it wouldn't have come to that. By the way, thank the kitchen staff for me. I swear that was the best meatloaf I ever had."

Diane nodded. "Yep, they've got it together back there. I'll even go as far to admit they're better cooks than I am." This was followed by another boisterous laugh before she turned to leave. Pausing at the door, she pointed her finger at Jack. "Remember what I told you… if you want her to come home, she needs her rest. A concussion isn't something to take lightly, so try not to keep her awake with all your yakking. And if I don't see you again, take care."

She waved the rose at them one more time and was gone. They could hear her talking to another staff member on her way to the elevator, followed by another of her contagious laughs.

Jack grinned. "I believe she's more than established herself as the unofficial boss of this floor. She's a definite keeper. Though I wouldn't want to get on her bad side."

Diane's visit a reminder he had yet to give Savanah her rose, he picked it up, intending to hand it to her.

Only to find her on the verge of tears.

Uh, oh…

Of course, this made him nervous. He placed the rose back on the chair, and sitting on the edge of the bed, he searched her face. "Okay, Vanababe, now what did I mess up?"

"Nothing, you did nothing wrong. It's only that I can't believe you were here all night. I told myself maybe it was all a dream."

"*Ah…* it wasn't a dream. In fact, I have proof."

He reached into his jeans pocket and, pulling out the note he'd left earlier, handed it to her. She read it out loud.

Vanababe, I left your phone on the table next to your bed.
If you need anything, call me. I'll plan to stop by later today.
Sweet dreams, love.

He watched a tiny line crease her forehead before she looked up at him. "I don't understand. There was no phone on the table."

Jack hesitated, unsure of how to answer.

It was obvious, at least to him, her mother was responsible for the missing phone. Nonetheless, Savanah had to figure this out on her own.

While tucking a strand of her hair behind her ear, he kept his answer vague. "After Stephanie got your phone from your mother, she gave it to me. I left it on the table so you'd see it when you woke up. I wanted to make sure you knew you could call me."

He gestured to the note. "So I left the note explaining this at the nurses' station in case it got misplaced. Unfortunately, the nurse forgot to give it to you."

She was shaking her head. "I did call you. And I heard what you said before you left. I meant to ask my mother if she knew where the phone was, but I forgot. I wonder what happened…"

Her voice fading mid-sentence, she looked down at the note in her hand before she glanced over at him.

Their eyes locked, a flicker of anger in his, a sudden comprehension in hers.

He exhaled a long breath. "Let's not worry about that now. I have a feeling it will show up when we least expect it."

Refusing to meet his gaze, she stared down at the note. Then she nodded. "You're right, it's just a phone."

Hoping to lighten the moment, he pulled the stuffed bear out of his pocket and handed it to her. "I almost forgot, this called out to me from the hospital gift store. I would think every ballerina could use a ballerina bear to watch over them."

As he'd hoped, she smiled. Granted, it wasn't a big smile, but it was a start. So, aiming for more, he handed her the rose, a little squished, yet still as beautiful. "And this is to make up for the rose that got left behind at the dance studio."

"Thank you." She held the rose to her lips. "But it didn't get left behind. I insisted on taking it with me because it was from you. When I realized I'd left it in the studio, I begged a paramedic to go back and get it for me. I'm pretty sure he thought I was crazy."

She frowned. "I remember having it in the emergency room. But I don't know what happened to it after that."

She turned to him, an anguished look on her face. "*Oh, Jack…* what am I going to do? Everyone expects me to put this behind me and act as though nothing happened. Yet I'm not sure I can."

She fingered the rose, fighting back the threat of tears. "Or else they've already decided my career is over."

A wave of tenderness washing over him, he smoothed the hair back from her face. "No one thinks that. And even if they do, you need to ignore them. Your chief priority now is to heal. And whatever you need, I'm here for you, okay?"

She nodded. Right before the words flew out of her mouth, surprising her more than him. "I wish we could dance. Everything feels right when I'm in your arms."

He glanced around the room, then back at her.

A slow smile traveled across his face. "Well, there doesn't seem to be enough room to dance. However, I may have a better idea."

She watched as he made his way to the other side of the bed. After he kicked off his boots and pulled down the blanket, he smiled over at her. "Now, if you move over a bit and give me some room, we'll be good to go."

Once he'd settled next to her, his arm wrapped around her, he smiled. "So, we may not be dancing, however, I believe this is a pretty good, if not better, substitute."

"It feels wonderful." Her sigh turned into a long yawn.

A smile came through in his voice. "Why do I have a feeling you're about to nod off on me? Before you do, there's something Stephanie brought to my attention. And this is that I never asked you to be my date for her wedding. I guess I assumed this, which I know is wrong. And I apologize. So, even though I'm late in asking, will you be my 'plus one' for the wedding? And for the rehearsal dinner as well?"

She lifted her face to his, a smile curving her lips. *"Hmm…* it would be a shame not to wear the dress I bought for the occasion. And I'll let you in on a little secret… I couldn't imagine going with anyone but you. So, in answer your question, yes, I'd love to be your 'plus-one' for Stephanie and Evan's wedding."

He laughed. "Well, if your dress is anything like the one you wore when we went out to dinner, I can't wait."

She settled more comfortably against him. "I can't wait either. Stephanie told me you're playing the song they chose for their first dance, and she's so excited." Her eyebrows raised, she gazed up at him. "She also said she asked you to sing, you refused. Why?"

He sighed. "The song she and Evan chose is meant to be sung as a duet. So, I have no plan of ruining the beauty of the song by doing it solo."

He pressed a kiss to her forehead. "I was more than happy to do a revised version for them. In fact, I already wrapped up the final score right before I came here." He smiled. "I think they'll like what I came up with."

"I'm sure they will." For a moment she hesitated, as though she was about to say something. Instead, she rested her head back on his shoulder, where even though she tried, she couldn't hold back another yawn. "I'm sorry, I don't know why I'm so tired."

He pressed a kiss to the top of her head. "Close your eyes, love. I'm not going anywhere."

In what seemed like only a few minutes, he felt her relax against him, her heartbeat settling into a slow dance with his.

So, he figured he might as well close his eyes, too.

Because, right now? There was no place else he'd rather be.

About twenty minutes later, on her way to meet a friend for dinner, Cora pulled her car into the hospital parking lot. She was dropping off a container of her homemade chicken soup for Savanah.

Earning her second place in a local cooking contest a few years back, the soup became her one claim to culinary fame. The promise it could cure anything, from the common cold to a broken heart, was one she took very seriously.

Heaven forbid you ask for the recipe.

After catching sight of Jack roaming the hospital earlier this morning, and what she felt was a very unsatisfactory meeting with Dr. Davis, she was now even more determined to get Savanah released from the hospital.

If ever there was a time for the soup to work its magic, it would be now.

When Cora walked into Savanah's room, Jack was the last person she expected to see. Thinking her mind was playing tricks on her, she blinked.

No question about it, not only was he real, he was sharing the bed with Savanah.

Dammit… what's going on here?

Now she wasn't one to swear, a habit she considered barbaric, especially in women. However, faced with a situation so out of her comfort zone, this was the one time she made an exception.

This was a hospital. Didn't they have rules pertaining to this kind of behavior?

And if they didn't?

Well, they should have.

She took a step closer. From what little she could make out, tucked against Jack and under the blanket, Savanah was asleep.

His cheek resting against the top of her head, Jack also appeared to be asleep.

She placed the container of chicken soup on the table. Then, with the angry pounding of her heart echoing in her head—a warning her blood pressure was about to escalate out of control—she closed her eyes. Finally, after exhaling a long breath, she moved closer to the bed.

As if she sensed her mother's presence, even while sleeping, Savanah threw aside the blanket. Giving a soft whimper, she rested her injured arm back on Jack's chest.

Jack's eyes flew open, and searching for the blanket, he pulled it over her, careful not jar her arm. After pressing a kiss to the top of her head, he murmured words of comfort until she settled back against him with a long sigh.

Once he was satisfied she was still asleep, he lifted his head, his gaze falling on her mother.

Their eyes met, his, steady and on guard. While hers blazed with anger, every inch of her quivering with rage, sending the message she wanted him gone.

It was a modern day stand-off.

Jack wasn't worried. She could send all the threatening looks she wanted. His only concern was for Savanah. After she told him she felt safe in his arms? He had no intention of leaving her side,

So, when her mother moved even closer, the furious look she leveled on him a sign this could lead to another heated exchange, he put his finger to his lips, shaking his head.

His voice was low, yet firm. "Please… just let her sleep."

The air between them heavy with tension, she said nothing. Then she let out a harsh breath. She was at a disadvantage. No matter how much she tried to rationalize her behavior, people would always see her as the villain.

So, she had no choice but to leave.

She was halfway out of the room when she came to a stop. Pulling Savanah's phone out of her coat pocket. She slapped it on top of the container of chicken soup. And after one last menacing glare in Jack's direction, she left.

"Thank you." In shock, by the time Jack got this out, she was already gone.

When Cora reached her car, she closed her eyes as she tried to calm down. She felt as if her sanity was slipping away, leaving her unhinged.

Because what just happened in that hospital room?

By leaving, hadn't she sent Jack the message she approved of his relationship with Savanah?

This is exactly what you did.

And this was a far cry from the truth.

Was she worried? You can bet she was.

Despite that, she wasn't ready to throw in the towel quite yet. She had one more option lined up. Hopefully, more information about this would be available by the end of next week.

She started up her car and headed for the restaurant. As she drove, she couldn't shake the memory of what she'd stumbled upon in that hospital room.

Seriously? What was Savanah thinking? Has she listened to anything you've said?

A car swerved into her lane, right in front of her. After she slammed on the brakes, for the rest of the drive, she kept her eyes glued to the road and a tight hold on the steering wheel.

The sooner she put an end to this whole mess, the better.

And Jack?

He found it hard to believe Savannah's mother had left without putting up a fight.

This had him holding his breath each time he heard footsteps in the hallway, expecting her to come charging back into the room, ready to call him out.

Finally, comforted by the sound of Savanah's even breathing, he rested his head back against the pillows and closed his eyes.

He wasn't going to worry.

At least not yet, he wasn't.

Hmm… you know what they say, never underestimate the power of an angry woman.

CHAPTER 41

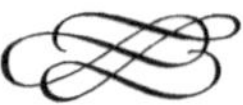

If there is anything better than to be loved, it is loving.
~ Anonymous

Four days had passed since Savanah's release from the hospital. And knowing what she knew now, she never would've tried to convince Dr. Davis she would be better off at home.

She was going stir-crazy.

To clarify, the definition of stir-crazy is a person distraught or restless from a long confinement such as prison. If you were to ask Savanah, she'd tell you she was that person.

No matter what the situation, her mother was always ready with her opinion, wanted or not. And how long she intended to stay was anyone's guess.

She had swept through Savanah's condo like a hurricane, nothing spared from what she considered her tired and true organizational skills. The pantry, refrigerator, and freezer were stocked with enough food for the next several months, the cabinets lined with shelf paper and organized for efficiency. Savanah's clothes were now sorted and arranged according to color in both her bedroom closet and dresser drawers. Her linen closet would pass Martha Stewart's inspection with flying colors.

She had warned Savanah at least three times against using the fireplace. Regardless of what people said, she had her doubts about the safety of this modern convenience. Her motto being better safe than sorry.

And if this was even possible, she'd found a way to over-clean. The roar of the vacuum cleaner at the early hour of eight in the morning had now become Savanah's daily wake-up call.

To get back into a routine, even with just the few warm-up exercises allowed, she went to the dance studio twice. Both times Léon had made an appearance, only to avoid her,

He hadn't inquired about her injury, or if she was okay. Neither had he offered any apology.

So she ignored him.

The highlight of the last four days were the texts and phone calls she received from Jack, the latter sometimes lasting until late into the night.

Savanah wasn't used to this slow paced way of life. She'd started dance lessons before she even attended elementary school. Even at that age, everything her life became everything about dance, leaving little time for anything else.

In fact, she never thought she'd say this, but she missed the bone weary aches and pains that came from the long hours of practice every day. As strenuous as this was, she reveled in the sense of accomplishment. And she missed that even more.

What it came down to?

She was bored. This explained her stir-crazy state.

However, things were looking up. With Savanah's repeated promises she'd call if she needed anything, along with a gentle shove out the door, her mother got in her car and drove away.

Wandering over to the sofa, Savanah sank into the soft cushions, the silence a welcome change. This lasted less than a minute before her phone chimed. She picked it up to see she had a text from Stephanie.

> Hey, I hope you're feeling better. It's been crazy
> here. I can't wait until my shift is over and it will
> be wedding time. I also wanted to make sure
> your plan was still in place. It's going to be
> great. I can't wait.

She sent her reply.

> So far, so good. And if there is anything else you need, let me know. I'll see you Friday night. Hang in there.

Stephanie responded within seconds.

> You've got this... it's going to be fine.

After she set the phone on the coffee table, she leaned back in the cushions and closed her eyes. She could only hope her text came out more confident than she felt. She was taking an enormous risk, one that could change her future forever.

Much later, after taking a shower and washing her hair, Savanah wandered into the kitchen. Scrolling down through her phone, she found the playlist she wanted and hit play.

Hungry, she scanned the contents of the refrigerator. Selecting a container labeled as pasta carbonara—one of the meal choices left by her mother—she popped it in the microwave. She was searching for silverware when her doorbell rang.

She sent up a silent prayer that it wasn't her mother, while preparing herself it very well could be. Then, filled with guilt for this thought, she tucked her still damp hair behind her ears, pasted a big smile on her face, and opened the door.

Almost obscured by the enormous bouquet he was holding, a delivery man gave her a big smile. "Hi, there. I have a delivery here for…" an eyebrow raised, he read the name on card tucked in the bouquet. "Vanababe? Would this be you?"

She laughed, nodding. "Yes, that's me."

"Then, here ya go. Enjoy." He handed her the bouquet and, bounding down the steps, ran back to his truck.

With the use of only one hand, she managed to carry the heavy bouquet over to the island, placing it next to a vase holding a single, fragrant pink rose.

Of all the flowers she'd received while in the hospital, this was the only flower she'd kept, leaving the rest for the nurses and patients.

She pulled out the card tucked in the bouquet.

*Vanababe, These are to replace the flowers you so gener-
ously gave away. You should always have flowers in your life. I
only ask you think of me when you look at them. Love, Jack*

She smiled, and closing her eyes, she pressed the card to her lips.
You don't need flowers… you only need him.

She was reaching for a vase on the top shelf of the cupboard—a decision she'd later admit was not one of her smarter moves—when her doorbell rang again. Startled, she lost her hold on the vase.

Though she struggled to maintain her grip, the vase slipped from her fingers. So she did the only thing she could, she closed her eyes and ducked. Hitting the countertop with a deafening crash, the vase exploded into a million pieces, the sound of shattering glass echoing through the room..

Oh, no…

She was almost afraid to move. With the sound of the crash still echoing in her head, she slowly peered down at the floor. A sea of broken glass surrounded her bare feet, peeking out from under her pajama pants.

Oh boy, you did it this time. Now what are you going to do?

About five minutes after the delivery man left, Jack pulled into a parking space close to Savanah's condo. After he searched the area to find no sign of her mother's car, he jumped out of his truck. Grabbing the two cups of Café Latte coffee and a bag holding two sour cherry scones from the passenger seat, he sprinted to Savanah's front door.

It had been a long day, filled with unnecessary delays and problems. But then it seemed like the entire week had been a struggle. So, he was more than ready for a break.

Right now, the only thing that made sense to him was to be with Savanah. She was all he could think about. He wanted to hold her in his arms, look into her eyes, and get lost in whatever kind of spell she'd cast over him.

Yeah, he was bewitched. And more than happy to admit to this.

There was only one problem. Even though they had talked on the phone and messaged each other, he hadn't actually seen Savanah since the last time he visited her in the hospital.

Her mother had made sure of that.

He'd foolishly thought after finding him and Savanah together that night at the hospital, she'd have a change of heart. Instead, she had gone into overdrive, taking on the role of overprotective mother bear, guarding her cub from danger.

And yes, you'd qualify as the danger.

He'd swear, it was as if she and Dr. Davis were in cahoots, their goal to separate him and Savanah.

Well, he'd had enough. This the reason he was now standing on Savanah's doorstep.

He pressed the doorbell. As if on cue, a loud crash came from inside the condo. But even more concerning was the long silence that followed.

He hit the doorbell again.

"Help... "

This faint cry galvanized him into action. He turned the handle, and, finding the door unlocked, he entered the condo.

His eyes swept the room before settling on Savanah. Their gazes locked, and a concerned frown creased his brow. "Vanababe? What happened?"

She burst into tears.

Not the response he'd hoped for, but relieved she appeared to be all in one piece, he set the coffee cups and bag of scones on the counter. As he started towards her, the crunch of broken glass beneath his boots stopped him cold. He glanced down. Shards of glass glittered across the floor.

But it was the sight of her bare feet that sent him into action. He scooped her up in his arms and headed for the sofa. After a slight hesitation, he changed course and carried her into her bedroom. After setting her gently on the bed, he shrugged out of his jacket, kicked off his boots, and settled next to her.

His hand sifting through the silkiness of her hair, he held her in his arms as she continued to cry.

He hadn't the faintest idea what went on in a woman's mind.

Not a clue...

But if he had to guess, Savanah's tears weren't about the broken glass. More likely, they were a delayed reaction to the draining events of the past few days.

Her world had been upended, the rug yanked out from under her, leaving her future uncertain.

So, he did what he could, whispering words of comfort as he held her.

Jack wasn't sure how long he held Savanah in his arms, only that when he'd first arrived, the sun had just dipped below the horizon. Now, the only light spilled from the moon and stars, scattered like diamonds across the night sky.

Savanah's tears now down to an occasional trembling sigh, he pressed a kiss in her hair.

"Hey..."

"Hey..." Her face burrowed in his shoulder, she kept shaking her head as she spoke. "I'm sorry, I wanted to put the flowers in water and I didn't think the vase would be so heavy. It was a mistake to think I could do that with this cast on my arm. Then there was broken glass everywhere, and I..."

"Shh... it's okay." He brushed her hair back from her face. "There's no need to apologize. After all you've gone through, you can cry as much as you want. My shoulder is yours, for as long as you want."

A slow smile curved his lips.

Uh, oh...

She searched his face. "What are you thinking?"

He shook his head.

"Jack... come on, tell me."

He hesitated, his gaze lingering on hers for a moment before he shrugged. "Okay, but remember, you insisted," he said.

Propping himself on his elbow, he leaned in, and brushing his lips over hers, his voice dropped to a husky whisper. "I love you, Savanah Jackson. From the moment I met you, all my dreams, my thoughts... they have all been of you. Holding you in my arms is something I once thought could only happen in my imagination. But here we are... and I find it's not enough."

His kiss caught the corner of her mouth.

"I want more…"

He dropped another kiss to her mouth, this one lasting a little longer.

"I want to hold you in my arms when as I fall asleep at night." he said, "and I want to find you're still there in the morning so I can kiss you awake."

A thrill surged through him as she fisted her hand in his shirt, pulling him closer. And this time, she was the one to initiate the kiss.

Outside, car doors slammed, followed by the sound of women's voices.

Jack lifted his head, a flicker of concern crossing his mind. But Savanah reached up, her fingertips brushing his lips. "Don't worry," she whispered, "it's just the neighbors. So, please, don't stop kissing me."

Everything now forgotten except for the woman in his arms, he leaned in to grant her request.

CHAPTER 42

Cora Jackson breathed a sigh of relief when she saw the parking space next to Savanah's car was vacant.

There was no black pickup truck parked there.

On her way home from dinner with her friend Doreen, she hadn't planned to stop by Savanah's condo. It was only after she had trouble reading the menu, and a search through her purse for her glasses was to no avail, she remembered setting them on Savanah's fireplace mantle.

She had met Doreen at a local consignment shop where they both volunteered part time. Besides rambling on about her son who, according to her, was the number one lawyer in the entire state of Ohio, she was also a huge gossip.

Doreen liked to talk, while Savanah's mother would rather listen. So it's no surprise their friendship worked so well.

Only recently, Doreen had suggested her son and Savanah should meet.

Cora shot down the possibility of that in record time. A lawyer? She didn't trust lawyers. As far as she was concerned, they rated right there at the bottom of the list with musicians.

And now, peering through the windshield at Savanah's condo, from what she could see, there didn't seem to be any lights on.

She glanced over at Doreen in the passenger seat. "*Hmm...* how odd. Even though Savanah's car is here, it doesn't look like she's home. I can't imagine where she'd be. Unless..."

Her mouth twisted into a frown. Still smarting from how Savanah had practically kicked her out of her condo earlier, she didn't even want to imagine what this could mean.

"Perhaps she's already gone to bed?" Busy checking her messages, Doreen didn't even look up from her phone.

Already halfway out of the car, Cora shook her head. "I doubt that. Wait here, I should only be a couple of minutes."

Before she pressed the doorbell, she gave the handle a good push. This sent the door flying open, almost taking her with it.

Mumbling under her breath that she needed to remind Savanah to lock her doors—as it was obvious she hadn't listened to her warning the first time—she made her way through the darkness into the kitchen and turned on the light.

The enormous bouquet on the kitchen island was the first thing to catch her attention. As she walked around the island to see if there was a card with the sender's name, the crunch beneath her feet alerted her to the broken glass scattered across the floor.

She froze, eyes wide as she struggled to understand.

What happened? Did someone break in? And where was Savanah?

Her heart now pounding in her chest, she inched open a drawer, grabbing the first thing she came in contact with.

This turned out to be a butter knife. Not much of a weapon, but it would have to do.

The knife clutched in her hand, she sent a nervous glance around the room. This was when she saw the two cups and bakery bag from Café Latte on the counter.

Her blood pressure skyrocketed out of control in a matter of seconds.

An intruder wouldn't have brought take out from Café Latte. This could mean only one thing...

Jack...

She groaned, yanked open the drawer, and tossed the knife inside with a clatter. Her failure to return it to its proper place—a clear sign of her distress—she slammed the door shut. Gingerly sidestepping the broken glass, she headed for Savanah's bedroom.

She came to a halt.

Are you sure you want to do this? Don't forget, ignorance is bliss.

After a slight hesitation, she called out... "Savanah?"

When there was no reply, she called out again, louder this time. "Savanah, are you here? Answer me."

When Savanah first heard her mother calling her name, she thought she'd imagined it. But the second time confirmed it was real. Eyes wide, she broke away from Jack's kiss, pushing her way out of his arms.

She was frantic. *"Oh, no, no, no...* Jack, it's my mother. Quick, you need to get up."

Not quite sure what was happening, Jack bolted upright in bed. Then, Savanah's words finally registering in his befuddled state, he groaned, slapping his forehead in frustration. "You've got to be kidding me."

This is also when he decided he'd had enough.

He dove across the bed and grabbed hold of Savanah just as her feet hit the floor. Once he pulled her back on the bed, his warning brushed right below her ear. "Oh, no you don't, I want you to stay right here while I take care of this."

His hope he'd come across more confident than he felt, he left the bed. Only to whirl around, and catching her chin in his hand, he captured her mouth in an all-consuming kiss.

One might say it was a kiss given by a man about to go into battle to fight for the woman he loved.

Which, if you were to ask Jack, was exactly what he intended.

He finally lifted his head, and satisfied with the dazed look in her eyes, his deep voice rumbled through her. "Hold on to that until I get back."

Her head spinning from the kiss—one that told her she had nothing to worry about, he would definitely be back—she fell back into the pillows and closed her eyes.

After combing his fingers through his hair, and giving a halfhearted effort to smooth the wrinkles out of his shirt, Jack headed for the kitchen. He could only pray he didn't come across as a man who, only seconds ago, had been in the midst of a passionate kiss with the woman he loved.

A woman who is also the daughter of your most formidable enemy.

He found Savanah's mother standing by the kitchen island. Arms crossed, and her mouth drawn in a thin line, she stared him down.

If he didn't know better, he'd swear she was putting some kind of curse on him. A possibility that had him tempted to run right out of the room.

Instead, his intent to maintain a show of civility between them, he jammed his hands in his pockets and sent her a big smile. "Hello, Mrs. Jackson. It appears fate has brought us together once again. If you're here to check up on Savanah, she's fine."

She ignored his greeting, waving her hand around at the broken glass. "Are you responsible for this?"

He hesitated. Then he nodded. "Yes, I guess you could say I am."

You're not lying. You rang the doorbell and startled Savanah enough to drop the vase.

She glared at him. "What do you mean, you guess? You either did, or you didn't. It's a shame, because not only was the vase expensive, it was also a family heirloom." After sending him a disgusted look, she marched over to the small kitchen pantry, yanked open the door, and pulled out a broom and dustpan.

He cleared his throat. "I will be more than happy to re-place it. You only need to let me know what kind it is." When she ignored this, he moved closer, carefully approaching her as one would confronting a wild animal. "Why don't you let me clean up the broken glass? It's the least I can do."

She shook her head, mumbling something he couldn't hear as she began swinging the broom around like a hockey player after a bad call. Rather than take the chance of getting hit by fragments of flying glass —or possibly, even the broom—he backed off.

The glass swept up and thrown in the trash, she tossed the broom and dustpan back in the closet. Avoiding his gaze, she then skirted around him to get to the fireplace.

She grabbed her glasses from the mantle. After she dropped them into her coat pocket, she sent Jack a curt nod. "I accidentally left my glasses when I was here earlier. Now that I have them, I'll check in on Savanah, say hello, and then I'll be off."

She sent him a pointed look. "I take it you will also be leaving soon?"

As this might send her over the edge, Jack resisted the urge to share that he was thinking of staying the night. Instead, he smiled. "That all depends on Savanah. Since she's still dealing with the effects of her concussion, my concern is that nothing sabotages her recovery."

Feeling extremely proud of how he evaded the question, he sent her another smile.

Her eyebrows shot up. "*Humph...* so now you consider yourself a doctor, too?"

He shrugged. "Oh no, ma'am... I'm far from a doctor. But I love Savanah and I will protect her however I can."

She cringed at his choice of words.

Love? Did this man even know what love was? There's no doubt he's confused it with lust.

She gave a frustrated sigh. His unwavering confidence, shown by the way he referred to Savanah as though she was his private property, had her even more determined to check on her.

Then maybe you can knock some sense into her. Concussion, or no concussion.

But before she could make a move, the front door slowly opened. Doreen peeked inside, a relieved look on her face when she saw Savanah's mother.

"Cora? Is everything all right? You said you'd only be a few minutes, but it's been longer than that. So, I thought I'd better check—"

Her words came to an abrupt halt at the sight of Jack. Giggling like a schoolgirl and fluffing up her hear, she turned back to Savanah's mother. "My goodness, Cora... who is this handsome young man? Now I understand why you had no interest in pairing my Jimmy up with Savanah."

She sent Jack a coy smile. "With a man like you, I'm sure she has more than enough to handle."

She peered more closely at him. "You seem very familiar to me. I swear I know you from somewhere. *Hmm...* let me think about this."

Finding her a bit intimidating, Jack took a step back, shaking his head. "I'm sorry, I don't believe we've met. As I'm sure I'd remember if we had." This the most he planned to give her, he softened it with a smile.

Before Doreen started asking Jack a million questions about things that were none of her business, Cora grabbed her arm and herded her over to the door. There she turned to get one more scowl in at Jack. "Please inform Savanah that I will be stopping by to check on her."

With Doreen protesting their sudden departure, she slammed the door behind them.

Jack could hear the two women arguing even before they got to the car. Once he heard them drive away, he'd locked the door.

He turned to go back to Savanah, only to find her standing right behind him. He wrapped his arms around her, and after pressing a kiss in her hair, he chuckled. "Did that just really happen?"

Her mouth twisted in a wry smile. "Unfortunately, it did. But maybe leaving without a fight is a sign my mother's opinion of you is changing for the better?"

He raised an eyebrow.

She frowned. "Jack, I'm serious."

His voice was gentle. "*Oh, love...* I know you are, yet..." He dropped a kiss to her mouth instead. "And who was the woman with her?"

"That's Doreen. She and my mother met while volunteering at a local consignment shop. I think my mother hangs around with her because she always knows the latest gossip."

"*Hmm...*" His fingers sifting through the silkiness of her hair, he couldn't tell you a single word she said.

Even without a hint of make up on her face, dressed in pink flannel pajama pants and a plain white tee shirt, he found her breathtakingly beautiful, so utterly desirable.

Her soft curves fit perfectly against his masculine frame as she clung to him, holding on as if she never intended to let go. Her eyes sparkled like the brightest of stars, her parted lips an unspoken invitation for a kiss.

And her scent—a sultry mix of vanilla and floral, with a hint of musk—flooded his senses until he couldn't even think straight.

All of this, hitting him all at once?

Never before had he felt such an overwhelming rush of emotions—this desperate ache for Savanah consuming his every thought.

And if he were to be honest?

This sort of scared the hell out of him.

"Jack? Are you going to answer me?"

He blinked. For a moment, he stared at her as he struggled to recall what they had been talking about. Then, with an almost goofy smile on his face, he shrugged. "I'm sorry, you've got me so bewitched, I didn't catch a single word you said."

The color rising in her cheeks at his unwavering scrutiny, she stumbled over her response. "I simply asked why you told my mother that you broke the vase. There was no need for you to take the blame." She shrugged. "And if I'm not mistaken, she just recently bought the vase from HomeGoods. I don't think that qualifies as being a family heirloom."

He gathered her closer before pressing a kiss in her hair. "She's already decided nothing I do will ever be right. So, let her believe I'm the guilty one. And if you think about it, if I hadn't rung the doorbell, you wouldn't have dropped the vase."

He released his hold, glancing over at the kitchen. "Speaking of vases, we need to get the flowers in one before they die. I also brought coffee and scones if you're hungry."

She smiled up at him. "Since my dinner is still in the microwave, that sounds wonderful. After the vase broke, I forgot all about it." She sighed, massaging her forehead. "This might explain the headache I have."

"Vanababe, that's not good." His stern expression enough to make her feel guilty, she let him lead her over to the kitchen island, where he pointed to a stool. "I want you to stay put while I fix you something to eat."

Remember what he told her mother? He loved Savanah and would protect her in every way he could.

He had never been more serious.

CHAPTER 43

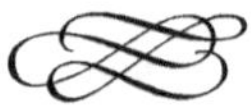

Don't panic, every roadblock has a detour.
~ Anonymously Yours

Jack's Friday morning started out on the wrong note the moment he opened his eyes. Feeling as though he'd only just fallen asleep, he checked his phone for the time.

9:00 a.m.

This had him diving out of bed, dragging his hands through his hair as he tried to get his bearings. He couldn't remember the last time he'd overslept. This was something he just didn't do.

He picked up his phone to check the time again.

9:01 a.m.

It didn't take long for him to figure out he'd set his alarm for 8:00 p.m. instead of 8:00 a.m.

He blamed this on a lack of sleep. Wide awake after he left Savanah a little after midnight, he had flipped through the TV channels, searching for something to watch. Or better yet, something to put him to sleep. He'd settled on the movie Erin Brockovich, the credits rolling down the screen before he finally turned off the TV and fell into bed.

Only to fall into a restless sleep, left feeling like he hadn't slept at all.

He checked the time again, if only to make sure.

9:03 a.m.

He should already be in his client's office for their nine o'clock meeting. However, as this was at least a twenty-minute drive, even if he threw on the first clothes he could find, and drove like a maniac, he'd still be about a half hour late.

Not the best way to make a favorable first impression.

After sending a text he was on his way, he got dressed, did a quick comb through his hair, and was out the door in less than five minutes. Only to be held up in traffic for another fifteen minutes because of a main line water leak.

Fortunately, he was able to convince his client he had his best interests at heart and there would be no more delays. And from that point on, his day improved. Even with a quick stop at the studio, he still finished up earlier than expected.

Now, out of the shower and towel drying his hair, all he could think about, all that mattered, was how in less than an hour he would be with Savanah.

His hair finally dried, and careful not to overdo the cologne, he got dressed. After one last glance in the mirror, satisfied with what his final look, he flipped off the bathroom mirror and headed for the kitchen.

It was 5:26 p.m.

If he left now, he would be early.

You've already been late once today, so why not switch it up and go for early?

Keys in hand, he headed for the door.

"Okay, I will call you Sunday morning. Love you, too."

Savanah ended the call with her mother and set her phone down on the bed. Sitting in the early evening silence, she tried to process the conversation they just shared

What are you going to do?

A car door slammed. Her heartbeat accelerating at the thought it might be Jack, she jumped up from the bed and hurried over to the window. Only to watch her neighbor start up her car and drive away.

She turned, her glance falling on the large box shoved in the corner of the room. Inside was over twenty years of memorabilia, all to do with ballet. Photos, programs, costumes, hair accessories, and all the other little things she'd collected along the way. There were even a few once vibrant bouquets, the flowers now dry to the touch, the ribbons faded.

She'd be willing to bet almost every pair of ballet slippers she'd ever owned were also in the mix.

Her mother had suggested she add shelves to display her most memorable items.

She had also asked if you planned to paint the walls pink. After all, your bedroom had been pink for as long as you can remember.

Savanah had shot down both suggestions. She planned to put the box in storage and went with a soft spring green—Ocean Mist—for the walls. She loved the sense of peace it gave her when she walked into the room.

However, not today. After the call she received from her mother? She needed more than a soothing shade of paint to calm her.

You need Jack…

She glanced over at the note he'd left, still on the pillow next to hers. When opening her eyes earlier this morning, it was the first thing she saw.

She'd read it so many times, she had it memorized.

Good morning, beautiful,

I woke in the early morning hours with you sleeping like an angel beside me. And even though the temptation to wake you with a kiss was almost too hard to ignore, I let you sleep.

But you can bet I'll collect on that kiss later.

I'll pick you up tonight around six for the rehearsal dinner. Afterward, I'd like to take you home with me, if only so I can hold you in my arms a little longer this time.

Keep me in your heart, as yours is always in mine.

Love, Jack.

Despite shaking her head, she couldn't contain her smile
If he keeps writing notes like this, you don't stand a chance…
She glanced over at the clock on the nightstand.

5:27 p.m.

This meant she had about a half hour to do her make-up, style her hair and get dressed. She'd decide later on what to do about the call from her mother.

After a long stretch, she headed for the bathroom.

Savanah took one last look in the mirror.

A touch of blush, a hint of burnished gold eyeshadow, two coats of mascara, and a light dusting of bronzing powder was her only makeup.

Her decision to wear her hair down, after only a few minutes with her curling iron, it now fell in soft waves over her shoulders.

The dress she chose to wear wasn't new, yet remained one of her favorites. Fitted, and falling right below the knee, the fabric was a rich burgundy brocade with a delicate raised floral pattern. The modest scooped neckline and three-quarter length sleeves were simple, yet elegant in design. Because of her injured arm, she couldn't pull the zipper all the way up on the dress. So, her plan was to enlist Jack's help when he arrived.

Her only jewelry was a fine gold chain with a teardrop garnet pendant and matching earrings she inherited from her grandmother.

Unfortunately, the reflection staring back at her showed her worried expression, not the excitement she'd hoped for.

Maybe a bright shade of lipstick would help?

After rummaging through the small basket of lipsticks on the bathroom vanity, she chose Forever My Love. It wasn't quite lipstick, more of a sheer gloss, but it always made her feel beautiful, boosting her confidence.

She stared down at the lipstick in her hand. Then she closed her eyes, a frustrated sigh escaping her.

You need more than a bright shade of lipstick to quell your inner turmoil.

What had she been thinking? She should've ignored the call when she saw her mother's name on the caller I.D. And yes, she understood her mother's need to call her right away to share such exciting news. If this had happened a month ago, she would be just as ecstatic.

But now?

She wasn't sure how she felt.

And Jack… what would he have to say about this?

Perhaps she should wait until after Stephanie and Evan's wedding to tell him?

She applied a coat of lipstick, and after studying the effect in the mirror, she nodded, her mind made up.

You'll tell him on Sunday. Tonight it will be only about you and him.

Now having settled on a plan, she turned off the bathroom light and headed for the kitchen to wait for Jack.

CHAPTER 44

*J*ack sprinted up the steps to Savanah's front door and hit the doorbell. As he waited, he gazed up at the sky.

A chilly March night, there wasn't a cloud in sight. This made it hard to believe the forecast for Stephanie and Evan's wedding tomorrow called for rain all day.

Hopefully, they were wrong.

He flicked a piece of lint from his sleeve. Then he cleared his throat. He was about to hit the doorbell again when Savanah opened the door.

He smiled. *"Hi…"*

"Hi…"

For a very brief moment, their eyes held. The first to look away, she stepped aside so he could come in.

Jack's smile had disappeared.

He'd be a fool not to know something was wrong. Unsettling thoughts racing through his mind, he watched as, still avoiding his gaze, she closed the door.

Savanah knew she was in trouble.

Hiding her emotions had never been her strong suit. And this was even more true with Jack. One look into his eyes, and she'd either burst into tears or start rambling, making no sense.

After tucking her hair behind her ears, she went with the latter, her words flowing non-stop. "You're early. But that's probably a good thing since it's Friday. You know how crazy the traffic is with everyone in a rush to start their weekend."

After sending him a glance that was so fleeting he almost missed it, she nervously ran her hands down the skirt of her dress before she spoke. "It's okay, though. I'm ready. At least as ready as I can be, since I couldn't do the zipper or fasten the hooks on the back of my dress with one hand." She shrugged. "So, I might need your help."

He opened his mouth to respond, but she didn't give him a chance. "You probably noticed I'm not wearing the cast. I wanted to take a shower, and it's impossible to wrap it good enough so it doesn't get wet."

She knew there was no reason to share all this with him, but she couldn't seem to stop. "I know I've only had to wear it for little over a week, but I can't wait until I can keep it off for good."

More concerned about her agitated state than the state of her dress —or that she'd removed her cast—Jack slowly inched his way over to her. He wanted to take her into his arms, shower her with kisses and tell her whatever had her so upset, he would make it right, But he decided it might be best to take it slow'

Giving her a reassuring smile, he brushed a stray curl back from her face. "Vanababe… even if you're not zipped and hooked up, you look absolutely amazing. If you turn around, I'll get you all fixed up. Then we'll put your cast back on before something happens."

She started to back away, a stricken look on her face. "You're right. It's in my bedroom. Let me go get it."

He grabbed her hand, turning her to face him. "Hey, that can wait. Instead, I want you to tell me what's going on. What's wrong? Whatever it is, you can tell me."

Drawn in by the tenderness in his gaze, when she took a step towards him, he saw this as an invitation to take her into his arms. Only to grow even more concerned when she remained rigid in his embrace.

He pulled her close, his soft murmur falling in her ear. "Let me in, love… it can't be that bad."

It can't be that bad?

She had a feeling he'd think differently when she told him about her mother's latest plan.

And now, her intention to wait until Sunday to tell him no longer seemed right.

You can't do that to him. It's only fair you let him know.

Her forehead pressed to his chest, she closed her eyes and took a deep breath before she spoke. "I've been invited to audition for the Seattle Dance Company."

He stilled, the kiss he was about to press in her hair coming to an abrupt halt.

"Seattle?" He pulled back, searching her face. "When did this all come about? And why Seattle, of all places?"

Then he nodded. "*Ah...* is this your way of dealing with what happened with Léon?" He shook his head. "Running away isn't the answer, love."

She pulled away, her eyes flashing a warning. "I'm not running away. This would be a promotion. My mother was able to—"

His harsh laugh cutting in, at the same time, he dropped his hands from her and took a step back. "*Ah, ha...* so your mother is behind this. Why am I not surprised?" Gazing heavenward, he groaned in frustration. "*My, God...* will she stop at nothing to keep us apart?"

Torn between defending her mother, yet understanding his frustration, she said nothing, leading to an uneasy silence between them.

Then she sighed. "Jack, she only wants what's best for me. If I want to pursue a career in dance, I have to take advantage of every chance I'm given. No matter where it takes me."

"And the further away from you, the better, it seems." Muttering this under his breath, he jammed his hands in his pockets and walked over to the windows, his back to her. His vision blurring, he blinked.

You need to calm down.

However, this was getting old. With no sign of a compromise in sight, he wondered if he'd been caught up in battle he'd forever have to fight, a war he'd never win.

You were so confident you and Savanah had overcome the odds. But with your track record, this doesn't come as a surprise.

"Jack?"

When he turned to see Savanah was watching him, he dragged his hand back through his hair, exhaling a long, drawn-out sigh. "When is this audition scheduled to take place?"

She had wrapped her arms around herself, her reply a whisper. "We leave on Monday. The flight, hotel… everything is all set up."

Eyebrow raised, he held her gaze. "We?"

"My mother and me." She held up her injured arm. "Because of this, she made plans to go with me."

For a long moment, he studied her, his expression unreadable, before he nodded. "*Ah…* of course she did." Shaking his head, a short laugh escaped him. "How generous of her. She certainly didn't waste any time, did she?"

"*Jack…*" Her brow creased as a wave of unease swept through her.

He shoved his hands back in his pockets. "Savanah, come on. You have to agree she's done just about everything she could to keep us apart. This is proof she has no plans to stop."

Even though she didn't like the direction the conversation was headed, she knew she had to say something. "My mother is the only family I have. And she's devoted her life to helping me get to this point in my career. I'm sure it wasn't easy to set up the audition, so the least I can do is check out what they have to offer."

Then she ruined it, her next words coming out more accusing than she intended. "Jack, I have to do this. I don't have a choice. Nor am I as brave as you, just leaving your home and father behind to go out on your own. I could never do that to my mother."

As soon as these words came out of her mouth, she knew she'd made a mistake. A pained expression on her face, her hand went to her mouth. "*Jack…* what I meant, is—"

He held up his hand to stop her. "No, there is no need to explain. You're right, family is very important. Believe me, there have been many times over the past years I've wished things were different."

His eyes drifted back to the window; where he watched as a couple walked by, holding hands before they shared a kiss. A fleeting expression of pain crossing his face at this, he turned back to Savanah. Again he studied her, his look searching.

Then he shrugged, a hint of resignation in the gesture. "I thought we had something special, a connection most people can only dream about. Instead, the longer we're together, the harder I have to fight for every moment with you. And it's only getting worse."

Her head jerked up at his words.

Had? You 'had' something special?

A sudden chill running down her spine, she shivered, hugging herself tighter for warmth. The desperation in her voice was unmistakable. "Jack, we do share something special...you have to know how much you mean to me. Yet you're not being fair. What is it you want me to do? Give up my passion for dance? Turn my back on my own mother?"

His expression softened. *"Oh, Vanababe...* I would never ask you to do either of those. I think you should do only what you want to do, not what you think others expect of you." He hesitated before his next words. "And until you figure out what that is, it might be better if I wasn't around."

Speechless, Savanah could only stare at him. She didn't understand. Just like that? He was going to walk out of her life?

Taking her silence as a sign she agreed, his voice became choked with emotion when he finally spoke. "Maybe I've asked too much from you, too fast. But this is only because I've never been so sure of anything in my life. And this will never change."

A wry smile twisted his lips as he shrugged. "But I need to know you're on my side. And right now—" He paused, a flicker of bewilderment crossing his face. "I really don't think you are."

All this coming at her with no warning, she couldn't think. Instead, she let her emotions get the best of her, the words flying out of her mouth. "If this is what you think, evidently you don't know me at all. So, you're right... it might be best if you left."

He groaned, taking a step in her direction. "Vanababe, I..."

Wrapping her arms around herself, she took a step back, shaking her head. "Please, you should leave."

In what felt like the longest journey of his life, Jack walked over to the door. His hand on the doorknob, he turned to her. He had to close his eyes at the stunned look on her face, her eyes bright with the tears he knew would fall as soon as he left.

He opened his mouth to say something, only to close it.

Just leave. Hell, you don't want to make things worse.

Before he opened the door, he waited for her to say something…anything. He'd take anything.

She was silent.

His smile bittersweet, the rough tone of his voice spoke volumes. "I hope you find what you want in Seattle. I wish you the best."

He slipped outside, softly closing the door behind him.

Savanah was in shock.

He would change his mind, right? Surely, after he thought it over, he'd realize how wrong he was.

She stared at the door, willing it to open. If they were living the perfect love story, this would be the part when the door would fly open, with Jack bursting back into the room. After taking her into his arms, he'd insist he hadn't meant a word he said, his emotional reaction only because her news was so unexpected.

He'd then assure her she'd be a fool not to check out what the dance company had to offer. And if it turned out to be what she wanted? He would support her decision.

Their differences aside, they would kiss, and everything would be as it should.

But this didn't happen.

No matter how hard she stared at the door, it remained closed.

Instead, she heard his truck start up. She rushed over to the window and watched as he backed halfway out of the parking space before coming to a stop.

Perhaps he changed his mind?

She held her breath, waiting. Instead, she could only watch as, with an almost angry roar of the engine, he drove away. And even after his truck had disappeared from view, she continued to stand by the window, hoping for a miracle.

Unfortunately, it appeared her time for miracles had ended.

Consumed with a crushing sadness, she wandered over to the sofa and sank into the cushions.

She shook her head. This wasn't happening. Jack couldn't have meant what he said.

Then, in a complete turnabout, she was furious. Hadn't he told her he loved her? When you love someone, you want what's best for them, right? He had to see this opportunity in Seattle could be her chance at becoming a principal dancer. A goal she'd worked for so long.

She stood, pacing the room. Coming to a stop, she closed her eyes.

You haven't been entirely truthful with yourself, have you?

Which also meant she hadn't been honest with Jack.

She walked over to the window to search the parking lot one last time.

Other than a man walking his dog, it was a quiet night, not a soul in sight.

This is when it finally hit her—he wasn't coming back.

And now, nothing felt right.

CHAPTER 45

Where there is food, there is love,
~ Unknown

The bells were ringing the quarter hour when Jack turned into the church parking lot.

He pulled into the space next to Jason's SUV and turned off the ignition.

There were quite a few cars in the lot, which didn't surprise him. He knew how Stephanie had agonized over the guest list. So, in order to avoid any hurt feelings, she had invited almost as many people to the rehearsal dinner as she had to the actual wedding.

A sudden thought occurred to him… what if she invited the fast-talking Dr. Davis?

For God's sake, forget about him. You've got more important things to worry about right now.

He leaned back in his seat and closed his eyes. His mind was running all over the place, reliving every moment, every word he and Savanah just shared.

Twice he'd nearly turned his truck around and driven back to Savanah's condo. In his mind, he had it all planned out—he wouldn't even knock. He'd just walk right in and tell her they needed to talk.

Then he'd keep them talking—for as long as it took, all night if necessary—until they figured it all out and they were back to the way they were.

Tapping his fingers on the steering wheel, a habit of his when he was worried about something, he groaned, dragging his hand down over his jaw.

Jack Buchanan, you are a fool. You gave the woman you love an ultimatum and then walked out on her. You've possibly messed up the best thing that ever happened to you.

A raindrop hit the windshield. Enough to galvanize him into action, he got out of the truck, hit the lock button, and took off in a sprint for the main entrance to the church.

He had no plans to stay, only to give Stephanie a brief explanation of what had happened. Then he would leave.

He had a lot of thinking to do.

They were finishing up with the rehearsal when Evan leaned over to whisper in Stephanie's ear. "Jack sent a text. He's in the vestibule and needs to talk to you. He also said he's alone. I thought he was bringing Savanah?"

"*Oh, no...* he was. I wonder what happened?" She put her hand on his arm. "I'm going to see what's going on. In the meantime, can you make sure everyone knows where Jake's Place is? And if they need a ride?" She pressed a kiss to his cheek. "I won't be long, I promise."

"*Hmm...* I'm going to hold you to that." A resigned smile on his face, he watched as she walked over to Jack. He was so looking forward to their honeymoon when he would have her all to himself.

But right now, he had a crowd of hungry people on his hands. He turned to see everyone was putting on their coats, getting ready to leave.

Rubbing his hands together, he raised his voice to get their attention. "I don't know about you, but I'm starving. So, Jake's Place, here we come. Who needs directions? Or a ride?"

Five minutes later, everyone accounted for and on their way to the restaurant, Evan settled in the front pew to wait for Stephanie.

His guess was another ten, fifteen minutes, just enough to get in a cat nap.

A smile passing over his lips, he closed his eyes.

After exchanging a hug, Stephanie gave Jack a big smile. "I'm so glad you made it. We just finished up. Now we can only hope it goes just as well tomorrow. Now everyone is heading to Jake's for dinner."

He nodded. "I see that. It looks like you have everything under control. My apologies for being late."

"That's okay." She glanced around them. "Where's Savanah? You didn't come together?"

Together? Remember this is what you told Savanah… you could make this happen? That didn't last long, did it?

He exhaled, his breath leaving him in a long sigh. "No, we didn't." Then he shrugged. "Unfortunately, I don't think we'll be seeing her tonight. And I'm not sure about tomorrow. We'd made plans to meet at the church in time for the ceremony. Hopefully, this still stands."

Slowly sitting in the pew, Stephanie gazed up at him. "*Oh, no…* that can't happen. Not after what—" She drew in a sharp breath, pressing her lips together. Again, she wasn't good at keeping secrets.

She sent Jack a tentative smile. "Do you want to talk about it?"

Talk about it?

Starting with what a fool you are? And how you might have lost the best thing you ever had?

He wasn't sure this was a good idea.

But one look at her concerned expression, it all came spilling out. "As soon as I saw Savanah, I knew something was wrong. She wouldn't even look at me."

He had no intention of telling her that Savanah turned her head in order to avoid his kiss. This was still too difficult for him to even think about

Dragging his hand through his hair, . "It turns out her mother sent her resume to a ballet company in Seattle. When they invited Savanah to audition, she made flight and hotel reservations for her and Savanah. The audition is Monday."

Stephanie raised an eyebrow. "Seattle? Why Seattle?"

"I looked up the company online. They're a larger operation than Cleveland's, with a very generous fan base. So, they're always on the hunt for new talent."

He abruptly came to his feet, his jaw tight with anger. *"My God…* will the woman not stop at anything to keep us apart? I thought she was coming around as she's kept a pretty low profile since Savanah's been home. Never did I suspect this."

Stephanie was shaking her head. "I don't understand. Savanah doesn't want to go to Seattle. She told me how happy she is here. And I know this is mostly because of you."

He sent her a wry smile. "I thought the same. Unfortunately, it appears we're both wrong."

Her brow furrowed, Stephanie was silent. Then she glanced over at him. "Did Savanah know her mother sent her resume?"

"I didn't ask. Only because if she did, I knew I'd have a hard time accepting she'd kept it from me. It was when she said her mother might be right, it made sense to see what Seattle had to offer, I lost it. I told her until she figured out what she wanted, it might be best if I wasn't around."

He shrugged. "Then she suggested I should leave. So, I did. And that's where we stand."

He groaned. His hands shoved in his pockets, he shook his head. "What am I doing? I shouldn't even be telling you this. Not now, with your wedding tomorrow. Don't worry, I'll figure it out."

Stephanie was furious.

Jack didn't deserve this—and neither did Savanah.

She stood, and placing her hand on his arm, her anger came through in her voice. "Savanah's not going anywhere. I don't know how, but we're going to fix this."

Then she gave him a bright smile. "But now? You're right. We have a rehearsal dinner waiting for us. And I'm starving." She laughed. "I heard Evan's stomach growling during the rehearsal, so I know he's hungry, too."

Jack hesitated. "I think it might be better if I bowed out."

He held up his hand as she began to protest. "No, you don't need my long face ruining your dinner."

A sheepish smile on his face, he shrugged. "To be honest, I came here hoping Savanah had come on her own. But after the words we exchanged, I can understand why she hasn't. But why should she? I didn't even give her a chance to defend herself. It's only…"

His words trailing off, for a few moments, they were both silent.

She smiled up at him. "Don't worry, The two of you will sort this out. In the meantime, you still have to eat. So, come to dinner with us. Please? I'll feel so much better if you do."

He frowned, massaging the back of his neck, .

Remember? This night is about Stephanie and Evan. Not about your messed up love life. So, get it together.

Offering his hand to help her out of the pew, he smiled. "Okay, for you, I'll stay."

She gave him a quick hug. "Thank you. It wouldn't be the same without you."

He pulled out his keys and turned to leave. "I'll meet you there."

She smiled. "Is that a promise?"

"Yes, I'll be there, scout's honor."

Stephanie slid into the pew next to Evan.

He opened his eyes, his arm going around her. "Well... hello there, beautiful. Is everything okay? "

She sighed, resting her head on his shoulder. "I guess that will depend on how much they love each other."

She gazed up at him. "Can we sit here for a few minutes? I have a feeling we won't have much alone time over the next twenty-four hours. So, we should enjoy this time while we can."

"Hmm... sounds like an excellent plan to me."

He pressed a kiss to the top of her head. "Have I told you how much I love you, Stephanie Bennett—soon to be Stephanie Marshall?"

He chuckled. "Just think, by this time tomorrow, you'll be stuck with me forever."

As he leaned in for a kiss, the love she could see shining in his eyes had her even more determined to get Jack and Savanah back together again. They deserved a love like she and Evan had.

Her head on his shoulder, they sat in the silence, breathing in the comforting smell of incense, mesmerized by the flickering votives on the altar. A moment they both needed during this hectic time, a blessing of their love.

When Evan's stomach growled, the sound magnified in the deserted church, Stephanie reluctantly rose to her feet, pulling him up with her.

She was laughing. "It sounds like you need nourishment. Come on, I'm hungry, too. I'll fill you in about Jack and Savanah on the drive to Jake's."

With the long list of wedding activities scheduled early the next morning, the rehearsal dinner ended at an early hour.

And much to Jack's relief, his brief response of an unexpected conflict seemed to satisfy any inquiries regarding Savanah's absence.

Even before he left the restaurant, a scheme had already taken shape in his mind. Now, waiting to turn out of the parking lot, he glanced at the dashboard.

8:39 p.m. Still early enough to put it into action.

Fifteen minutes later, he parked his truck in front of a small brick bungalow. The address, 310 Buckeye Trail, was clearly visible on the plaque above the front door. Encouraged by the lights shining from the windows, he got out of his truck. Before he could change his mind, he took off in a brisk walk to the front door.

Hands deep in his pockets, he turned, staring out at the street. Besides the distant sound of a dog barking, the neighborhood had settled into a peaceful silence. Hoping to take advantage of this moment, he drew in a huge breath, exhaling just as slowly.

He knew this was a gamble, but he had to try something, anything.

What's that famous quote again?

Fight for the one you love?

That's exactly what he was about to do.

A car came down the street. When it slowed as it passed by, he pressed the doorbell. The last thing he needed was someone calling the police to report him for trespassing.

Savanah's mother would love that, wouldn't she?

There was no answer, so he rang the doorbell again.

This time, the porch light went on, followed by the clicks of at least three locks. Clearing his throat, he pasted a smile on his face.

He was as ready as he'd ever be.

Cora Jackson had been in a restless mood ever since her phone call with Savanah about the Seattle audition. For one of the few times in her life, she wondered if she'd handled everything all wrong. Everything being Savanah and this Jack she was so crazy about.

This feeling of doubt so unlike her, she was frowning as she plopped into her recliner.

She turned on the TV and scrolling through the channels, finding nothing of interest, she turned it off. She set the remote in the basket with her current knitting project, a pink baby blanket. She planned to give it to the young pregnant girl who recently started working part time at the consignment store.

She maneuvered her way out of the recliner to get a drink of water from the kitchen. Once she was back in the recliner, she pulled out the baby blanket and added two more rows before tossing it back in the basket.

She turned on the TV, then turned it off again.

She picked up the blanket again. Working at a furious pace, she added another row before she realized she'd skipped a stitch. She ripped out the row, folded up the blanket, and stuffed it back into the basket.

Maybe a cup of tea was in order?

In the kitchen, her tea basket in front of her, she was pondering her options when the doorbell rang.

She glanced over at the clock above the kitchen sink. It was a little past nine. Wondering who would be stopping by at this late hour, she grabbed her phone to check the security camera monitoring the front door.

"Dammit..."

This was the second time in less than a week she'd sworn out loud, all thanks to the man now standing on her front steps.

Jack Buchanan...

Well, whatever he had to say, she wasn't interested.

He rang the doorbell again. Now beyond irritated, and her most intimidating frown in place, she marched across the room. After she undid the three locks—and yes, she knew this was to the extreme, but one can never be too safe—she yanked open the door.

For a very long, tense-filled moment, neither said a word.

Relieved she hadn't slammed the door, or worse yet, began accusing him of every crime in the book, Jack was the first to speak. His gaze unwavering, he smiled. "Mrs. Jackson, I hope I'm not stopping by too late."

He paused, taking a deep breath before his next words. "I think we need to talk."

This was followed by another long and uncomfortable silence, this one even longer.

Finally, after a very long and dramatic sigh, she stepped back and waved him inside.

It was a start…

Forty-five minutes later, Jack stepped into the elevator of his condo building and hit the button for the tenth floor. He looked down at the two banana muffins on the plate he was holding.

Yeah, some might only see them as muffins, but to you? They're as good as gold…

Closing his eyes, he chuckled.

Baked goods seemed to play a big part in his relationship with Savanah. Who would've thought? First the scones, and now these muffins.

As he was leaving, Savanah's mother had insisted he take the muffins with him. They were her own prize winning recipe and a cure-all for everything, she told him.

Curious, he pulled back a corner of the plastic wrap covering the muffins, broke off a small piece, and popped it into his mouth.

"Hmm… not bad." He could definitely taste the banana. Prize winning? He could agree with this. Though a sour cherry scone would always be his first choice of favorites.

Maybe it's true what they say? Feeding someone is a way of showing your love?

Sounded good to him. He'd be more than happy to believe the muffins had worked their magic, a truce now in place.

He polished off the rest of the muffin on the way to his condo.

He had one more task to complete.

But this could wait until morning.

CHAPTER 46

*J*ack set his coffee cup back on the counter. From where he sat, he had a good view out the window.

It wasn't looking good.

All morning, angry clouds had been hovering over the lake, hinting at the threat of rain. It appeared the weather forecast for Stephanie and Evan's wedding day was turning out to be everything they said it would be.

However, it was still early, only a little past nine. So, things could change.

He picked up his phone. The number he'd punched in—at least a half hour ago, maybe even longer—was still on the screen. One swipe of his finger and the call would go through.

So, just do it.

He tossed the phone back on the counter. Dragging his hand back through his hair, he groaned.

This is ridiculous. What do you think is going to happen? You're not a kid anymore, you're a grown man.

A very successful man, by the way. Living the life he'd always envisioned. With the woman of his dreams.

Well, maybe things were a little shaky with that part of his life right now, but…

He jumped up and, grabbing the coffeepot, re-filled his cup. One thing at a time, he needed to get back some of that energy and confidence he had last night after his talk with Savanah's mother.

He took a drink of coffee, and drumming his fingers on the counter, he glanced over at the phone.

Just pick up the damn phone and call him. For all you know, he might not even answer.

In one quick move, he pressed send. The connection made, he set the phone on speaker mode and set it back on the counter.

His heart pounding in his chest, he waited.

After three rings, and a silence that seemed to go on forever, a voice he remembered so well came over the line.

"Hello?"

This single greeting transported Jack back in time, an image of his father flooding his mind. He could see him, seated at his desk with the usual stack of papers in front of him. At the sound of Jack's hesitant knock, he'd wave him in, regardless of what he was working on.

This had been Jack's favorite place to be when he wasn't playing the piano. With the sound of his father's voice as he talked on the phone, a comforting presence in the background, he'd do his homework. Or simply take the time to recharge after a sometimes challenging day at school.

Despite his father's gruff exterior, and busy schedule, he'd always made him feel welcome.

And now, it wasn't until this exact moment he realized how badly he needed that feeling back in his life, how desperately he wanted to recapture those cherished memories. The happy times—and even the ordinary moments—before his mother and sister's deaths.

And this phone call could be the first step in making this a reality.

He swallowed. "Dad… it's me, Jack." His voice coming out all gruff, he had to clear his throat. "I'm glad you picked up. I want to thank you for sending the piano. I… well, I can't tell you how much it means to me."

After a silence that seemed to go on forever, and the long sigh that followed, his father finally responded. "Let's just say Elenore Cromley isn't one to take no for an answer. But to be fair, after thinking over what she had to say, I'll admit she was right.

He cleared his throat. She also suggested it was about time I let you know how proud I am of you. Which I am, son. More than you could ever know."

Jack barely choked out his reply. "That's all I've ever wanted. From both you and mom. If only—"

His father, sensing his emotional state, interrupted him. "I'm know your mother would say the same. So, can you forgive an old man for his stubbornness? Because I'd like to stay in touch, hear all about what I've missed over the years."

It was more than Jack had expected, as his father had never been good at apologizing. And it left him speechless. As the tension drained from his body, he settled more comfortably on the kitchen stool, glancing at his watch. "Sounds good. I've got about an hour before I have to leave for a friend's wedding."

"A wedding, huh? So, how about you? Do you have someone special in your life?"

"As a matter of fact, I do. However, I could use your help. It appears I've gone and made a mess of things. And I'm not sure how to fix it."

A loud laugh greeted this. "I don't know a man on earth that hasn't voiced those same concerns when it comes to the woman in their life. So, tell me, what did you do?"

"Dragging his hand through his hair, Jack chuckled. "Oh boy, it might be best if I started from the beginning when I stopped off at our local coffee shop and…"

It's understandable he was a little late getting to the church. Who would've thought he and his father would have so much to talk about?

Hoping to discover even a hint of blue in the overcast sky, Savanah glanced out her bedroom window. Only to find her view obscured by the large raindrops bouncing off the glass.

She sighed.

This certainly wasn't looking good.

She picked up her phone and checked the screen.

No word from Jack - no text, no message, no nothing.

With a long, weary sigh, she tossed it back onto the bed. Wandering into the great room where she'd started a fire in the fireplace earlier, she held her hands towards the flames. Comforted by the heat, she closed her eyes.

Unable to sleep, she'd tossed and turned all night, only to drift off moments before her alarm went off. That, along with constant threat of tears, left her an emotional and exhausted wreck. She couldn't stop thinking about what Jack said.

"I think you should do only what you want to do,
not what you think others expect of you. And until
you figure out what that is, it might be better if I
wasn't around."

This triggered another wave of tears.

Because he was wrong. Her life would never be better without him.

He *was* her life…

Brushing away tears with a swipe of her hand, she glanced at the microwave clock. With only thirty minutes to get ready before her ride showed up, she headed for the bathroom.

One look in the mirror—her pale complexion, along with the dark circles under her eyes—confirmed she had work to do. If she intended to win Jack over, she needed to look her very best.

She splashed her face with cold water, and set to work, applying her makeup in record time. She was adding a final coat of mascara when her doorbell rang.

The faint chance it might be Jack, her heart gave a little leap. Tossing the mascara on the vanity and giving one last check in the mirror, she hurried over to open the door.

Her heart sank.

It wasn't Jack.

Instead, without a word—and what could almost, but not quite pass as a smile—her mother brushed past her and marched inside.

Savanah closed the door, and leaning back against it, she closed her eyes.

You love your mother, but she's the last person you want to see right now.

She watched as she removed her raincoat, dripping from the rain, and drape it over a stool by the island. After she walked over to the refrigerator and took out a bottle of water, she caught sight of the fire in the fireplace.

She took a big drink of water before shaking her head. "As I've told you before, gas fireplaces can be dangerous. I hope you read the instructions?"

Savanah shrugged. "It seemed like the perfect day for a fire." Her arms crossed over her chest, she tilted her head.. "Is that why you're here, to warn me about the dangers of gas fireplaces? Because a call or text would've been just as effective and a lot less work."

Now fluffing up the throw pillows on the sofa, her mother sent her a long look. "Now there's no reason to be sarcastic. And, yes, I suppose I should've called, but this was a spur-of-the-moment decision."

Savanah laughed out loud. She didn't believe this for a moment. Her mother never did anything without a plan.

She watched as she sent another glance around the room before she nodded. "It's coming along. With a few more well thought out pieces of furniture, you should be set."

Savanah rolled her eyes. "Mother, whatever you want to say, *please*... just say it." She glanced at her watch. "My ride will be here in about fifteen minutes, and I don't want to be late for Stephanie and Evan's wedding. So, you need to make it quick."

Her mother frowned, a spark of warning in her eyes. "Is this any way to talk to your mother? I thought I raised you better than that."

A frustrated groan escaping her, Savanah began removing her robe as she headed for her bedroom. She grabbed her dress from the hanger and stepped into it. As she struggled to pull up the zipper, she realized her mother had followed her. "Do you need help?"

Savanah shook her head. "The cast can make things difficult, but I've learned to deal with it. So, no... I don't need help."

Ignoring this, her mother pulled up the zipper. After fastening the hook, she sighed. "You haven't changed a bit. You were stubborn as a child, and now you're even more headstrong as an adult."

She walked over to the nightstand and picked up a photo of a six year-old Savanah in her first professional performance. Her mouth twisting in a smile, she set it down, her eyes meeting Savanah's in the mirror. "I wish you'd take a stand with this Jack of yours instead of letting him fill your mind with foolish ideas."

Savanah whirled around. Her eyes flashing in anger, her voice carried a clear warning. "It doesn't matter what you think of Jack. I love him. In fact, I'm madly in love with him. He makes me feel safe, and so loved. When I'm sad, he makes me laugh. Or if I'm worried about something, he knows what to say to make me feel better. He is the kindest and most unselfish person I've ever known."

A wistful smile curved her mouth. "He's the best thing that's ever happened to me." She shrugged. "I would do anything for him… *anything*."

In the silence that followed, she realized how true this was. If monopolizing her life was one of Jack's 'foolish ideas' she was all for it.

Savanah frowned at her mother. "What kind of silly ideas are you talking about? That Jack loves me for who I am, not who he wants me to be? While you've been so focused on molding me into the dancer you once dreamed of becoming, you haven't seen how miserable I've been."

In the past, the shocked expression on her mother's face, would've prompted an apology. But now she couldn't seem to shut up, everything she'd kept bottled up, coming out all at once.

She let out a long sigh, her voice softening. "Mother, you know as well as I do that there are so many dancers who are more talented than me. No matter how hard I push to get to the top, there will be someone waiting to overtake me."

She shook her head. "Don't worry, I'm not giving up dance. I just need to go about it differently. "

A wistful smile curved her lips. "I want to teach beginning dance— those early days when the students are wide-eyes and enchanted by it all. The ballet slippers, costumes, recitals, everything." She shrugged. "I want to make a difference, use what I learned to inspire others."

Her mother sank down on the bed. This told Savanah she was out of her element. How many times had she been told beds were to be used for sleeping, not sitting? This was what chairs were for.

She ran her hand over the quilt, an actual smile on her face when she gazed up at Savanah. "Your grandmother made this quilt. She gave it to me when I got married. At the time, I never thought it would last longer than my marriage."

Unsure of what she was leading up to with this last comment,

Savanah sent her a warning glance in the mirror. "A quick reminder, the time is now down to eight minutes."

A frown settled back on her mother's face. "I had an unexpected visitor last night. Jack came to see me after he left the rehearsal dinner. But I imagine you're already aware of this. Tell me, was this something the two of you planned, hoping to win me over?"

Turning from the mirror, Savanah stared at her. "Jack? My Jack? When? And no, I knew nothing about this."

A pained expression on her face, her mother nodded. "Yes, 'your Jack' told me you argued because of the interview I arranged with the Seattle dance company."

Savanah sat next to her mother on the bed, ignoring her frown. Creasing her dress before she even left the house was another no-no in her mother's rule book of life.

She peered over at her mother. "And what else did Jack have to say?"

Her mother frowned. "Unfortunately, a lot more than I wanted to hear. However, some of what he said—not everything, mind you— might be right. It's possible I've been a little overbearing."

Savanah rolled her eyes. "A little? Mother, it seems the older I get, the more controlling you are."

Her mother gave her a long, piercing look—one that, when Savanah was younger, warned a lecture was inevitable.

After a huffy sigh, it appeared this still held true. "I want you to listen to me. It was because of a man I quit dance. His name was Robert Danzier."

She stared into space for a moment, then sighed, shaking her head. "He was so handsome. Every dancer in the city, maybe even in the country, was infatuated with him. So, when he singled me out, I was ecstatic. I fell madly in love, foolishly believing his promises meant he felt the same."

She shrugged. "Less than a year after we met, with no warning, he left. He joined another dance company and replaced me with a woman from a fourth-generation family of dancers. I'm sure he thought this would guarantee him a permanent place among the elite of the ballet world."

After a few moments of silence, she continued. "When I discovered

I wasn't the only dancer he discarded to advance his career, I filed a report against him. An investigation followed, and, they banned him from all the top studios. But this meant my reputation was also questioned. The stress was unbearable—I. I couldn't walk into the studio without having an anxiety attack, let alone dance. So, I decided to take a break."

She shrugged. "We both know a break in the dance world is an enormous risk. As you pointed out, there's always someone younger, more talented, waiting to take your place.

So, my career as a dancer ended almost before it had begun."

"I'm sorry that happened to you," Savanah said, resting her hand on her mother's. To her surprise, she didn't pull away, unusual for a woman who'd never welcomed any show of physical affection.

"Yes, it wasn't a good time. But never did I think you'd be the one to suffer because of something I did before you were even born."

Suffer because of something she did?

Confused, Savanah peered more closely at her. "What do you mean?"

"About a week ago, I became suspicious of Léon's comment about a dancer I once worked with. So I called her. This is when I discovered Léon is not Léon Pantonelli. Instead, his name is Robert Danzier, like his father. Given his father's troubled past, he changed his first name and used his mother's last name. This explains his treatment towards you. He's seeking revenge for his father. I guess some grudges never die."

She frowned, shaking her head. " With this last stunt Léon pulled, Gayle had no choice but to put him on probation. I heard he was furious, insisting it was a lack of talent that caused your fall. When the other dancers stepped forward in your support, he even threatened to leave."

She shrugged. "Yet, where can he go? He's run out of options.. So, if he's really serious about dance, he'll need to clean up his act."

She gave Savanah's knee a quick pat. "Perhaps now you can understand why I sent your resume to the Seattle company. It would be a fresh start.

She frowned. "And all this talk about not being talented? That's nonsense."

Savanah was silent. Only because she didn't know what to say. As she'd suspected, Léon wasn't who he claimed he was. And now, more than ever, she wanted nothing to do with him. Or with the studio, for that matter.

When your worst nightmare turns into reality, it's time to move on.

Her phone rang. Coming to her feet, she sighed. "Mother, that's my ride, so I need to go. After missing the rehearsal dinner last night, I can't be late for the wedding. I'd never forgive myself if I was."

She took one last look in the mirror, grabbed her purse and evening shawl, and headed for the door.

It appeared her mother had already moved on. The calculating expression on her face as she gazed around the room hinted at another project.

Uh, oh…

She groaned. "Mother, please, don't get crazy and start rearranging everything. Yes, the place needs work, but I'm determined to do it my way."

Busy rearranging the sofa pillows, her mother sent her a bright smile. "Don't worry. I only want to get the feel of the place."

She sent Savanah a vague wave. "Go… have a good time. And make sure you give Stephanie and Evan my congratulations." After she picked up another throw pillow, placing it at the other end of the sofa, she turned to see Savanah had already left.

Good… now she could measure the windows for blinds. One could never have enough privacy.

She was humming as she searched through her purse for her tape measurer. The home sale at Macy's ended this weekend, so she needed to work.

CHAPTER 47

The taxi driver sent Savanah a glance in his rear-view mirror. "So, is this a family wedding?"

She shook her head. "No, a good friend."

She frowned.

At least you hope Stephanie still wants to be your friend.

Now that she had time to think about it, her refusal to go to the rehearsal dinner seemed childish. Embarrassing even. But after Jack gave her what she felt was a very unfair ultimatum, how could she have spent the evening in his company pretending nothing had happened?

You know that would've been impossible. And now, trying to process what your mother disclosed about Léon has left you so confused, you don't know what to believe anymore.

She kept her face turned towards the window, blinking back the tears that kept popping up without warning.

The driver, picking up on her mood shift, changed the subject. "Well, your friend chose an impressive church for her wedding ceremony. It's one of my most requested wedding destinations. The interior is magnificent." He shook his head. "Nope, they don't build them like this anymore. It would cost a fortune."

When Savanah only nodded, one hand on the wheel and squinting through the raindrops hitting the windshield, he frowned. "Too bad about the weather. From what they're predicting, there's a good chance the rain will be with us all day."

He eyed her in the mirror. "You know what they say about rain on your wedding day, don't you?"

"No, I'm sorry I don't."

"Well, believe it or not, the rain is supposed to bring you good luck." He grinned. "And who can't use a little extra luck in a marriage?"

Savanah laughed. *"Hmm…* why does this seem more like a way to calm a hysterical bride, her dream of a sunny wedding day gone awry?"

The driver chuckled. "I believe you may be right."

The rain had now intensified; the drops pounding the windshield and blurring the world around them. Thinking about what the driver just told her, Savanah smiled. Stephanie and Evan didn't need any extra luck. Even a torrential downpour wouldn't ruin their wedding day. Being around them was enough to believe in the power of love.

Hopefully, you haven't ruined your chance to share a love like this with Jack.

Uncertainty filling her, she gazed back out the window.

After the driver pulled up behind the passenger van provided by the hotel Stephanie had reserved for out-of-town guests, he turned to Savanah. "I see they have ushers with umbrellas to escort you into the church. Since it's raining harder, you stay put until I wave one over. We're next after the van, so it shouldn't be a long wait."

An usher, an umbrella in each hand, came sprinting out of the church and over to the van. The possibility it could be Jack, she tried to get a glimpse of his face. But the over-sized umbrella blocked her view.

Another usher escorted a guest into the church, only to return moments later to take on the next one.

The driver glanced at her in the mirror. "I've gotta hand it to them, they're very organized. Now that everyone is out of the van, I'll try to flag down the next available usher."

He grinned. "Who knows? Maybe the two of you will meet, and it will be the start of a beautiful friendship. I've found weddings can be magical—after all, that's how I met my wife. We'll be celebrating twenty-eight years next month."

Halfway out of the car, he paused, turning back. "I always say the right person is out there. And once you find them, everything will fall into place.

With a playful wink, he shut the door behind him.

Jack was standing on the front steps of the church. Sheltered under the umbrella he was holding, he scanned the vehicles lined up at the curb.

He wondered which one Savanah was in.

How was he so sure this was even a possibility?

Well, to be honest, he wasn't.

So, why didn't you take a chance, show up at her condo, and insist she accept your offer of a ride?

Who was he trying to kid? This wouldn't have gone over well. Not when he'd made it very clear they had no future together unless she put him first in her life.

He groaned, mumbling under his breath.

"A bad move... a terrible move."

He should've tried to be more understanding when she told him about Seattle. Instead, so wrapped up in how this could affect him, he'd responded by giving her an ultimatum.

What were you thinking?

In his defense, he had been so damn frustrated, leading to his anger.

He sighed, running his hand through his hair. This was so unlike him. How had falling in love turned him into such a jerk, hurting the person he loved the most?

And now? So much depended on what happened in the next few hours.

The rain had intensified, now a torrential downpour. But this was fine with him. In fact, he viewed this as a blessing. Running back-and-forth with the umbrella, battling the wind and rain, left him little time to think about his impending meeting with Savanah.

If only he could shake the nagging thought he'd gone too far.

A sharp whistle made him jump, and opening his eyes, he saw the driver of the next vehicle waving for his attention.

His umbrella a shield against the rain, he took off in a sprint.

The car door flew open, revealing a glimpse of the driver's face as he peered in at Savanah. He grinned. "I grabbed the best looking usher of the bunch and he's going to take over from here. It was a pleasure driving you, and I hope you have a great night."

After he left, Savanah took the hand offered by the usher holding the umbrella. Once he helped her out of the car, he refused to let go of her hand, linking his fingers with hers. She looked up, her breath catching in her throat.

"Jack..."

At the sound of his name—spoken by the one person whose voice always sent his heart beating a little faster—Jack tightened his grip on Savanah's hand, unwilling to let go for even a moment.

He was torn. This wasn't how he'd pictured their reunion. In his mind, it had been more laid back and in a less hectic environment. Perhaps they'd share a meaningful glance during the church ceremony. Or maybe at the reception, when he'd casually stroll over to join her. This would've given him more time to get over the awe that robbed him of words whenever she was near.

But fate, as it often did, had other plans—throwing them together in the midst of a driving rainstorm.

The driver beeped his horn, a sign he was waiting to leave. Coming to life. Jack shut the car door and, taking Savanah's arm, moved her away from the curb.

Unfortunately, in his haste, he lost his grip on the umbrella. Determined to keep her sheltered from the rain, he made a grab for it. But as he flipped it back over her, a river of water rolled off the top of the umbrella and right down her back.

Her face scrunched up in shock, she let out a little shriek.

Jack was horrified.

Again, this wasn't part of his plan. He had hoped to wow her with his suave demeanor, not with how clumsy he could be.

As had happened so many times since they first met he launched right into a frantic apology. "*Oh, my God...* I'm so sorry, sweetheart... so, *so* sorry." Still holding the umbrella, he began shrugging out of his jacket. "Here, take my jacket so you don't get chilled."

She pressed her fingers to his mouth, shaking her head. "Jack, it's okay. I'll be fine. And as we've already found out, a little water won't hurt us."

Mesmerized by her touch and the smile she gave him, his gaze swept over her, everywhere. The silky fabric of her dress, a delicate shade of coral, showed off her curves in a flattering silhouette. She'd chosen to wear her hair down, and now damp from the rain, it framed her face in a riot of wispy curls.

A fine gold chain with a dainty diamond studded ballet slipper pendant and diamond stud earrings were her only jewelry.

She was the most beautiful woman he had ever seen, perfect in every way.

Given the opportunity, she did the same.

His look was flawless. With the immaculate cut of his dark gray tuxedo, crisp white pleated shirtfront, and the single pale pink rose boutonniere, he was the perfect model of sophistication. But it was the crooked tilt of his bow tie and the mussed state of his rain swept hair that tipped him right past charming and over the edge into irresistible.

And, sexy... so, so, sexy...

She wanted to run her fingers through the unruly waves, maybe even move in closer for a kiss. And the lopsided bow tie?

She'd leave that for later, when they were alone.

Her imagination taking off with where this could lead had her voice coming out all breathless. "You look nice."

Jack chuckled, bringing on that now familiar rush of heat to her cheeks.

Nice?

Really?

Surely you can come up with something better than that.

The word 'nice' didn't even come close. It fell flat—too ordinary.

Even in everyday life, she wouldn't think of describing him that way. Impressive, smooth, charming, and even handsome would be a much better fit.

Hands down, he was the perfect man.

Jack was smiling. By her reaction, it was obvious their unexpected encounter had her just as rattled as him.

This was good… really, really good.

But then he turned serious, searching her face. "Savanah, there's so much I want to say, starting with an apology—"

She moved closer, erasing the space between them. "No… not now. I also have something I'd like to say. But it can wait. Please, let's enjoy Stephanie and Evan's wedding day."

A sudden tap to the umbrella sent more water cascading around them, followed by a cheerful male voice. "Hey, Jack… I don't know who you're hiding beneath that umbrella, but you need to get a move on. We've got less than twenty minutes before the ceremony starts. So, in order to get everyone in the church and seated on time, we need to pick up the pace. You can pile on the charm later."

They both peered out from under the umbrella, just in time to catch Jason's wink as he sprinted off.

Jack smiled. "It appears I'm shirking my usher duties. So, before I get into more trouble, possibly dragging you down with me, let's get you inside." He pulled her close, sheltering her under his arm. "Stay close so you don't get more wet than you already are."

They took off in a mad dash, with Jack lifting her off her feet a few times to avoid the huge puddles left by the rain.

Once they were inside the church, he removed his jacket and, before she could protest, draped it over her shoulders.

"Jack, I don't—"

He cut her off, shaking his head. "You're shivering, sweetheart. So please, keep it on. I'll feel so much better if you do."

After he seated her in one of the pews, he dropped a kiss to her cheek before he whispered. "I'll be back." Then, his lips coming dangerously close to hers, a smile crept into his voice. "And, Vanababe? Nice? Nice doesn't even come close to capturing how I'd describe you. Absolutely breathtaking is more like it."

With that, he was gone.

The ushers had rolled the white aisle runner in place, bringing on that hushed excitement that take place right before a wedding ceremony is about to begin.

Savanah closed her eyes. She wasn't going to cry. At least, this was her intention. However, since she'd cried at almost every wedding she could remember, the chance of this happening was pretty slim.

The rustle of clothing alerted her someone had slid into the space next to her. She didn't even have to open her eyes to know it was Jack, the scent of his cologne drifting over her, calming, and so familiar.

She opened her eyes, met with his tentative gaze.

He whispered. "Is it okay I sit here?"

That he even thought he had to ask, she almost burst into tears. Nodding and blinking like crazy, she turned her head, looking anywhere but at him.

As surprising as this may see, Savanah's tears didn't come as a surprise to Jack. There wasn't a single woman he knew that didn't cry at weddings. He'd swear it was as though they couldn't decide if they were happy or sad.

Maybe a little of both?

He pulled out a handkerchief and after he tucked it in Savanah's hand, he leaned in to whisper. "Here, I learned early in life that a man should never be without a clean handkerchief in case of moments like this."

She turned to give him a watery smile, her move sending his jacket sliding off her shoulders. When he reached over to pull it back up, she snatched his arm, panic in her voice. "Oh, no… you should be with the other ushers right now, shouldn't you? But you didn't have your jacket."

She shrugged off the jacket. "Look, they're just now lining up. If you hurry, you can join them before Stephanie starts her walk down the aisle."

He pulled the jacket back over her shoulders. "No worries, we're fine. There are limitations to my usher duties. I'm more of a backup guy, ready to help in case of an emergency."

He was smiling as he brushed back a loose curl framing her face. "I guess this means you're stuck with me. I hope this is okay?"

With Savanah's emotional state almost at an all-time high, it's no surprise this brought on a flood of tears. Thinking it might be in his best interest to keep his mouth shut, Jack waited until she blotted away the tears before he reached for her hand.

She didn't pull away.

Filled with relief like none other, he linked their fingers together.

Again, he had no intention of letting go.

CHAPTER 48

$\mathcal{E}$van and Stephanie were now officially husband and wife.

As the guests began filing out of the church, a brilliant ray of sunlight burst through the clouds, transforming the rain drenched church and grounds into a glittering fairytale-like setting.

In a state of awe, the consensus of the guests was that a special kind of magic had played a role in this astonishing transformation. Anticipating more surprises to come, everyone was in high spirits as they made the short walk to The Regency for the reception.

Once they were in the foyer of the party center, Jack pulled Savanah aside. "There's something I have to do. I'll catch up with you in a little bit, okay?"

He didn't want to leave, not when everything was going so well. But there was a promise he needed to keep. He'd explain it to her later.

With a quick kiss to her cheek, and he took off in a run, only to stop and turn back. Still standing where he'd left her, Savanah raised her hand in a tentative wave.

He didn't even pause to think, erasing the distance between them. And before she could utter a single word, he swept her into his arms and captured her mouth in a fervent, lingering kiss that left her breathless.

At the sound of a scattering of applause, Jack stepped back. His lips curved into a smile at the sight of Savanah's flushed cheeks. Leaning in, his breath warm against her ear, he whispered, "Now that we've captured everyone's attention, I'll be off…"

A quick kiss to her cheek, and he was gone.

Left on her own, Savanah set out to find Stephanie and Evan. Finally spotting them chatting with a guest, she waited until their conversation ended before she approached them, calling out.

"Stephanie?"

Stephanie whirled around, a smile lighting up her face. "Oh, Savanah… I'm so glad you're here."

After they hugged, Savanah stepped back, her gaze traveling over Stephanie from head to toe. Clasping her hands to her heart, she sighed "Oh, Stephanie, you are stunning. Your dress, your hair, everything…

She turned to hug Evan. "And you are so handsome. Together, you are the perfect bride and groom.

Stephanie grabbed her hand before she gazed up at Evan. "Give us a minute, okay? I promise I'll be right back."

Evan chuckled, pressing a kiss to her cheek. "Now that I know you're mine for the rest of our lives, I believe I can spare you for a few minutes." Then he smiled at Savanah. "We missed you last night."

"I know. And I'm so sorry, I…"

Stephanie cut her off, pulling her aside to avoid a group of women making a bee-line for Evan. Watching as they surrounded him, she laughed. "It will be interesting to see how he handles this."

Then she turned to Savanah, a frown flitting across her face. "Jack told me a little of what happened, so I understand why you didn't come to the rehearsal. I convinced him to stay for the dinner, but it was obvious he would've rather been with you. He looked miserable."

She searched her face. "I saw you sitting together in church. Does this mean you worked things out? I hope so. And your plan… it's still on, right?"

"We're going to talk later." A frown creased Savanah's brow. "And, about that… I've been thinking, perhaps we shouldn't…"

Stephanie interrupted her, shaking her head. *"No, no, no…* don't even say it. And remember, you promised."

She laughed. "It's going to be amazing. I can't wait to see the expression on Jack's face."

She glanced over at Evan. His bewildered expression a cry for help, she was grinning as she turned back to Savanah. "I think Evan has reached his limit. He looks a little overwhelmed. So, I better rescue him before he runs off and I never see him again."

These words had barely left her mouth when she was enveloped in a warm embrace from behind, Evan's whisper tickling her ear. "I'm right here. And I have no plans of running off anywhere, Mrs. Marshall. Nope, not a chance."

"Mrs. Marshall…" Gazing up at him, a sigh escaped her. "I love the sound of that."

Then she pointed her finger at Savanah. "Remember, a promise is a promise."

As she watched them leave, Savanah hoped the smile she gave them was more upbeat than she felt.

With the cocktail hour in full swing in the Garden Room, Jack was able to slip into the Grand Ballroom unnoticed.

After he closed the door behind him, he took a moment to check out the now transformed room.

Stephanie had outdone herself.

All the months of planning had paid off, her dream of turning the ballroom into a beautiful summer rose garden had now become a reality.

Floor-length white tablecloths with rose-patterned toppers in various shades of pink covered the round tables. The fine white china place settings, crystal glassware, and mirrored chargers sparkled in the light from the clear rose-tinted glass luminaries at each place setting.

The centerpiece for each table was a miniature version of a two-tiered wedding cake displayed on a vintage cut crystal cake stand. Adorned with realistic fondant roses in a range of shades from deep rose to pale pink, each cake was unique in both design and flavor.

A cookie from Sweet Abby's, sealed in a cellophane bag and tied with a pink satin ribbon, held the place of honor at each place-setting.

Jack leaned in to get a closer look.

In the shape of a bride and groom, decorated to resemble

Stephanie and Evan, the attention to detail on each cookie was amazing.

The sound of voices drifted in from the hallway.

This a reminder he had only a few minutes before the guests began filing in, he made his way over to the grand piano.

He pulled a small gold charm shaped like a grand piano from his pocket. It had been given to his mother by the same person who gifted her the piano, and she had kept it with her whenever she performed. She claimed it brought her good luck.

When he began entering piano competitions, she had passed the charm on to him, making him promise to carry it with him whenever he played. He took that promise to heart, tucking it in his wallet for safekeeping.

Following her death, overcome with grief, he packed the charm away with his other treasured childhood keepsakes. Only after Savanah found his name scratched inside the piano, he remembered he still had it.

Once he made sure no one else was in the room, he tucked the charm right next to his initials, along with a whispered warning.

"Okay, this is your chance. Show what you've got."

His mission accomplished, he gave a quick tap to the microphone to make sure it still worked. He also checked that the sheet music was his version of Stephanie and Evan's song.

Not that he needed it. Given the time he'd spent on the revision, he was pretty sure he could play the song blindfolded.

Satisfied everything was as it should be, he was about to leave when he noticed the place cards on the tables. Curious to see if Stephanie had seated him near the piano as promised, he circled the closest table.

Sure enough, there was a place card with his name.

He checked the card for the seat to the left of his.

Elenore Cromley.

He laughed out loud.

Well, this promises to be an interesting evening.

Then, almost holding his breath, he glanced over at the place card on his right.

Savanah Jackson

His confidence at an all-time high, and a huge smile on his face, he sauntered out of the ballroom.

That good mood he was in?

Not only was it still there, it had grown even brighter.

Jack found Savanah in the ballroom, waiting to learn her table assignment. She was chatting with the guest ahead of her in line, laughing at something he said.

Though he couldn't hear their conversation, Jack found himself laughing too, swept up in a wave of pure, unadulterated joy.

You want to spend your life making her laugh…

Slipping his hands into his pockets, he shook his head in wonder. What were the odds? In a world of billions, they'd found each other.

In the past, that another man was responsible for her happiness may have made him jealous.

Remember Dr. Davis?

But now? This gave him a reason to love her even more. Because, at the end of the day, he would always be the man she loved.

The urge to sweep her up in another kiss surged through him, but he found he needed a minute. Closing his eyes, he exhaled a slow, calming breath.

"If you want even half a chance with her, you'd better get over there and talk to her before it's too late. A woman like that gets scooped up fast."

This coming from a guest standing next to him, Jack turned, an eyebrow raised.

The man gave a hearty laugh. "Come on, don't play dumb with me. You've been staring at her for the past five minutes." He nodded in Savanah's direction. "The beautiful woman in the peach colored dress, right?"

When Jack shrugged, the man nodded. "I thought so. If she has you this infatuated, she could very well be the one."

He took a big swallow of his drink before he sent Jack a wry smile. "Take it from someone who's been there, you'll wish you'd seized the moment.

Jack studied him for a moment. Then he chuckled.

"Hmm… you know what? You're absolutely right." He reached over to pat him on the shoulder. "Thanks for the advice."

He walked over to Savannah, slipping behind her. His hands resting on her waist, he nudged her ear with his mouth.

The memory of the kiss they just shared still fresh in her mind, a shiver ran through her at his touch. She relaxed against him, a ghost of a smile on her lips.

He pulled her even closer, his whisper brushing across her cheek. "Hey beautiful, are you looking for someone to escort you to your table? If so, I think I know the perfect man for the job."

Her mouth curving into a smile, she gazed up at him. *"Hmm…* and who would this be?"

He took a deep breath, his voice dropping to an even huskier whisper. "A man who didn't believe in love at first sight until he met you."

His eyes, full of emotion, held hers, leaving her speechless. And for what felt like forever, they didn't move.

Jack was the first to speak. *"God,* I can't believe how much I've missed you. I want…" He fell silent. He wished he'd never agreed to her request they talk later. The uncertainty was killing him.

But she seemed to understand, her response coming in a long sigh. "I know, I've missed you, too." His mouth now dangerously close to hers, she closed her eyes, anticipating his kiss.

"Good evening everyone, may we please have your attention? If you've yet to find your table assignment, please do so now. Once everyone is seated, dinner will be served."

This announcement was enough to bring Savanah back to earth, and opening her eyes, she fell right into Jack's knowing grin.

What are you doing? You were ready to kiss him like there was no tomorrow. And you can bet he knows this.

Jack attempted to conceal his grin. But he was so happy. And relieved… so, *so* relieved. The way Savanah was gazing up at him, her cheeks flushed and a dazed look in her eyes?

He saw this as a definite invitation for a kiss. Giving him even more reason to hope.

He dropped a kiss to her forehead. Not the kiss he'd like to give her, but it would have to do for now. Then he reached for her hand.

"Come, our table awaits us."

CHAPTER 49

A reception without friends
is like a party without a cake.
It just doesn't feel complete.
~ Anonymous

Of the nine people at their table, Jack and Savanah were the last to arrive. Jason and Darcey, Paul and Sasha, and Joe and Beth had already taken their seats. Assigned the seat next to Jack, Elenore Cromley rounded out the group as the ninth member.

After Jack introduced Savanah, Paul was the first to speak. Leaning back in his seat, he flashed a teasing grin—a warning of what was to come. "So, Savanah… I believe Jack told us you're a dancer? A ballerina, if I'm not mistaken. Did he mention he's also quite the dancer?" Massaging his chin, he looked over at Jack. "*Hmm…* Correct me if I'm wrong, but wasn't that in that article about you for—"

Laughing, Jack raised a hand in protest. "*Whoa…* stop. You, of all people, know you can't always believe what you read in the news." He grinned. "You better be careful, Paul. I've got far more stories about you than you could ever dig up about me."

Paul waved this off before he winked at Savanah. "I bet he also didn't tell you he has a great voice, did he?" He sent a nod over at

Jason. "Ask Jazz. He's been trying to get him to go solo ever since he joined the band. Unfortunately, he refuses, said it's not his thing."

Jason frowned, shaking his head. "One of these days, I'll wear him down. You all know how it bugs me to see an amazing talent go to waste."

"I'm not sure about singing, but I can vouch for his dancing skills." Savanah shot Jack a teasing smile. "No matter the time or place—coffee shops, parking lots, deserted banquet rooms, middle of the night…"

Sasha leaned forward, resting her arms on the table, an excited smile lighting up her face. "Oh my, how romantic. Do tell."

Paul groaned. "Oh boy, here we go." He looked over at Jack. "What, now you've become the new and improved twenty-first century version of Fred Astaire?"

Jack shrugged. "I guess you'll have to wait and see, since I'm not one to brag about my accomplishments. " With a raised eyebrow, he jerked his head toward Paul. "Unlike some people at this table tonight."

Jason burst out laughing before turning to Paul. "Jack did mention he took tap lessons when he was a kid. Who knows? Maybe he'll start a new trend."

Paul snorted. "This I'd like to see."

A pained expression on his face, Jack shook his head. "Come on, enough already. Give me a break. I agreed to play for Stephanie and Evan's first dance tonight, didn't I?"

Darcey smiled at him. "Yes, you have. And we're all so proud of you. But getting back to romance—I agree with Sasha. The more, the better."

She glanced over at Savanah. "So, tell us… what kind of magic did you work on Jack? The Jack we all know and love made it quite clear he had no interest in dating." She shook her head. "I can't tell you how many times he refused my attempts to fix him up."

Sasha was nodding. "Same here. Right from the beginning, he let me know that was a no-go." She grinned over at Jack. "But, do you remember what you shared with me a short time ago?"

Indeed, he did. She was referring to the time she stopped by the studio with dinner for the band, knowing it would be a late night.

When she started dropping hints about a woman from her book club whom she thought would be perfect for him, he wasted no time letting her know he wasn't interested.

This was also the one and only time he told anyone about his chance meeting with Savanah at Café Latte.

So, yes… he remembered exactly what he'd told her.

And now you can bet he wished he'd kept his mouth shut.

He groaned, running his hand down over his jaw. "*Geeez…* I don't think anyone would find this interesting."

Paul looked up from the dinner roll he was buttering. He chuckled. "Oh, I disagree." Then he glanced over at Jason. "What do you think, Jazz? Are you as curious as I am to hear what Jack had to say?"

Jason leaned back in his chair, a big grin on his face. "Absolutely. I'm always interested in hearing Jack's views on love. Or anything else, for that matter."

All eyes were now on Jack.

It only took one glance around the table for him to realize he wouldn't be able to shrug this one off.

Perhaps you'll think twice before blurting out any personal details in the future.

He sighed, sending Sasha a resigned smile. "Of course I remember, Sasha. I told you I'd met someone. But before I could get her name, she vanished into thin air. So I made a vow—no matter how long it took— I'd find her."

And even though he shrugged, there was no mistaking the huskiness in his voice. "And be it fate, destiny, or perhaps even a hint of magic?" He reached for Savanah's hand, his lips brushing over her fingers in a kiss. "I found her."

Naturally, this sparked a flurry of questions. Beginning with why did Savanah run away? And why hadn't Jack gone after her? This led to the subject of sour cherry scones and the role they played in that initial meeting.

After Jack and Savanah had each shared their versions of what happened that day in the coffee shop, sprinkled with plenty of good-natured banter, the consensus was clear—it couldn't have been more romantic.

Jason came to his feet, and after reaching for his wineglass, his gaze traveled around the table. "If there was ever a moment deserving of a toast, it would be now. So, raise your glasses."

Once everyone had a glass, he spoke. "Here's to beautiful women, great friends, and good times. May we always have a reason to celebrate each other."

His glass was halfway to his mouth when Darcey tugged on his arm. "Aren't you forgetting something?"

Confused, he stared at her. Then a smile tweaked the corner of his mouth before he leaned over to press a kiss to her cheek. "*Ah, yes…* and love, we can't forget love. Cheers."

The glasses were no sooner back on the table when Jack also stood. "I'd also like to say a few words."

Paul groaned. "*Damn…* now?" He craned his neck, searching the room. "Can't it wait until after dinner? Look, they're serving the salads."

After Jack shot Paul a look that had him raising his hands in surrender, Jack pressed on. "Don't worry, I'll keep it short."

After clearing his throat, he sent a smile around the table. "There is a very important person at our table whose generosity has changed the lives of so many people, me included. And that would be Elenore." Placing his hand on her shoulder, he smiled down at her. "Her encouragement gave me the push I needed to rediscover my love for the piano."

He paused, shaking his head in disbelief. "And, then, to have the piano here at The Regency? What can I say, except that I hope it brings others the same joy it brings me."

A wry smile tugged at his lips. "She also made me realize some people will never change. And I should accept them as they are and hope for the best." His eyebrow raised, his glance went to Paul. "And believe me, with some people, this is no simple task."

Paul grinned. "Like they say, if it ain't broke, don't fix it."

Once the laughter had died down, Jack turned back to Elenore. "Elenore… I thank you from the bottom of my heart." He leaned over and pressed a kiss to her cheek. "I only hope I can make you proud."

Overcome with emotion, a rarity for Elenore, it was a few moments before she could respond. "Oh, Jack… you already have. My hope was the piano would help you see your past in a different light. And you've done so much more than that. So please don't feel the need to thank me. If anything, we should be thanking you for the loan of your beautiful piano. And remember, this is what it is, a loan. When the time comes you want it back, say the word, and it's yours."

After taking a moment to gather his thoughts, Jack smiled down at her. "Thank you. And you're right—I think I've finally figured it out. I owe so much to that piano, it shaped who I am today. Playing again is an experience I can't even begin to describe." He grinned. "Let's just say I'm now a true believer in second chances."

He raised his glass. "So, Elenore, this toast is for you . For your generosity, and all you've done for others, we thank you."

Glasses back on the table, Jack turned to Paul. "I'm done. So, go for it."

Paul acknowledged this with a brief wave, more interested in the basket of rolls Sasha passed to him. After selecting the roll he wanted, he turned to Evan's friend Joe, who was seated next to him. "So tell me, what are your thoughts about the last cover shot Evan did for us?"

Joe nodded. "The kid has talent, and people are starting to notice. He has a way of capturing the perfect shot at the right time. There's also a lot of emotion in his shots. By chance, did you see the young boy in the wheelchair taking photos at the church? Tragic story, lost his whole family in an accident. Evan got him a camera, and it turns out the kid has a knack for it."

Paul laughed. "I saw him at the church. I also saw the little dog he was trying to hide in his backpack."

Joe nodded. "Yep, that's Oreo. Again, this was Evan's doing. He's a down-to-earth kind of guy. A perfect match, he and Stephanie bring out the best in each other."

As the servers arrived with their salads, the table's chatter was reduced to a murmur. Half listening to the conversations swirling around him, Jack picked up his wineglass.

After taking a sip, he glanced at Savanah, his knuckles lightly grazing her cheek in a caress.

"Hey…"

She smiled.

"Hey…"

Resting his forehead against hers, he didn't even stop to think, the words slipping out straight from his heart. *"Marry me..."*

"Jack..." She pressed her fingers to his lips, shaking her head.

He sighed. "I'm sorry. But I only need to be near you, and those two little words sneak out on their own." With a shrug, he sighed again. "I guess I'm holding on to the hope one of these times you'll say yes."

Switching gears, he grinned, reaching for her hand to link their fingers together. "*Sooo...* after the rave reviews you gave for my dance moves—which, by the way, I find totally flattering, coming from a pro like you—does this mean you'll dance with me tonight?"

She laughed. "I'm not sure. What's in it for me?"

Watching the server refill their water glasses, Jack smiled. "Whatever your heart desires, Vanababe. Name it, and it's yours. But first, let's eat. I'm starving"

He reached for his napkin, almost tipping over his water glass. Frantically righting it, he sent Savanah a sheepish look.

She burst out laughing. "Oh, Jack... what am I to do with you?"

He grinned. "That's simple... Marry me."

CHAPTER 50

$\mathcal{D}$arcey smiled at Savanah in the mirror of the ladies' lounge. "I love your dress. It's such a beautiful color."

"Thank you. I got it at Chic Boutique." When Darcey nodded, she laughed. "Why do I get the feeling you already knew this?"

Darcey grinned. "Guilty as charged. I'm sure you've already noticed nothing gets by this group of friends. At least not as long as Sophie's around. She's a sweetheart and would do anything for you. But she can't keep a secret for the life of her. However, if you're on the lookout for a perfect outfit? Or that special dress? She and her Aunt Louise are who you go to for help.

She smiled. "I'm so happy about you and Jack. He's such a sweetheart. And you make such a beautiful couple. The way he looks at you?"

She sighed. "It's so obvious he's fallen head over heels in love with you."

Then she leaned in closer and, even though the only other occupants in the room were two teenagers who were giggling about something in the corner, she spoke in a whisper. "Jason and I know what you have planned tonight."

At the look of panic on Savanah's face, she placed her hand on her arm. "Don't worry. We're the only people Stephanie told. Except for maybe Evan." She stopped to think about this before she nodded. "Yeah, I'm sure he's in on it, too."

She grinned. "I can't wait to see the expression on Jack's face. He's going to be so surprised. If you pull this off and he agrees to sing? You just wait… he has this crooner kind of voice, makes you want to melt."

Guilt written all over her face, she shrugged. "I heard him singing while he was working on something for a client. He didn't know I was listening. Jason has been trying to get him to sing solo since he joined the band, but he refuses."

She sent Savanah a knowing glance. "Then you came along." She laughed. It's amazing what love can do, isn't it? Look at you and Jack— in what is usually a boring and unpredictable month of March— a song and a dance have changed your lives forever."

Before Savanah had a chance to respond, Darcey glanced down at her watch. "*Oh, geeez…* we better get back out there. I'm sure both Jason and Jack are wondering what's taking us so long."

She was about to open the door when she turned to Savanah and gave her a big hug. "I can't wait. I know you'll be great."

Savanah followed her out of the lounge. If she had been nervous before, well… now she was even more so.

Great? You'd settle for an okay at this point.

She could only pray.

Jack set two drinks on the table, a scotch and soda for him and a chardonnay for Savanah.

After a quick glance over at the entrance to the ballroom, he sent Jason a vague smile. "I'm sorry, did you say something?"

"*You* haven't heard a thing I've said, have you?" When Jack responded with a blank stare, Jason grinned, shaking his head. "Let's try this again. Tell me how you'd like to handle the introduction. Do you want to leave it up to me? Or would you rather do it yourself?"

When he realized Jack's attention had wandered again, he sighed. "Or here's an idea, why don't we take our chances and ask a random guest to play the song for Stephanie and Evan's first dance? Make things interesting? Though I'm not sure how Stephanie will feel about this."

After giving him a long look, Jack groaned, raking his hand through his hair. "Sorry, I guess I've got a few things on my mind. Whatever you want to do is fine with me. Just let me in on what you decide. I don't want to make a complete fool of myself." He frowned. "Something I seem to do a lot of lately."

Jason nodded. "*Ah ha...* now I see where this is going. Did you two get a chance to talk?"

Jack sent him another blank stare. "Talk? Talk to who?"

Jason rolled his eyes. "Don't play dumb with me. You know damn well who I'm talking about."

Shoving his hands in his pockets, Jack shook his head. "Not yet. Later is the plan." He shrugged. "Her idea, not mine."

"*Hmm...* left you hanging, huh?"

His glance shifting to the entrance to the ballroom, Jack nodded. "Exactly."

"I'm sure she's nervous about the song." The moment this left his mouth, and confronted with Jack's confused expression, Jason wanted to kick himself.

Again, let this be a reminder you're not good with secrets.

He cleared his throat. "Forget what I said. What I meant—you're overthinking it. From my experience, women take on a whole new personality at weddings."

He shrugged. "Since I haven't a clue what that's all about, I've learned to just roll with it."

This was when he realized Jack was no longer listening. A faint smile on his face, his attention was on Savanah as she and Darcey made their way over to them.

Jason chuckled, shaking his head. "Man, never had I thought I'd live to see the day. When you fall, you fall hard."

After replying to something Darcey said, and giving her a brief hug, Savanah walked over to Jack.

"*Hi...*" She slipped her hand in his.

"*Hey, beautiful...*" Taking her hand, he gracefully twirled her into his arms. A smile flitted across his face. "Before I forget, I don't think we finished our earlier conversation—when I asked if you'd share a dance with me tonight?"

She glanced at the now empty dance floor, then back at him, a wary look crossing her face. "Remember our deal? Only if we have the right music."

He chuckled. "*Ah...* so now it's the 'right' music? I guess we did agree on that, didn't we? So, again, tell me. What kind are we talking about?"

A wistful smile curved her lips. "A love song... one with a happy ending."

Tilting his head, he studied her. Then he nodded. "*Hmm...* that's easy. I happen to know a lot of those—enough to last a lifetime."

She leaned back, smoothing his shirtfront with her hand before adjusting his bowtie, smiling when he closed his eyes at her touch. "They have to be with only you."

He nodded. "Yes, always. That's a crucial rule, as far as I'm concerned. Though, as you can see, we can dance anywhere, no matter the music."

That's when she realized—his fingers pressed firmly against her back to keep her close—he had been leading her in a slow dance around the edge of the dance floor in time to the dinner music being piped through the ballroom audio system.

He twirled her again, his whisper brushing her ear. "Don't look now, but it seems we're being watched again." He chuckled. "Should I do something fancy?"

She scrunched up her face, holding up her arm with the cast. "Do I need to remind you?"

His whisper brushed over her cheek. "So, what you're saying, you'll settle for a kiss instead?"

Unfortunately, Jason and Darcey joined them before she could reply.

A big grin on his face, Jason patted Jack on the back. "Are you all set for the big reveal?"

"*Yoooo-hooooo... Jason.*"

They turned to see Stephanie was waving to them from where she and Evan were in a conversation with the band members.

She beckoned for him to join them.

"Uh, oh... looks like it's showtime." Jason pointed his finger at Jack. "So, flex those fingers while I make sure we're all on the same page."

He pressed a kiss to Darcey's cheek and took off in a sprint to the stage.

Once he and Savanah were seated at their table, Jack drummed his fingers on the table. He felt anxious, which made little sense.

Savanah noticed this, and leaning closer to him, she spoke in a whisper. "Are you nervous? I always get butterflies right before I have to dance. I've been told it's a good thing." She shrugged. "But, who knows? Maybe this was made up by the same people who tell you to break a leg before you dance. Or it's good luck if it rains on your wedding day."

"What?"

He looked so confused, she laughed. "This was my driver's words of wisdom today." Determined to make her point, she leaned in closer. "I guess what I'm trying to say—if you have faith in yourself, everything will fall into place."

"*Hmm...* words of wisdom, I'm sure."

That's when she noticed the quirky grin spreading across his face—a grin she'd come to know well, a sure sign he was amused at what she said. Naturally, this had her flustered.

"Jack, I'm being serious right now."

His grin still there, he trailed his fingers along the line of her jaw, nudging up her chin. His kiss brushed her lips, his only reply those two familiar words.

"*Marry me.*"

She sighed, closing her eyes. "*Jack...* you promised."

His sigh mirrored hers before he shrugged. "You're right, I did. But this seems to be the one promise I can't keep. I love you, Savanah Jackson, and I want you in my life for always."

She studied him for a moment, then whispered in his ear. "Whatever happens next? Remember, I did it for us." With that, she turned to say something to Darcey.

His fingers brushing the cheek where her kiss had landed, Jack shook his head.

Whatever happens next? What the hell is that supposed to mean?

Then again, whatever it was, she did say she was doing it for them.

This should be enough, right?

CHAPTER 51

I never really thought that much about the song
until I heard you sing the words.
~ Anonymous

The lights dimmed, a drum roll echoing through the Grand Ballroom.

This was followed by a brief silence before Jason came striding out onto the floor, microphone in hand.

He walked the floor, his arms extended in a greeting as he waited for the applause to die down. Then, coming to a stop, he grinned around the crowded room. "Thank you, thank you. I can see we have a very enthusiastic crowd here tonight. And why wouldn't it be, since we're all here to celebrate Stephanie and Evan, now the new Mr. and Mrs. Marshall."

After gesturing for Stephanie and Evan to join him on the floor, this bringing on a big round of applause, he grinned. "And now, before we get this place rocking and rolling, we're going to start off with Stephanie and Evan's first dance as husband and wife. However, there are a few things I'd like to say."

Another drum roll followed, this one longer. Shading his eyes with his hand, he shouted out to the drummer. "Hey, I thought we discussed this. The plan was one drumroll, then we'd move on. Your time in the spotlight was over."

The drummer responded with a set that went on for close to thirty seconds, the grand finale a clash of symbols loud enough to send the crystal chandeliers shaking.

After another enthusiastic round of applause from the guests, Jason sent a salute to the drummer. "Well, there you have it, Carson Reese on the drums, folks. You've just had a small sample of what you can expect from the newest band in the area, The Wedding Crashers. And don't worry, it's not all drums. They play everything from slow to fast, nostalgic to new age, country—you name it, there's something for everyone."

He walked over to another band member. "This here is Luke Hilton, the band's fearless leader. We've known each other for what has it been, Luke? Ten years?"

Luke laughed before leaning in closer to his microphone. "More like fifteen, going on twenty, Jazz. Long enough to think of you as my older brother."

Jason groaned, dragging his hand down over his jaw before he turned to the crowd. "Older brother? I don't think I like the sound of that. And just to be clear? Our ages are less than a year apart." His voice dipped to an exaggerated whisper. "Believe it or not, he's also very single, ladies."

Luke laughed. "Ah, no, no, no… don't you start on me, Jazz. You know music is my only love."

Jason rolled his eyes. "Yeah, I used to say the same thing. But one of these days, the right woman will come along and that will change. Trust me, I know what I'm talking about."

After blowing a kiss over to Darcey, he went on to introduce the other three band members before he returned to the center of the dance floor.

He sent a warm smile out to the guests. "So, let's get back to why we're here tonight—to celebrate Stephanie and Evan. And what better way to start than with their first dance as husband and wife?"

"But this is no ordinary dance. You all know Jack Buchanan, our close friend and the drummer for Banded Together. Turns out, he has a hidden talent for the piano. When Stephanie learned this, she asked if he would play the song she and Evan picked for their first dance. Jack did better than this—he put together his own version of it. And he nailed it. A well-known classic, I'm sure you'll recognize it the moment he plays those opening chords. So, without further ado, with Jack Buchanan on the piano, we give you Stephanie and Evan's first dance. Enjoy…"

"It looks like this is my cue. Wish me luck, beautiful." After whispering this in Savanah's ear, Jack came to his feet.

She smiled, giving his hand a gentle squeeze. "You're going to be great. Break a leg."

He chuckled, leaning down to whisper. "You realize if that happens, you'll definitely have to marry me. So you can take care of me."

For a millisecond, he saw something in her eyes that had him holding his breath, waiting. But when her only answer was a kiss to his cheek, he made his way over to the piano.

Once he took a seat, he checked to make sure everything was in order. And yes, he had already done this. But it had been a long time since he'd played solo in front of an audience. So, he wanted his performance to be flawless.

Instead, confusion set in.

Everything was different.

He remembered the microphone being on his left. Now it was on his right.

And the sheet music? His scribbled version, written only for piano, was no longer there. Instead, someone had replaced it with a new and neater sheet of his version, along with another sheet of the lyrics to match.

He took a closer look at the sheet music. Yes, the score was his. However, what was the reason for including the sheet music with the lyrics? He'd made it very clear to Stephanie he would not be singing.

The agreement was he'd play the piano, nothing more.

So, who made these changes? It couldn't be Stephanie, as she would've said something by now. She was terrible at keeping secrets.

He glanced over to where she was standing with Evan.

She smiled and waved.

Well, there you have it… she looks pretty innocent.

He raked his fingers through his hair. None of this made sense.

This was when he remembered where he was—center stage, in a room full of people waiting for him to either say or play something. He cleared his throat, then had to clear it again before finding his voice. "Good evening everyone. As Jason mentioned, my name is Jack Buchanan. When Stephanie asked if I would provide the music for their first dance tonight, I wanted to give her and Evan something they could truly call their own. So, what I'm about to play is my rendition of their chosen song—'Endless Love' by Lionel Richie."

He glanced over at Stephanie and Evan, raising his hand in a salute. "This is for you. I love you guys."

Then, his hands hovering over the keys, he took a deep breath.

"Excuse me…" A woman's voice came from somewhere in the room.

A very familiar voice. Not one he'd expect to hear right now. Every nerve in his body on high alert, he waited.

But when there was only silence, thinking his imagination was messing with him, he raised his hands again.

"Excuse me, Mr. Buchanan?"

There was no doubt about the voice this time.

Savanah…

He dropped his hands to the keys, sending a dreadful clash of notes echoing through the ballroom. His heart joined in the fray, thundering in his chest.

He shot a glance over at Stephanie and Evan. Their blank expressions told him they were as clueless as he was.

So, grabbing the microphone, he headed for the table he'd shared with Savanah.

Her chair was empty, Savanah was nowhere to be seen.

Now he was even more confused.

My God… you're losing it. But don't panic, she has to be here somewhere.

He did a slow turn, dragging his hand back through his hair as he scanned the room. However, with the chandeliers dimmed, and the only other lights shining on the dance floor and piano, it was difficult to make out the faces in the crowd.

The microphone raised to his mouth, he peered out into the maze of tables. "Hello? Are you still here?"

"Here... I'm over here."

He whirled around, an almost ridiculous feeling of relief flowing through him when he saw Savanah. About twenty feet away, she looked scared to death.

He'd later admit he'd never wanted to kiss her more than in that moment. It took almost every ounce of control he had to keep from rushing over, sweeping her into his arms, and doing just that.

It would be an unforgettable kiss, you would've made sure of that.

This enticing thought tucked in the back of his mind, he tried to hide his smile as he sauntered over to her. When he was only a few feet away, he came to a stop.

He crossed his arms over his chest, his tone of voice teasing. "Well, well, well... hello there."

With her plan now a reality, Savanah's hands began to shake. Between that and the pounding of her heart—to the point this was all she could hear—she somehow returned his greeting.

"Hi..."

Jack responded to her tentative whisper with a reassuring wink before he shifted his attention to the guests. "*So...* this is a most unusual situation. Never has such a beautiful woman interrupted me as I was about to play at an event." He shook his head. "Nope, never. But I must say, I like it. And now I'm curious to know more."

Once again, he addressed the guests. "And what about you? Are you with me on this?"

After receiving a resounding yes, he turned back to Savanah. "Well, there you have it. Would you like to start out by telling everyone your name?"

She spoke, or more like whispered, into the microphone he held. "Savanah... my name is Savanah Jackson."

Jack nodded.. "*Ah, Savanah... A* beautiful name. Almost as beautiful as you. And tell us, Savanah, what is your claim to fame?"

This took her by surprise, her eyes going wide. "My claim to fame?"

A smile tweaking the corner of his mouth, he nodded again. "Yes, tell us... what makes Savanah Jackson special?"

She gave a breathy little laugh. *"Oh, my...* I don't know. Right now, I'm a ballerina for a dance company here in Cleveland." She shrugged. "I'm far from special."

"Hmm... so you're a ballerina?" He held her gaze while shaking his head. "And I disagree. I can see you're very special." This sending a flood of color to her cheeks, he smiled again.

Then he took a step back, his hand raised in denial. "Whoa... wait a minute, is this why you interrupted me? You thought this might be a way to show off your dance skills?"

Horrified, her hand flew to her mouth. *"Oh, no, no, no.* I stopped you because I was a little confused about what you were about to play."

A frown creased his brow. "I don't understand. You don't like the song?"

Again, she shook her head. This was turning out to be much harder than she thought it would. She certainly hadn't expected him to ask so many questions.

It was also clear, by the smile he was trying to hide, he enjoyed he had her so flustered.

Nope, he had no intention of making this easy for her.

Well, as they say, two can play at this game.

She took in a deep, fortifying breath before gesturing with her hand to make her point. "No, I absolutely love the song." But someone very knowledgeable about music told me," here she sent him what he took as a very flirty smile, "that it's regarded as the greatest love song ever written. However, it's only when sung as a duet that it becomes the masterpiece it is."

He nodded. *"Ah, yes...* an interesting observation. And this someone you know? He must be an absolute genius. Because he's right."

"Yes, I've found he's been right about a lot of things." This remark coming across as even more flirtatious, he took a step closer. He didn't know what she was up to, only that it was working. She had him ready to do whatever she asked.

Is she's trying to tell you something?

The possibility she was, it took him a moment to collect himself. Then he gave a little laugh before he turned to address the room. "I... uh... sorry. Now where were we?"

A guest shouted out. "The song, Jack, you were telling us about the song. You can flirt with the girl after you're done."

He waited for the laughter to die down before he acknowledged this with a wave. "Thanks, I'll be sure to take your advice. But before we move on, a brief history here. As Savanah already pointed out, the song 'Endless Love' was first recorded as a duet sung by Diana Ross and Lionel Richie. In the song, they both declare their 'endless love' for each other. Thus the name."

He sent Stephanie and Evan a thumbs up. "A great choice, by the way. But you already know that."

He turned back to Savanah. "As you can see, I'm going solo here. So, a duet isn't an option. And if I sang the song by myself, the total effect of the words will be lost."

Unaware she'd taken another step closer, she nodded. "I understand. Although what if someone offered to sing with you?"

In response, Jack had also moved closer. His arms still crossed now more out of necessity to keep from making a move he might later regret—such as pulling her into his arms and giving her a kiss under the watchful eyes of everyone in the Grand Ballroom—a slow smile curved his lips. "Wow… I've never had anyone request something like this. Give me a minute."

He bowed his head as if deep in thought. Then, comprehension dawning, he glanced over at her. "*Hmm…* out of curiosity, do you have someone in mind?"

His gaze was so intent, he had her so she couldn't even think. It didn't help the room had gone silent, as if everyone was holding their breath, waiting for her reply. Even with all the dance recitals in her past, never had she felt so exposed.

And you expect to sing? You're in big trouble.

Obviously, she'd made a mistake. This hadn't been such a good idea after all.

"Well?" Waiting for her answer, Jack searched her face.

She took in a deep breath and looked right into his eyes. "Me. I can do the duet with you."

He stepped back in disbelief. Then, assuming she was kidding, he was chuckling as he answered. "You?"

"Yes, me." A little insulted by his reaction, she waited for him to say more. When it became obvious this wasn't going to happen, she panicked.

This was not what she'd expected. In fact, she wondered if this might be the time to make another quick exit.

Instead, she did the only thing she could in the circumstances. Her head held high, she sent him a brilliant smile. "It's okay, I understand if this is something you'd rather not do. So pretend I never asked. I guess I thought it would be nice…" Her voice trailing off, she turned to walk away.

Now caught up in this unprecedented drama unfolding in front of them, and unhappy with the outcome, a long groan rose from the guests. The same guest who yelled out before even jumped up out of his chair to express his disproval. "Come on, Jack. Let the girl sing."

This sent Jack into motion. He caught up to Savanah, and grabbed her hand, gripping it firmly in his. "Savanah Jackson, forgive me. My silence was only because you took me by surprise. That being said, I'd be honored to sing a duet with you. However…"

He turned, calling out to Stephanie and Evan. "Are both of you okay with this?"

After a thumbs up from both Evan and Stephanie, he turned to address the room. "Well, folks, it looks like we'll be singing a duet. Give us a few minutes to get in sync. Then we'll give Stephanie and Evan their long awaited first dance."

A thunderous round of applause cheering them on, they made their way to the piano.

He didn't even try to hide the kiss he gave her.

CHAPTER 52

*O*nce they were both seated at the piano, Jack turned to Savanah.

He was grinning. "Vanababe, what have you done?"

Overcome with a sudden shyness, she avoided his gaze, running her hand down over the skirt of her dress. Dismayed to see it was still shaking, she hid it in the folds of the fabric.

He reached over, caressing her cheek with his fingertips. "*Hey,* look at me."

Her head held high, she sent him a sidelong glance.

This, of course, had his grin growing even bigger. "*Sooo…* are you going to tell me what you're up to?"

She shrugged. "We hoped it would be a nice surprise."

"We? And, pray tell, who is this we?"

She sent a brief glance over to where Stephanie and Evan had left the dance floor and were chatting with guests at a nearby table.

"*Umm…* me and Stephanie."

He nodded. "*Ah…* Stephanie, your partner in crime. And you really want to do this? Sing a duet with me?"

"Yes, I do."

"*Hmm…* but didn't you tell me—even though you love to dance— you don't enjoy being in the spotlight? You're happiest when you perform as part of a group. Yet now, if you do this, I guarantee all eyes will be on you."

She gazed up at him. "But I'll be with you. With you, I'll be okay."

The trust shining in her eyes sent a wave of tenderness flooding through him, the words escaping him in a husky whisper. "I love you Savanah Jackson."

For a moment, one that felt like it would never end, she remained silent. Then, after a long, trembling sigh, she leaned her head against his shoulder, whispering the words he'd patiently been longing for. "I love you, too."

And now Jack was the one having a hard time.

To get his emotions in check, he began fiddling with the microphone, adjusting the sound. Once he confirmed everything was ready to go, he reached for the sheet music before smiling over at Savanah.. "I'll replace my version with the original. If I don't, you might find it hard to follow along."

She took the sheet music from him and put it back. "No, it's fine. I'd rather do your version. If this is okay with you?"

He didn't understand. "You've seen my version? How?"

Guilt sent the color rising in her cheeks. "Stephanie persuaded Jason to give her a copy of your version, and with a little help from the pianist at the dance studio, I'm pretty sure I've got it."

He burst out laughing. "*My God*, Jason was in on this, too?"

She grabbed onto his arm, looking up at him. "Yes, but please don't tell him I told you. He made me promise I wouldn't."

She sighed. "But I can't lie to you."

And this time, he couldn't resist. His fingers trailing down the side of her face to catch her chin, he leaned in for a kiss.

"*Ah, love…* if I could, I'd sweep you up in my arms and take you home with me. Right now, song or no song."

Now she was flustered. "Jack, *please…* we're here to sing. Then we'll see what happens."

This taken as a promise, he nodded. "Okay, beautiful… I'll start off with the first line. You jump in whenever you're ready. Then we'll see how it goes from there. And if you get nervous, hum, or do whatever feels comfortable. I'll carry us through.

She hesitated, as though she wanted to say something. Instead, clasping her hands in her lap, she closed her eyes and took in a deep breath.

Then she looked over at him and nodded. "Okay, I'm ready."

Caught up in her eyes, again he let the moment carry him away, his whisper brushing across her cheek. "*Marry me…*"

"*Jack…*" Shaking her head, at the same time she couldn't fight the laughter bubbling up in her throat.

If you were to ask Jack, he'd claim this was the reaction he was going for, his only goal to help her relax.

Hmm… yet, let's imagine he'd waited only a few minutes before he gave Jason the sign they were ready to begin.

Her response may have surprised him.

To what was now his second drum roll of the evening, Jason came striding out onto the dance floor. "So, are we ready to try this one more time?"

Once the applause ended, he chuckled, shaking his head. "I don't know about you, but I can't wait to see what's going to happen next."

He held up his hand. "But, before we move on, if there is anyone else who has something to say to Jack, this will be your last chance. I'll give you twenty seconds to make yourself known. Starting… now."

His gaze glued to his watch, after what felt much longer than twenty seconds, he raised his arms up to the ceiling and gave a loud shout.

"*Hallelujah…* On that note, let's hear it for Stephanie and Evan, the featured couple of the night. May this dance be the start of a lifetime of many, many more."

A silence falling over the room, Stephanie nodded over to Jack. His fingers coming down on the keys, the opening notes of the song traveled through the room. Mesmerized, Savanah watched as his fingers danced over the keys, each note flowing into the next with an effortless beauty.

This also sent her into a brief panic. What had she been thinking? She never should've let Stephanie talk her into this. Instead, now Stephanie and Evan's first dance, Jack's piano debut, and even her own future all hinged on this single performance.

She had to sing as she'd never sung before.

Closing her eyes, she shut out everything except the words as Jack sang them.

"My love…
You're the only love in my life,
The only one that's right…"

Jack's voice lived up to everything Darcey said it was, and more. Imagine Matt Dusk, Mike Broussard, Harry Connick Jr. and Michael Bublé, all rolled into one. Then throw in a little of Josh Groban for a touch of classic pop.

She opened her eyes, falling right into the tenderness of the smile he sent her as he sang. She wanted to put her head on his shoulder and stay in the moment forever.

She almost missed her cue to join in.

In fact, she did miss it.

"Savanah?" It was at Jack's questioning whisper, along with the gentle nudge of his elbow, she came to life. This had the words flying out of her mouth, surprising even herself at how effortlessly her voice blended with his.

"My love…
Two hearts beating as one.
And even though our life has only begun,
I want to share all my love with you."

And now their roles had reversed. Almost in shock, Jack found he was having trouble remembering the words. His fingers stumbling over the keys, this left Savanah to carry them through the next stanza.

"My love…
My one and most precious love…
With every breath,
And every journey we take,
Our love will only grow stronger."

Not that Jack hadn't thought Savanah could sing. He just didn't expect her to be as good as she was. As she sang the lyrics in perfect harmony, matching him note for note, it was as though they'd performed this song together many times before.

He'd describe the tone of her voice as a mezzo-soprano, yet deeper and full of passion. And if he could? He'd be more than happy to let her sing solo while accompanying her on the piano.

But remember, this song is at its best when performed as a duet.

Savanah watched Jack play the next two stanzas before, his hands dropping from the keys, he nodded over at her. And together, they sang the final chorus as it was originally meant to be sung, the last word slowly fading into silence. As though they were reluctant to let the moment end.

This gave Evan the opportunity to twirl Stephanie around one more time before he dipped her almost to the floor. Where he gave her the perfect kiss for their first dance as husband and wife.

"And, yes…
You will always be the only one,
Our love will never end.
My love, my love, my endless love,
Two hearts beating as one.
Our true love,
Our forever love…"

Caught up in the beauty of the moment, at first, there was only silence. Then the guests came alive and, rising to their feet, erupted into a thunderous round of applause.

This turned into a chant, calls for an encore rocking the room.

Before Savanah had a chance to even look at Jack—given she was desperate to know what he was thinking right now—he grabbed her hand and pulled her up from the bench. After the briefest curtain call on record, she almost had to run to keep up as he led her through the maze of tables.

He continued at this fast pace even after they left the Grand Ballroom and were halfway down the hall.

Savanah was laughing. "Jack, you need to stop or slow down. These heels I'm wearing aren't intended for a marathon."

When this didn't stop him, she tugged on his hand.

"Jack, please…

He finally came to a halt, and framing her face in his hands, his voice was between a whisper and a sigh. "My God, I love you. I've wanted to do this from the moment I realized it was you trying to get my attention back in that ballroom."

His mouth crashed down on hers in an all-consuming kiss.

Obviously, he approved.

The thought crossing her mind this was the best answer he could give her, she returned the kiss just as passionately.

Jack lifted his head. A moment he wanted to keep in his memory forever, his gaze traveled over her face, taking in every detail. Then, after shaking his head, he pressed the softest of kisses to her mouth. "Savanah Jackson, the more I get to know you, the more you amaze me. Why didn't you tell me you can sing?"

Before she could answer, he kissed her again. He watched as her lashes fluttered open before he spoke. "So, tell me… what other surprise do you have brewing in that beautiful mind of yours?"

She laughed, shaking her head. "Nothing, I swear there's nothing else. To be honest, I still can't believe I went ahead with this. When I told Stephanie if I hadn't taken up dance, my second choice would be to sing, I never thought she'd take off and run with it."

Her look was one of disbelief. "This was after she hadn't even heard me sing. She told me, if I said I could sing, that was good enough for her." She hesitated before gazing up at him, an earnest expression on her face. "I almost said something the night you came to see me in the hospital. Remember when we talked about how the song was a duet? Then I chickened out."

She shrugged. "All my life, I've been told I'm a dancer. So I had no reason to believe I could do anything else. Until Stephanie convinced me otherwise."

Her wistful smile tugging at his heart, he pressed a kiss in her hair. *"Ah, Vanababe…* I am so glad she did. A talent like yours should never be hidden. You are one amazing woman, love."

His head lowered for another kiss, the sound of voices had them both glancing over to see Stephanie, Evan, and Darcey bearing down on them.

"Darn, it looks like they found us…" This coming in a sigh against her cheek, Jack dropped a kiss to her mouth before he grinned, calling out. "So, what do you think of the incredible job this woman did?"

Her hands pressed to her heart, Stephanie was beside herself, jumping up and down with excitement. *"Oh my gosh…* the two of you are meant to sing together. I'll admit I was a little skeptical at first, yet something told me I'd be making a big mistake if you didn't sing. And boy, was I right."

A teasing glint in his eyes, Evan shook his head as he pulled her against him in a hug. "And here comes more of that woman's intuition of yours again."

Stephanie laughed. "I haven't been wrong yet, have I? And, just think, you have the rest of our life to put up with all my spot-on predictions."

He pressed a kiss to the tip of her nose. "Sounds like the ideal life to me."

She smiled up at him before she turned back to Savanah. "And a heads up—Jason is already talking about songs and recordings. He—"

"Hold on, did I hear my name mentioned? Because after what I just witnessed, and whatever you're plotting, I'm in."

They all turned to watch as Jason approached the group, a server trailing behind with a tray holding glasses of champagne.

Stephanie laughed, giving a light punch to his arm. *"Ah, ha…* I believe I won this bet fifty times over. Isn't that right, my-not-always-right-big-brother?"

Busy handing around glasses of champagne, Jason made a face at her. "Since this is your wedding day, I'll let you have the win. But either way, I believe this moment calls for another toast." Once he saw everyone had a glass, he raised his. "Here's to a lifetime of making beautiful music together. And to the best first dance."

He winked over at Darcey. "Since ours, of course."

After returning her glass to the tray, Stephanie grabbed Evan's hand. "We've cut the cake, made the required speeches, and we've had our first dance. So, now it's time to have some fun. I want to dance every crazy wedding dance there is with my new husband."

Evan groaned. "Be warned, once you see my pathetic attempt at fast dancing, you'll wonder what you got yourself into.

She reached up to give him a kiss. "Bad moves and all, I will always love you."

After watching them leave, Jason turned to Jack. "Are you planning on joining us?"

His arm wrapping around Savanah, Jack hesitated. "Give us a few minutes, okay?"

"Gotcha." Jason gave him a thumbs up before he turned to Savanah. "And you?" He shook his head. "We need to talk. Because there is no way we'll let you to hide that amazing voice of yours. It's just not going to happen."

Darcey gave Savanah a hug. "Just a warning, even though he can be overly persuasive when he wants something, he means well. And I agree, you have too beautiful of a voice not to share. It was such an honor to be the first to hear you and Jack sing together tonight. Definitely a moment Stephanie and Evan will never forget."

Jason grinned back at them as he and Darcey headed for the ballroom. "But right now, since it isn't every day your sister gets married, I'm ready to do some celebrating. I hope you'll join us."

After they left, her hands slipped under Jack's jacket, and resting her cheek against his chest, she gave a long, contented sigh.

This had him pulling her even closer, his words a murmur in her ear. "I'd like to make a suggestion…"

She leaned back, her mouth curving into a smile. "You would? And will I like this suggestion of yours?"

He chuckled. "*God*, I hope so." After tucking a stray curl behind her ear, he gazed down at her. "I think we should leave. If we walk back into that ballroom, they'll want you to dance. Or sing. And we'll never get away."

He hesitated, searching her face. "Unless you'd like to stay?"

After taking a moment to think about this, she reached up to smooth the lapels of his jacket as she nodded. "I agree. We've already more than made our presence known tonight. So, it might be best if we left. Though, I was hoping to dance with you again." Her smile was teasing. "I'd like to see some of those dance moves your friends were talking about."

He chuckled. "If you haven't already noticed, Paul and Jason have a tendency to exaggerate the truth at times. But I promise, the next time you ask, we'll dance. Music or no music. For as long as you want."

He lowered his head, his lips brushing over the curve of her cheek. "But right now? I don't want to share you with anyone. I don't care where we go or what we do. As long as it's with you."

After he pressed a soft kiss to her mouth, his voice dropped to a whisper, the deep, seductive tone enough to send a tremor through her. "I want to have you to myself for a while, maybe even catch the sunrise together. I've wanted this from the moment I turned to find you standing behind me in line at Café Latte."

How could she resist such a tempting offer? Whatever he wanted, she was all in. Not that she had a choice, as her heart had already made this decision for her.

This gave her the courage to do what she'd fantasized about since she saw him at the church.

She reached up and yanked at his tie until it came undone. After unbuttoning the top two buttons of his shirt—her cast making this a little difficult—she grabbed the ends of the tie and pulled him down to her for a kiss.

This caught Jack completely off guard. However, within a heartbeat, he drew her up against him and kissed her back.

He was smiling when he lifted his head. "I'm going to take that as a definite yes. So, let me tell Stephanie we're leaving."

After a quick kiss to her mouth, he began walking away, only to turn and point his finger at her. "Stay right here, don't leave."

He had no reason to worry. The only way she'd even consider leaving would be with him.

To pass the time while waiting for Jack to return, Savanah wandered over to examine the large photo collage chronicling The Regency's history. Displayed on the wall just outside the ballroom, it offered her a clear view of the entrance, ensuring she wouldn't miss Jack's return.

"Please... will you just leave me alone? Go put your moves on someone else."

Startled by this loud command, she turned just in time to see a woman storm out of the ballroom. Seconds later, a man followed, his voice oddly familiar and filled with frustration..

"Lucy, come on... You can't leave, not in the state you're in. Exactly how much have you had to drink?."

Savanah's eyes widened.

Dr. Davis?

And who is Lucy?

His date?

Sinking back against the wall, hoping to remain unnoticed, she watched as Dr. Davis caught up to Lucy, grabbing her arm.

Lucy jerked her arm free, whirling around to face him. "I will be fine. And, no... I'm not drunk. Even though I'm beginning to think it might be better if I was." Her voice breaking, she wailed, "I just want to go home."

He stepped in front of her, blocking her way. "Okay, so you're not drunk. But you're a mess—" He had no plans to let her know about the streaks of mascara down her face, made worse by her attempts to wipe away her tears with her hand.

No, he wasn't stupid. Give him some credit.

She glared at him. "Gee, thanks for making me feel so much better. And yes, that was supposed to be sarcastic. Now, if you'll get out of my way—"

Before she was finished, he silenced her protests with a kiss. She abruptly pulled back, and for a brief moment they stared at each other. Then with a low growl, he pulled her roughly against him and claimed her mouth again, the kiss deepening into something new and unspoken.

She gazed up at him, wide-eyed. "What just happened here?"

Pressing a soft kiss to her forehead, he sighed. "Lucy, I've wanted to kiss you for I don't know how long. But I didn't want it to be a casual fling." A smile tweaked the corner of his mouth. "Unfortunately, you've never shut up long enough for me to try.."

Bewildered, she shook her head. "I... what I mean is... I..."

He chuckled. "Ah, this is promising. You're speechless—a miracle I'm not sure will last much longer. Let me take you home, Lucy, so we can see where it goes. I believe we're two of a kind."

The warmth of his voice sliced through her doubts, the steady grip of his hand a promise he had no intentions of letting go.

Two of a kind?

She almost laughed at the thought—could this be true? For months she had brushed him off, thinking he was out of her league. But now, caught up in the tenderness of his gaze, the truth settled in. This was real.

Throwing her arms around him, she kissed him with a passion that matched her racing heart.

Laughing, and hand in hand, they hurried down the hallway. leaving Savanah staring after them in stunned silence.

No sooner had Lucy and Dr. Davis disappeared around the corner, Jack appeared, carrying Savanah's purse and evening shawl.

As he gently draped the shawl over her shoulders, his breath brushed over the curve of her neck, sending a shiver down her spine

"Did you miss me?" he murmured, his voice low.

She laughed, still thinking about what she'd just seen. "Yes, terribly. Though I think I may have just witnessed a miracle. Tell me, who's Lucy? Because it seems she and Dr. Davis have suddenly discovered each other."

Jack was skeptical. "Lucy and Dr. Davis?"

After she described what she saw, he burst out laughing. *"Wow…* who would've guessed?"

With his arm tucked around her, they headed for the exit, a thoughtful look on his face. "It just proves there's someone for everyone —and you, Savanah Jackson, are my someone."

A warmth spreading through her at his words, she reached up and pressed a soft kiss to his cheek.

"As you are mine," she murmured, "always."

CHAPTER 53

True love is where each partner
secretly suspects they got the better deal.
~ Unknown

Jack had stopped for a red light. His fingers tapping on the steering wheel in time to The Piano Guys version of Just the Way You Are, playing from his truck's audio system, he glanced over at Savanah.

She wore a preoccupied expression.

He reached over, linking their fingers together. "You've got a pretty serious look going on right now," he said, his voice amused, yet genuinely curious. "What are you thinking about?"

Resting her head back against the seat, she smiled at him. " I was just wondering what you must have thought when I interrupted your performance tonight. To then almost demand you sing a duet with me."

He laughed. "I was surprised at first. But you were so serious, I decided even if you turned out to be a terrible singer, I'd go along with you." He grinned, shaking his head. "At the same time, a little voice in my head assured me I had nothing to worry about. You'd rock it."

She was curious. "How could you be so sure?"

He smiled. "With you, I'm sure about everything."

When this was met with silence, he shrugged. "I can't quite explain it. I only know being with you just feels… right."

Before she could reply, he turned into the entrance of Lake View Towers, the high-rise condos where he lived. After he pulled up to the main entrance, he turned to her. "So, here we are. The place I've called home for the past few years."

He nodded over at the man about to approach them. "And here comes Mike, the concierge." After he opened the door and jumped out of the truck, he turned back with a grin. "You'll find he takes his job very seriously."

"Welcome to Lake Towers." This greeting accompanied by his huge smile, Mike opened the passenger door. After he stepping aside to let Jack help Savanah out of the truck, he sent her a wink. "I see you're with one of my favorite residents. This tells me you must be pretty special since I can't remember the last time he brought—"

Jack cut him off with a laugh. "Okay, enough already. You don't want to ruin my 'man-about-town' image, do you? Not after I've finally convinced her what a great catch I am. But you're right about one thing—she is very special."

"Man-about-town image, indeed." This had Mike chuckling as he opened the door to the lobby. After he ushered them inside, he turned to Jack, all business-like. "I'll park your car in its usual spot, he said. "Enjoy the rest of your evening, folks."

Already on the way to the elevator, Savanah's hand tucked back in his, Jack sent him a nod. "That would be great. Thanks, Mike."

Jack hit the elevator button for the tenth floor and turned to Savanah. "Mike's a nice guy. From what he's told me, he took on this job after he retired because he missed interacting with people. He started a few weeks after I moved in."

He smiled down at her. "Chester and Sophie Mazzori own the condo I live in. After they had twin boys, they decided to rent out the condo and buy a house." He grinned. "That's where I came in."

Savanah nodded. "I met Sophie tonight when Darcey introduced us. I also got to meet her Aunt Louise when Stephanie insisted I check out Chic Boutique to find a dress for the wedding."

Jack chuckled, shaking his head. "Ah, yes… the Chic Boutique. I'll let you in on a little secret. Most of us guys are terrified of that little shop because it's where all the latest gossip is shared. So, we dare not do anything wrong. No one wants to become the latest topic of conversation."

Savanah laughed. "I'm sure it's not that bad." Her head tilted, her glance was teasing. "But now I'm a little concerned. Maybe I should stop by again to see if they have any scandalous stories about you."

In one swift move, he pulled her back against him, wrapping his arms around her. A smile on his lips, he pressed a kiss to the curve of her jaw. "I assure you, my record is impeccable."

He'd lowered his head, ready to capture her mouth in another kiss, when the elevator doors slid open. His resigned sigh brushing across her cheek, he reclaimed her hand.

She watched as he unlocked the door to his condo, waiting until he opened it before she reached up, her fingers brushing his cheek before catching the corner of his mouth in a kiss. "I really do love you, so much."

She slipped past him into the condo.

Leaving him standing there, a goofy smile on his face.

Jack flipped a switch, turning on the lights.

Music, a must have with any musician, he chose one of his favorite playlists and adjusted the volume. Satisfied with the results, he turned to see Savanah was gazing around the room, checking it out.

He hung back.

Given that twenty-four hours ago he wasn't sure if she'd ever want to see or talk to him again, now that she was here, he was in no rush.

She could take her time.

He didn't mind waiting.

If you could, you'd make this night last forever.

He removed his jacket, tossing it on the chair. As he reached his tie, he paused, remembering how Savanah had used it to pull him close for a kiss. A thrill running through him at the memory, he wondered if he should leave it on.

After all, that was quite the kiss...

He ran his hand through his hair. *Nah...* he had a feeling there would be plenty more moments like this in their future.

He planned to make sure of this.

The tie joined the jacket on the chair.

Rolling up his shirt sleeves as he headed to the kitchen, he chose a bottle of wine from the wine cooler. When he turned to set the bottle on the counter, he saw that Savanah had finished her inspection and was now watching him.

Their eyes met. Perhaps it was his imagination, but there was something different in the way she was looking at him. Almost as if she'd finally figured it out, knew what she wanted.

And he sincerely hoped that it was him.

His gaze holding hers, he sent her one of those slow, knowing smiles of his. "So, love... what do you think?"

What did she think?

She wondered how he'd react if she told him her surroundings were the least of her thoughts right now. What had her complete attention was how sexy he looked. With his hair all tousled, the top buttons of his shirt undone and his sleeves rolled up, he came across as so incredibly desirable, it was a struggle to keep from rushing right into his arms.

It's all too much... do you even know what you're doing?.

She was out of her comfort zone, having never reached this stage of a relationship before. With her dance schedule taking up a major part of her time, pursuing any relationship more seriously wasn't even an option.

But then again, no one had intrigued her enough to even want more.

Then along came Jack...

Stalling to regain at least some of her composure, she walked over to the fireplace, her focus on the massive oil painting above the mantle. Contemporary in design, the bold brushstrokes of vivid colors appeared to almost leap out of the canvas.

Not at all what she'd expect Jack to choose.

Her intention to ask him about this, she turned to find he had come around the island, and leaning against it, his arms crossed, he looked as though he hadn't a care in the world.

He raised an eyebrow. "So, tell me… you must have an opinion. Or maybe, like me, your mind is on something else?"

The teasing tone in his voice, along with what he insinuated, sent a rush of color to her cheeks. And the fact she knew he was aware of this had her becoming even more flustered.

She didn't understand. He seemed so sure, so relaxed, while she was a bundle of nerves. Her heart pounding so fast and so loud, she wouldn't be surprised if he could hear it all the way across the room.

Unbeknownst to her, his heart was racing just as fast, if not faster. Now that he finally had her with him in the privacy of his home, you'd think his confidence would've kicked in to carry him through. Instead, he was hesitant to make any kind of move, lest he'd do or say something wrong.

He put part of the blame for this on their failure to discuss the quarrel they had, the subject of Seattle still a nagging reminder in the back his mind.

Remember, she promised you'd talk about this later. Well, it's later, so…

But what was he thinking? He had no plans to bring it up. Not when everything felt so right.

Pushing this thought aside, he watched as she gazed around the room again before she spoke. "This is an amazing space. I can understand why Sophie and Chester don't want to give it up."

He nodded. "You'd think that, wouldn't you? Yet last night at the rehearsal dinner, Chester mentioned they were thinking of selling, furniture included. If I was interested, I only had to let him know."

She glanced over at the painting, then back at him, her expression skeptical. "Even—"

He cut her off with a laugh. "I know what you're going to say. No, the painting isn't my choice. It was here when I moved in. A friend of Sophie's, a popular French artist she met in Paris, painted it. I've considered taking it down, but I have no idea what to replace it with."

He grinned. "And, honestly? It's grown on me over time."

She laughed. "It is very eye-catching. But like you, it's not my style either."

"*Ah*… another thing we have in common." He slipped back around the island and held up the bottle of wine. "Is this good for you?"

She nodded, though in her present state, he could give her a glass of apple juice and she probably wouldn't notice the difference, totally captivated by everything about him.

The sudden need to be closer, she approached the island, watching as he searched through a drawer for a corkscrew. Her head tilted, she smiled at him. "But what you said about Chester wanting to sell... would this be something you'd like to do?"

Fingering the corkscrew, he contemplated telling her that this decision depended on her. He wouldn't care where he lived as long as she was with him.

Instead, the reminder he'd vowed to take it slow, he shrugged. "I don't think so. It's a great place, but not what I'd pictured in my future."

"And what would this be?" She leaned against the counter, her gaze searching.

He laughed, reaching over to tap her nose with his finger. "My goodness, all these questions." When this sent the color rising in her cheeks, he was quick to assure her. "But I love it. You can ask me anything. In fact, I'd be disappointed if you didn't."

She laughed. "I'll have to remember that for future reference."

Relieved she was laughing, he raised an eyebrow? "*Ah*... so you think we have a future together... that's good to hear. Very good."

Before she could respond, he smiled, waving the corkscrew for emphasis. "As far as what I picture in my future—especially now that it seems you'll be a part of it—I'd say I want the same as most people... a home, family, a bunch of kids, maybe even a dog or a cat."

He grinned. "Or both."

His mouth curved into a wry smile. "I guess I'm not the 'cool kind of guy' I used to be." He paused his battle with the corkscrew his expression serious. "And you? What do you want in your future?"

You, I want you...

She panicked, at first thinking she'd said this aloud. Walking over to the wall of windows, after taking in the view of Lake Erie and the Cleveland skyline, she turned to smile at him. "Like you, I want the same. But maybe just one dog or one cat. Not both."

He nodded, his tone playful. "Duly noted. One dog or one cat, no more." He winked at her before pouring the wine.

When he came over to hand her a glass, she pressed a soft kiss to his cheek. "Just so you know, I'm one of your biggest fans. And I think you're really cool. I also agree this isn't a family kind of home." She hesitated, peering more closely at him. "Out of curiosity, when you say a bunch of kids, exactly how many are we talking about?"

"Hmm…"A glimmer of a smile crossing his face, he took her glass, setting it on the coffee table with his. Pulling her back against him, he wrapped his arms around her. The deep rumble of his voice sent a shiver through her. "I'd like to think this would all depend on you, love. I'm more than willing to compromise."

Not the reply she had anticipated.

She glanced up at him, only to realize this was a bad move, the intensity of his gaze a sign of how serious he was. Struggling for words, she turned her attention back to the view. "This is so beautiful. Even on a cloudy night like tonight, you can still see the city lights."

Even though this wasn't the response Jack had hoped for, he nodded. "Yes, the view is always different. But when there's a storm? It can be overwhelming. Nature can put on quite a show."

A silence falling between them, they watched the city slowly coming to life, the lights growing brighter against the darkening sky.

When Savanah stirred against him, giving a long sigh, Jack pressed a kiss to the top of her head. "What are you thinking that merits such a dramatic sigh?"

Her head resting on his shoulder, she gazed up at him. "Are you ever afraid? Not just of storms. But making a mistake that could come back to haunt you later in life?"

He tried to hide his smile at the seriousness of her question, but she saw this and laughed. "Jack, I'm serious."

"I know you are, and I'm sorry for laughing." He searched her face. "But what kind of mistake we're talking about here? I hope it's not about being with me?"

She shook her head vehemently. "Oh, no, no… you are the best thing that's ever happened to me. I…" Her words trailed off as she pressed a soft kiss to his mouth before leaning back against him again.

Jack was having a hard time. The only thing on his mind at the moment was the woman in his arms. He didn't want to talk about the view outside his window. Or about dogs, or cats. Or even kids.

And definitely not about mistakes. Heaven knows he'd made more than his share over the years.

This wasn't because he didn't care. Of course he did. The thought of having children with Savanah, or even discussing the possibility, had never felt so right.

And after what happened earlier tonight at the reception, their voices blending in perfect harmony? His desire had only intensified... every kiss, every touch leaving him craving more.

So, yes... talking was the last thing on his mind.

He tightened his hold, dropping slow, gentle kisses down the slender column of her neck. "Any time you are afraid, or worried about making a mistake, I'll be here for you. Whether it's now or in the next hundred years."

She was smiling as she leaned back to look at his face. "That's a long time—a hundred years."

"*Mmm*... Even then, with you? It still wouldn't be enough. Which means we need to take advantage of every moment we can. Like right now..." His mouth swooped down to cover hers, the kiss that followed sending a tremor through both of them. His anticipation now off the charts, he buried his face in her hair.

"Maybe four? As an only child, I've always wanted a big family."

He lifted his head, his mouth curving into a smile at the hushed tone of her voice. Reaching for her hand, he turned her to face him. "Ah, yes... four seems like a good number, doesn't it? Very doable."

He brushed her hair back from her face, tucking it behind her ear. "I believe this should go on record we've now made our first major decision, no?"

When she nodded, resting her cheek against his shirtfront, he pressed another kiss in her hair before he spoke. "I have another suggestion I'd like to make."

Laughter bubbled up in her throat as she gazed up at him. "You do?"

Lost in her eyes, he rested his forehead against hers before he nodded. "Yes, since my record for suggestions until now has gone so well, I'm ready to aim higher."

She couldn't hide her smile. "Aim higher? *Oh, my*... what do you have in mind?" At the same time, she reached up to wrap her arms around his neck, a groan escaping her when he had to duck, just barely avoiding a direct hit to his jaw by her cast.

She tried to hold back her laugh, but failed. "Oh, no… are you okay? I'm so sorry. Maybe we…"

The possibility this moment could end here was unacceptable to him.

Nope, it just wasn't going to happen.

"No, I'm fine. I'm more than fine." His hands drifting down her back, he pulled her closer. "Now, where were we? *Ah, yes…* I remember. I was about to tell you my newest suggestion."

A smile touching her lips, she nodded. "I'm listening…"

"Good, because after thinking about it, I've decided it's only fair that you know this isn't the only room with a great view. I'd say the master bedroom might be even better. And with the king sized bed? So comfortable, with more than enough room for two."

He nodded. "It could be a practice run for those possible four kids we've already decided on."

As soon as these words came out of his mouth, he wanted to yank them back. And bury them. Deep… really deep.

A practice run? Did you just say that? You need to fix this, and fast. Otherwise, any chance at romance will be long gone.

Unfortunately, he only dug himself in even deeper. "What I mean is… I… well… being with you is all I've been able to think about. Never have I wanted anything as much as I want this with you." He groaned, burrowing his face in her hair. "Oh, Vanababe… I'm sorry. As you can see, I'm not good at this. I…"

"I think you're doing just fine." A smile curving her lips, she claimed his mouth in a kiss.

He had his answer.

CHAPTER 54

Before Savanah realized what Jack had in mind, he scooped her into his arms. Her head nestled against his shoulder, she gave a contented sigh as he carried her down the hallway. "I've always dreamt of being swept off my feet by the man who's about to make mad, passionate love to me... the man I love."

He slowed his pace, his whisper a soft caress against her ear. "Let me be that man, Vanababe. Forever."

"Always..." after her lips joined his in a kiss, he continued on to the bedroom.

As if she were made of the finest porcelain, he gently lowered her onto the plush carpet, her feet sinking into its softness.

She turned, her gaze sweeping the room. Despite its sleek, masculine decor, everything about the room radiated comfort and luxury. The oversized king bed, the panoramic view of water and sky from the wall-to-ceiling windows, and the soft, instrumental music drifting from hidden speakers created the perfect romantic ambience.

She smiled at him. "You're right, it's a beautiful room."

Caught up in her spell—because how else could he explain the sudden overwhelming need to cater to her every desire—Jack pulled her into his arms. His mouth capturing hers in another kiss, he began moving them in a slow dance towards the bed.

At least, that was his intention.

Instead, he was about to discover she had something else in mind.

She murmured, "I need to tell you something,"

Already grappling with the tiny, stubborn hook at the back of her dress, his fingers fumbling in the dim light, his response was distracted. "*Mmm…*"

The hook freed, his lips found the sensitive skin at the nape of her neck. The brush of his mouth sent an electric shiver down her spine, their bodies reacting as one.

Afraid she would slide right down to the floor, she leaned against him. Her mind racing with the magnitude of what she was about to say, she inhaled a steadying breath.

"*Jack…*"

He groaned in response, his words a soft murmur against the warmth of her shoulder. "I swear, the taste of you is like an aphrodisiac. I will never get enough of you."

She tugged at his arm. "Jack, please… there's something I really want to say.

He leaned back, his gaze traveling over her face, a mix of curiosity and concern in his eyes. He wasn't too sure what was happening here. Was she having second thoughts? Was he moving too fast? Too soon?

His hands tracing over the curves of her back, he pressed the hard length of his body against hers, his breath a deep whisper against her lips. "I'm listening…"

The slight roughness of his touch ignited every nerve in her body, but it was the steady beat of his heart against her own that gave her the courage she needed.

"My answer is yes."

Jack froze, his heart pounding in his chest. Then realization dawned… she'd finally given him the answer he wanted. Overcome with emotion, he wanted to sweep her into his arms, devour her in a kiss.

After all, this was what he'd been waiting for… that one simple, but very important word that promised she would always be his. Yet, knowing his future—no, make that their future—hung on this moment, he needed more. He needed to hear her say it again.

He framed her face in his hands, his response a hoarse whisper, "Say it again."

Her smile was radiant. "Only if you ask me again," she replied.

His thumbs caressed her cheeks, the love shining in her eyes almost blinding, this is exactly what he did.

"Marry me?"

And wouldn't you know it? When she opened her mouth to respond, overwhelmed by a flood of emotions—joy, love, excitement, and so much more—her voice failed her.

Instead, she nodded—and that was enough for him. Tumbling her back onto the bed, he claimed her mouth in a kiss that sealed the vow they'd made.

Neither Savanah nor Jack could tell you how long they remained wrapped up in each other's arms, their tears mingling with laughter, their kisses falling like promises in between.

Propped up on one elbow, his gaze roamed over every inch of her face. He wanted to burn this moment into memory—every second, every word, every kiss. When a shy flush rose in her cheeks under his scrutiny, he shook his head.A tentative smile touched her lips.

"What's wrong? Are you having second thoughts?"

"No, that will never happen." Then, after tucking a strand of her hair behind her ear, he hesitated. Maybe he was asking for trouble, but he couldn't stop thinking about the possibility she might leave. He needed to know what she'd decided.

So, he just let it out. "Vanababe, we need to talk about Seattle. More importantly, I need to apologize. I had no right to give you an ultimatum like I did. I—"

She pressed her fingers to his mouth, silencing him. "Stop… it's okay. I understand. If anything, I should apologize to you for telling you when I did."

He groaned, regret in his voice. "No, it's not okay. But the thought of you leaving, well… I'm ashamed to say I went a little crazy." He shook his head. "I certainly didn't handle the news very well."

He pressed a kiss to her temple. "*My God…* you need someone who supports you, not someone barking out orders, trying to run your life."

"Barking out orders? Is that what you were doing?" A smile tweaked the corner of her mouth as she brushed his hair from his forehead. "Funny, I didn't see it that way. Well, maybe at first I was angry. But then I realized how lucky I am to have someone who loves me as much as I love them."

Her eyes wide, she shook her head. "And then I discover you went to see my mother?"

"*Ah*... so she already told you about that, huh?"

A slow smile traveled across his face. "That had to be the smartest decision I've ever made. Once she realized how serious I am about you, but wanted her blessing, she finally accepted I wasn't the bad guy here. Granted, a long lecture followed, but I think we understand each other now."

He chuckled. "She even sent me off with a plate of her banana muffins."

She laughed. "Those muffins are her answer for everything. You said you have a freezer full of sour cherry scones? Mine is filled with banana muffins."

"Yeah, it seems I've had a pretty busy couple of days." He linked their fingers together, bringing her hand up to his mouth for a kiss before he continued. "This morning I got up the courage to call my father to thank him for the piano. And this time, instead of getting sent to his voicemail, he answered. It was a good conversation, lasting for over an hour."

He paused in thought before he smiled. "Yeah, it felt good. I found out he knows more about my life than I thought. So now, the plan is to keep in touch."

A teasing glint in his eyes. "We even talked about you."

She smiled. "I'm so glad you finally talked. He has to be so proud of you. And me? What did you tell him about me?"

"I asked him for advice. I told him I goofed up and wasn't too sure of how to make it right. I only knew I couldn't lose you."

She took in a deep breath, her gaze holding his. "You won't. I've decided against the Seattle interview," she said, "Instead, I'll take this time to sort things out, decide what I really want." She shrugged, holding up her arm with the cast. "A lot depends on what happens with this."

"And I will be there to support you no matter what you do." He sealed this with a kiss.

She laughed, her eyes sparkling with happiness. "Oh, Jack... this is the first time in my life I feel like I have choices, my choices. And it feels wonderful."

She drew his face down to hers, their lips meeting in a kiss that was both a promise and a plea. "The one thing I'm sure of is you. And how much I love you. I can't wait to marry you, Jack Buchanan. The sooner, the better."

His reaction wasn't what she expected. Scrambling off the bed, and raking his hand through his hair, he let out a deep groan. "Damn... This isn't right. I don't even have a ring to give you." Before she could respond, he headed for the door. "But wait..." He left, leaving her staring after him.

Almost in a sprint, he headed over to where he'd left his tuxedo jacket. Reaching into the pocket, he pulled out the piano charm he'd left in the grand piano earlier.

He returned to the bedroom and settled next to her. After removing her necklace with the ballerina slippers pendant to add the piano charm, he fastened the necklace once more around her neck. His fingers tracing the intricate carvings of the charm, the soft brush of contact sent her pulse racing, shivers running down her spine.

Very aware of this, he cleared his throat. "This belonged to my mother. Given to her by the same person who gifted her the piano, she believed it brought her good luck. So, she passed it on to me. Remember when we first arrived at The Regency and I left you for a few minutes? This was to tuck the charm next to the heart and initials I'd carved inside the piano."

He shrugged. "Unsure of what would happen with us, I figured I could use all the luck I could get. And look where it brought us. So, now I want you to have it."

He jerked his head towards her, a determined look on his face. "But it's not intended to replace an engagement ring. I will—"

She silenced him with a kiss.. "Thank you, I love it. And I don't need a ring.. That I have your love is more than enough."

His husky whisper brushed over her jaw to linger at her mouth.

"Enough to make love to the man who has been dreaming about this moment with you for so long?"

Her lips curved into a playful smile. "*Hmm…* would this be the same man who suggested this could be a good time to get in some practice for those four kids we talked about?"

His face buried in the curve of her shoulder, he groaned. "Something tells me," he murmured, "that you'll never let me forget I said that."

"Of course not," she grinned, this melting into a sigh as the kisses he trailed down her throat grew more intense. A slow heat spreading through her body, her next words came out all breathless. "Just so you know, I'm more than willing to go along—"

His mouth met hers with a fierce urgency, silencing her with a kiss that demanded everything.

He watched as Savanah struggled to unbutton his shirt, the cast on her arm making this a challenge. Sensing her frustration, he caught her hand in his, and together they freed the remaining buttons. Shrugging off the shirt, he let it fall to the floor.

His hands drifted to her back, the sharp, metallic hiss of the zipper slicing through the silken fabric of her dress echoing in the hushed silence. With each discarded garment, their kisses grew more passionate, their touch a kindling for the flames of desire between them.

Her scent, warm and intoxicating, filled his lungs, while the silkiness of her skin beneath his fingertips only made him ache for more. His mouth became more demanding, his hands roaming over the curve of her back, leaving a trail of heat in their wake

The need to feel her against him, under him—consumed him. Aligning her more intimately, he lifted himself over her. Her soft curves pressed against him was electrifying. Each brush of skin against skin brought a wave of pleasure so intense, it drowned out everything else. Leaving only the desperate need to lose himself in her completely.

He wanted to love her.

Be loved by her.

Not only tonight, but the rest of forever.

And Savanah?

Never had she felt such a desperate need to get closer to someone—a longing that consumed her completely. Her heart pounded against her ribs as her fingers glided over Jack's skin, tracing the contours of his body. His whispers brushed her ear, sending shivers cascading down her spine.

It was no wonder she felt so utterly overwhelmed.

Yet, like Jack, it was never enough—she wanted more. Drawing him closer, she whispered his name against his lips as she wrapped her arms around him.

Their gazes locked, the raw hunger in his sent a deep shudder through her. He pressed the softest kiss to her mouth, then lingered there, his whisper brushing against her lips. "You are the air I breathe, the light of my life. I will always—*always*—love you."

"Then show me," she pleaded, a hint of desperation in her voice. "Love me now."

With one swift push, they became one, bodies and hearts entwined until nothing else existed, conscious thought no longer possible.

The passion that followed was a dance as ancient as time, their love a living testament to the vow they'd made.

And yet, there was one memory of this night. A moment Jack would carry forever, tucked away, in his heart

He finally had his answer…

She said yes.

CHAPTER 55

I'll never finish falling in love with you.
~ Unknown

*M*esmerized by the sound of Savanah's heartbeat mirroring his own, Jack nestled his face in the warmth of her shoulder, teetering between a dream and reality. A mellow saxophone jazz rendition of *"The Power of Love,"* a favorite from his playlist, drifted through the room.

A slow, lazy smile curved his lips

Could this moment be any more perfect?

Beneath him, Savanah shifted, taking in a deep breath. Lifting himself to his elbows, he watched her eyes flutter open. Their gazes locked, and the world—and everything else—settled into a haze, leaving only the two of them. Her lips curving into a smile, she lifted her face to his.

"Hey…" her whisper grazed his mouth.

"Hey…" Lost in the love shining in her eyes, this was all he could manage at first. This was the woman he'd been waiting for--the one who held every hope, every dream, every joy of a lifetime together. Trailing his fingers down her cheek, he spoke in a low husky murmur. "I love you. And every day, I fall even deeper… over and over again."

"I love you, too." But then she hesitated, a flicker of hesitation in her eyes.

Sensing her unease, his voice softened. "What's on your mind, love?"

She bit her lip, her voice barely a whisper. "Do you ever wonder if this all happened too fast to be real?"

His heart skipped a beat, a sudden tightness gripping his chest. Why would she think this?

For a fleeting moment, doubt crept in—what if she was right, and the obstacles they'd faced were an omen of what lay ahead?

But then he felt the steady beat of her heart against his, a wave of certainty washing over him. Never had he been so sure of anything in his life.

Plain and simple, they had this.

He pulled her close, his voice gentle but firm. "No, this is more real than anything we ever could've imagined." A mischievous smile tugged at his lips. " Picture us telling this story to those four kids of ours one day—how it took just one heartbeat to fall in love."

His grin grew wider. "Well, that, and a sour cherry scone."

His gaze roamed over her face as he smoothed her hair back from her forehead. There was a husky tenderness in his voice and eyes. "Stay with me tonight? I want to wake up and find you next to me. I've dreamed of this from the first time I looked into your eyes."

Trailing her fingers across his chest, she smiled. *"Hmm...* will you make me breakfast if I do?"

His lips already brushing slow, feathery kisses along her jaw, he drew back enough to meet her gaze. Then he grinned. "You're in luck. I just so happen to have enough sour cherry scones and banana muffins to feed you for days."

Laughter bubbled up in her throat as she gazed up at him. "Oh, Jack... I do love you... *so* much."

"I love you, too."

Then his hands were in her hair, his mouth capturing hers in a kiss, again, and again, and again.

CHAPTER 56

"**A**re we almost there?"

Seated in the passenger seat of Jack's truck, Savannah's voice vibrated with excitement.

Even with the blindfold he'd insisted on—his way of keeping it a surprise, he'd claimed—she couldn't stop the smile tugging at her lips. It had lingered there since his call earlier that day to let her know he would be picking her up at seven for dinner.

He also said she should wear her best dress.

Best dress?

When she'd asked what he meant, he chuckled, suggesting she wear the same dress she wore for their first date. Then, cut off by another call, he'd given her a quick "I love you" before his promise to see her soon.

The week following Stephanie and Evan's wedding, she and Jack had spent every spare moment together. Their days passed in a blissful, romantic haze, their nights filled with whispered promises and a passion that felt like it belonged in a dream. A single glance from him, or the brush of his hand, was all it took to have her falling in love all over again.

She didn't know how she'd ever lived without him.

She sighed. Whatever he had planned, she knew it would only make her love him even more.

But, the blindfold?

She hadn't seen that coming...

The sound of his fingers tapping on the steering wheel to the beat of music playing from the speakers, a sudden craving for his touch flared within her.

Sliding her hand on the console between them, her voice was a soft murmur.

"Jack?"

Like Savanah, Jack couldn't seem to stop smiling.

This beautiful woman had transformed his life, his priorities no longer the same. To wake up and find her curled up and asleep next to him was the most amazing feeling in the world.

And the nights?

What could he say? Except that the passion between them, a beautiful testament of their love, had changed him forever, taking him to a place he never wanted to leave.

She was everything to him.

The sun. The moon. And all the stars.

He smiled as he reached for her hand. "Sorry, I had to merge into the other lane. Won't be much longer now."

A frown flitted across his face. "Since you're not wearing your cast, I don't dare take my eyes off the road. I can't risk an accident—not with you."

She tilted her head towards him. "The doctor said it's okay to take it off for special occasions. "I figured this qualifies as such, no?"

He nodded. "Absolutely. But, when you say the doctor... this wouldn't be—"

She cut him off with a long and exaggerated sigh. "No, it wasn't Dr. Davis." A smile tugged at her lips. "I must say, I find it very flattering you're jealous. No one has ever felt like that about me before."

He chuckled. "I guess we can add this to our list of firsts, as I've never had a reason to be jealous until now. There's just something about that guy…"

She shook her head, the blindfold shifting at the move. "You have nothing to worry about… *ever*."

Another sigh escaped her. "So, how much longer now?"

Though he knew she couldn't see this, he grinned, shaking his head. "*Tsk, tsk*… So impatient. This is a whole new side of you I haven't seen yet. And no, there will be no hints. Don't you want to be surprised?"

"It just feels like we've been driving for hours."

He glanced over at the dashboard clock and chuckled. "It's only been about twelve minutes, love. Five more minutes and we'll be there."

After a short silence, she smiled. "I bet we're going to Jake's Place, aren't we?"

He flicked on the turn signal. "We're here, so we'll soon see if you're right."

Savanah tilted her head, straining to hear something familiar. But, beyond the crunch of gravel beneath the truck's tires, there was only silence.

She frowned. "This sounds too quiet to be Jake's."

He chuckled, his voice teasing. *"Hmm…* you think so?

He turned off the ignition, the hum of the engine fading into silence. After his fingers brushed over her cheek in a soft caress, she heard the click of his door opening. This was followed by the sound of gravel crunching under his boots as he rounded the truck and opened her door.

One glance to find her lips parted in what he saw as an invitation, he captured her mouth in a lingering kiss before her feet even touched the ground.

His hand on her arm to guide her, his whisper fell right below her ear. "Not much longer, love."

To avoid tipping her off with the steps at The Regency's main entrance, he'd chosen to use the back door. Once inside—the echo of their footsteps on the polished hardwood floors magnified in the silence —he guided her down the hallway to the Grand Ballroom and ushered her inside.

Dropping his hand from her arm, he whispered. "Stay right here. I'll only be a minute."

Jack couldn't believe how nervous he was. He could feel his heart racing, his stomach tied in knots.

Everything had to be perfect.

He flicked on the chandelier, and turned on the music, adjusting both until he captured the romantic vibes he was aiming for.

Then he hurried over to the sunroom, where he did a quick scan to ensure everything was flawless—the fire crackling in the fireplace, clusters of candles tucked between the vases of red roses arranged throughout the room, and the table set for an intimate dinner for two.

Satisfied, he returned to Savanah.

He cradled her face in his hands, pressing a soft kiss to her lips.

"See? I'm back... ready, love?"

"*Yes, yes...* can I take off the blindfold now?"

Already leading her towards the sunroom, he chuckled. "*Hmm...* just a few more steps."

She stopped short, and clutching his arm, a huge smile spread across her face. "*Oh, my gosh.* Is this what I think it is? Where we had our first date?"

Laughing, he untied the blindfold and slipped it off, watching her eyes flutter open before she gazed around the room. When she turned to him with a look of awe , he shrugged. "I thought of taking you to Jake's, but—"

Before he could finish, she walked right into his arms, her whisper cutting him off. "*Oh, Jack...* this is perfect."

He gazed down at her, a tenderness in his voice. "I wanted it to be just like our first date, but better. Darcey suggested the candles and roses, and our dinner's compliments of The Regency head chef. Turns out, under that gruff exterior, he's a hopeless romantic."

He guided her to the table. Once they were seated, and a server had appeared to pour the wine, Jack nodded towards a card propped against her water glass. "I believe that's a message for you."

Reaching to move the glass closer to her, he almost tipped it over. Mumbling an apology, he sent her an embarrassed smile before he grabbed the card and handed it to her. "No harm done."

At his eager nod, she read the card aloud, her eyes widening in surprise.

"Marry Me?"

She stared at the card, then turned to him, her hand flying to her mouth.

He had already dropped to one knee, and was holding a small jeweler's box in his hand."

Now, Jack had rehearsed this moment at least a dozen times, maybe more. Again, he wanted this evening to be perfect, a memory they'd cherish forever. And even though Savanah had already said yes a few days ago, for him, they weren't officially engaged until she had a ring on her finger.

Call him old-fashioned, but this is what he believed.

He cleared his throat, his voice steady but filled with emotion. "Vanababe… from our first date to this moment, every second with you has been unforgettable. I found this quote—Love is a lot like dancing, you just need to surrender to the music.' You will always be my dancer, as I promise to be your music. And, together, the love songs we share will carry us through a lifetime."

He removed the ring from the box and, his gaze locked with hers, slid it on her finger. "So, my love, for one last time… Marry me?

A soft laugh escaped her, nothing more.

He peered more closely at her before tipping his head back with a groan. "*Damn*… it wasn't romantic enough, was it. I should've said more. What was I thinking?"

Half-laughing, half-crying, she threw her arms around him. "What you said is more than enough. And, of course, again my answer is a yes." Her voice softened. "It's been a yes since the moment I turned to find you in line behind me at Café Latte. I love you so, *so* much.

"I love you, too."

The sound of someone clearing their throat, they turned to see a member of the catering staff—a plate in each hand—had arrived with their dinner.

Dropping a kiss to Savanah's cheek, Jack took her hand. "Since Darcey's been raving about the menu she and the chef put together for this dinner, I know we're in for a real treat. So, let's eat. Then I want to dance the rest of the night away with you, love."

Her smile radiant, she pressed a kiss to the corner of his mouth. "That sounds wonderful."

He retrieved their wine glasses and raised his to hers in a toast. "But first, a toast—You are my forever and always. With you, I am home—I love you, Vanababe."

Much later, after lingering over dessert, Jack and Savanah sat at the piano. The catering staff had already left, but not before they thanked them and the chef for making the night so magical.

Glancing down at Savanah, her eyes closed, her head resting on his shoulder, Jack grinned. He ended in mid-song, and with a sharp flick of his wrist, went right into a glissando, his fingers gliding over the keys in a perfect slide.

Savanah bolted upright, her eyes wide.

He laughed. "*Hmm...* so that got your attention, huh?"

Languidly stretching against him, she smiled. "I'm sorry. But listening to you play puts me in a trance." "She gazed up at him. "Remember, you did promise to teach me how to do that."

His expression turning thoughtful, he nodded. "Tell you what... I'll teach you on one condition."

Her eyebrows raised, a smile tugged at her lips. "*Hmm...* not a suggestion, but a condition? I"m intrigued. Tell me, what would this 'condition' be?"

"You set a date for our wedding." A wistful smile touched his lips. "I don't want a long engagement. I want to be married to you, the sooner, the better."

She studied him. Then she nodded. "Well, as a matter of fact, my mother—"

He groaned, dragging his hand down over his chin. "Please let this be good news, because I don't—"

She laughed, pressing a quick kiss to his mouth. "Stop, listen to me. She asked if we'd set a date, and I told her we were leaning towards August or September."

"*Hmm...* either sounds good to me." He peered more closely at her. "You do mean this year, right?"

She smiled. "Yes, I promise it will be this year."

"Good. I'm going to hold you to that." He checked his watch, then stood, reaching for her hand. *"Whoa… I didn't realize it was so late. We should leave before the kitchen crew arrives. But, not until we share one last dance."*

He picked up his phone, hit a link, and *"Can't Help Falling in Love"* filled the room.

Still holding her hand, he gave a half bow. "May I have this dance?"

Twirling her not once, but twice across the dance floor, his sure steps were a testament of his new-found confidence. With each beat every sweeping turn grew bolder until it felt like they'd covered every inch of the floor.

The music slowed and time seemed to stand still. Her head resting on his shoulder, her hand in his, they swayed gently to the music.

When their steps stilled, his hands drifting down her back to pull her closer, he whispered. "I love you,"

She looked up, eyes sparkling. "I love you, too."

He dipped her low, almost to the floor. Then, as the last notes faded, he pulled her up and sealed the moment with a a passionate kiss.

So… what happens when fate brings two strangers together through the magic of love and music?

"You dance… like you've never danced before."

~

LET'S BAKE SOME SCONES

*E*veryone loves scones, right? Contrary to popular belief, these delightful pastries aren't only limited to afternoon tea. With so many variations, some might even consider them to be a dessert. This recipe is a close copy to the scones from Café Latte that worked their magic on Savanah and Jack.

Enjoy …

Sour Cherry Scones

Scone Ingredients:
2 cups all-purpose flour
1/3 cup sugar
1 teaspoon baking powder
1/2 teaspoon salt
1/4 teaspoon baking soda
1 stick (8 tablespoons) cold, unsalted butter
(cut in small pieces and frozen)
1/2 cup dried sour cherries* coarsely chopped
2 teaspoons orange zest
1/2 cup, plus 2 tablespoons sour cream
1 large egg

Glaze Ingredients:
   1-1/2 cups confectioners sugar
   2 tablespoons butter, melted
   2 tablespoons hot water, or more if needed

*To soften the cherries, soak them in hot water for about 30 minutes, then press between paper towels to remove most of the moisture.

Directions:
   Line baking tray with parchment paper.
   Mix flour, sugar, baking powder, salt, and baking soda in a medium bowl. Use your fingers (or pastry blender) to work in butter until mixture resembles coarse crumbs, then toss in sour cherries and orange zest.
   Whisk sour cream and egg together in a small bowl until combined.
   Stir sour cream mixture into flour mixture until large dough clumps form. Shape dough into a ball. (Dough may seem dry, but will come together. Do not over-work dough).
   Place dough on a lightly floured surface and pat into a 7- to 8-inch circle, about 3/4-inch thick. Use a sharp knife to cut into 8 equal triangles; place on the prepared baking tray, about 1-inch apart. Refrigerate for 30 minutes.
   Meanwhile, set oven temperature to 400F and adjust oven rack to the lower-middle position.
   Bake scones in heated oven until golden, about 15 to 17 minutes. Remove from the oven. Let cool on the tray for a few minutes before lifting onto a wire rack to cool.
   Whisk all of the glaze ingredients together until smooth, adding additional water if needed to drizzle over the scones.
   Allow to set completely before serving.
   Yield: 8 Scones

Dear Reader,

March, a Song and a Dance is the ninth swoon-worthy novel in my Twelve Months, Twelve Love Stories series. Savanah and Jack's story is close to my heart, and I'm so excited you're here to share it with me. If you're new to the series, don't worry—each book can stand on its own, but trust me, the nine so far will have you hooked.

To my loyal readers who've danced through this journey with me— thank you. You are the inspiration that keeps me writing, the spark of every late-night plot twist.

Here's to love, laughter, and the next story,

L. B. Joyce

P.S. The recipe included in this book? It's all mine—created and tested with love. Every recipe in the series has earned five-star raves so far, so give it a whirl and let me know what you think—I'd love to know if it wins you over, too.

ABOUT THE AUTHOR

L. B. Joyce lives in Chagrin Falls, Ohio. A freelance artist by day, with designing Christmas ornaments her specialty, she's also a writer by night. She loves getting lost in a good book, has redecorated almost every room in her house more times than she'd like to admit, loves baking up a storm in her kitchen, hates housework with a passion and will drive just about anywhere because of her fear of flying.

To keep up with news of the first nine books of the Twelve Months, Twelve Love Stories series - *A Million Decembers, For the Love of July, February's Angel, Promise Me November, An Unexpected June, A January to Remember, September's Moonlight Serenade, Goodbye Heartbreak, Hello May, and March, a Song and a Dance-* along with the first book of the new *Holidays in White Oaks Valley* series, *A Grand Slam Kind of Christmas,* make sure you check out the website/blog at: lbjoyceauthor.com

Visit on Facebook: https://www.facebook.com/LBJoyceAuthor/

Or Email: lbjoyce12@gmail.com

ACKNOWLEDGMENTS

Endless Love ~ Written and composed by Lionel Richie

The Music of the Night ~ Composed by Andrew Lloyd Webber
Lyrics by Charles Hart, Richard Stilgo

Can't Help Falling in Love ~ Written by Hugo Peretti, Luigi Creatore, and George David Weiss

Greensleeves ~ Composer Unknown

The Power of Love - Written by Candy DeRouge, Gunther Mende
Lyrics by Jennifer Rush, Mary Applegate

Book Cover – *Soxsational Cover Art*

www.ingramcontent.com/pod-product-compliance
Lightning Source LLC
Chambersburg PA
CBHW071917130726
47909CB00014B/2052